Also by Diana Peterfreund

SECRET SOCIETY GIRL: AN IVY LEAGUE NOVEL

PRAISE FOR

Secret Society Girl: AN IVY LEAGUE NOVEL

"The action is undeniably juicy—from steamy make-out sessions with campus hotties to cloak-and-dagger initiations." —*Washington Post*

"[A] tell-all book about secret societies at Ivy League schools... Think *The Da Vinci Code* meets Bridget Jones." —*Toledo Blade*

"*Secret Society Girl* succeeds.... Peterfreund's descriptions of the ambitious Amy Haskel's collegial life are both vivid and amusing." —*New York Observer*

"[C]heerful, sensible, with just enough insider's scoop to appeal to the conspiracy theorist in everyone... Readers will cheer on the not-so-underdog as she faces male alumni and finds that membership does indeed have privileges." —*Tampa Tribune*

"Thanks to a quirky, likable protagonist you'll be rooting for long after you've turned the last page and a provocative blurring of fact and fiction, *Secret Society Girl* provides the perfect excuse to set aside your required reading this summer and bask in a few hours of collegiate nostalgia." —Bookreporter.com

"Fun to read—full of quirky characters and situations." —*Booklist*

"[A] frothy summer read for anyone interested in the collegiate antics of the secret rulers of the world." —Bloomberg News

"The plot is a winner." —*Kirkus Reviews*

"A fun, breezy, beach-perfect diversion...unfailingly hip, with a myriad of cultural and intellectual references to everything from *Eyes Wide Shut* to Aristotle's *Poetics*." —*Winston-Salem Journal*

"*Secret Society Girl* is a blast! Fun and witty, with an engaging theme, heartfelt situations, intriguing dialogue, and a cast of characters that you'll be cheering for, it's a story you won't want to put down." —TeensReadToo.com

"Very smart...exceptionally well-structured. Witty and suspenseful, *Secret Society Girl* is an original concept expertly executed." —Romance Divas.com

"Absolutely captivating, *Secret Society Girl* takes us into the mysterious, rarified, and delicious world of an Ivy League secret society—but even more, into the life of a fascinating and dauntless young woman. Diana Peterfreund has such a bright, original voice, and she has written an unforgettable novel." —*New York Times* bestselling author Luanne Rice

"A warning label should be put on the cover of this book: Get comfortable, because once you pick it up, you won't be able to put it down. *Secret Society Girl* has it all: razor-sharp wit, nail-biting suspense, and pitch-perfect storytelling that will leave you begging for more.... The Ivy League has never been this fun." —Cara Lockwood, bestselling author of *I Do (but I Don't)*

"Chick lit heads off to the Ivy League in Diana Peterfreund's superfun, supercool debut novel, *Secret Society Girl*. Of course, I'd like to tell you all the reasons why I loved it, but then I'd have to kill you." —Lauren Baratz-Logsted, author of *The Thin Pink Line*

Under the Rose

AN IVY LEAGUE NOVEL

Diana Peterfreund

DELTA TRADE PAPERBACKS

UNDER THE ROSE
A Delta Trade Paperback Book / July 2007

Published by Bantam Dell
A Division of Random House, Inc.
New York, New York

Cover photo by Craig DeCamps
Cover design by Lynn Andreozzi

Book design by Carol Russo

Library of Congress Cataloging-in-Publication Data

Peterfreund, Diana.
Under the rose : an Ivy League novel / Diana Peterfreund.
p.   cm.
ISBN 978-0-385-34003-8 (trade pbk.)
1. Women college students—Fiction. 2. Greek letter societies—Fiction.
3. College stories. 4. Chick lit. I. Title.
PS3616.E835U64   2007
813'.6—dc22   2007002434

Printed in the United States of America
Published simultaneously in Canada

www.bantamdell.com

BVG   10 9 8 7 6 5 4 3 2 1

For Jacki, who has always treated me like a daughter

I hereby confess:
I didn't understand what it
meant to be a Digger.

When you picture the secret society of Rose & Grave, I know what you see. Commanding statesmen, wealthy entrepreneurs, sly spies. Shadowy, secretive, and always in control. Those who have sought to infiltrate our brotherhood have vanished without a trace. Those who have dared to reveal our clandestine ways have learned the true meaning of the term "cloak-and-dagger." We have suffered much to cultivate our image, and we will stop at nothing to maintain it.

From the first years of our existence, our order has been protected by a massive network of the rich and powerful across the country and around the globe. Now, those who displease us are quick to discover how deeply our tentacles have stretched, and those upon whom we shower goodwill live as one of the elect. Indeed, our detractors say favorites of Rose & Grave have made a deal with the devil—and we don't proclaim them wrong.

As far as the outside world is concerned, there is no history of Rose & Grave. We are eternal and unchanging, a centuries-long line of monolithic and omnipotent clubs.

Each has sought to continue the work and uphold the traditions, the prejudices, and the champions of the one before. There has never been dissent. There has never been attrition. There has never been... a traitor.

No, really, there hasn't. Honest. I swear.

———

Don't believe me? Then step inside for a moment, and witness the truth. Grab a taste of absolute power. Steal a kiss from your wildest fantasies. Take a gander upon that which few eyes have seen.

But be careful. You've heard what we like to do to outsiders....

The Rose & Grave Club of D177

1) Clarissa Cuthbert: *Angel*
2) Gregory Dorian: *Bond*
3) Odile Dumas: *Little Demon*
4) Benjamin Edwards: *Big Demon*
5) ~~Howard First: *Number Two*~~
6) Amy Haskel: *Bugaboo*
7) Nikolos Dmitri Kandes IV: *Graverobber*
8) Kevin Lee: *Frodo*
9) Omar Mathabane: *Kismet*
10) George Harrison Prescott: *Puck*
11) Demetria Robinson: *Thorndike*
12) Jennifer Santos: *Lucky*
13) Harun Sarmast: *Tristram Shandy*
14) Joshua Silver: *Keyser Soze*
15) Mara Taserati: *Juno*

I hereby confess:
We aren't like other
college students.

1.

Stragglers

It was shopping period at Eli University, and lest you think this is one of those books about fashion, let me enlighten you. The students at Eli were not shopping for Prada, but for Proust; they weren't hunting for good bargains, but rather, for gut classes; and they would happily surrender Fendi at forty percent off to secure a Fractals section that wasn't all the way up on Science Hill.

As a senior, I found this shopping period especially poignant. It was my penultimate chance to discover the hidden gem seminar, the one I'd look back on in the cold, post-Eli future as being one of those bright college days the song* speaks of. My last chance, in many cases, to take the famous lectures given by the college's most notorious luminaries.

"What? You didn't take Herbert Branch's Shakespeare class?" future employers will say with incredulity. "Why, Amy Haskel, what were you *doing* there at Eli?"

And I will not be able to tell them, because I swore an

---

* Cole Porter. Keep up.

oath never to reveal the truth: that while other Literature majors were shopping the Branch class, I was crouching in the shadows on a cold stone floor, garbed in a long black hooded robe and a skull-shaped mask, rehearsing an esoteric initiation ritual that required me to lie in wait for an inno-cent classmate to wander by so I could leap out, pelt his face with phosphorescent dust, and yell "Boo."

As if I'd admit to something like that anyway.

"Hey, Lil' Demon!" I called down the stairs. "I sort of wanted to shop a seminar this afternoon, so can we non-speaking parts adjourn for the day?"

Keyser Soze, a.k.a. Joshua Silver, popped up from be-hind a tower of human remains. "The Branch class? I wanted to take that, too." Figures. Branch was a brand-name profes-sor at Eli, and it would suit Josh's political aspirations to add the scholar's reputation to his C.V.

Lil' Demon, currently levitating over a pool of blood, raised one perfectly plucked eyebrow and blew a strand of chestnut brown hair (she'd had it dyed over the summer) out of her eyes. "I should have gone union," she said with a sniff. "You people just don't understand show business."

(By the way, that thing in *Us Weekly* about Lil' Demon over the Fourth of July weekend is categorically untrue. Odile Dumas wasn't "servicing" any ex–boy-band members in Tijuana; she was with me and the other Diggers at a patri-arch's pool party on Fire Island. And, say what you will about the starlet, she has better taste than to get down with a bunch of scrawny tenors. If that were her style, we had more than enough singing groups right here on campus.)

Thorndike, poised below her and wielding a wicked-looking pitchfork, tapped Lil' Demon on her Pilates-honed and designer jeans–encrusted behind. "Can't let the Team-sters in the tomb," she reminded her. Demetria "Thorndike" Robinson was our resident power-to-the-people expert, so she'd know. "But I'm with them anyway," she continued. "There's this Racial Strata of the 21st Century symposium I wanted to hit at three."

A chorus of voices erupted from the other costumed participants about classes they were missing. Bond, our club's British contingent, wanted to ensure his seniors-first spot in a college poetry seminar, Frodo needed to go to a board meeting of the Eli Film Society, Big Demon had scheduled some physical therapy at the gym, Kismet was tutoring Swahili, and Graverobber, who I don't think I'd ever witnessed in an Eli classroom, needed to see a man about a horse. Which he owned.

Lil' Demon sighed, unhooked herself from her safety harness, and dropped to the floor. "Fine, but don't blame me if the new initiates think they're getting shafted on their ceremony."

"With these special effects, I doubt it," I replied. Lil' Demon had somehow managed to cajole some FX guy at her studio into lending us a bunch of old monster-movie stuff for the initiation we were holding tomorrow for the Rose & Grave taps who had been abroad during our junior year. No offense to previous clubs—society jargon for each year's class—and their sublime efforts at scaring the pants off the neophytes, but there was something about stuffing the taps into the same coffin that had once housed Bela Lugosi that added a certain air of authenticity to the proceedings. It would be one hell of a night, rehearsal or not.

I shoved the mask off my face and breathed in cool air. Acting was so not my thing. Some might say I lacked the basic requirement: the ability to conceal my true emotions at any given time. Others would argue I didn't have the necessary charisma.

Someone tugged at my hood. "Hey, 'boo."

Speaking of charisma . . . I turned to see Puck grinning at

me from beneath his hood. Of course Lil' Demon wouldn't hide *that* face under a disgusting mask. Who'd want to cover up a masterpiece like George Harrison Prescott? "Are you going to that thing at the Master's house later?"

If you're going, I thought. "There's supposed to be free cookies," I said. "And booze." Somehow, we'd moved away from the railing, back into one of the corners. We have a funny habit of doing that. Puck leaned against one of the skull sconces gracing the wall and his robe fell open, revealing a very faded, much washed T-shirt, and a whole lot of check-out-how-much-lifting-I've-done-this-summer shoulders. Ah, George. I like his shoulders. I like the way they connect his arms to his chest. I like the arms and the chest they connect. I like his collarbones. I like the way he kissed me in the bar last spring. . . .

"Bugaboo!" Soze shouted from the landing. "Are we going to the Branch class or what?"

Bugaboo. That's me. "Yes!" I called back, but I didn't take my eyes off Puck. "Why wouldn't you go?" I asked him.

"They do this thing . . . a presentation on the history of Prescott College." He rolled his eyes. I like his eyes. They'd looked like copper pennies when he asked me to go to bed with him. "I think I've got it down pat by now."

They hadn't even blinked when I told him no.

"Because it's starting in about three minutes!" Soze yelled.

Crap. "Coming!" I cried back down the stairs. I turned back to Puck, forcing myself to remember *why* I'd told him no. "Yeah, well, I've got it down pat after three years of living there, and I'm not even a Prescott."

I'd said no because he wasn't just George Harrison Prescott. He was also a "Puck"—society nomenclature for the knight in every club who had slept with the most people.

And right then he was my friend, and what's more, my

society brother. "Look, come early, grab a few beers, then slink out before they get into the lecture."

He quirked a brow. "Slink out with me?"

Soze stuck his head into the shadows. "Now or never, Bugaboo."

Tell me about it.

———

George decided to accompany us to the Shakespeare seminar. Raise your hand if you're surprised. So off we went, three little Diggers, into the bright sunny world of Eli University that lay beyond our gloomy tomb. George checked to see if the coast was clear, and we sneaked out the side door and proceeded to affect the easy stroll of three students who'd just emerged from the nearby Art and Architecture building.

You see, that's the real trick of being in Rose & Grave: getting in and out in the light of day without shouting to the world that you're a member. It's worth it, though. For the price of a little secrecy and a few bizarre rituals, we're given a unique connection to fourteen other people we might never have known—or liked, if we did know them. (I plead guilty to one such early prejudice, having held an entirely untenable distaste for one of my fellow members before I actually got to know her. Persephone bless Rose & Grave.)

We cut across High Street and through the gate onto Old Campus, otherwise known as freshman central. The powers that be at Eli think it promotes class bonding if the freshmen aren't isolated in their assigned residential colleges right off the bat, so they stick them all together in the dorms on our largest and most picturesque quad. Five-sixths of the frosh make their home there. (Two colleges keep their freshmen to themselves, due to space constraints, and trust me, you can tell who those freaks are just by looking at them. A common refrain here is "I don't know that person. Must be in Strathmore or Christopher Bright Colleges.")

I've been told by my Digger big brother, Malcolm Cabot (a.k.a. Lancelot), that the beginning of term is the most dangerous time for Diggers in terms of secrecy. The Rose & Grave tomb is right across the street from Old Campus, and there are a thousand freshmen who have heard all about secret societies and are dying to stake them out. Today, however, Old Campus was dangerous for another reason: the student activities gauntlet.

"Brace yourself," Josh said, as we were bombarded with a sheaf of brightly colored brochures. Russian Chorus, Club Crew, The Party of the Right, the Campus Crusade for Christ, the Women's Center, and the Solar Car team Ad Lucem ("toward the light" in Latin, because we're pretentious like that). Every organization on campus was out in full force, promoting their group and trying to make themselves look as sexy as possible for the freshmeat who hadn't yet filled up their schedule.

"Join the Society for Creative Anachronism!" said a kid in an oversized suit of armor, brandishing a papier-mâché sword in George's face.

"Too late," George replied. "I live it."

Josh rolled his eyes and steered our friend away before he started discussing how creatively anachronistic Rose & Grave could get. (George is our most reluctant Digger, and coming from me, that says a lot.)

On my left, a Young Democrat and a Tory were wrestling over table space. (Yes, we have Tories at Eli, despite the fact that loyalty to the Crown went out two hundred and thirty-one years ago.) On my right, the gonzo journalists were encroaching on the turf of my old charge, the *Eli Literary Magazine*. I wandered off the path to pay my regards to the new editor-in-chief, junior Arielle Hallet.

(Yes, we've got the same initials, and yes, I've heard the jokes about how they don't even have to change the rubber stamp.) I'd passed her the reins just last week, after we'd gone to press with the freshmen clips issue that kicked off every year. "You hanging in there, Ari?"

She shrugged, and fanned herself with a few copies of my crowning achievement, last year's commencement issue. "It's hot as balls today. You haven't seen Brandon, have you? He's on lemonade duty."

I tried not to cringe at the way she was wrinkling the pages. Or at the mention of my ex-boyfriend's name. "No, I haven't seen him." Yet. This year. Or since he dumped me in May.

But the look on Arielle's face made it pretty clear that no more needed to be said. Josh grabbed my arm and saved me from my self-inflicted awkward moment. "Class. Come on. Time to reminisce about your abandoned activities later." Abandoned was right. Josh had no clue. "You're a senior now. You've moved past this stuff."

Then he caught sight of a truly pathetic attempt at stenciling by the Mock Trial team. "Aw, man, they totally messed up our sign!"

"Yes, Josh, you're a veritable model of moving on."

George, for whom the term "student activities" has always meant a more private affair, was urging us forward when we all ran smack into a phalanx of a cappella singers who were doing the Eli equivalent of the Jets and Sharks routine right there on the flagstones.

"Hi there!" said a bubbly young moppet, shaking a head of braids in George's face and sticking out her chest, where the name of one of the school's several dozen a cappella groups was featured prominently. "Do you sing?"

"Um . . ." George said, looking at her T-shirt. "I—"

Sure they'd caught a live one, her packmates descended

in full force. "Do you sing? Do you sing? Do you sing?" they shouted, waving their CDs. "Come to our show! Audition for us! You don't need experience!"

"Back off, bozo," I hissed at a bass who was bellowing his mantra at me. "Or I'll make you a soprano. We're not freshmen, and we aren't interested."

The Greek system at Eli is notoriously chill. We've got a few frats and sororities, but not many students join, and Panhellenic rush is practically imperceptible in the melee of other student activity groups. Secret societies are only for seniors, so freshmen looking to get their fix of "joinerism" invariably get sucked into the madness of Singing Group Rush.

Think secret societies are a lot like frats? Here's the difference:

1) You join a secret society at the end of your junior year, after you've spent almost three years getting a taste for the college, defining your place in it, and deciding what kind of activities you want to take part in. It's not like Rushes, where they trap freshmen into an activity commitment of four years or more before they've even unpacked.
2) There's no Rush period for societies. They don't pretend they're crazy about you if they aren't interested.
3) You usually don't even know what society is interviewing you until the night they offer you membership. At least, I didn't, though I was a special case (more on that later).

Just past the singers, a blessedly quiet trio was handing out pamphlets advertising a prayer group. I caught sight of another Digger in the group. "Jenny, where have you been?" I called. "Odile about went nuts."

Jennifer Santos, a.k.a. Lucky in Rose & Grave parlance, looked at her companions and then back at me, her eyes wide. She came closer and spoke in a low voice. "What happened to 'discretion,' Amy?"

"What happened to rehearsal?" George replied, but Jenny, as usual, ignored him.

"Look, I had a prior commitment."

Josh folded his arms. "We're more important." Subtext: Besides, you're a senior and it's time to put away childish things.

"No," she said. "You're not. I've been with these guys for three years."

"You took an oath saying we'd come before everyone," Josh argued.

Her eyes narrowed. "I've made a lot of promises. Some are more important than others."

I stepped between them. "Okay, guys, let's calm down. I'm sure Jenny's memorized her part."

She gave me a cool, clear gaze. "You bet I have."

Just then, another member of Jenny's group joined our tight little circle. The newcomer was tall, with blond hair that fell to his shoulders, and dark, slashing eyebrows. "Is there a problem, Jennifer?"

"No," she said. "These guys are seniors, and they're not interested in what we have to offer them."

"Pity," the young man said.

Josh held up his hand. "Whatever, dude. I've got my prophets, and you've got yours."

The boy turned on him. "I would like to know what exactly it is you worship, Joshua Silver."

"Same God as you, man."

"Knowing what I do about your kind, I doubt that."

This time, both Jenny and I put our hands on the shoulders of our respective friends and pulled them away from each other. The words coming out of Josh's mouth were not exactly godly and beating up a classmate over religious differences would hardly help his political career. George jumped in to help me save Josh from himself.

"Jenny, see you later?" I called, as we dragged Josh away. She glared at me, as if I had no right to speak to her in front of her other friends. Boy, was I going to bring this up the next time the Diggirls got together. Oaths of secrecy were one thing, but Jenny took it all a step or two too far.

The ranks of student activity promoters thinned out toward the far end of the quad, and we squeezed into the English building and slipped into the lecture hall right as the carillon in the Hartford Tower chimed three o'clock.

Professor Branch was already at the front of the class, pontificating on his own brilliance and mastery of the field and checking out the cute young things who had come to worship him this semester. We found three seats together near the back of the room and sat. I scoped out the area around us for a stray syllabus, and a girl with dark curly hair seated next to the podium at the front of the room started arguing with the professor about one of the assignments.

He didn't take too kindly to it.

George nudged me. "Check it out: Mara Taserati."

One of our missing members, in the flesh. I watched the girl go head-to-head with the famous scholar and realized why the Diggers found her so attractive. Like most of the women that comprised my tap class—the first ever to include females—Mara was a power player. Ranked high in the academic and political strata of the student body, she fancied herself a young Ann Coulter. She hadn't been on campus last semester, so though we'd been given word she'd accepted the Rose & Grave tap, she'd never been initiated into the Order.

"Did you know she'd be here?" I whispered back.

"No, I'm just *really* into Shakespeare. What do you think?" He held open the pocket of the oxford he wore over his T-shirt and flashed me a glimpse of glossy, black-edged paper. "Check it out, Boo." Standing, he sauntered toward the front of the auditorium. George, being George, soon had the eye of every female in the joint. He reached the podium, swiped three copies of the syllabus, gave Professor Branch a little salute, and returned. He winked at me from behind his copper-rimmed glasses and passed me a copy.

"Wow, what a maneuver, George," Josh said, with mock admiration. "I don't think I've ever seen anyone disrupt a lecture so thoroughly."

"Keep watching."

But nothing happened for the next forty-five minutes, aside from a truly illuminating lesson on the theory that, owing to his fictionality, spoiled college kid Hamlet was actually a more real person than any of the real college kids gracing Professor Branch's lecture hall. Maybe after our uncles killed our dads and married our moms, we'd catch up. We were gathering our bags when I heard the gasp.

Mara Taserati was staring into her bag, her hand clamped over her mouth. When she didn't make any further move, the other students shrugged her off. Josh and I, in unison, leaned back in our seats and waited while the room emptied out around us. George braced his hands behind his head and put his feet up on the row of chairs in front of him. Far below us, Mara reached her hand back into her bag and drew out a square white envelope, edged in glossy black and sealed with a dollop of black wax.

I knew what was in that envelope. Once upon a time, I'd received one just like it.

She raised her eyes to our row. George stood, slowly, and his infamous knowing smile took on a whole new meaning. "Welcome back, Mara," he said in a voice that made me realize why Odile had given him a speaking part in these proceedings. "How was your trip?"

Even from twelve rows away, I could see her shiver.

I hereby confess:
There's something rotten
in the state of Digger.

2.
Party Lines

Is it possible to feel nostalgia for something that's not over? The start of senior year at Eli seemed engineered to evoke that emotion at every opportunity. Special receptions, teas, parties, barbecues, meetings, lectures, symposiums, brunches—everything proclaimed "The best years of your life are coming to an end!"

Actually, my roommate, Lydia, had a different explanation. "They're priming the pump for the alumni giving fund. Wait and see."

I maintain that if they expect to hit me up for extra dough after my monthly student loan bill, they're unfamiliar with the twenty-thou-a-year—in Manhattan!—editorial internship I have waiting for me after graduation. (That is, if I go to Manhattan. More on that later.)

Tonight's Prescott College reception was par for the course, but as I'd told George this afternoon, at least there would be free beer.

I stood in front of my desk, brushing my hair with one

hand and scrolling through my "welcome back" message from the dean of the Lit department with the other. My hair had grown out a bit over the summer, and in August, I'd capitulated to Odile's prodding and gotten funky red highlights. She said it would match my tattoo. Of course, not many people saw said tattoo, so my correlated coloring hadn't gotten the appreciation it deserved from anyone who wasn't one of the five "Diggirls."

In her adjoining bedroom, Lydia was singing. If ever a girl loved shopping period, it was my best friend. But I don't think I'd ever seen her as happy as she was when she got back to the suite earlier. I wandered out to the wood-paneled common room, but her bedroom door was still shut, its whiteboard decorated with a blue ink smiley face sporting orange ink pigtails.

Singing and pigtails? Yeah, I was going to hear about this later on for sure. (Unless it was about something going on in her own secret society.) But as long as she was busy...

I ducked back into my room, carefully angled my computer screen away from the door, and minimized my Eli mail window.

A moment later, I was logged on to my *other* e-mail account. One new message.

From: Lancelot-D176@phimalarlico.org
To: Bugaboo-D177@phimalarlico.org
Subject: good luck tomorrow!

how's my favorite little sib? all set for the stragglers? do me a favor, and try not to tear apart the foundations of the society at the initiation. i know that's what you're famous for. give poe a hug for me, huh?

"Hey," Lydia said, sticking her head in. "Ready to go?"
"Yeah, just a minute," I responded. "I'm reading an

e-mail." I took a deep breath. *Don't ask from whom.* How was I to explain my sudden kinship with the wildly popular and recently graduated Malcolm Cabot? But Lydia made it easy on me.

"Okay." She ducked out.

everything's great up here. it's so beautiful, bugaboo, i wish you could see it. i've been making a few friends, but we rarely talk about anything but fish. (that reminds me, give hale a heads-up to expect a large shipment of halibut.) i won't lie; it's been a bit of a letdown after the kind of closeness I had w/ the d's at e, but I guess that's the point. nothing is ever going to be like r&g. i'm going into juno at the end of the month. should be a fun trip. you know what they say about alaska: five men for every woman. though they never do mention how many men for every man. ;-)

on the homefront, the latest report says i'm suffering from *exhaustion*—

"You know," Lydia said, very close. I jumped a foot. She stood beside me, idly rooting through the earrings scattered across the top of my dresser. "If we get there after all the Master's seven-layer cookies are gone, I'll never speak to you again."

Could she see? The text was small, and there were no incriminating graphics on the page. Just to be sure, I alt-tabbed back to the mailbox and minimized.

A second before the screen disappeared, I caught sight of another bold subject heading in my in-box. *New mail.*

WARNING: AMY HASKEL

Lydia waved a hand in front of my face. "Ames. Let's go."

I slammed the laptop closed.

Lydia jumped back. "I wasn't snooping!"

Who sent that? Who was using my *barbarian* name to send me e-mail on the secret Diggers-only, society terminology–only, society time-stamps–only e-mail? It had to be from another knight of Rose & Grave. Only they knew of our secret domain or the configurations of our e-mail addresses. This had better be some kind of joke—something worth the two dollar fine for using barbarian names in society missives.

"There's no reason to freak out," my roommate continued.

But there was. Because Phimalarlico webmail was only supposed to come from others in the phimalarlico.org domain. It was a "virtual tomb"—no one but Diggers inside, heavily password-protected, no barbarians allowed.

Lydia was still talking. "Ten seconds and I'm leaving without you."

"No, wait!" I cried. "I promise, ten seconds, I just have to—"

Lydia rolled her eyes and stalked out, murmuring, "Ten—nine—eight . . ."

I opened my laptop again.

From: amy.haskel@eli.edu
To: Bugaboo-D177@phimalarlico.org
Subject: WARNING: AMY HASKEL

YOU THINK ITS OVER BUT ITS NOT
FROM WITHIN DOTH PERSEPHONE ROT

I closed the window as the hairs on the back of my neck rose. Leaving aside for a moment the lack of apostrophes and phenomenally bad sense of rhythm in the poem (you can take the girl out of the editorial office...), it was one seriously chilling message.

And it apparently came from me. Which meant someone out there, who knew my society identity—which, I guess, could be any Digger—had hacked into my regular e-mail in order to send it to me. What was I supposed to do? If I told the other Diggers, it would seem as if the security leak was my fault, as if I'd somehow been less-than-discreet about my society e-mail.

"Two, one and a half, one!" Lydia warned from the common room.

"Coming!" I called, and rushed to meet her.

We'd "squatted" during the housing lottery last spring, betting on keeping our top-pick junior suite rather than risking a crappy draw that might lead to a less-than-desirable senior year rooming situation. Like something on the fourth floor. It might be great for our calves, but so not worth the hassle.

Lydia stood near the door, arms crossed, foot tapping. "Can you tell me what was so important, or is it verboten?"

I fingered the Rose & Grave pin I was wearing inside my pocket. "Some bizarre *Salon* op-ed."

"Aren't they *all* bizarre?"

"Says the woman addicted to Daily Kos?" I replied as we lumbered down the steps of the entryway and into the Prescott College courtyard.

The air was still late-August warm and all the windows of Prescott were open, showering snatches of hip-hop music, scholarly debates, video game sound effects, roommate squabbles, and cello tuning onto the students milling about on the lawn. The cacophony was a signature start-of-term sound, one I would no doubt associate with Eli for the rest of my life.

Beneath a yellow pool of light from a lamppost, a group of students kicked around a hackey sack. Nearby, a circle of outdoor types sat tailor-style in the grass, drinking from Nalgene bottles and reminiscing about the bonding they'd done on their freshmen outdoor orientation trips. In a small stone niche, two black-clad Theater majors were smoking and arguing about whether their company should start out the year with Ibsen (too trendy), Sartre (too light), Miller (too chaste), or Williams (too avant-garde).

We arrived at the Master's house, and if the crowd we glimpsed inside was anything to go by, we'd definitely missed the seven-layer cookies. At the door, we were met by George Harrison Prescott, who was holding fast to the arm of a pretty, dark-haired woman.

"George, let go of me. I'm perfectly capable of walking by myself," she said, then proceeded to tumble off the stoop.

Lydia and I were right in position to catch her.

"Excuse me, I'm so sorry," the woman said quickly, straightening her body, her skirt, and her hair. I glanced at George, who was wearing an expression I'd never seen before. His jaw was all tight. It did wonderful things for his cheekbones, which already deserved kudos.

"Mom, these are some of my Prescott College friends. This is Lydia Travinecek and Amy Haskel. Ladies, this is my mother, Kate Anderson Prescott."

The woman eyed us. "George Harrison doesn't have *girl* friends," she said coolly. "Like father, like son." Then she turned and marched toward the drama couple—who had moved on to a discussion about whether or not Shakespeare was too obvious—to bum a cigarette.

I swallowed and looked at George, whose permasmile was back in place. "Long story," he said with a shrug.

The door opened again, and out came a very distinguished-looking man in his mid-forties. He glanced quickly around the corridor before his gaze landed on our little group. When his eyes met mine, his eyebrows raised, and I got a good look at the copper-colored eyes George had inherited. "You!" the man said.

"You're looking young, Mr. Prescott," I replied. The last time I'd seen this man, he'd been wearing Academy Award–quality aging makeup, a gray wig, and a mask made of roses.

His eyes flashed toward Lydia, and a scowl turned down the corners of his mouth. Oops, right, Barbarian-in-Vicinity. Alert, alert.

"Where did she go?" Mr. Prescott asked George, who cocked his thumb at the stone nooks, then stuck his hands in his pockets as Mr. Prescott took off after his ex-wife, some-time lover, and decades-long sparring partner.

"It's dead in there," George said to us. "Now at least. Amy, are you going to Clarissa's thing?"

"Um..." I hadn't quite been able to explain to Lydia why my sworn enemy was now sending me party invites and showing up in our suite for impromptu chats. She probably suspected I'd gone shallow in my old age. Or maybe she figured it was one more Digger-inspired change that had come over me since being tapped. She'd adjusted splendidly to the sudden location switch of my summer internship from Manhattan to D.C. (mostly because it meant we could stay together over the summer). However, we'd enjoyed a strict moratorium on all secret society–related conversations since May, and activities skirting that topic—such as a party with a Digger friend—might be dangerous. Whenever I brought up anything that could be construed as heading in the direction of society talk, she clammed up faster than a biochem major after mid-terms. And I thought Rose & Grave valued secrecy! Evidently, we had nothing on Lydia's brothers.

My roommate, however, was even now on her way into the Master's house.

"They're out of the cookies," George warned, and Lydia slumped.

So, it was off to Clarissa's shindig. Clarissa Cuthbert lives in a very swank penthouse on the top floor of one of the classier apartment buildings in town. Her dad is some sort of Wall Street bigwig who thinks nothing of throwing money at a problem. The Cuthberts had even donated a very valuable Monet to Eli upon their daughter's admission to the university, though the ongoing campus debate about which came first, the admission or the donation, was not one I participated in anymore, for two reasons:

1) Clarissa is a fellow knight, and also a friend.
2) She told me the truth last year. (The donation, and it doesn't bother her, either.)

Clarissa is also rather notorious for her champagne-tasting parties, to which I'd never before rated an invitation. Apparently, all it took to pass the bar around here was an initiation to an elite society, and of course, the subsequent bonding over a vast misogynistic conspiracy that almost ruined us both. Clarissa and I were pretty tight these days.

But try explaining that to your barbarian best friend.

"I don't get it; why is it we like this bitch now?" Lydia asked, as we were ushered into an apartment scented with calla lilies and lit by hundreds of floating tea lights. A man in white tails offered us slender glasses of rosé champagne from a silver tray.

"What's not to like?" George said, taking his. "Thank you, my good man."

Clarissa Cuthbert, a vision in white silk and salon-sprayed tan, met us a moment later. "Darling!" she cried, air-kissing me on both cheeks as if we hadn't spent the afternoon together in a darkened tomb. "George, sweetheart!" Same for him. She turned to my roommate. "Lydia, right? We met last spring."

"Hi," Lydia said. "Nice digs."

"Thank you! Canapés are on the back sideboard." She turned to point and her long, perfectly highlighted blond hair swung over her shoulder, revealing for a moment the edge of the Rose & Grave tattoo on her shoulder blade. George looked at me and raised his eyebrow. Lydia clamped down on my arm. Crap.

POSSIBLE RESPONSES

1) "What tattoo? I think there was something in her hair."
2) "Roses. How cliché."
3) Deny, deny, deny.

But, as it turns out, Lydia's grip had not been inspired by the tat. "Oh, my God, Amy. Don't. Look."

Of course, I looked. Across the room, picking through a tray of chocolate-dipped strawberries, stood Brandon Weare. His hair was even longer this year, and streaked with golden highlights. His tan had deepened over the summer, like always. Brandon. From what I heard at the Lit Mag, he'd just gotten back to campus. He hadn't been at school in time to help me on the frosh issue. Luckily, I'd had Arielle for backup. It was little more than a clips issue, so no biggie, but—

Lydia's grip on my arm grew tighter. His plate loaded with fruit, Brandon crossed the room and joined a group of attendees. One turned and smiled at him. She had straight black hair. She had wide-set black eyes. She had an eensy waist. And as I watched, she snagged a strawberry and brought it to his lips.

I threw back the champagne.

"Maybe she's helping him because his hands are full," Lydia suggested.

The girl kissed a trace of chocolate from the corner of his mouth.

"Or not."

The two of us shuffled behind a shoji screen. "Okay, game plan," I said, steeling myself. "I've seen him, so the initial shock has passed."

"Right. Step one achieved without public humiliation."

"So the next question is: Approach him or wait for him to approach me?"

"Tough call. Approaching him puts the power in his hands," Lydia said, "but in this crowd, he might not see you at all, and the resulting ego blow would be—"

"Crippling." I nodded. "It's a dilemma."

The screen shook slightly. "Knock, knock," George said. "Is this some kind of private summit usually reserved for group trips to the ladies' room?"

"Ah, a wingman!" Lydia exclaimed.

"Negatory." If I was going to appear on anyone's arm, it wouldn't be George Harrison Prescott's. Brandon had broken up with me after discovering I'd hooked up with George mere minutes before I'd agreed to make our friends-with-benefits relationship official. I doubt such a display now would improve my rating on the slut-o-meter.

"What are you two plotting?"

"George," I said, "be a darling and get us more champagne."

As soon as he was gone, I slipped out from behind the screen and sashayed across the room, head held high. With my snazzy red highlights, I was hardly about to blend into Clarissa's "Martha Stewart is my godmother" white décor. He'd see me, and he'd stop me to say hi.

But not before Clarissa did. "Amy, honey, come meet my good friend from camp!" One perfectly French-manicured hand on my elbow later, there I was, face-to-face with long black hair, wide-set eyes, eensy-weensy waist, and—dear Lord, those boobs couldn't be real, could they? "This is Felicity Bower and her boyfriend, Brandon. Felicity and I spent six summers together at Camp Lake Hubert for Girls."

And that simply couldn't be her real name, either. "Hi, I'm Amy Haskel," I said in as strong a voice as I could muster.

Felicity's eyes got even bigger, but it was Brandon who spoke. "Hi, Amy. How was your summer?"

And then he hugged me.

I pulled back right before my major organs went into emergency shutdown. "It was good." I swallowed. My throat was parched. Jesus, where was George with that champagne? Where was George with that body and that face and those eyes? Felicity was blinking at me. "I was in D.C., working for a think tank." Was Brandon taller? What was up with the five o'clock shadow on his chin? Who did he think he was, Keanu Reeves? Did Felicity actually go for that shit? "We were putting together narratives by exploited women."

"Wow!" Felicity said. "What an amazing job! How did you score that one?"

"It sort of fell in my lap, last minute," I offered lamely. The kind of last minute that comes of knowing a Digger patriarch. Of course, the society owed me after screwing up my first job. A waiter passed by and I swiped another glass of champagne.

"Man," Felicity said, "all I did this summer was house-sit my uncle's place."

Clarissa heaved a dramatic sigh. "Woe is you, lounging in the Hong Kong mansion."

Felicity blushed, beautifully. Of course. "Well, I almost died of boredom until I met this one." She ruffled Brandon's hair. "And then my uncle totally made it all up to me when he lent us his yacht for our cruise around Fiji."

Okay, she totally knew about me and Brandon, so she was just doing that to be a bitch. As soon as he saw the focus of my gaze, Brandon caught her hand and pulled it down.

(I'm not ashamed to admit he's a far better person than I am. Had he treated me the way I'd treated him, I would have basked in showing off my new, drop-dead-gorgeous, rich-as-Pluto significant other in front of him.)

"No dates for me this summer," Clarissa said, oddly oblivious to the tension. "After Mom found Dad in flagrante with the dog-walker, she went on this whole I-am-woman-hear-me-purr kick. Completely cut the Y chromosome out of her existence. Except for the divorce lawyer, of course."

"What happened to your dad?" I asked. There was no love lost between Mr. Cuthbert and me, not after the way he and his Rose & Grave patriarch cronies had sabotaged our tap class. Of course, he'd sabotaged his daughter at the same time. I wondered exactly how daddy dearest and his dog-walker had gotten caught.

"Considering the heinous details of the case," Clarissa began, then shot me a look reminding me, as if I needed it, never to get on the bad side of the Digger named Angel, "we suffered obvious emotional trauma such that...well, let's just say my father readily arranged to keep us both in the manner to which we'd become accustomed." She stopped the latest server. "Beluga, anyone?"

"Actually, we'd better get going," Brandon said, slipping

an arm around Felicity's waist. "It was nice meeting you, Clarissa." He nodded at me. "See you later, Amy."

And then they were gone, before I had time to figure out whether it was a *see you around* kind of "see you later" or an *I'm going to call you so we can discuss this* kind of "see you later." I wasn't given much chance to ponder it either, as we were immediately set upon by the Prescott College contingent—George and Lydia.

"Well?" Lydia asked.

"He looks different, he smells different, and he's dating a girl named Felicity." Still quite the hugger, though.

Comprehension dawned chez Clarissa. "So you know that guy pretty well?"

"Biblically."

She groaned (though George was grinning). "Total social faux pas. So sorry, Amy."

I took a deep breath. "I'm fine."

"Felicity?" Lydia cocked an eyebrow.

I glared at her in warning. "I said I'm fine."

"Which is more than I can say for some of my other guests." Clarissa gestured to Jenny Santos, who was sitting on a white couch looking disdainful. I don't know what that girl's deal is. If you're going to take part in something, shouldn't you commit yourself? She'd skipped out on our rehearsal earlier, and now she was acting too good for a fellow Digger's party. And while I could dismiss the former as merely overextending her activities, I'm not quite sure what motivated the latter. If she didn't want champagne, Clarissa no doubt had plenty of fancy French spring water.

"She's been hiding out all evening," Clarissa said. "George, want to come with me and get her circulating?"

George began to edge toward the sideboard. "I think I'll pass. That girl has always looked at me like she's Salome and I'm John the Baptist."

If he used lines like that more often, Jenny would probably like him better. Clarissa went off to cheer up our resident party-pooping Digger, and Lydia and I found space to perch on the edge of a wingback chair.

"So what do you think was up with George's parents?" Lydia asked over the din of the party. "His dad acted like he knew you."

"I think we met move-in day freshman year," I lied smoothly. "Or maybe he got me mixed up with one of the billion girls always dangling off his son." I knew all about George's divorced parents' long-term love-hate (or at least lust-hate) relationship, but George had told me that in confidence, Digger to Digger. The report wasn't for Lydia's barbarian ears, or even, as far as I was concerned, for other Diggers until George felt like sharing it himself. Had I not spent last spring keeping the secret of my society big sib Malcolm's sexual identity?

Malcolm's e-mail made him sound so lonely up there in Alaska. I understood his desire to take a gap year before starting business school, especially given the trauma of coming out to his ultra-conservative governor father, but did he have to do it in such an isolated locale? That reminded me, I didn't finish reading his e-mail.

Or figure out who had sent me the other one. I looked over at Clarissa and Jenny, whose company had grown. "Excuse me for a minute," I said to Lydia, who was already waving to a fellow Debate Team member near the cheese fondue, and crossed the room.

The knot of girls on Jenny's couch had only two things in common:

1) A small tattoo of a rose inside an elongated hexagon somewhere on their bodies.

2) The fact that they'd once taken on a group of
   powerful and vicious men and lived to tell the tale.

Other than that, we didn't look as if we'd be friends at all, and I wondered if—extreme circumstances aside—we really were. Sure, we'd bonded as taps and at various society events over the summer, but once we got into the schedule of classes and regular meetings, what would we have to talk about? A club of Diggers was supposed to offer one another support and advice. But what did a Hollywood starlet like Odile Dumas have to say to a computer whiz like Jenny Santos? What kind of support could a radical activist like Demetria offer to a socialite like Clarissa Cuthbert?

Still, you'd think I was the only one questioning stuff if you saw the enthusiasm with which they greeted me. "Hey, chica!" Odile called, pulling me down next to her. "We were talking about Mara. One more girl for our little revolution, eh?"

"I saw her this afternoon," I said. "She's kind of intense."

"She's a classist bitch." Demetria sniffed. "Did you read her column in *The Ivory Tower* about how they never should have let women into Eli?"

"Sounds like a girl the patriarchs would like," I said. "Did she really write that?" *The Ivory Tower* is this crazy conservative paper on campus.

"Yes. Said the school was at its height before they sullied the student population with an excess of estrogen. Wonder what she thinks of breaking the gender barrier at our club?"

"I wonder why she even accepted the tap," Clarissa said.

"You expect a hypocrite to act rationally?" Jenny asked. "She thinks women shouldn't be at Eli, but she's a student here. If she really believed we don't belong here, wouldn't she be cooling her heels at Wellesley or someplace?" She toyed with the end of her long, dark braid and tucked her chin into her chest, as if the outburst had sapped all of her socializing strength. "Sounds less as if she's saying what she really means than that she's parroting the words of her cronies." And then she clammed up completely, as if afraid to say more on the subject.

"I don't know," I said. "She didn't seem the submissive type in class today. Took on Professor Branch and everything."

"Well, we'll get the scoop tomorrow," Clarissa said.

I twirled the glass in my hand. "Hey, guys?" I said, tentatively. "I have to tell you something. Before I came here tonight, I was checking my D-mail, and there was this message...."

They all froze. They all looked down at their drinks. And then Jenny said, "So, you got it, too?"

I hereby confess:

Paranoia loves company.

3.
Skulls and Drones

I'll be the first to cop to a certain affinity for overthinking. Most of the time, it's served me well. (Cf. academic success culminating in admittance to and continuing high GPA at Eli University.) Occasionally, it's gotten me into trouble. (Cf. habit of constantly attributing mysterious occurrences to the shady machinations of misogynist Rose & Grave patriarchs. But sometimes, it really is their fault. After all, they tried to ruin my life last semester, so a little healthy wariness isn't a bad thing.)

But if every girl in the club got a mysterious e-mail, I sat up and took notice. When the club convened before the straggler initiation a few days later, we discussed the bizarre rhyming e-mails and what they could mean. Each Diggirl had received a two-line message sent from her regular Eli account to her Digger-mail; the time stamps showed each e-mail had been sent two minutes apart. When assembled by order of the time stamps, the couplets formed the following ditty:

YOU THINK ITS OVER BUT ITS NOT

FROM WITHIN DOTH PERSEPHONE ROT

THEY WONT LOSE THAT FOR WHICH THEY FOUGHT

PRETTY SOON THEYLL SNATCH YOUR SLOT

TO SEE WHAT KIND OF DOOM YOUVE BROUGHT

CUT THROUGH THE WEB IN WHICH YOURE CAUGHT

LEARN OF THE THIEF WHO CAN BE BOUGHT

FOR THEY HAVE FOUND YOUR ONE WEAK SPOT

BEWARE OF POISON IN YOUR DRAUGHT

OR IGNOBLE DEATH SHALL BE YOUR LOT*

"What do you think?" Thorndike asked, after pasting the lines together on her laptop.

"That whoever it is needs to brush up on diction," I said. " 'Draught' is pronounced like 'draft.' Totally wrecks the rhyme scheme. And don't get me started on the lack of punctuation."

"Plus," Lil' Demon added, pointing at line four, "this part sounds kind of dirty."

Thorndike slapped Lil' Demon's hand away from the screen. "Can you get sex off your mind for one second?"

Lil' Demon pursed her full lips and winked saucily down at Thorndike. "Oh, come on, you thought it, too. *Snatch?* Please."

Lucky blushed. "Moving on, what do we think it means?" For the moment, at least, she'd dropped her derision in favor of helpful discourse.

"Haven't the foggiest," Angel said. She turned to me. "Really? Draft?"

I nodded. "Who could have sent this? It had to be another

---

*All [sic], naturally.

Digger, right? Someone who knows our society names and e-mail addresses?"

"Great," Clarissa said. "That narrows it down to about 700 living patriarchs."

"Well, probably fewer than that who know anything about computers," Jenny said. "I wouldn't credit this to anyone older than D150 or so. If it even *is* a Digger," she added under her breath.

"Or it could be a patriarch willing to pay off some geek in the IT department," I said. "Honestly? It could be anyone."

It was a sobering thought, but Lil' Demon was rarely one for sober. "All right, ladies. Let's discuss this with the guys after the initiation. Costumes, places, let's get moving."

Little did we know that, post-ceremony, a badly written poem would be the last thing on any of our minds.

———

The tomb kitchen on the lower level had been converted into a makeup trailer, which had rendered our aged caretaker, Hale, a quivering mess. "Hollywood types invading the tomb," he was muttering from his place outside the entrance to the kitchen. "Never would have stood for it in the good old days."

"There, there, Hale," I said, checking out my costume in the ancient, diamond-dust mirror hanging floor to ceiling at the dead end of the downstairs hall. The Rose & Grave tomb housed the coolest stuff. The mirror's gorgeous carved wood frame featured various scenes from the tale of Persephone and was crowned at the top with a giant carving of a rose. Its reflection was a bit on the wavy side, but that was to be expected in such an antique. Almost a shame they kept it down here in the basement.

"They'll be gone in an hour or so," I said. "And plus, it's not like they're seeing anything important, just hanging in the kitch—" He glared at me from under his bushy gray eyebrows and I shut my lip. Probably wouldn't do to characterize our caretaker's main domain as the least important part of the tomb. Hale took extraordinary pride in being the Diggers' caretaker, as his father had been before him. No one in the society knew who we would hire after he succumbed to the ravages of age, since Hale had no kids and the position wasn't exactly one we wanted to advertise for on Craigslist.

"Oh, Hale," I said quickly, walking toward him and putting my hand on his shoulder in a gesture of comfort. "I meant to mention this to you: Apparently Lancelot, D176, got a huge catch of halibut in Alaska. He's sending some down for our deep freeze."

"You heard from him?" asked a voice behind me, and I turned to find myself face-to-face with Death.

Or Poe, in Grim Reaper makeup. Same diff, as far as I was concerned. Damn, where had he come from? He's an Olympic-class lurker, this one.

"Yeah, the other day," I said.

Poe frowned (or maybe it was just the spirit gum) and jammed his hand in his pockets. "Oh. How's he doing?"

Poe hadn't heard from him? "Good. He, um, told me to say hi." Actually, that wasn't what Malcolm had written at all, but I have my limits when it comes to Poe. After all, four short months ago, the guy standing before me had stuck me in a plywood coffin and threatened to dump me in a pool. (I don't swim.) No love lost around here.

"He owes me an e-mail." Now Poe crossed his arms over his chest. "So, how was your summer?"

"Good," I said. "I was in D.C."

"Yeah. Working for that patriarch."

Oops, bad topic. Poe had lost his own patriarch-bestowed internship at the White House after (eventually and reluctantly) siding with me and the other active Diggers in our battle last spring. I wasn't sure what he'd been up to this summer. (Though whatever it was, judging from his arms, he'd gotten a tan. Looked good on him, actually.)

"So, how's...law school?" Last I heard, Poe had been scheduled to start as a 1L at Eli Law this fall, which meant this campus was stuck with him for three more years. Bummer.

"Fine."

The conversation was going swimmingly. We stood in silence for a second or so, and then Poe, in a misguided attempt to jump-start the exchange, said, "Lil' Demon asked me to play the Reaper tonight. Guess she couldn't find anyone in the *current* class she liked enough to take on the role."

Yeah, because insulting my club would definitely warm me up. "Or maybe she thought no one else had the requisite air of depression and desperation." I smiled. "Planning on drowning anyone this evening?"

He matched my grim smile, and this time it wasn't the makeup. "Only if you get close enough, Bugaboo."

Asshole. I opened my mouth to respond, but Angel interrupted me. "Bugaboo, your turn in the chair," she called, and I shot Poe one last, withering glare and departed.

"Who was that?" she asked me as the makeup artist started in with the airbrush. "I couldn't tell under the goop."

"Poe. Remember?"

She looked back at him. "Really? Jeez, what did he do over the summer? Take up bodybuilding?"

"Don't know, don't care. He should have spent the time getting a personality."

"He's got a personality," Thorndike interrupted from

the chair next to mine. Her artist gave her a warning glance and gestured dangerously with the palette knife. "It's just not a pleasant one."

The girls all laughed, and I noted Poe shrugging into his robe in the opposite corner of the kitchen, back turned. He hunched his shoulders at the sound. *Oh, damn.*

Whatever, Amy. He's a jerk. Save your sympathy for someone else.

Lucky dropped by as I was tying the hood on my robe. "Hey, Bugaboo, I already talked to Soze, but I wanted to tell you that my—um, friend...he didn't mean what he said at the bazaar. It just came out wrong." She looked down at her hands. "He sometimes doesn't realize how it sounds. I hope you don't think I—"

I put my hand over hers, my earlier annoyance for her lack of commitment vanishing. "Of course I don't. You're one of us. I trust you. And we can talk about it more if you want." I checked the swiftly emptying kitchen. "After the initiation." She was always so much friendlier inside the tomb than when I saw her in the barbarian world. Better take advantage of it while I could.

Half an hour later, we were at "places," waiting for the show to start, which meant I was back to crouching in a dusty corner with my bag o' glitter, wishing I'd done more thigh workouts at the gym.

"Yo, 'boo," Puck whispered across the way. "See anything yet?" He'd had been given the role of Quetzalcoatl in the festivities, proving perhaps that Lil' Demon's true talent lay in casting choices, because the shirtless-loincloth outfit was an excellent look for the boy. Feathered headdress, scale makeup, and all.

"No," I whispered back.

"Good." He slithered over to my side of the hallway (and I say that literally, as those FX guys had somehow applied a

long tail to his outfit—which was, no, *still* not a turnoff) and
slid down the wall next to me, crossing his legs beneath him.
I spotted gym shorts beneath the loincloth. Damn. "About
last night—"

Oh, no, *please* don't ask about Brandon! "Yeah?"

"I wanted to apologize."

Huh?

"For my mom. She's not usually like that." He fiddled
with some of the beading on his ceremonial bracelets.

"Oh. That's okay." I cocked my head to one side. Was
that the chanting in the Firefly Room starting up?

"We got some news." He took a deep breath. "My dad's
pregnant. I mean, his wife. They're having a baby. And let's
just say he's known for a lot longer than he's been acting like
it where my mom's concerned."

I couldn't even work up a token expression of surprise.
Disdain, however, was available in surplus.

"Romantic, huh?" Puck said.

"Depends on your definition of romance."

"I try not to have one." He leaned into me, and let his
voice drop to a low, husky timbre. "I find it's better for everyone involved if I keep myself open to . . . new interpretations."

"How magnanimous," I said. "And kind of kinky." Which
would have sounded a lot smoother if my hands hadn't gotten all clammy at the thought and dropped the bag of phosphorescent dust.

He looked down at the glitter scattered across the floor,
then at me. "Slick move, Amy."

"Ooh, best stick with 'boo, at least in the tomb. That will
be two dollars."

"Stupid fines," he whispered against my hood.

I shifted my face ever so slightly toward his. "Tell you
what, I'll say 'George' and then we'll be even." But then

neither of us said much of anything, what with the fact that our mouths were busy and all.

Now, you'd think cold tomb floors are not the most pleasant place to lie, but if you've got George Harrison Prescott—I mean, Puck—on top of you, you'd be wrong. Even with the random jabs and pokes from the quills on his costume, I was chock full of pleasure. Every time I kiss him (which has been twice now) I'm struck by the puerile nature of all the silly games men and women play. Why the coy drama? I want him and he wants me; who needs subtext?

Everything was going along beautifully in the first base department, and we were blithely and completely irresponsibly (considering the timing) headed to second when the explosion happened.

We froze at the din, and stared at each other as the floor of the tomb shuddered beneath us. Puck bit his lip. " 'Boo, your face—"

"Get up," I said, yanking my robe out from underneath him. "Get up now!"

Together, we rushed toward the balcony and looked down to see billows of smoke emanating from the Firefly Room. Several figures stumbled out, coughing, and Keyser Soze rushed down the hall, wielding a fire extinguisher. "Outta my way! Outta my way, folks! The last thing we need is the fire department up in here."

"What happened?" Puck shouted down as we rounded the stairs. From what little I could see of the room, there appeared to be no raging inferno inside, but that had been one hell of a bang.

"Pyrotech issue," Lil' Demon gasped. "It's okay, it's okay. The grips got it out."

"Bugaboo," Thorndike said, pointing her pitchfork at me. "What's all over your face?"

"Whatever it is," Lucky said, waving her hand around to

clear the smoke out of the air, "it's the same stuff on Puck's chest."

I looked at Puck, whose body was smeared all over with phosphorescent dust. It was streaked on my robe and my hands as well, an obvious testament to my backstage activities.

Thorndike raised an eyebrow in my direction, and her disapproving expression was helped enormously by her devil costume. *Playa*, she mouthed in warning.

"Move it, girly," Hale cried, shoving Thorndike aside to join Soze on extinguisher duty.

"Dear Lord," came a voice through the haze. "What kind of show are you people running here?" I saw a curly head emerge from the smoky darkness. "I'd never expect the Diggers to be so sloppy!" Mara Taserati surveyed Lucky, Lil' Demon, Thorndike, and me clustered at the foot of the stairs. "So the rumors are true," she said.

Um, what did she think? She was a girl, too.

"Apparently they're *all* true," said Angel, joining us and crossing her arms over her chest. The rubber asp forming the bulk of her Cleopatra costume slipped down one shoulder, exposing more than just her tattoo.

Soze clapped his hands. "Okay, guys. Fire's out. Let's go back now."

Mara snorted inelegantly. "Right, more endangering of my life? I'm not up for that, thanks."

"I'm with her," said a boy I assumed must be Howard First, another straggler. "I don't know if I want to be a part of this until you guys get your acts together."

The Grim Reaper glided up and placed hands on both of their shoulders. "The Play is in progress, Neophytes. Come this way." Figures Poe would be able to stay in character throughout the crisis.

But Howard shook him off. "Forget it, dude. I have strict standards when it comes to the protection of my body."

"Is that what you were doing in that Colombian jungle last spring?" Thorndike asked. "Adhering to your strict standards?"

"Actually, no," he replied. "I was inoculating children." And with that bit of rampant holier-than-thou-ism, he made a beeline for the door.

Poe raised his eyebrows at me. Okay, so the scene did remind me a lot of what I'd done after he'd hit me with the water guns at my own initiation, but how was I supposed to defend the society in this case? Poe had been tricking me with super-soakers. I don't think that explosion was a trick.

Here goes nothing. "Howard, wait!" I cried, running forward. "Look, don't go. It's just part of the initiation game— all of it. You should have seen the crap they pulled with me in April. They threatened to drown me, they threatened to rape me—"

"And this somehow endeared them to you?" he asked.

"Well, no, not as such but—"

"Look—uh, Glow Girl, or whatever part you're supposed to be playing—this isn't really my type of gig, okay?"

"Then why did you accept the tap?"

"Jungle fever?" he suggested.

Well, Kurtz, welcome to a whole new heart of darkness. "Look, I didn't think it was my thing, either." And my enemies would agree with that. "But it's been—"

"Get out while you still can, man," interrupted Graverobber. "Before any *vows* are taken. I wish I had. These cats don't have the same cachet they used to." He leaned against the wall. "Word is, the endowment's drying up as well."

Like Mr. Greek-shipping-heir Graverobber needed any extra dough! "Back off," I hissed. I turned to Howard. "As you can see, we'd really love some new blood in the brotherhood."

"As you can see," Graverobber echoed, "the word 'brother-hood' is a bit of a misnomer."

"Both literally and figuratively. You two are at each other's throats." Howard shook his head. "I don't have time for this drama. I've got MCATs to study for." And with that, he turned and walked out the front door.

Everyone stood and stared with their mouths open. I turned to Poe. "What do we do now?"

"Same thing I did last year. Go beg."

"Me? I didn't even start the fire. Where's his big sib?" Weren't there any other patriarchs on campus, or were we only blessed with this creep?

"Cutting up cadavers at Berkeley," Poe said flatly. "Oaths of loyalty clearly don't cross the Continental Divide."

Oh, for Persephone's sake! I grabbed Graverobber's arm and yanked him after me in pursuit of our stray straggler.

"Howard!" I cried, as we sprinted down the steps and through the (open) gate. "Come back! Let's talk about this."

A bunch of freshmen at High Street Gate gave us weird looks, so Nikolos grabbed Howard's elbow and pulled him into the alley next to the tomb leading to the sculpture garden. Once we were well hidden by building shadow and the drooping branches of a willow, I pushed back my hood. "Look here," I said. "You accepted the tap. We put you on the list we sent out to all the patriarchs. You're in. How can you go back on it now?"

"That was April." He shrugged. "I've had a long summer to think it over, and with all of my commitments right now, I don't know how much I can devote to you people."

But he hadn't decided that until he'd gotten inside and took a good look at us. Why did I have to be the one begging this jerk to come back? I didn't care how many third-world children he'd inoculated.

I elbowed Nikolos, and he sighed, but rallied. "Your

commitments? You're the one senior on campus who's still involved in activities? Can you not spare a little time for us? We will definitely make it worth your while."

Howard chuckled. "A little? You're a senior, right? Totally new to all of this. You don't know how much time we're talking about." He began ticking things off on his fingers. "I'm a freshmen counselor, I'm doing my biochem thesis, I'm on the board at the Jewish Students Center, and I volunteer at a lab downtown a few nights a week. Unfortunately, it wasn't until I was inside that tomb that I realized how much more those things matter to me than a bunch of strangers in weird costumes."

"We don't always wear the costumes," I pointed out, to little avail. We wouldn't always be strangers, either.

"Look, sweetheart, I know the guy who was grooming me to fill his spot in Rose & Grave, and he was a mess last year. Something happened where he almost lost his place in school. . . . I didn't get the details."

"So you think you'll avoid that by denying us?" Nikolos asked.

"Getting out before I get in too deep sounds good to me," Howard replied. "These meetings of yours are going to start taking up a couple nights a week—all night long. Wait and see. And then, when you're struggling to finish your thesis on time, ask yourself if it was worth it. I'll be seeing you. Or," he added, giving my black robe the up-down, "maybe not."

And then he was gone. I rubbed my temples in frustration, then glanced in dismay at my glitter-covered hands. Great. More mess to deal with. "Now what?" I turned to Nikolos. "Should we keep following him?"

Nikolos pulled at the tie on his robe and slipped it off his shoulders. "I'm not going to do it in this outfit," he said. "I feel somewhat responsible. I probably shouldn't have said those things to him back at the tomb. Let me try to catch him and make this right."

I nodded, glad to see Nikolos was willing to shoulder some of the responsibility. Still, I didn't have much hope. I watched him take off after our straggler, though he still hadn't caught up by the time they turned the corner off of High Street and onto Elm.

Stunned, dejected, and yeah, a little concerned Howard First might actually be onto something, I returned to the tomb, to find Mara holding court.

"Don't you find it disheartening?" she was asking Poe. "So many of our brotherhoods have fallen by the wayside, been gobbled up by the PC police. If you ask me, it's these newfangled organizations that are truly the elitist ones. For all that students rail against the secret societies, who is really the one propagating racist doctrine on our campus?"

"Your newspaper?" Thorndike suggested.

"The administration is more intent on founding yet another alliance of people based on the color of their skin and cultural heritage—the Southeast Asian Alliance, the Muslim Student Alliance, the Northwestern Nepalese Students' Union—rather than on what brought us all here in the first place, intellectual meritocracy! A fervent desire to drink from the fountain of knowledge."

"You know, that's an interesting point," Soze said.

Lil' Demon frowned. "Isn't it the fountain of *youth* and the *lamp* of knowledge?"

Lucky shrugged. "That sounds about right. At least, there's a lamp on the seal of my Eli throw blanket."

Mara droned on. "There's such a lack of respect for the traditions of this noble institution."

"Rose & Grave?" I whispered to Angel.

"No, I think she's still talking about Eli as a whole."

"Well, there's plenty of respect-lacking going on for

Rose & Grave right now." I hung my head. "I think we lost Howard." All eyes turned in my direction. "Graverobber is still working on him but—"

"Because he's such a good advocate," scoffed Thorndike.

"He's the only person who volunteered," I argued.

Soze raised his hands. "Hey, I was on extinguisher duty."

"So what do we do now?" I asked. "If we really lost a straggler. If he chooses the 'new' organizations—as our neophyte here so carefully elucidated—over us."

Mara waved her hand in the air. "Excuse me, miss? I'm not a neophyte. They just initiated me. I'm Juno now."

I looked at Poe. "Come on. You're the one who knows all the policies and procedures of this outfit. Tell us what the game plan is."

But Poe just laughed. "Right, because after that spectacular display of spitting all over my advice last spring, I'm going to completely relinquish all rights to say 'I told you so'." He pulled off his robe, and began to peel the Death's-head makeup from his face. "You guys made this bed; I hope you like lying in it."

Quoth Juno: "Where's the party? There's supposed to be a party after this, right?"

Quoth Lucky: *"From within doth Persephone rot."*

Quoth the Middle-Eastern-guy-I-later-recognized-as-Harun-Sarmast-our-last-straggler as he stuck his head over the balcony: "Um, guys? I've been waiting up here with my blindfold on for a while. Anything wrong?"

I hereby confess:

I'm not proud of my Hit List.

4.
Assignations

WHY I DON'T LIKE SUNDAYS
(THIS ONE IN PARTICULAR)

1) Upon waking, am smacked upside the head by
   calendar date and thereby reminded of all the things
   I need to do before Monday (usually comprising
   term paper, test, problem set, etc.).
2) Often regret whatever I did Saturday night. (This
   week it was attending an early October Jane Fonda
   marathon at the Eli Film Society, which was
   Kevin's—a.k.a. Frodo's—idea, though he'd ducked
   out somewhere in the middle of *Barefoot in the Park*.
   By the end, I thought someone had roofied my Solo
   cup, but then I realized it was just *Barbarella*. George
   had intimated he'd show up as well, but he'd
   obviously found someone better to do. Ugh.)
3) Always find a huge debate waiting for me on the
   D177 e-mail loop. (These are usually started by
   Graverobber, about the deplorable state of the

society—like he would have anything to compare it to!—and seconded by Juno. It's as if they insist the pot get stirred immediately prior to our Sunday meetings. Though this week, I was more than willing to get into a debate about the future of the society. I found it far preferable to the official event on the docket....)

4) My C.B. is tonight. Gulp.

The C.B.s, or Connubial Bliss reports, are a rite of passage for every Digger. Each of us is assigned one evening starting in late September to stand up in front of all of our brothers and discuss our love lives, soup to nuts. It's supposed to be some sort of bonding experience—as if, after carefully detailing all the sordid details of romances gone wrong, the rest of the club will somehow think it's made us closer, rather than giving us juicy fodder with which to earn us a spot on a Matt Lauer show of the future.

We'd had two already: Josh Silver's and Clarissa Cuthbert's. Josh, being first, wasn't quite sure exactly how much information was too much, but thankfully we'd stopped him short of any description of bodily fluids. Though single at the moment, he'd had a bunch of girlfriends over the years, none who'd really knocked his socks off. Perhaps, he explained, that was the reason why he'd never been able to remain faithful to any of them. Every single one of his serious relationships had ended when Josh had failed to keep it in his pants.

"This," George had whispered to me from our position on one of the leather couches in the Inner Temple, "is why I don't get into relationships. No heartache if you were never trying to be faithful in the first place."

But Josh remained hopeful. "I like having a girlfriend," he'd insisted. "It's nice to know there's someone who will be there for me."

"Even if you're not there for them?" Demetria had asked. Nikolos snorted, which, I was learning, was his standard reaction whenever he thought discourse in the tomb was growing too girly. This occurred with annoying frequency (cf. his firebrand e-mails). Unfortunately, no serious discussion ever took place on the topic because Nikolos didn't see any cure to what he perceived as the problem, except to get rid of the Diggirls, full stop. This had been his argument for the past six weeks, ever since we'd lost Howard.

Clarissa's C.B. was every bit as dishy as one would expect. Of course, she discussed her misspent youth, including the thirty-year-old boyfriend she'd hidden from her parents while in high school. Odile had nodded in silent empathy, having no doubt played the ingenue to plenty of would-be movie moguls in her time. (No one could wait to hear her C.B. and find out if the rumors about her and the various movie stars and hip-hop artists were true.) A sample of the type of anecdote to which our club was subjected:

Clarissa: I mean, who amongst us hasn't tried anal?
Most of the Rest of Us (I bet you can guess who wasn't included in that number!): *(raises hand)* Um, me?
Clarissa: And after a few weeks, he asked me if I'd get a Sphinx Brazilian.
Jenny: A what?
Odile: Bikini wax. *All* of it.
George: *(grins)* Cool.
Jenny: *(looks horrified)*
Clarissa: *(not even pausing)* But after I did it, I felt prepubescent. I haven't seen that part of me since I was eleven. I wasn't in the mood for sex until it had grown back.
Nikolos: *(snorts)*

See how that might be a tough act for me to follow? I didn't know how I'd deal with another night of Nikolos's snorts. And what if they snickered at my more embarrassing anecdotes? At least I'd already fallen in the middle of the statistics in the "virginity lost" and "partners had" categories.

Still, I doubted my tale of prom after-party sex in the bedroom of the host's kid sister was going to impress anyone. I'm pretty run-of-the-mill for a Digger. Especially since there was only one orgasm involved, and it wasn't mine. I bet Odile had done it on the top of the Eiffel Tower at midnight, or maybe on the Concorde. George had probably done it on the space shuttle. Would not surprise me a bit. As for Jenny, I was beginning to get the impression she was still a virgin. Not that there's anything wrong with that. Quick C.B. and then we can all go home and study. I was all for it, especially now that it was October and classes were in full swing.

Not to give you the impression we only talked about sex! Before the C.B.s began, we'd tested the waters of knightly bonding with reports that amounted to recaps of summer vacation. I told everyone about my summer spent transcribing and editing narratives by exploited women, an experience I still hadn't wrapped my mind around. I'd always figured I'd move to New York after graduation and work in publishing. All of a sudden I was gathering Peace Corps brochures from the Eli Career Center and looking into graduate school programs. All of a sudden I couldn't picture myself in a cubicle, a realization I sheepishly shared with the other knights. But they were surprisingly supportive. I'd have thought with the Diggerly emphasis on ambition, the other knights would scoff at a career path that wasn't fast track. I was wrong. Demetria had told me all about an upcoming project she was running for Habitat for Humanity, and Jenny—in one of her increasingly infrequent talkative phases—explained that she'd gone through a similar enlightenment after being involved in an Indonesian clean water project her church had sponsored two summers ago.

I'd spent my whole life getting my resume in order. Maybe it was time to turn it into confetti.

I swung my legs over the side of the bed and padded out to our common room, bypassing my computer for the time being. If I was going to deal with "Graverobber's" griping, I needed sustenance. I reached to the top shelf, where we hid our contraband hot pot behind a large hardback of *Art Through the Ages*, and filled it with water from our purifying pitcher. (I will never understand who the fire marshal thinks he's kidding with his surprise inspections every semester. He knows we have coffeepots and stuff in here, and we know he knows. It's all such a game. Demetria tells this story about sophomore year when he came into her suite while she and her roommates were huddled about the hot pot, smoking— another no-no—and waiting for their soup to warm. He just shook his head and wrote them a ticket. Demetria claims she used it for rolling papers.)

What was I going to say at this thing? I plugged in the pot and plopped down on the couch, drawing my knees up inside my oversized sleep shirt and pondering the issue at hand. How embarrassing would it be to let everyone know that a week in my arms caused number two on my Hit List, a faux-beatnik named Galen Twilo, to pack up his dog-eared copy of *Howl* and burn for a *different* "ancient heavenly connection to the starry dynamo of . . ." whatever-it-was.

Or would I open up the wound from number three, the supposed love of my short life, Alan Albertson, who'd abruptly left me for someone named Fulbright? Or Brandon, number five, who I couldn't manage to hold on to for longer than a few days. How about that one-night stand I'd had in

between the two of them, that Spring Break mistake I don't
remember well enough to report his full name?

I could imagine why these C.B.s were so popular with
male-only clubs. The double standard was in full force, once
again. A man having anonymous sex was a *Penthouse* letter. A
woman doing it was something different altogether. And
there was probably nothing I could say that would impress
George enough to keep him from sorta making plans with
me and then sorta standing me up. I leaned my head back
and began massaging my temples. Five minutes in, and the
day already sucked.

The door to Lydia's bedroom opened and out walked a
very rumpled-looking Josh Silver.

He stopped dead in his tracks when our eyes met, and for
a second we just stared at each other—me a bumpy T-shirt
lump on the sofa, him in a wrinkled button-down he'd obviously unwadded from a corner of Lydia's boudoir.

"What are you doing here?" he hissed.

"I live here," I replied. "Did you not notice the pictures
of me in her room? No, wait, don't answer that. I don't want
to know what you were busy noticing instead."

Lydia came to the door in her silk bathrobe. *Silk!* "Oh,
Amy, you're up. This is Josh."

"Hi, Josh," I said, extending my hand from inside my
tee. "Nice to meet you."

"Nice to meet *you*," he said, taking my hand in his.

"Oh, wait!" Lydia said. "What am I saying? You guys totally know each other."

We froze, mid-shake.

"Remember, Ames?" Lydia said. "At that political reception last January?"

I looked to Josh. Go with it? "Yeah, I think you look
vaguely familiar."

"Funny, I was just about to say the same."

"I'm going to go hop in the shower," Lydia said, then began to coyly toy with the felt-tipped marker attached to her whiteboard by a thin piece of yarn. *Lydia, coy!* "You, um, want to stick around for breakfast, Josh?"

"Sure."

Lydia left. The second the door closed behind her, Josh looked at me.

"Amy—"

"No."

"Amy—"

"*No.*"

"Amy—" He stopped. "Wait, 'no' what?"

"No, I'm not getting involved. This is barbarian matters, Josh."

"Oh." He plopped down beside me. "I thought you meant 'No, you can't see her.' "

"I like that one, too." I crossed my arms. "This is weird."

"That's my assessment."

"How did you … meet?"

He brightened. "It's a funny story, actually. It was at the inductee ceremony for Phi Beta Kappa last month."

My legs shot out of the bottom of my oversized T-shirt. "Phi Beta Kappa? But—"

"I know, that's what I thought, too." Josh nodded, getting into his narrative. "My dean called me in to her office to give me the news and I was all 'Thank you so much for the honor, ma'am, but I'm afraid I must decline, as I am already in a secret society.' "

I blinked at him. "Isn't Phi Beta Kappa just an honor society now? I think it doesn't conflict with our oaths."

"Yeah, I know that *now*," Josh said, rolling his eyes. "After they all had a nice good laugh at my expense."

I shook my head. We were getting way off track here. "Wait, let me get this straight. Lydia is in Phi Beta Kappa?"

"Yeah. Didn't she tell you? The induction was the day of Angel's champagne party."

"Two dollars," I said evenly. And no, she hadn't. But she *had* been ebullient that day, and this explained it. Why would Lydia keep such great news a secret from me, her best friend?

Josh was apparently wondering the same thing, considering the raised eyebrows he was currently pointing in my direction. And then, it clicked. She was keeping it from me because I was keeping Rose & Grave from her. So not fair. She got two secret societies to my one? (Lydia's secret society freaked me out, quite frankly. They almost destroyed our suite during their initiation last year. Of course, she'd never stand for me grilling her about it.)

"So anyway, that's where we met. I mean, we'd known each other from class and stuff, but for some reason, after the ceremony we just clicked. Bonded."

Knowing Lydia, seeing him in Phi Beta Kappa probably convinced her he was good enough for her.

"And now what?"

He looked at me quizzically.

"Is she your *girlfriend*?"

He looked down at his lap. "Yeah. I guess she is."

I shot to my feet.

"Amy—" He grabbed at my arm, but I whisked it away and made a beeline toward my bedroom.

"I'm getting dressed."

"Amy, your oath!"

"I'm getting dressed!" I yelled, and slammed the door.

What was I going to do? Lydia needed to know what she was getting herself into before she started to regret all of this coyness and Sunday morning sexy bathrobe wearing and cutesy little brunch invites. But what was I supposed to say? *Yes, this Josh fellow seems like a lovely guy, but I have it on good authority he's never been faithful to any of his girlfriends.* If I knew Lydia, she'd try to bludgeon my sources out of me.

Why I Don't Like Sundays (Especially This One): reason number five . . .

———

Brunch with Josh and Lydia got stickier than the dining hall's sweet buns when Lydia left the table for a second helping on her Eli breakfast sandwich. The Eli breakfast sandwich is the best thing our dining halls offer: greasy fried egg, greasier fried bacon, and a greasy, half-melted slice of cheddar on a greasy English muffin. It's to die for. Josh—who had, apparently, hopped in our shower while I'd been getting dressed—stared intently into his cornflakes. I concentrated on the opinion column in the *Eli Daily News* and munched a bagel. Neither of us saw it coming.

"This seat taken?" A loaded tray slammed down beside me. I looked up to see George frowning at our little tableau.

"At the risk of reaching critical mass," Josh said, "go ahead."

George sat down hard and began to pound the bottom of the ketchup bottle until the contents spurted out over his sandwich. But he wasn't watching the delectable he was currently drowning in condiment. Instead, he was staring daggers at Josh, whose wet hair was leaving little rivulets on the collar of his day-old shirt.

Oh. I smiled and returned to the newspaper, perfectly willing to let whatever dreadful and delicious conclusion George might have jumped to stand for the time being. That would teach him to stand me up! "Josh," I said, in the sweetest tone I could muster, "be a darling and pass me a napkin."

He gave me a curious glance, but did.

"So, Josh," George said, after a bite of ketchup-drenched sandwich, "you never did get back to us about that trip we wanted to take over Thanksgiving Break. You know, the one where we all go up to Canada for the cheap lap dances?"

"Oh, *really*?" I bit my lip to keep from grinning and turned the page to the comics section. Ooh, *Doonesbury*. Out of the corner of my eye, I saw Josh give a non-committal shrug, but I wasn't sure it was for my benefit. After all, we weren't under the seal of Rose & Grave right now. If I thought Josh, not Soze, and George, not Puck, were going on a strip-club lost weekend, I could tell Lydia just fine.

Of course, George played right into my hands. "Look, if I'm interrupting the two of you—"

And then Lydia came back and ruined everything. "George, scoot over," she said, bumping his tray and setting hers back down. "They were out of the kind with bacon." She pouted. "They always make too many lacto-ovo veggie ones." Josh sighed and switched his bacon-laden sandwich for hers, and she beamed at him. They were so cute I could just vomit.

George snorted. Great, another snorter in the club. I looked at him and he shook his head, then winked at me. "Nice try, Boo."

When Lydia, Josh, and I left the dining hall, I found George waiting for me in the Prescott College Common Room, legs slung over the armrest of a leather love seat. He waved, and I latched on to any excuse to depart from the company of the lovebirds.

"What do you want?" I asked.

"Is that any way to greet your brother?" He feigned hurt.

"No doubt the way you would prefer I greet you isn't very sisterly, either."

He nodded and moved over on the seat. "That's true. Sit down and talk to me."

"Where were you last night?" I sat down, but at the farthest edge. There was a recommended minimum safety distance when it came to tête-à-têtes with George Harrison Prescott. Also, I preferred an immovable barrier between us, like a table, or a mountain. Otherwise, I could muster little resistance to getting horizontal, even in a place as public as the Prescott College Common Room at brunch time.

"Would you believe me if I said studying?" He watched me shake my head. "But I was. I was studying. All the time spent in the tomb has been taking a real toll on my working hours. I had a paper due last week and I got an extension until Monday because of our Thursday meeting. But we have another meeting tonight. Last night was the only time I had to work on it."

"What was the name of your paper?" I asked. "Sarah? Mandy? Amber?"

He clutched his fist to his heart. "I find your lack of faith disturbing. It was called 'The East German Uprising of 1953, and Its Effects on the USSR and Other Nations of Eastern Europe.' And you, dear Boo," he added, leaning forward, "should not be acting jealous."

"Oh?" I crossed my arms. "*You* get the exclusive on that?"

He waved his hand back at the dining hall. "Tiny lapse in judgment." Apparently, hundreds of thousands of years of male evolution are tough for even George to overcome. "But my point is, I have always been . . . available to you, for whatever. You're the one who's not interested in what I have to offer." He leaned back. "*You're* the one who left me standing outside your door last May."

Silence spread between us in the wake of that remark, and I studied George carefully. Had Prescott College's most popular player actually been hurt when I turned down the chance to stare at his much-observed ceiling? He'd acted with equanimity at the time, but maybe, like so much of the devil-may-care attitude George presented to the world, it was a show. After all, I was one of the few (I supposed) privy to his tale of woe about his parents and their traumatic ongoing affair. When he'd told me shortly after initiation, he'd intimated it was only our Digger connection that made him feel comfortable sharing the sordid details of his upbringing. But maybe I had broken down the barriers of the most gorgeous and eligible bachelor at Eli, and maybe I'd broken a little more than that when I'd rejected his offer.

"You shot me down," he added, "to get, of all things, a *boyfriend.*" He rolled his eyes. "Yeah, I figured it out. Your whole short, doomed relationship with that guy from Calvin College." So George had been paying attention to my awkward exchange with Brandon and his new girl after all.

I raised my eyebrows.

"Clarissa told me." Now he shook his head and laughed, swinging an arm around my shoulders. "Don't you see, Boo? You're not the girlfriend type. This is not a bad thing. You're like me!"

"And that's a good thing?" I snapped back. George and I might have been equally unable to deal with commitment, but there the similarity ended. Gorgeous, rich, charming George Harrison Prescott could have the women (and gay men) of the world at his feet with a crook of his finger. My face hadn't exactly launched any ships recently.

"Would you really prefer that whole deal Josh has with your roommate?" he asked. "Lie to her for a few weeks or months, then cheat on her? Tell me you think it's not headed in that direction."

He had me there. "But there are good relationships, too."

"I'm sure there are," he said. "But I know I'm already one strike against a relationship. How does it have any chance with me involved? It's doomed from the start. You're the same way."

"You think I doom relationships?"

"Ask me again after I hear your whole C.B." He put a finger to my chin. "You know I'm dying to learn all about you."

Crazy shivers spun through my system and I clamped my thighs together. "Why are you saying all this?"

"Why do you think?" He flung himself back to his side of the couch. "I like you. I'm interested in you. I'm pretty sure you feel the same way about me, and yet I think you're playing hard-to-get because of some sort of outdated idea of what romantic relationships should look like. And," he added, standing up, "I have a strong personal interest in making sure the thesis of your C.B. tonight makes you sound as desirable and sexy as possible, rather than reading like a laundry list of broken dreams."

Now, if that wasn't a promise, I don't know what was. "If you had your way, my C.B. would suddenly acquire an extra entry," I said to his retreating back.

"Say the word, babe." And then he was gone.

Interesting. Laundry list of broken dreams, huh? And here I'd been laboring under the impression that George didn't know me very well at all; that to him, I was another conquest.

Was I dismissing him unfairly? Had I bought into his player persona so fully that I didn't recognize when he was actually trying to make a connection with me? I figured if I didn't sleep with him, there were easily half a dozen others who would gladly take my place. I automatically assumed every time he ditched the Diggers for another event, it was because some pretty young thing had agreed to see his etchings. But maybe I'd pegged him all wrong.

I stood up and my gaze caught on one of the bookshelves

lining the Common Room. A thick burgundy volume stuck out from the shelf, and on its spine in silver lettering was embossed:

The East German Uprising of 1953:
Its Effects on the USSR and Other Nations
of Eastern Europe

Or maybe not.

I hereby confess:
They'll get our respect
when they deserve it.

5.

Apple of Discord

It's more complicated than you might think to choose an outfit in which to publicly report on your sexual experiences. You have to veer away from anything that screams "slutty" or, at the opposite end of the spectrum, "frumpy," and Persephone help you if the ensemble bears any resemblance to something worn in any of the following fetish-fantasy situations: schoolgirl, librarian, secretary, or Lara Croft. A white T-shirt makes you look like a candidate for *Girls Gone Wild: Cancún*, and low-rise jeans are out, for fear there might be any peeks at a thong. I finally settled on a pair of sleek brown pants and a cardigan over a not-low-cut sleeveless top, and boots (ankle, not dominatrixy) with a low heel. There. Not too conservative, not too outlandish.

Kind of like my love life, come to think of it.

At precisely five past six (VI in Diggers-time, which always runs five minutes off the rest of the world) I filed into the tomb with the others. First, we ate. Tonight, Hale had made us Cornish hens stuffed with wild rice and tarragon. Would it be awful of me to admit that so far, my favorite part about being a Digger was escaping dining hall food a couple nights a week?

"Nervous?" Angel asked. She was at my right, carefully dissecting the poultry on her plate with a skill indicating just how much time she'd spent in debutante class. My family was more of a chicken tenders type. "Don't be. We'll love you no matter who you've fucked."

"Or how?" Lucky prompted from my other side. "Personally, I think this whole tradition sucks. Does it really foster brotherhood for us to stand up and recount our sexual experiences in front of one another?"

"Or," said Big Demon, "in some cases, lack thereof? Is that your real worry here, Lucky?"

She shot a forkful of mashed potatoes at the jock, and, I'm proud to report, rather impressed him with her aim. "What I'm saying is, I wish we could get past all this adolescent junk and on to the real mysteries."

"What do you mean?" Frodo asked. "Like, 'Ten Little Diggers' or other *Murder She Wrote* stuff?"

"Dude," said Soze, "*Ten Little Indians* was Agatha Christie."

"*Dudes,*" Lucky mocked, "I mean *mysteries*. Divine revelation beyond human understanding? The secret rites of an organization only open to initiates?"

Puck shook his head, leaned over, and tugged on Lucky's endless and ever-present braid. "You're starting to sound like our girl 'boo here."

Ah yes, ridicule the resident conspiracy theorist. That'll get you laid, Puck. Still, I couldn't help but thrill at his casual "our girl."

Poe looked up from the corner, where he was partaking of his meal at a decent distance from our club, a physical reminder of his patriarch status. "You're *enjoying* the mysteries, Lucky," he grumbled, slicing his asparagus into perfectly bite-sized chunks. "Next week you'll enjoy the mystery of chateaubriand."

I swallowed a bite of Cornish hen and rolled my eyes. Poe had been inviting himself to our mealtimes a little too often for my appetite, and his M.O. was always the same. Come in, grub food, sit apart from the rest of us, and channel Oscar the Grouch. Okay, so there was a standing invite for patriarchs to share in the food they helped provide through their donations. Did that mean he had to crash every one of our dinners? There should be some kind of limit for patriarchs who happened to live in town. Rumor had it Poe had spent his graduate summer cutting grass or something. I'm sure that had to have paid better than a government internship—you'd think the kid could afford some groceries. (Though, considering the cooking of most recent grads I knew, eating Hale's food might be reason enough to turn townie.)

Graverobber tapped his silver against his water glass and an audible groan sounded around the table. "Before we get to the main event of the evening," he said with a nod toward me, "I'd like to once again broach the topic of—"

Thorndike cleared her throat. "As Uncle Tony for the evening, I'd like to once again remind the club that this particular topic is tabled tonight." Under her breath, she added, "Just one whine-free meeting is all I need to die happy."

"Oh, I doubt that," Juno said. "I'm sure you have a variety of other pet issues to shove down our throats before you even begin to get happy."

The other Diggirls began to bare their teeth at our newest compatriot. Suffice it to say, Juno (a.k.a. Mara) had not endeared herself to the other girls in her weeks of membership. This time, I didn't chalk it up to personality differences. She had managed to piss off each of us. I will say this for her: She was an equal opportunity firebrand. She corrected my grammar, questioned the authenticity of Lil' Demon's breasts, called Angel bourgeois, told Lucky that Dvorak was a scam, and suggested to Thorndike that *Brown* v. *Board of Education* had been a bad decision.

We all just *loved* her.

"Look, we can table it as much as you like, but that doesn't make the facts go away," Graverobber said. "We're hemorrhaging patriarchal support left and right, and the donations this year have been way down."

Thorndike twirled her finger in the air. "Woo-hoo. As long as the Tobias Trust is still in the eight figures, I'm not ready to worry about funds." She pointed at the feast spread before us. "Hale's not going to have to switch over to lentils and cabbage any time soon."

"Frankly, I find your grasp of the financial details leave something to be desired," said Juno. "Much of our prestige is derived from our wealth. If we lose that—"

"Right," I said. "If we lose some of our big secret wealth we can't tell anyone about anyway? Please."

Part of me wanted to think if we gave Juno some time, she'd grow on us. It hadn't taken the rest of us that long to bond, but then again, we'd become fast friends under extreme circumstances. Were we simply being too cliquish for her? Was her prickly nature due in part to a perception that the rest of the Diggirls were already a closed group, and if she couldn't join us, she'd try to beat us? If so, aligning herself with the biggest misogynist in the club was a good step along that path.

"Besides," I continued, "most barbarians already think we've got twice the money we do, and about ten times the power. We could be bankrupt and they'd still say we owned half the world."

"I agree with Bugaboo on that point," said Soze. "I don't think our money situation is an issue at present. I myself was surprised to learn its true value at the initiation, but, like Thorndike, I don't think we're about to go broke. What concerns me," he said, "is our perceived influence if we continue to alienate the patriarchs. How are we supposed to groom next year's taps when word on the street is that the Diggers can't get their own alums to give them internships? Don't mistake me, I am fully committed to our Order, but I worry for next year's tap class."

"I had a patriarch internship," I argued.

"Yeah, a terrific little patched-up, last-minute affair," came the voice of Poe from the corner. He scowled at me. "Everything worked out just grand for you. But how many of the rest of us were screwed?"

I looked around at the show of hands and ducked my head in guilt.

But Angel lifted her chin. "I lost my job because of my father. He could say it was a patriarch trick, but the old man and I would have had it out either way. And there are six women sitting in this room who would have been out a lot more if we'd given in to their demands last spring. Are we paying a price? Yes. But it was worth it. Didn't we prove beyond a shadow of a doubt that there are many more patriarchs who support this step than condemn it?"

"Yes," said Poe, "but are they the ones coughing up the big bucks?"

"Or handing out entry-level positions at CAA?" Frodo added.

"I think we've been through a trying time," Soze said, ever the politician. "And we need to work a little bit to get back in good graces with our base. At the risk of being crucified for actually expressing this opinion, there is something to be said for the idea that maybe the patriarchs who voted to let the change go through *might* not have been people who were all that committed to the society to begin with."

"Much as I hate to admit it," said Lil' Demon, "Soze may be right. A lot of people picked up that *Maxim* spread I did, but they weren't the ones buying my CDs or going to my movies. My true fans hated that I was sullying my image. Maybe the patriarchs who didn't care if there were women in Rose & Grave also didn't give a shit whether it ruined us or not." She shrugged. "Not that I think it's ruining us."

Graverobber snorted. Of course. "If we have to keep pussyfooting around the topic, we're never going to get anywhere. Of course it's ruined. We've lost one tap already. If things don't start turning around in here, I might start thinking he had the right idea."

For a moment, we all gaped at him, even Poe. "You wouldn't," he whispered from his corner. "Your oath."

"Oh, please, like we haven't had attrition before?"

"Not for decades." The law student's face was stricken, reflecting all our shock. "Maybe even for a century."

Thorndike cleared her throat. "No one's making any hasty decisions they'll live to regret. We know the issue is out there; we've been arguing about it since school started. And we will figure out a way to fix it. No quitting, okay?"

I nodded. "And before we go about setting up a false dichotomy of 'involved patriarchs hate women' and 'slacker patriarchs say *Go girls!*' let's remember that my internship—however it might have been arranged"—I shot Poe a dirty look—"was, in fact, arranged by one of the members of the board of trustees. A more involved Digger you couldn't hope to find. Those are the people we need to be reaching out to."

"As well as trying to win back those we've alienated," Soze said. "I've done it before for candidates in much more dire straits. Before you dismiss us for lack of current alumni connections, remember our club alone wields some significant firepower."

"My dad thinks we're cool," Puck said. "And, historically,

the Prescott contributions have been no small part of the Trust."

Graverobber slumped against his seat, conceding the point. We'd dodged the bullet for another meeting. But how much longer before his threats to quit took shape in reality?

The danger of attrition was twofold. First, the obvious: We'd tapped a person for a reason. We clearly wanted him to be One of Us. Anytime we lost a tap, we lost every bit of potential he offered us in terms of future accomplishments, influence, and money. We lost a dynamic team member, a valuable brother, and someone with a potentially entertaining C.B. No matter how much Graverobber pissed me off, I couldn't deny that when he bothered to speak on any other topic, he had many worthwhile things to say. And we were all still smarting from Howard's dis on Straggler Initiation Night. I'd only spoken with him for a few moments, but he still seemed like someone I'd love to get to know. Now whenever I saw him around campus, I felt a definite pang of regret for what could have been. Had we all handled ourselves better, he might have been our brother. (I'd had to steel myself on several occasions from walking up and saying hi. I wondered if he would recognize me sans cloak and glow-in-the-dark face paint.)

The second danger was to our storied secrecy. For instance, Howard had been in the tomb and seen much of our initiation before opting out. How much worse would it have been had he been a fully-fledged Digger before he quit? Someone like Graverobber, for example, who was not only fully initiated, but understood so much of the day-to-day running of the society? He had access to all the Phimalarlico e-mail, had explored the entire tomb with the rest of us last spring, and at this point had even sat in on several C.B.s. I couldn't imagine a guy like that on the loose, no longer bound by his oaths.

Assuming, of course, they were oaths he'd ever taken seriously. Here I was about to tell my deepest, darkest secrets to the room, and I wasn't even sure I could trust them all.

"Not to veer away from such a scintillating topic," Angel said, proceeding to do exactly that, "but has anyone given any more thought to that weird e-mail we got?"

"*You* got," Big Demon corrected. "Whoever was threatening didn't see fit to send it to anyone but the girls."

"If they were even threatening," said Juno. "It was just a nonsense rhyme." I got the distinct impression our newest female knight was a bit jealous she hadn't been included on the Diggirl list. But she hadn't even been a Digger yet.

"You think so?" Lucky asked, playing with the wishbone on her plate. "But who could have sent it, and why?"

"Who cares?" said Graverobber. "You haven't gotten any more messages and nothing dreadful has happened. It was a prank. Probably some other society who got their hands on our club's roster."

"If you say so, Graverobber," said Lucky. "I'm surprised you of all people are so dismissive, considering your constant insistence that this society is indeed rotting from within. What if it's *not* a nonsense rhyme?"

Soze considered this. "Do you want to look into it, Lucky? You can track down users and stuff, right?"

She scowled. "Like I have time for another project?"

I smiled at her. "That will teach you to volunteer."

But Lucky closed down. "It's a lesson I've already had, thanks. And if no one here thinks it's important, then why should I spend my time on it? You can all go to the devil just fine without my assistance."

Um, *okay.* This chick PMSes like no one's business. One second, she's fun and kind of snarky, and the next second—*boom*—the bitch is back. I never knew what to expect from her. It was all Dr. Jenny and Ms. Hyde.

"Are we all done with dinner?" Thorndike asked to diffuse the tension. She pointed at the grandfather clock (no, not an atomic one) in the corner of the room, which was nearing the all important VIII marker. "I think Bugaboo here has some juicy stories for us."

There was a ripple of chuckles around the table, and I felt a corresponding turbulence deep in my stomach as we adjourned from the dining room and filed up the stairs to the Inner Temple. The round, domed room had become one of my favorite places on campus in the few short months since I'd been tapped into Rose & Grave. Eli had some gorgeous architecture, but this secret room thrilled me more than all of the Gothic glory of the library or the carved marble starkness along the Presidential Plaza or Memorial Hall. This room was mine—or ours. I was one of the few people who ever got to appreciate its deep blue ceiling, dotted with tiny gilt stars, the rich wood paneling scarred by centuries of Diggers scraping their chairs against the walls and regularly decorated with art, relics, and trophies the members had "crooked" from the college over the years. I was one of the few given the privilege of sinking into the cushy couches we'd been using during the C.B.s. Today, they were arranged in a semi-circle facing the large oil painting of the voluptuous nude we called Connubial Bliss. It was before this portrait I would stand as I spoke about my experiences.

I stood to the side a bit as my brothers got ready to call the meeting to order. Thorndike, this evening's Uncle Tony, donned a long black hooded robe, took her seat on the dais at the top of the room, and turned a pedestal so that the wooden engraving of Persephone faced the room. She struck a small gong thrice, once, and twice. "The Time is VIII. I hereby call to order this, our Seven thousand, one hundred, and twenty-ninth meeting of the Order of Rose & Grave."

Keyser Soze, our club's Secretary, took his seat to the

right of the dais, and the other Diggers, including me, followed suit, each perching on one of the couches.

"In honor of Persephone, the Keeper of the Flame of Life and the Consort of the Shadow of Death, we, her loyal Knights, salute and honor her image."

"Hail, Persephone," we intoned. Well, most of us. I was sitting next to Lucky, and I noticed she didn't intone a thing. She didn't even whisper it. She noticed me staring and rolled her eyes. Clearly, we'd entered the Hyde phase.

"*Omni vincit mors, non cedamus nemini,*" Soze said.

Thorndike continued with the rather arcane calling-to-order ritual, which included a list of fines incurred in the previous week by members for various infractions:

Lil' Demon: cursed before the altar of Persephone—$3.
Puck: used barbarian names when Bond had beat him in Kaboodle Ball last Thursday—$2.
Graverobber: twice caught without his society pin—$10. ("Get a tattoo like ours and you'll be golden," Angel suggested.)

After that, there was a sort of group-bonding activity in which we turned to our fellow knights and messed up their hair. I liken it to that moment in church where you shake hands with the people next to you in the pew. We sang a few traditional songs (singing is really big at Eli, no matter what activity you're involved in), which tended to be, at once: spooky, ribald, and filled with literary allusions.

Next up, Bond reported on the developing plans to steal back a small bronze statue of Orpheus that had been recently pilfered from our courtyard. Thanks to some recent surveillance, we were pretty sure the thieves had been Dragon's Head, and Bond and Lil' Demon had been combing through the archives in the Library to find records showing how to break into Dragon's Head and retrieve our property. This tradition of "crooking" from other societies was one of the oldest we had. The tomb was chock full of memorabilia from generations of Diggers who'd been trading trophies back and forth with all the other societies on campus. I thought most of the stuff was junk, myself, but I'm sure to the class of 1937, the mangy stuffed lion's head they'd swiped from the tomb of Book & Key represented a triumph of criminal ingenuity.

And the other societies weren't the only targets of our raids. I'd been amused to learn upon my induction into the Order of Rose & Grave that many of the most infamous items-gone-missing over the years could be found within the hallowed walls of the tomb. From what I could discern, the university turned a mostly blind eye to all of the shenanigans, so long as we kept our thievery confined to objects like champion crew boats, weathercocks from the roof of the president's office, and the like. A few years ago, a valuable World Clock had disappeared from a college dining hall, and the benefactor as well as the college dean were so upset that it seemed like all fun and games had come to an end. With the heat on, the club decided to ditch their booty and found an opportunity to kill two birds with one stone when the local campus tabloid printed an exposé about Rose & Grave. Magically, the clock appeared in the tabloid's minuscule office the following day, and an anonymous tip to campus police pointed the way hence.

I knew the story well. The editor of every publication at Eli had heard how the tabloid editor had been dragged into the provost's office to explain himself. The clock's presence in the tiny basement office was ridiculous, of course. No one believed they could have hidden such an enormous piece of equipment in a space hardly big enough to contain the rumors they collected. Naturally, the editor redirected the blame back at the Diggers ... and mysteriously, the case against the thieves—whomever they might be—was immediately dropped.

Interestingly enough, the club portrait of D169 hanging in the tomb's room of records features fifteen young men standing around the usual table showcasing the usual society paraphernalia. But behind them all is a World Clock.

We hadn't chosen the target of our club's big caper, but it was early yet in the year.

"This evening, to honor Persephone, we will hear the Connubial Bliss report of Knight Bugaboo. All agreed?"

There were sounds of assent in the room, and I took my place before the painting. I liked Connubial Bliss. She was not a beautiful woman, but she had a certain stark appeal. Her pose wasn't openly seductive, nor pornographic (like some other nudes we'd found in the tomb's collection), but rather a casual nakedness. In her hand she held a pomegranate, which, I'd learned, was a more accurate interpretation of Eve's apple. Persephone wasn't the only woman of myth who'd lost paradise by eating pomegranate.

Her gaze looked a bit beyond the viewer, her expression stoic, and at times I thought it was a little sad. Angel had said she looked aloof, as if she was above the adoration heaped upon her by the hormonal adolescents who usually used this room. Puck had said she looked sexy. So, clearly a naked Rorschach test.

I turned and faced my audience. "Most Sacred Goddess Persephone, Uncle Tony, and my fellow Knights of Rose & Grave ..." And then I stopped. "Um, what is *he* doing here?"

I pointed to Poe, who had, of course, taken a seat in the most shadowy section of the room. He looked affronted. "What do you mean? I can come to meetings."

"Oh, no." I folded my arms. "I don't want him here."

"I'm a member of this organization," he said. "I'm bound by the same oaths as the rest of these people."

"He's not in our club," I said. "I don't think—"

"But we always let the patriarchs sit in on the meetings if they want," Angel said. I shot her a look. Dude, show a little Diggirl solidarity, huh? She hadn't had that creep breathing down her neck when she was reporting on *her* sex life. Why should he get the honor of hearing about ours if we didn't get to hear his in return? (Um, not that I'd want to!)

And I still had my ace to play. "I don't feel comfortable. Isn't the idea of this evening for me to feel completely comfortable?"

"What exactly is it about me that makes you uncomfortable sharing your intimate history, Bugaboo?" Poe said with a cold satisfaction.

"What is it about you that makes everyone uncomfortable in general?" Lucky snapped. There we go! A little support.

I stood there, looking at the club, who were approximating a tennis match audience. Poe, me. Poe, me. Poe, me.

Thorndike cleared her throat. "This is Bugaboo's presentation. If the knight feels ill at ease in the presence of the patriarch—"

"She shouldn't," Poe argued. "I'm here like the rest of you, to participate in the experience of Rose & Grave."

"Haven't you gotten enough experience that you don't need to horn in on ours?" I glared at him. He glared back.

"I think," Thorndike said, "we should take a vote." She rapped a gavel against the wooden top of the pillar by her throne. "All those in favor of restricting the C.B. reports to the members of the current club, say 'Aye.' "

Everyone looked at one another. It was a momentous vote. I'm sure half of them thought I should drop the whole issue with Poe. Yeah, he was a jerk, but he was always hanging around the tomb, devouring our food and sulking. We'd almost gotten used to him. And he'd proved last year that when push came to shove, his oaths really did mean something. However, I could see it on each of their faces. They were all thinking of patriarchs they would rather not have around when it came time to do their own reports.

"Aye," said the women.

"Aye," said the men.

"Aye." Angel shrugged and joined in.

"Aye," said Puck. "We'd never want 'boo to be *uncomfortable.*"

"Aye," I said, and smirked at Poe.

Thorndike took a deep breath. "The motion is passed." She looked at Poe. "We request that Patriarch Poe of D176 leave the Inner Temple for the duration of the meeting."

And then she tapped the gavel thrice, once, and twice on the pillar.

Poe didn't look at her. He kept his cold gray eyes on me, and for a moment, when the last crack of the gavel sounded through the room, I thought I saw him flinch.

"Fine," he said, shrugging to his feet. "I'm out of here." His stately walk across the room was accompanied by not a single glance at any of the Diggers who'd just thrown him out. At the door, he paused. "If you guys hope to win back the favor of the patriarchs, let me give you a gentle hint. This is *not* the way to make it happen."

The door closed behind him and we all sat (or in my case, stood) in silence. Connubial Bliss frowned down at me. I ignored her. It was bad enough I had to put my love life up to the scrutiny of my own club members. Poe was over the line.

"Okay," Puck said at last, breaking the tension. He

rubbed his hands together in anticipation. "Enough of that. Bring on the sexy stories."

I smiled, and he grinned back. *Sexy stories, huh? Without you in them, how sexy could they be?* As I stood there, watching him do his best to get the rest of our brothers back on track and winking at me with those copper-colored eyes, I knew as sure as the painted chick behind me was naked that someday soon, I would have a story with George.

And I'd be super-glad I'd waited until *after* my C.B.

————

From: Lancelot-D176@phimalarlico.org
To: Bugaboo-D177@phimalarlico.org
Subject: Re: C.B.s and other indignities

no matter what you said in your e-mail, i can tell your c.b. went well! you survived! i knew you would! i'm sorry this whole patriarch thing is dragging out. i can speak from experience that it's no fun when the people you look up to are turning their backs on you. but our decisions are correct. i know it. hang in there. i think soze will steer you right. he's the best choice for club secretary because he knows how to win the hearts and minds of the alums. and if things start to get real sticky, you've got poe right there on campus to help you guys out. i know he would love to be involved.

things here are going well. there's something so open about this landscape. all the old bullshit begins to seem so unimportant. maybe you should rethink your whole grad school idea and come live with me in the wintry north? i promise you, that thing they say about the male population is *not* just the stuff of legend. :-)

I think Malcolm may have been spending too much time with his *Brokeback Mountain* DVD. But all in all, a sweet e-mail. Maybe if it had been him in the Inner Temple last night instead of Poe, I wouldn't have been so adamant about current-members-only. Malcolm wouldn't hold my C.B. against me. And the rest of my club—who would later have to offer up their own peccadillos—didn't judge me for the mistakes I've made in my relationships, for breaking the heart of a wonderful boy like Brandon, for engaging in illicit activity with some guy I didn't even know. Heck, George was probably proud of me for it! I could confess anything and they wouldn't hold it against me, like I didn't hold admissions of cheating against—

I heard a thump and a giggle through the wall separating my room from Lydia's.

—against Josh. I mean, not yet anyway. Besides, everyone makes mistakes.

There was a bit of rustling and then, "Shhh! What are you doing?" A little squeal of pleasure.

Didn't they have a Monday morning class to get to or something? They were supposed to be so smart and high-achieving and Phi Beta Kappa and all—didn't they have *work* to do?

I certainly did. I had yet to schedule a meeting with my thesis advisor to discuss my senior project. Unfortunately, I still didn't have a firm topic. Or any topic. I clicked over to my word processing program and reviewed my notes. Not exactly impressive. Certainly not worthy of honors in the major, and definitely nothing that would stand out on a grad school application. But, what was three-fourths of a literary degree worth but to make the flimsy look substantial? I began to edit.

There was another giggle from the vicinity of Lydia's room. I rolled my eyes and kept typing. They'd been sequestered in there all morning, and I'd bet dollars to donuts there was no political science summit going on.

Right after I pressed *Save*, there was a knock at our suite door. I stilled, waiting to see if there'd be any rustling through the wall to signal they'd get it. But Lydia and Josh were clearly not in any position to be pulling themselves together and answering the door. I sighed, and fingered my messy topknot. Fine. Some of us were doing homework, and some of us were hooking up, but whose right to refuse interruption seemed more valid? The couple's. Of course.

I padded across our parquet floor and opened the door. Behind it stood Brandon Weare.

"Hi, Amy" were the first two words I'd heard from him in more than a month. "Can we talk?"

I hereby confess:
I'm scarred by the experience.

6.
Significant Others

THINGS I WANTED TO SAY TO BRANDON

1) "Of course. Can we talk about your beautiful girlfriend?"
2) "What's wrong with me? Why didn't I love you when I had the chance?"
3) "You couldn't maybe have come at a time when I looked positively smashing?"
4) "Sure. It wasn't bad enough that my roommate and my society brother were getting it on while I'm trying to do my homework. I need more romantic torture today and a tête-à-tête with the ex fits the bill."

THINGS I DID SAY

1) "Brandon. Wow. Hi. Come in."

And then I put my hand to my hair in the universal girly gesture of "Oh, look what a mess I am, I usually look so much better than this," and ushered him into the room. I took a seat on the couch. He hesitated, then sat across from me on the coffee table. (Pinprick #1)

"How have you been?" he asked.

"Good. You?"

"Busy." He smiled sheepishly and began folding a stray piece of paper on the table. "Working my ass off on my thesis. Have you started yours yet?"

I shook my head. "No. I need to soon, though. I was just e-mailing my advisor about our meeting."

"What are you going to write about?"

"I haven't decided yet," I admitted. Brandon and I used to talk about our Lit papers all the time. I wondered if he now had those conversations with Felicity. I wondered if he proofread Felicity's papers for her and then sent them back to her in the shape of little paper airplanes.

Brandon folded a nose onto the airplane he was creating out of a "subscribe to *Cosmo*" postcard. Yeah, that's exactly what he did. Brandon flirts with aerogami. I watched his hands. His summer tan had faded, and they were back to being the pale olive color I remembered. I'd always loved how his skin looked against mine. At the thought, my skin flushed with heat.

To get my mind off its train of thought, I said, "I'm thinking maybe something with feminist theory. Maybe some sort of examination of female myths from several traditions."

He nodded without looking up. "That's so you." After a moment he launched the airplane, and it dove straight to the floor. "I know we haven't talked for a while."

"Yeah." And I don't think that was my fault. The ball was totally in his court after his little "see you later" comment at Clarissa's party. Probably too busy making four-fold stingers with *Felicity*.

"Your summer sounded really interesting when you told me about it at the party."

Me, huh? Not *me and my stunning, rich girlfriend, in whom I found solace after you broke my heart*? Maybe he was about to tell me it had been nothing more than a summer fling. A rebound. They weren't together anymore.

"Amy?" he asked, and he waved a hand in front of my face. He was smiling, but it wasn't the special smile he used to give only me. (Pinprick #2) "Your summer?"

"It was amazing," I said. "Really made me think a lot about my plans. I don't think I ever could have learned as much running for coffee as an intern at Horton."

"So, no more Manhattan editing position for you?"

"I haven't decided," I said. "Maybe I'll go to grad school. Sometimes I think I'd like to do something really important and life-changing, like I did this summer, but full time. But I don't know if I have that in me. I don't know if I'm the type of person to do important things."

Time was, Brandon would have responded with something like, "You're very important." But today, he just said, "You have to do what's right for you." (Pinprick #3)

He must be over me. Otherwise, he'd still believe I was capable of moving the world. That's the best part of being loved. Someone attributes to you all kinds of abilities they're fooled into thinking you possess.

Or maybe that's the worst part. I guess it all depends if the person you love lets you down or not. I'd let Brandon down. He'd attributed to me a return of affection, devotion, and loyalty. I hadn't lived up to it.

"So," he continued, "how's . . . everything else?"

"Like?" I asked, leaning forward.

"Like the stuff you don't talk about?" he prompted, pulling at an imaginary society pin on his shirt.

"I don't talk about it." I shrugged. "But...it's been good."

The smile reached all the way up to his eyes this time. "I'm glad to hear that."

I understood his need for paper airplanes. I was dying for something to do with my hands right now. "So, to what do I owe the pleasure?" I asked. "Is there anything specific you wanted to discuss?"

"No. I just missed you, Amy." (Pinprick #4)

Amy. Amy. Amy. No one said my name like him. No one had said my name like *that* in months. Even George only called me Boo. "We used to talk a lot," said I.

"We used to be really good friends," said he.

"And then we screwed it up." There. I said it. And then, before we could back away from the big black hole we were edging around, I ploughed forward. "But I need to know. How did we screw it up? I mean, do you think it was when we tried to have a relationship in May? Or maybe if we hadn't slept together back in February—"

"No." He put his hand up and I closed my mouth over the rest of my outburst. "I think," he began, "I would have screwed it up no matter what happened. Because I liked you, Amy, and I couldn't stop pushing for something serious."

He *liked* me? Last spring, he'd claimed he *loved* me. I'd been downgraded. No longer a hurricane in his life. Just a minor breeze. (Pinprick #5–5,000)

The door to Lydia's room opened and out walked Josh. He nodded at us and hurried past, clearly sensing this was a private convo. And then, at the door to our suite, he turned to me and held up five fingers, his expression inquisitive.

I nodded once. Yes, Brandon was number five on my Hit List. And Josh knew it. Josh knew everything about me, and I knew everything about him. Including the fact that, even now, he was probably plotting to cheat on my best friend, the woman he'd left giggling back in her bedroom. And one wonders why I have little faith in relationships.

"So we were doomed," I said, my voice flat.

Brandon chuckled. "Yes. Doomed. That's suitably dramatic."

Ouch. "How's Felicity?" I asked, because as long as you're going to indulge in pain, you might as well get it all over with at once. But even as I said it, a little part of my brain crossed its non-existent fingers and prayed, *Please say "Felicity who?"*

"She's good." He started in on another plane. "You'd like her, Amy."

I snorted. "I wouldn't like her."

But he didn't ask me why not, and so I never got the chance to tell him I would never like his girlfriend because she was the living embodiment of how I'd disappointed him, of how I couldn't be the girl he wanted me to be, and how I couldn't love him the way she clearly did.

I hoped she loved him. I've never known a man so worthy of being loved. I thought I'd kill Josh if he hurt Lydia the way I feared he would. I *knew* I'd kill Felicity if she broke Brandon's heart. Only I got to do that and live.

What he did say was "Are you seeing anyone?"

I broke into a weak laugh. "No. I don't see people. Learned my lesson on that one, I think. I'm not the girl-friend kind of girl."

He studied me. "I don't think you know what kind of girl you are."

Oh, please. I know and he knows, and apparently George knows, too. I don't do relationships. If I did, there would never have been a Felicity. "And you're the one who always says I think about that too much!"

Josh returned, and his second intrusion seemed to kick-start Brandon. "I'm going to stop by the Lit office with some coffees," he said. "Want to go with me and deliver them?" It was a tradition at the *Eli Literary Magazine*. The old editors (like Brandon and me) would bring the new editors coffees when they were heading into crunch time. "Ari said they'd be in this afternoon."

So he did have some pretense to visit. "Sure. Let me go change." I went into my room, and as I closed the door behind me, it struck me that I was shutting out a man who'd already seen me naked plenty of times. The world would be ideal if ex-boyfriends disappeared like puffs of smoke, and you never had to run errands with them again.

So I got dressed. I wore my nicer (read: tighter) pair of jeans, my push-uppiest push-up bra, and a bright pink sweater with a deep V-neck. Of course, there was the usual carri-witchet over the placement of my pin. Strap of my bag, where Brandon had once before spotted it? Belt loop, where it would be nice and subtle?

"Screw it," I said to the mirror, and attached the damn thing to the sweater's neckline. I pulled on my ankle boots, grabbed my wallet/key/cell phone-on-a-carabiner combo, and marched out the door. "Ready?"

He looked from my neckline to my face and shook his head, a smile flickering over his mouth. "Sure."

Do you know what I dislike? Aside from the obvious thing where I walk down the street with my ex-boyfriend on a spurious coffee-procuring trip? The thing where said ex-boyfriend is an utter genius who is not only completely over me, but also can see through absolutely every attempt I make to look fabulous and carefree about how much he's over me. And doesn't give a fig that I am a Digger, and therefore a member of a super-cool club he could never hope to penetrate.

So there I was, in line at the coffee place, listening to Brandon rattle off the very specific orders of the new Lit

Mag editors. (Frankly, if you're going to go with some sort of caramel mocha confection, you're kidding yourself by making it with fat-free soy. It's like ordering a Big Mac, large fries, and a small Diet Coke.) We moved down from the ordering section to the waiting-for-coffee section, and it's there I saw Jenny. She was standing with that blond kid from the freshman bazaar. Her head was thrown back, laughing, she was practically beaming at him, and the look in her eyes was one I'd only seen on her face in the glow of a computer screen. I'd known Jenny for a good half a year now, and I didn't think I'd ever seen her laugh like this.

Gone was the air of wariness and derision I was so accustomed to. There was no Ms. Hyde present this morning. Granted, we've all had our rough times in the tomb, but I should at least be able to recognize a fellow Digger's expression of joy, should have seen it at least once—during a good song, a good lobster tail, a last-minute Kaboodle Ball victory? I'd observed our resident snorter, Nikolos, looking happier to be hanging out with the other Diggers than Jenny ever had.

And that's when I realized it: Jennifer Santos was miserable being a Digger. She hated it. I made the command decision not to go up and talk to her because, in this moment, she was really happy, with the kind of elation I'd never once witnessed inside the tomb. And now I knew those dirty looks she always gave me when I ran into her outside were actually her begging me not to remind her of how we knew each other.

The real attrition threat was not Nikolos. It was Jenny. How could I have missed this?

I began to back away very slowly, hoping the bright fuchsia of my make-Brandon-miss-me sweater wouldn't attract the attention of my fellow knight, and slammed right into

Brandon. For a moment we stood frozen, half falling, shoulder to shoulder, back to chest, butt to things very much not butt.

"Ouch!" He put his hands on my waist and held me. Held me for a whole, unnecessary second after I was completely steady on my feet again. And then his hands were gone, leaving behind them a whispered imprint, a ghostly pressure and warmth so vivid I swear I thought I could feel every whorl on his fingertip. Even through my sweater.

Of course, his outburst and that second of hesitation were all it took to gain the attention of every eye in the place, including Jenny's. I watched her face fall into its usual dour expression and bit my lip. Behind her, the blond guy's gaze dropped to my neckline and he frowned.

"Hi, Jenny," I said.

"Hi, Amy." Behind her, I saw the guy give me a once-over, and his lips curved into a slow, contemptuous smile. My psychic powers must have been on in that coffee shop, for I came to my second blinding flash of insight for the morning—Jennifer Santos had broken her oath of secrecy and told this person about my C.B.

And no, I wasn't simply overreacting because of my uncomfortable situation with Brandon and all the leftover stress I'd been feeling about my report and how the other Diggers would take it. Honestly, I knew without a doubt this was the case. I *knew* it. This guy's expression couldn't have been any clearer if he'd been holding up a neon sign saying "I know who you did."

"Who's your friend?" I asked, straightening and looking him right in the eye. *Have you told him what sluts you think we all are?*

"This is Micah Price," she said. "Micah runs the prayer group I'm in. Micah, this is Amy Haskel. I tutor her in fractals."

I don't know a fractal from a fraction, but sure. "Nice to meet you," I said, and held out my hand.

He didn't take it. Of course, last time I ran into Micah Price, he'd practically pummeled Josh into the pavement. Thinking back on it, perhaps I should have let him. Would have saved me from all that through-the-wall giggling.

Brandon stepped forward. "Hi, I'm Brandon." He pumped Jenny's hand and then gave Micah a little punch on the shoulder. Jenny raised an eyebrow in my direction but I was in no mood to play nice. *She'd told her boyfriend about me.* I was fighting my better instincts to keep my oath, knowing it may well break my best friend's heart, and Jenny had told her snobby blond boyfriend all about me. For what? A funny anecdote? Bragging rights about all the cool stuff she'd heard in the Rose & Grave tomb? My throat began to burn. She wasn't just any Digger. She was a Diggirl. Didn't that mean anything to her?

"Well, we should go," Jenny said quickly, as the laser-powered glares I was shooting in her direction finally hit their mark. "See you later."

"You bet," I replied, my voice like ice.

I leaned against the counter and watched them leave. Brandon stood beside me. "You know that guy?" When I shrugged, he went on. "He's bad news."

"How bad can he be? Super-Christian, runs a campus prayer group?"

Brandon shook his head. "It's not a prayer group so much as a cult. He lived across the entryway from me freshman year. Sometimes I would hear him talking in there. Nothing he was saying sounded very Christian to me."

"So, like what? Intolerance and stuff?"

Our coffee order came up and Brandon began fitting the cups into the cardboard carrier. "Yes, that, and ... other stuff. Don't get me wrong; I love a good prayer group." Who doesn't? "But he didn't seem to be so much about God or the Bible as he was about himself. About following *him* on his . . . crusade. I don't know. Tell your tutor to be careful around him."

"She's not my tutor."

He handed me a coffee cup. "Amy, don't you think I know you've never taken fractals in your life? I'm a math major. If you needed help, you'd ask me." He stopped. "Wouldn't you?"

"Not this semester."

We headed toward the entrance, and though Brandon was balancing way more coffee than me, he held the door open as I stepped through. "I'd like to change that, if I can."

I swallowed, trying to clear my throat of all the sentences threatening to rush out at once. *I don't think that's a good idea*, and *Why are you doing this to me now?* and *Where the hell can all this lead except to make me feel miserable that I gave you up* and *Aren't you smug that finally you've gotten me pining for you?*

I was still trying to formulate an appropriate response when Brandon grabbed my elbow and pulled me back under the awning. "Wait," he whispered.

Oh, God. No. I may not be the best person in this relationship, but I could take the high road when the situation demanded. Brandon was happy with Felicity, and I would not be the one to let him jeopardize that in some moment of weakness brought on by tight jeans and a tighter sweater. "Brandon, I don't think—"

"Shh." He peeked around the entrance. "They're still out there. Can you hear?"

Oh. As soon as I paid attention to something other than my heartbeat and my ex's proximity, I could.

"Micah, no! It's not like that," Jenny was saying, practically . . . sobbing?

"This is what we agreed on, Jen." His voice was perfectly even, as if he were discussing the weather. "I fail to see how anything has changed. You were the one that told me—"

"Not here, please. And not now. Seriously, it's not right."

"You promised me you would. You swore it. Were you lying? Were you lying to *me*?" And there was a hint of emotion in his voice, a carefully reined anger that slipped a bit on the "me."

"No, of course not. It's just so hard. So much harder than I thought it would be. I'm not sure I want to do it anymore."

"I don't understand. I love you, Jen. Don't you know that? I trust you."

"I know. I know you do." Her voice broke on her words.

"And you love me...don't you? Don't you love me? If you love me, then why is it so hard to do what I want?"

Enough! "That bastard," I hissed and would have stormed out of the foyer, but Brandon put his hand in front of me.

"You'll humiliate her."

"I plan to eviscerate him." Betrayal or not, she was my Diggirl, and I was going to show my support. I'd teach this budding sexual predator that "no" meant *no*. I'd sic the full force of the Eli Women's Center on his ass. But Brandon held me firm, and I didn't move.

Jenny spoke again. "I can't talk to you about this now."

"When, then?" Micah said. "No more waiting. You've been putting this off forever."

"It's not forever. I'm just not ready."

There was a long pause, and then he said, "Well, I'm ready, so I don't care if you are or not."

"I've changed my mind," said Brandon, and his hand formed a fist. "Get him."

We spilled out of the entrance and Jenny looked up. Her

cheeks were stained with tears. She looked at me for one second, her eyes burning with hatred, then turned and sprinted off.

Micah smirked at Brandon, and also departed posthaste. The jerk was probably well aware Brandon Weare would not fight him on a crowded city street.

"Should I go after her?" I asked him.

Brandon's jaw was clenched tight. "If you think she'll talk to you. I don't think she will." He watched Micah walk away. "But I'll tell you what I do suggest. Get your *people*— and I know you have them—get your people to do that guy some damage. Soon." He took the coffee from my hand. "I'm going to go deliver this to the Lit office. Chase down that girl, or find your friends, or something. I'll see you later."

No! That's what he'd said to me last time, and it had been a month and a half before I saw him again. "When?" I couldn't help but blurt out.

He looked down at the coffees. "I don't know, Amy. Maybe when you call me?"

———

I power-walked back to Prescott College, cell phone in full gear. Jenny's phone rang and rang, but Brandon had been right. She clearly didn't want to talk to me. Maybe she'd take a call from another Diggirl. But that route dead-ended as well. Clarissa's phones sent me to voice mail, Odile's message said she'd be out of town until Wednesday, and Demetria's land line (she refused to sign her soul away to a Cingular contract) had a busy signal. (Seriously, who doesn't do call-waiting these days?)

Okay, no problem. I'd wait until Jenny calmed down somewhat and try her again. Or maybe I'd even give Josh a heads-up on the issue. He may not be a Diggirl, but he was close enough, and I was sure he'd love any excuse to give

Micah a little smackdown. But when I got back home, it was to find Lydia alone on the couch, chewing the end of her highlighter and smiling dreamily into her Locke.

"Where's Josh?" I asked.

"Eleven-thirty lecture," she murmured, and proceeded to highlight a line I'm sure she'd had memorized since freshman year. She glanced up at me. "Anything wrong?"

Nothing that couldn't wait until the next time I saw Jenny. I schooled my features into a more casual expression. "No. Why?"

"I thought Brandon was here."

"Oh, that. He was. It was fine."

Lydia nodded. "I'm glad to hear it. I hope you guys can move on and be friends."

"Sadly, I think that's up to him. I'm the one who hurt him, so I'm pretty much consigned to taking whatever friendship he's willing to let me have."

Lydia pursed her lips. "Brandon's a good guy. I'm sure he wants to be your friend."

"I don't know if I can be his friend—not really. I doubt we were ever just friends. There was always the tension, and then the outright flirting, then all the naked stuff. And then we were kind of together. I don't know how to be friends with him without the sexual element. Maybe I just don't do the *boy* friend thing."

"Especially not at your current pace with Monsieur Prescott, *mon ami*."

"You ain't just whistlin' 'La Vie en Rose.'" I plopped down on the couch next to her. "But that's a whole other headache. I think I'm having a day where I wish all men would simply spontaneously combust and leave our planet alone." Starting with Micah.

"Mmmm," Lydia sighed. "I'm not." She stretched out her feet and wiggled her toes. "Josh is . . . sublime."

I rolled my eyes.

"No, really, Amy, if only you knew." Ha. If only *she* knew. "I know it's only been a couple of weeks, and yes, rationally I know it's my brain exulting over the whole pair-bonding thing and going nuts, but I don't think I've ever known a guy like him before. We can lie around for hours and talk about nonsense or issues and it feels so comfortable. I don't worry if he'll think I'm an idiot if the subject matter changes from what we should do in the Middle East to whether the new *Star Wars* movies are any good. Which, you know, they're not."

"Right."

"But it's amazing. I feel as if I can tell him things I've never told anyone." Her eyes widened. "Except you, of course."

"Of course."

She broke into a smile. "And it's so weird, but I feel as if he can tell me things he's never told anyone, too."

Except me. Of course.

"That's great, Lydia," I said, and meant it. Or hoped I did. "I'm really really happy for you. I hope this works out."

"Thanks, hon. I know the last thing you probably want to hear about right now are my romantic adventures."

"No, actually, it's nice to think there is a purpose to all of this." And nicer to hope that maybe this time Josh would hold himself in check.

Lydia dropped her head on my shoulder. "I think there is. Right now anyway. Ask me again when I'm single." I chuckled, dislodging her from her perch. "Okay, back to 17th-century political theory."

The phone rang and Lydia grabbed the receiver. "Lydia and Amy's Den of Sin."

Great. When she said stuff like that it was *always* my

mom. We were sitting so close, I could hear the person speak on the other end.

"*Lydia, it's Josh.*"

"Oh, hey there, cutie."

"*Are you alone?*"

"Um, no, Amy's right here." There was a *click*. "Josh?" She looked at me. "That was weird."

And then my cell phone rang. I answered it, careful to hold it up to the ear facing away from Lydia. "Hello?"

"Firefly Room. Now." And then the line went dead.

I hereby confess:

I am my brother's kept woman.

7.
Connubial Bliss

Within fifteen minutes, Soze had managed to collect most of us in the tomb's Firefly Room. Lucky was there, looking a little puffy around the eyes and absolutely refusing to recognize my presence, and so was Puck, who had his feet upon an antique hutch in the corner. He'd tracked down Thorndike despite her lack of cell phone, and Bond, Big Demon, Frodo, Juno, and Graverobber rounded out the party.

"Okay, I'm not going to mince words or waste any time calling us to order. Hope you guys will forgive me for dispensing with tradition." Soze laid his cell phone open in the middle of the table. "But we're here to talk about this." He pressed a button.

The tinny, static-filled voice of Kurt Gehry burbled out. "*... absolutely unacceptable ... would never have stood for it back when Rose & Grave actually meant something to its members ... last straw. If you think the patriarchs of this organization are going to stand idly by while you and your pathetic excuse for a club sell off our traditions to some idiot off his medication, then you are not worthy to bear the title of knight. We hold you completely* *responsible for this fiasco, and if you do not root out this traitor and stop them before they cause any more harm, then we will do it for you. By any means necessary."*

The patriarch's voice cut out, replaced by the recorded options on Soze's voice mail for save, replay, and delete.

"I shudder to think this man holds a high position of political power in our nation," Thorndike said. "Now, would someone please explain what exactly he's raving about?"

"This," Soze said, and opened the screen of his laptop. We all leaned in to look. A browser window was open, showing the homepage of a website called "secretsofthediggers.com." It looked like your standard conspiracy-theorist website, focusing on the alleged omnipotent actions of our shady, secret, and elite society with lurid Day-Glo colors and a disturbing emphasis on exclamatory punctuation. Nothing I hadn't seen before. Except for this one had a big, bold, flashing paragraph front and center:

WATCH THIS SPACE FOR AN EXCLUSIVE EXPOSÉ WITH AN ACTUAL CURRENT DIGGER!!! APPALLED BY THE SOCIETY'S SECRET CONTROL, THIS MEMBER WOULD LIKE THE WORLD TO KNOW THE SOURCE OF THEIR EVIL POWER!!! EVERYTHING *THEY* DON'T WANT YOU TO KNOW, REVEALED HERE!!!

Frodo blinked at the screen. "This is it? This is what we all got called in here for? Methinks the guy running this site isn't the only one who's acting a little unbalanced."

"Yeah," said Big Demon. "The phrase I'm searching for is 'Who cares?' Isn't it just going to be the usual Men in Black, woo-woo stuff? Since when do we even care what these lunatics print about us?"

Soze tabbed over to his Phimalarlico mail, then clicked

on the group heading for patriarch postings. There were dozens of new messages. "Every patriarch with an e-mail account got an 'announcement' from this fellow telling them exactly what they—personally—could expect from this exposé. And judging from some of these e-mails, it was very personal indeed. This knight apparently has a vast amount of information, whoever he—or she—"

"*Or she!*" I rolled my eyes. "Of course they think it was one of us. Rose & Grave was fine until they let the chicks in, after all. It could be any disgruntled patriarch."

"The reason they think it's one of us," said Thorndike in an odd, choked voice, "is because we're the ones with the most access to the tomb. We're the ones with easy access to the Black Books where the Uncle Tonys describe, in detail, what has happened at every meeting—every C.B.—we've ever had."

"That's correct," said Bond. "I remember looking through them with Lil' Demon when we were researching how to get into Dragon's Head to steal back that statue."

It instantly occurred to everyone in the room that Lil' Demon was very conveniently out of town. Thorndike began to sneeze, and then blew her nose.

"And they think it's us for another reason," Soze said. "This guy didn't send an announcement of the upcoming article to the patriarchs for fun. It was a threat. And alongside a threat comes—"

"Blackmail," said Lucky. "They think we're trying to get back at them for not supporting us this year."

"Makes sense, if you ask me," said Puck with a shrug. "They're betraying the society, so why is it still our job to keep their secrets?"

"Right, because an attack like this would make them feel so loving and conciliatory," I said. "Do they really have such a low opinion of us?"

"Says the woman who takes pleasure in kicking the alums out of the tomb?" asked Juno. "Of course they do, and we haven't been working very hard to convince them otherwise. The question is, what to do now?"

"Try to stop them, clearly," said Graverobber. "Didn't think it was possible to piss off the patriarchs any more than we already have, but clearly I was underestimating how low we could sink. Stealing secrets from the tomb?"

"You're one to talk, Grave*robber*," I sneered. "I think a person threatening to quit should go high on the suspect list. If you quit, you have nothing to lose."

"But do you think he's a thief?" Jenny asked me with a penetrating glance. "Do you think he could be bought like that?" I was surprised to see her actually taking his side. I was surprised to see her meeting my eyes, to be frank.

"Explain my motivation for selling anything to this nutcase," he snapped. "Unlike some of you, I hardly have a cash flow problem."

"Assuming it was one of us." Soze's tone immediately mollified the room. He clicked back to the website. "Which, though I'm not ruling it out, I'm not going to take for granted, either. So let's not start pointing fingers until we have more evidence. Patriarchs come and go from this place all the time. Yes, we have a record of their visits in our guest book, but that doesn't mean a thing. You don't know how long the traitor may have been sitting on this information before he decided to go public."

"Or she," Graverobber corrected.

Thorndike groaned. "While we play pronoun games, the clock is ticking. What's the plan?"

Soze looked at Lucky, who piped up. "I've checked out the site's Whois, of course, but it's a private registration, which I figured it would be. I've got a couple more tricks up my sleeve for tracking down this fellow, but frankly, I'm not sure how far it's going to get us. The problem with a paranoid conspiracy theorist is, well, he's already paranoid. He's sitting in a bunker somewhere with an aluminum cap on his head, certain the CIA and the FBI and whatever are trying to track him down. He's probably got himself pretty well hidden." She sat down at the computer. "But like I said, I'll try."

"Great." Soze looked around the table. "Anyone else?"

"I've got some friends in the radical community," said Thorndike, then stifled a cough. "It's a long shot but sometimes they know people who know people. Fringe of all stripes tend to hang together."

"And they're fine working with The Man?" Juno mocked. "You retain any street cred whatsoever after joining Rose & Grave?"

"I'm starting my revolution from the inside," Thorndike said, then sneezed. Lucky glanced at her for a moment, then returned her eyes to the screen. The rest of us took two steps away from Typhoid Thorndike.

"Shouldn't our focus be on rooting out the traitor in our midst?" Bond asked in clipped tones. "It seems as if that would be much more useful in the long run. Has anyone considered Howard?"

"Howard's not a Digger," said Frodo.

"No, but he was a tap. I doubt this website fellow would concern himself over a technicality."

Soze shook his head. "Howard doesn't have access to the Black Books, but your point is well taken. We do need to find out who's behind this. But I'm not sure how. It's not as if we can fingerprint the books. The patriarchs are sure it's one of us. I'm thinking it may be a patriarch trying to get us into trouble again, maybe weaken our support base a little more than it already is." He gestured with his phone. "This particular trustee is already our biggest detractor, so his reaction is no surprise, but he's not the only patriarch going postal."

The White House Chief of Staff had been the force behind last year's conspiracy to deprive all the new taps and the
senior club of their internships as punishment for participat-
ing in initiating the first female members. And as Poe could
attest, he wasn't afraid of carrying through on his threats.
Not only had the senior been denied his White House summer job, he'd been rendered unemployable anywhere on the
Hill. It was unheard of for a Secretary of Rose & Grave to be
forced to spend his graduate summer gardening.

The next fifteen minutes were devoted to strategy,
though all of our theories and plans were hampered somewhat by the realization that someone standing in the room
(or one of our missing members) could be responsible for
our current plight. As the conversation waned, I started
thinking that maybe Soze had a point. If there was a patriarch determined to ruin this club and start afresh with next
year's taps, then causing all this internal strife was no doubt
exactly the way to accomplish his goals.

Pretty soon, the room emptied out as each of my fellow
knights departed, task in hand. Lucky remained bent over
the laptop. I approached gingerly, as one might a wild animal
that might suddenly a) bolt, or b) snap your head off. My
anger at what I assumed to be her betrayal paled in the face
of our current issue—and more, in the wake of what I'd seen
outside the coffee shop.

"Lucky—"

"I'm really busy right now," she snapped. Apparently, we
were going with option b.

"Fine. We can talk later."

"I'd prefer if we didn't talk at all."

"Yeah, I'm getting that," I said, becoming somewhat
snappy myself. "And though you can be as difficult as you
want out there in the barbarian world, inside we're supposed
to support one another. I just want to help you."

"Do you even know what a firewall is?" she asked.

"You know what I mean."

Her fingers stilled on the keyboard and then she slowly turned and faced me. "I don't care who you think you are, Amy Haskel, or what you think you heard. If you want to pretend it's different in here, then that's your problem. I know I'm under the same judgment in here as I am outside. I'm not going to let myself be corrupted just because a bunch of silly men in robes tell me it's okay. And I'm not going to pretend any of you have *my* best interests at heart just because you took an oath to a minor goddess that doesn't exist." And then she turned back to the computer, and commenced typing.

Damn. Why did she join at all if she despised us so much? I took a deep breath. "You know, I never really thought it had anything to do with gods or goddesses. I thought that silly wood engraving was a symbol of this thing we made, all one hundred and seventy-seven years of us." Okay, that was the definition of graven image, but bear with me. "This isn't my religion, Lucky, and no one is asking for it to be. No one is asking it of you, either. But when I make a promise to someone, on anything, it's not about the thing I'm swearing by, it's about me. I made a promise, and I'm going to keep it. So I *do* have your best interests at heart. I do because I promised I would." I turned to walk away. "And you owe us two dollars for using my barbarian name."

I was halfway to the door when she spoke. "Coffee."

I turned around. "What?"

Lucky sat in a leather armchair three sizes too big for her and stared down at the end of her braid. "I, um...I spilled my coffee earlier. I could really use some caffeine. So if you wanted to, um, make us some coffee, I'll be done here by the time you get back and we can talk."

I laughed. "You chew me out and then ask me to fetch

you coffee? Luck, if you think that would work on anyone who didn't really like you and want to help, then you have a very odd grasp of the human spirit." I headed to the kitchen.

Now, if I were Hale, where would I hide the coffee? I was crouching in front of the pantry, shoving aside bags of potatoes and onions, when I heard footsteps behind me.

"Wow."

I stood and spun to see George standing in the doorway, jaw hanging open. Damn, where did he come from? I hadn't heard him on the steps. He came toward me, his eyes glinting behind his glasses. "Turn around, 'boo."

I furrowed my brow but did as he asked, slowly rotating until I faced him again. This time, his mouth was closed, and his face shone with appreciation.

"When," he began in a teasing tone, "did you get that lovely bit of ink on your backside?"

My hand flew to the waist of my low-rise jeans. Oh, right. There, framed perfectly by the top of the fuchsia lace thong I'd donned for Brandon's benefit, sat the tiny hexagon of my Rose & Grave tattoo. "Last spring," I said. "With the other girls."

"I love it," he whispered. "More than the other girls." And with that enigmatic statement, his hand slipped around my torso and he traced the spot with his thumb. "Why the hell have you been hiding it all fall?" He shifted and arched his head over my shoulder until he could see my back.

"I haven't been hiding it," I replied. "You just haven't been looking in the right places."

"I concur." He spread out his palm, flat against my back. "I've been woefully ignorant of all your right places." And there it was, just a tiny touch of pressure, and I listed forward against his chest. He buried his face in my hair. "You look amazing today, 'boo."

Brandon hadn't thought so. Oh, irony of ironies that

now the clothes I wore for my ex enticed the man responsible for screwing up the relationship in the first place. But that and other thoughts soon fled. How did George manage to do this? He was barely touching me—just the one hand against the small of my back and his jaw against my cheek—but I felt dizzy with anticipation. My hands went out to grasp the shelves, and I felt the unmistakable ridged metal of a coffee can.

Right. Coffee. Oh, hell, who needed coffee when I could just stand here and drink in the pheromones of George Harrison Prescott? My skin burned. If he would just shift slightly, if he would just move the hand he had anchored against my back, if he would just make the slightest gesture at all, I'd be his in a flash.

But he stood there, holding me, breathing deeply, his body almost, but not quite, touching mine.

Your move, Amy.

"We shouldn't do this here," I said at last. Because I'm a chicken.

"Those things you said last night at your C.B.," said Puck, as if I'd never spoken. And now his hand began to move, ever so slowly, down over my jeans-encased butt. "I sat there and listened to you talk about all those boys you were with—"

"*All those?*" I said on a breath. "You should talk."

He chuckled against my skin, and it felt like lightning. "Fine. That moderate number of boys you were with. And you know what I thought?"

Tell me tell me tell me tell me tell me.

I heard boots on the steps.

"Caffeine withdrawal is not a pretty picture, Buga—" Jenny swung into the kitchen and stopped dead. "*Miércoles.*" Her expression flashed with shock, then resentment. "Excuse me." And she turned and ran.

Crap. Crap crap crappity crap. I dropped my head back against the shelf as George pulled away from me. "I wish she hadn't seen that."

"Why? Might do her some good."

I bit my lip. "No, you don't get it. Earlier today I saw her arguing with her boyfriend."

Puck raised an eyebrow. "Luck's got a boyfriend? That's impressive."

"Not if you saw the boyfriend. He's a slimeball. He was being a total jerk to her and I'd just broken down that little shell of hers and convinced her to let me talk to her about it when you . . ."

"When I what?" Puck asked. "She acts like I did something to her personally. Always has."

"She doesn't approve of you."

"So? I don't approve of her, but I've never been mean." His jaw was doing that tight thing again and I wanted to kiss away the tension. "Whatever. I am who I am, and she's not the first person who has decided to judge me for it. There are plenty of people who hate me just for being a Prescott. My name is on a building down the street, and there's no way to escape that. People like Lucky will decide I'm evil for breathing their air, and there's no way to escape that, either."

"Don't worry what she thinks. She disapproves of all of us, I'm pretty certain."

"That wasn't quite the ringing endorsement I was looking for," he said, pouting.

"Sorry," I said. "What would you prefer? *'Why, Puck, how could anyone dislike you? You're a veritable icon of sexual power!'?'*"

"That's more like it. I'm used to being one of two things: a Prescott or a player."

According to your mother, it's one and the same. But I bit my lip to keep from saying that out loud, and pushed him away.

"Trust me here, the last thing Lucky needed to see right now was me getting cozy with a guy." Especially a guy like George. "She's going through a rough time." I walked past him to the door of the kitchen, but Jenny was long gone, and now the hall stood empty. I stared at my reflection in the diamond-dust mirror until George came up behind me and put his arms around my waist. I had to admit it: Those two people in the mirror looked good together.

"And regardless of how she treats you, you're going to help her?"

He didn't know the half of it. If my hunch was correct, Jenny didn't simply disapprove of us, she was telling our secrets to her barbarian boyfriend. Funny that she'd been put in charge of rooting out whoever was selling the patriarchs out on secretsofthediggers.com. "That's what we swore to do, Puck. She can judge the rest of us, but right now, I'm going to be her friend."

He looked back at the stairs. "Fine. I'll leave you to your prior engagement, however ill-advised I think it is. I make a habit of not going out of my way to be nice to people who don't return the favor."

"So a lot of people are nice to you, then?" I teased.

"And in return, I'm *excessively* nice to them." He leaned toward me and put his mouth near my ear. "The next time I see you, Bugaboo, we are picking up where we left off. No more waiting."

I'd heard a similar sentiment earlier today. Funny, from Micah, it had been the most despicable threat. From George, the most delicious promise.

————

It was a promise he didn't get a chance to fulfill for quite some time. Okay, several days. Okay, two. But, trust me, when you're waiting to have George Harrison Prescott's hands on your body, time passes very, very slowly. (Especially given that it had also been two days since Jenny had spoken to me. She'd disappeared from the tomb, and failed to respond to seven e-mails and three voice mails. And those were just from me—who knew what the rest of the Diggirls had said to her after hearing my account of the coffee shop confrontation? According to reports, she wasn't returning any of our calls. It was indeed possible our concern had spooked her.)

And so it happened that one evening I was sitting at my favorite study spot, the window seat in the tomb's Grand Library, looking out at the moonlit courtyard. Connecticut was shuddering into fall, which meant lots of dismal, gray gloom transitioning us from verdant summer into the fiery brilliance of New England's peak. Today's weather was the sort I'd come to associate with New Haven. It spit rain all day, and the ground slushed with the results, soaking shoes and socks and the flares of everyone's jeans and making them rethink that after-dinner section up on Science Hill or the screening at the Film Studies Center. I could feel the dampness as I sat there, legs crossed beneath me, a middle volume of the tomb's leather-bound set of *The Golden Bough* open on my lap. Time was running out to find a thesis topic, but I kept getting distracted. The rotten evening was the perfect chance to dig in, uninterrupted.

Ever since Monday, being present at the tomb usually meant an automatic conscription into Josh's latest campaign to appease the patriarchs and find the traitor before he caused a permanent break between the club and its most devoted supporters. We hadn't gotten much further in our search, as Jenny's efforts had turned up zilch, and everyone seemed too devoted to the cause to be responsible for the leak.

However, I happened to know that Lydia had taken advantage of the storm to trap Josh in her room for the evening. Bless her. The miserable weather and Josh's efforts would keep everyone else away as well.

But clearly, I'd underestimated a certain man's persistence.

The chandelier flickered to life above my head and I looked to the door to see Puck with his hand on the switch. "Ah, you are here after all." I hadn't even heard the front door open.

The sudden pounding of my pulse signaled: *This is it.* But I could play it cool. "Did Lydia tell you where to find me?"

"Not exactly." He smiled and crossed to me. "Lydia said she thought you'd gone to the library. Her boyfriend said he was sure you were having a *grand* old time."

"And then, no doubt, he sent you over here to conduct an investigation."

"Precisely. I think there was something about strip-searching anyone I found inside." He sat beside me and tapped the book in my lap. "What are you doing here so very late at night? No life?"

I checked my watch. It *had* gotten late, hadn't it? I was surprised that even Lydia and Josh were still awake. They'd usually "gone to bed" long before this hour. And let's not question why it took so long for George to come looking for me. "Studying. I take classes, you know. Or you would, but you opted out of Branch's Shakespeare."

"I decided the Nabokov seminar was more my style." He tilted his head. "*Bugaboo, light of my life, fire of my loins. My sin, my soul, Bugaboo. The tip of the tongue taking a trip down the palate to—well, burst, actually—at last, through the lips. Bug. A. Boo.*" He leaned in to kiss me.

"Gross," I said. "Humbert was a pedophile."

"A damn eloquent one. Besides," he said, and nibbled on my lower lip, "you're legal."

Can't really argue with that. I smiled and kissed him in earnest. "What are we doing?"

"What we should have done a damn long time ago, 'boo."

"What, and lay our private doings open to the society during my C.B.?" I teased, scooting down on the seat so he had an easier time reaching me. Man, this boy could kiss.

"Mine or yours," he mumbled, kissing down my jawline to my neck. "It's all going to come out eventually. And I don't care. Spend the night with me."

"Okay."

Simple as that. Because when a guy like George Harrison Prescott is this determined to hook up with you, when he walks through the rain and quotes ecstatic literature and kisses you like he hasn't seen a girl in years—well, there's only one acceptable answer. And that's to accept. Not to overthink it, not to weigh the options, not to determine where this fit into the scope of your orderly C.V., and definitely not to start figuring out exactly where you would fall on his lengthy C.B. This wasn't about my friends, or my future, or anything else but what I wanted...now. Within these walls, he was neither the reluctant legacy nor the school's most infamous heartbreaker, but rather, an infinitely charming fellow Digger, fellow Prescotteer, and the guy I'd wanted to tap ever since I laid eyes on him.

George Harrison Prescott: accept or reject? No contest.

I stretched my legs out and tangled them with his as he fought for leverage on the slim window seat. Beyond the lead-veined window there was nothing but private courtyard and wintry dying garden and moonlight, and we were alone in the tomb of Rose & Grave, which is as good as being alone in the world. Here we were, set off five minutes from the rest of the population, separated from the students of Eli by our society names and the secrets we shared.

"It's not as cold out as I thought," I said.

"Huh?"

I bopped him on the nose. "Your skin. It's not cold."

"I bundled." And then he began to unbundle me, starting with the scarf around my throat.

I loved this moment of hooking up with a boy, when you haven't yet relinquished all sense of rationality, but you're not by any means acting like you would in front of your parents. Our clothes were on, but we were horizontal; we weren't completely mussed from making out, but my skin was flushed and he was removing his glasses and laying them on the table to my left. I'd seen George without his trademark glasses before, of course, but never from an inch or two away. I thought his copper-colored eyes were gorgeous before, behind the matching copper frames. Without them, and staring into mine, those eyes would have taken my breath away if I'd been able to breathe in the first place. Men should not get the kind of genetic advantages bestowed upon this boy. Or at least not without a big warning sign tattooed on their foreheads.

He shifted his leg slightly, and suddenly, I forgot all about his eyes. "George," I murmured.

"Open your wallet, 'boo," he said into the tender skin of my throat. "Because I have a feeling you're going to owe these fine Diggers a lot of money pretty soon." His hands slid up under my sweater and I arched beneath him.

"Then we should probably adjourn to someplace more comfortable."

He lifted his head. "I have the perfect place."

And then, before I had a chance to gather my books or slip my shoes back on, he was pulling me out of the Grand Library and up a flight of stairs.

"Um, I can assure you this is not the way out," I said.

"And I can assure you all I'm looking for tonight is a way *in*." He reached our destination and held open the door with a flourish. "Milady."

The Inner Temple. I hesitated. "You're serious? What if someone comes into the tomb?"

He grabbed me around the waist and drew me inside. "I guarantee everyone's gone home for the night. Besides, you think we're the first to think of it? The first to do it?" He pushed my hair to the side and began kissing the nape of my neck. "I bet a ton of guys used to bring their dates in here to show off. Nothing so sexy as knowing what kind of power the guy you're with is wielding. Knowing you're with a Digger ..."

"Yeah," I replied. "But I'm a Digger, too. How do you plan to impress me?"

"Oh, I'll think of something." And then he kissed me. And I know I've gone on about George's kisses in the past, but indulge me one more time. He's phenomenal. I've never ever been kissed this way. Not to get too technical about it, but the man kisses as if he's doing way more to you than just kissing you.

My body got that impression as well.

WAYS IN WHICH "PUCK'S" REPUTATION IS WELL DESERVED

1) The aforementioned kisses.
2) The tremendous skill he possesses in removing a girl's clothes in a manner so subtle that, addled as she is by the kisses, she isn't even aware of what he's

doing until she's standing, half-naked, underneath the star-studded dome of the Inner Temple and he's moved his kisses south.

3) The things he does south, mainly to breasts. Quite astonishing, actually. Wow. *Wow.*

4) The way—

That's about as far as I got with my list before my knees buckled beneath me.

"Whoa there, 'boo." He chuckled against my bare skin and steadied me as I sucked in a breath and tried to make my stomach look like I'd ever taken advantage of the free Pilates sessions at the Eli gym. But it was tough to maintain the proper concentration when George Harrison Prescott dropped to his knees before me, anchored his hands on my butt, and began to nuzzle my belly button.

"Take your pants off," he said.

"Okay."

"Look at you," he said, and rocked back on his heels, watching me. "So agreeable all of a sudden. To what do I owe the pleasure?"

"The pleasure." I slipped my jeans down over my hips and received another jolt of happiness when his eyes widened. The load of laundry I'd done yesterday was totally worth it. "Fuchsia. Just for you."

"Very nice." His face expressed something far greater than approval, however. I kicked off my socks and pants and hooked my fingers beneath the straps of the thong.

And then I hesitated. "Wait a second—"

"Oh, I agree. Leave it on."

I stabbed him in the chest with my finger. "You're still clothed. What, planning on bolting and leaving me here in my skivvies?"

"Hardly." He pointed at the closet in the rear of the room. "With all the robes in there, it would be a pointless prank."

Good call. "Then I think you're overdressed."

He spread his arms. "Help yourself."

So I did, because peeling material off of George's Adonis body is not exactly an undesirable task. I'm embarrassed to admit how many times I've imagined him naked, and happy to report the reality blew them all away. And once he was naked, and I was nearly so (he flatly refused to let me take off my panties), all teasing went out of the proceedings. The point of no return.

Then I learned George's kisses were merely a prelude to the rest of the tricks in his repertoire. I've lived twenty-one years on this planet, and I think I've been around the block a couple of times (my C.B. audience can attest to this fact) and I never even knew some of the things he proceeded to do to me were physically possible. For instance:

Exhibit A: The throne on top of the dais is an antique, intricately carved affair, covered as it is with bas-relief scenes from the Grecian underworld and crowned by two large globes on the front of each armrest, which, it turns out, are great places to hook your calves when you're in particularly intimate positions wherein you are on the chair and he is . . . well, *not* on the chair, but rather, on the dais. On his knees. It was a gorgeous piece of furniture really, probably part of a set along with that diamond-dust mirror down near the kitchen. The only thing that might have improved upon the whole experience was if we'd had the mirror nearby. But I digress. I'd never thought of the straight-backed throne as particularly comfortable, but now I don't know if I'll be able to consider it at all without immediately breaking out into a sweat.

Exhibit B: Sex on the conference table may be a bit of an old saw in the corporate world, but sex on the Rose & Grave conference table, beneath the starry dome, surrounded by wood paneling and oil masterworks and George, George, George...I think I owe the good Diggers a couple hundred bucks. At one point, I grabbed his shoulders and stopped him.

"Do you think this place is bugged?"

"That would be fun." He swiveled a bit, demonstrating a move I swear is illegal in three out of five states.

"George! It's not funny. I'm creeped out by the idea that this could wind up on tape."

"Smile for the camera, 'boo." He chuckled, then reached down between us and made me gasp. "Come on, you think we'd still be forced to do all that transcribing in the Black Books if they had the Inner Temple wired?"

"Good point," I managed to get out in between labored breaths.

"Then again," he said, and rolled us both on our sides, "see that third star over there? Looks suspiciously like a lens, don't you think?" He pulled me on top of him and grabbed my hips. "I think this is my best angle."

I promptly came, so it was clearly my best angle as well.

Exhibit C: We ended up on the floor of the Inner Temple, lying on top of an unused robe, directly beneath the oil painting of Connubial Bliss. And I still had my underwear on, mere technicality though it was. George seemed fascinated by it, constantly running his fingers beneath the straps at my hips and in the back, obviously pleased as punch the flimsy scraps of material weren't in the least impeding his current activities. And I had to say, I was with him on that one. I'd always figured thongs were supposed to be sexy for the boys only; I'd never realized what a turn-on they were for me until George showed me their full potential.

"Remember what I said the other day?" His voice sounded gruff and breathless. "About what I was thinking during your report?"

"Yes," I murmured, looking down at him through half-closed eyes.

"This is it. This is what I wanted. I saw you standing here in front of this painting, talking about those other guys, and I wanted you. Right here. Like this. This is my fantasy, 'boo. You are...my fantasy." He squeezed his eyes shut, and I felt his chest shudder beneath my palms as his breath caught.

So I took over, happy to oblige any and all of this man's fantasies. Because it was no longer a secret he'd satisfied all of mine.

I hereby confess:

What happens in the tomb
stays in the tomb.

8.
Weird Sisters

Over the years, I'd heard many rumors about the wonders to be found in George Harrison Prescott's bedroom, including, but not limited to: black satin sheets on the bed, mirrors on the ceiling, and a jukebox that only played Barry White.

Negative on all three. Well, there was a little mini-jukebox (which I later learned was a present from his father on the occasion of his father's wedding), but it held a variety of songs by a variety of artists, and as far as I knew, "Fight for Your Right to Party" didn't count as a make-out song. The sheets were standard university-issue blue, there was a normal mirror hanging on the inside of the closet, and I was spooning with George on the narrow single bed. His arm was draped loosely over my waist and the stubble on his chin was scratching my shoulder blade.

THOUGHTS I HAD THAT MORNING

1) Wow, did I really do all the things I did last night?
2) My thighs feel a little stiff.

3) This is nice. I could hang out here and cuddle with
   George all day.
4) Except I have that seminar at 10:15.
5) And I have to pee.

One moment more of relaxing in George's arms, feeling our entire bodies pressed up against each other, back to chest, thigh to thigh. One moment more of hearing his breath in my ear and relishing his warm hand on my belly. And then I stretched a little and slipped out of bed.

I was buttoning my jeans when he blinked awake. "Morning."

"Hi." Dude, was that shyness? Wherefore had I suddenly become shy in front of George Harrison Prescott?

"Are you leaving?"

I giggled. Strike two. "Yeah, I've got work to do."

He rolled onto his back and put his hands behind his head. "But I'll see you tonight?"

My heart rate skyrocketed.

"At the meeting."

Of course. The Thursday meeting. "George, I always go. Besides, it's lobster night at the tomb."

"Good point." He smiled, but didn't move from his prone position. "See you later, Boo."

And that was it. I left his room, got out of the suite without any of his suitemates noticing me (no grist for the Prescott College gossip mill, thank you very much), and made it back to my suite. Lydia's door was closed; I was safe. It was over.

But it wasn't over. Not by a long shot.

The next few weeks passed in a flurry of sexual activity. Ostensibly, I was still taking classes, writing papers, doing problem sets, and working on getting together a thesis topic. But I can barely remember classroom discussions and I'll be the first to admit my papers weren't exhibiting their usual level of literary passion.

Josh had stepped up his efforts to discover who was responsible for the leak to the website, and though we each devoted plenty of time to trying to find this guy (or girl, as Nikolos insisted on reminding us at every opportunity), the identity of our leak persisted in eluding us as efficiently as Jenny eluded every Diggirl who tried to corner her into a private conversation. (And, to be honest, shitty as it sounds, the more often she avoided us, the less we all felt inclined to speak with her about it. We already knew how she'd respond.)

We'd decided, en masse, that a formal confrontation, which was the standard club M.O., would be too much for our shy brother to handle, so the best thing to do would be to go to her one by one and express our concern that perhaps her boyfriend failed to treat her with the proper respect. A girlfriend intervention. But she proved a slippery little sucker. It was nearly impossible to contact her outside the tomb, and we never caught her alone inside, or without the trappings of one of Josh's top-priority electronic missions to track down the traitor.

We weren't getting very far on that front. Once, when Lydia was out of the room, I asked Josh if he thought it had anything to do with the strange Phimalarlico e-mails all the Diggirls had received at the begining of the year. After all, the patriarchs had also received mysterious e-mails on the private account. And the weird poem had included the lines "Cut through the web in which you're caught/Learn of the thief who can be bought." Could that not be a reference to our current scandal? After all, we were dealing with stolen information sold to a website.

"Or maybe it was an even more pointed reference," I went on. "Remember what Jenny said to Graverob—er, Nikolos the day we found out about secretsofthediggers.com? We still have no idea who sent those e-mails, or what they mean, but what if they were a clue? It's the first time this has occurred to me. What if the 'thief' is a play on his name?"

Josh laughed, thankfully ignoring my slip of the tongue. "That's a bit obscure, Amy. You've been reading too much Dan Brown. But I like your first idea. I'll ask Jenny to do a little digging into the source of those e-mails."

"You don't think it could be Nikolos?"

"He might be the most inappropriately named member of our group," Josh replied. "One guy who never needs to be a thief. And even if money isn't the motivation, Nikolos is probably the last guy who'd be interested in further angering the patriarchs. He wants them back on our side, remember?"

I nodded. "So then, who doesn't have a huge trust fund, and possesses a yen to piss off the patriarchs?"

He met my eyes. "You mean, aside from you?"

The only thing I could guarantee was it was neither George nor myself. We were far too busy to bother with anything so mundane as selling society secrets.

Let me lay it on the line for you: George Harrison Prescott is *insatiable*. We hooked up between classes, after Rose & Grave meetings, before dinner in the dining hall. We hooked up in his room, in my room, in an entryway bathroom shower stall, in the library stacks, and, on one incredibly ill-advised occasion, in the Prescott College Common Room. On the very same couch, I might add, where I had previously resisted his considerable charms.

It never got old. We'd be in the middle of some fascinating political debate at a society meeting, and all of a sudden I'd catch myself reminiscing about some particularly enjoyable interlude, flush scarlet, and look over to Puck, who was almost always watching me, and certainly knew exactly what kind of naughty thoughts were going through my head. As soon as we were released from the tomb, we'd sprint back to his place, and stay awake until the wee hours doing everything but debating. Or we'd be sitting there in the dining hall, having lunch with all our Prescott College friends, and I'd feel his hand on my thigh. His gorgeous copper eyes would glint at me, and next thing I knew, I was talking about some non-existent reading I had to do that afternoon and George would mention a load of laundry and off we'd go— this time to hook up on the counter near the griddle in the momentarily abandoned Prescott Buttery.

George never ran out of places where he wanted to have sex with me, nor out of ways in which to do it, and, to my credit, I didn't spend much time thinking about who else he might have done there or how. I didn't spend much time thinking at all. Brandon would have been so proud of me; he'd always insisted I overanalyzed every situation I was in, destroying it before it ever had a chance to blossom. But with George, I was living entirely in the moment. He was beautiful and fun and sexy as hell, and I really didn't care what else he was up to as long as he kept making me feel the way I felt whenever we got together.

Besides, we were together so often that, oversexed as the boy is, I don't think he had the time or the stamina for anyone else.

Halloween, always momentous on the Eli campus, came around again, and since it was our last, the seniors I knew went all out. Most of us Diggirls raided the tomb's costume supply for our outfits. Lucky, of course, kept to her new policy of avoiding the rest of us and was nowhere to be found. Thorndike, who still hadn't shaken off the latest in her series of colds, rallied in the getup of an Amazon queen, though the rest of us advised her that the skimpy costume was unlikely to protect her from the elements.

"The reason you keep getting sick," Angel said, holding up a stunning Georgian ball gown, "is that you don't take care of yourself. Explain again what you have against wool?"

"It's a matter of sustainable agrarian models. Small farms are fine—" Thorndike paused to sneeze.

"The reason you keep getting sick," Lil' Demon interrupted, "is because you won't take those supplements I gave you. With a vegan diet like yours—"

"I'm not taking anything that quack gave you, okay?" Thorndike snapped. "And to be honest, I don't think you should, either. Just because it worked wonders on Jessica Simpson—"

"That may be a reason to avoid it on its own," I added.

Thorndike continued. "I was reading up on the ingredients the other day, and I think—"

Lil' Demon paused in her efforts to wriggle into a mermaid costume and pinched her thumb and forefinger together. "Zip it. Are you a medical professional? No. You're not even studying the sciences. Last I checked, you were majoring in Ethnicity, Race, and Migration."

"And what's your major this week?" Thorndike asked. "You know you do have to declare it sometime before graduation, don't you?"

"American Studies." Lil' Demon smiled sweetly. "And I think I may actually have a thesis topic. Even Errol Flynn over there will like this one."

Juno looked up from the floor, where she was strapping on a pair of thigh-high, Three-Musketeer–style boots. A cutlass hung from her hip. She twirled her silent-screen mustache. "Oh, do tell!"

"I'm writing about the development and spread of collegiate organizations," Lil' Demon said. "I've been doing a lot of reading in our own history books, and it's fascinating. Phi Beta Kappa gives rise to Rose & Grave, gives rise to other societies, gives rise to fraternities and sororities throughout the . . . " She trailed off as she took in our expressions. "What? I'm not going to tell any of the *secret* stuff!"

"Of course you aren't," Angel said, but she sounded far from convinced.

"Exactly how much research have you been doing?" I asked. My eye had landed on several pieces of faux Pilgrim wear, and I was busy constructing a wardrobe for Hester Prynne—if Hester Prynne had been a bit more of a sexpot. Long skirt, warm hooded cape, and a corset top emblazoned with the requisite "A." "And what does our noble Secretary think of your efforts?"

A nervous giggle ran through the room.

"He's getting more paranoid than you are," Lil' Demon replied to me. "It's quite impressive, really. But I refuse to change my behavior because of all this nonsense. We start letting it affect how we run stuff in this tomb and the terrorists really *have* won."

This time, the laugh was genuine.

"Seriously, though, you should see some of the stuff I've found. Maybe, if I have some time, I'll do a report on the secret, historical stuff for the rest of the club."

"That's a great idea," said Juno. "What kind of stuff are you talking about?"

She shrugged. "Past scandals, stuff that would make the shit that went down last spring look like child's play. You think the patriarchs are up in arms now, you should see what kind of crap they tried to pull when clubs started tapping minorities. The factions almost tore this place apart."

Angel pulled on a high, powdered wig. "The jury's still out on seeing how together we'll be by the end of the year."

On the way out, we ran into Lucky, who appeared to be making a beeline from the Grand Library to the front door.

"Hey!" I called. "Wait up!" She stopped and turned, her expression carefully neutral. "I'm getting the impression, Lucky, that you've been making yourself scarce recently. Come on, let's go get you a Halloween costume and you can come out with us."

"I don't participate in Halloween," Lucky said stiffly.

"Why?"

"Why do you care?" she snapped.

I held my hands up. "Whoa, there. Chill out. I just thought it would be fun. You never hang out with us anymore—"

"It's devil worship." She glared at me. "So you go ahead and honor demons. I'll pass, thanks."

"Okay, fine. Then how about we meet up tomorrow? We can get some coffee or something."

"I said, I'll pass."

The other Diggirls, clustered on the landing, began to rumble with protestations, and I leaned in closer. "Lucky, are you angry at me? I really think we should talk about this. I honestly didn't mean to overhear what you were talking about with that guy. So if you want me to keep my nose out of it, I will, no matter how much I would rather do other-wise. But please understand I'm only trying to help."

"Help me do what?" she cried. "Turn into the kind of people the rest of you are? No thanks."

At that, the other girls gasped.

"Look here!" I shouted back. "I've never judged you, and believe me, if I wanted to, I could. I could say plenty of stuff about how narrow-minded you're being, and how rude, and what poor decision-making skills you seem to have . . ."

"Oh, yes," she replied in a voice dripping with disdain, "go ahead and attack my morals from *your* position in the gutter. You were looking plenty high-minded in the *kitchen.*"

"Me?" I cried. "You started it. This has nothing to do with different values. I respect yours. Lucky, all I ever wanted to do was talk to you because I thought your boyfriend was pressuring you into something you didn't want to do."

She straightened. "You don't know me, you clearly don't know my boyfriend, and most of all, you haven't the slightest idea what it is *I want to do.* So stay out of my life, Bugaboo."

With that, she left. The other four joined me.

"You guys have some sort of issue I don't know about?" said Thorndike, looking after Jenny's retreating figure.

"Same old story from a few weeks ago," I said. "I accidentally saw her in a fight with her boyfriend"—and she saw me getting cozy with George—"and I don't think she's taking it too well."

"I'm going to go out on a limb here and figure the rest of us would get similar treatment?" Angel asked. "She practically tore your face off. I didn't know she had it in her."

"Better you than me," said Lil' Demon. "I've been in a couple of catfights in my time, but that girl? She'd have Lindsay Lohan cowering."

"She's not usually like that, is she?" Juno asked. "I always got the impression she was sweet and quiet."

"Yes on the latter, not so much on the former," I grumbled.

"Don't worry." Angel put a brocade-clad arm around my shoulder and squeezed. "She'll calm down by the next meeting. You two can patch things up."

"You think?"

"Sure. You're Diggirls."

We left the tomb and headed to Clarissa's apartment to put the finishing touches on our hair and makeup (Odile is a master at eyeliner). Some of the party vibe had worn off after my altercation with Jenny, but the other girls did their best to lift my spirits. Mara, especially, seemed in a great mood, but she was probably just celebrating the fact that, for once, she wasn't the odd Diggirl out. And yes, I have to admit Mara was growing on me. I still found her blunt opinions and truculent nature a bit irritating, but who was I to hold that against her? If the other knights could put up with my conspiracy-theorist leanings, then why couldn't I give a free pass to the Queen of the Eli Political Union? (Also, Clarissa popped a bottle of Krug, and really, that just makes everyone friendlier.)

Unfortunately, I'd already promised to spend the evening attending the annual Eli Symphony Orchestra's Halloween concert with Lydia, so I took my leave of the other girls and, all costumed up, began to hoof it home through the cold but clear purple twilight. My roommate and I had hardly been spending time together at all in the last few weeks. She was busy with Josh, I was busy with George, and we were both ridiculously busy with the demands of our classes, not to mention our respective societies.

Our secret society radio silence still held, but I was beginning to see chinks in the armor. My best friend had been dropping a few hints about planning a trip for our last spring break (when all Diggers historically hold a retreat on our private island), and when I'd demurred, things had grown a little chilly.

For the two weeks following, she'd taken all of her phone calls in her bedroom, left the suite early on society evenings, and made several references to Eli "traditions" I'd never heard of. They could only pertain to society-specific activities. I'd have to remember to ask Greg or Odile if, in their research, they'd come across a mention of any campus society that incorporated into their initiation rites the raw-hamburger "blood" or feathers I'd found on our suite floor last spring, or if they even knew any of the terms Lydia had been throwing around. I myself have been guilty, upon occasion, of letting Digger jargon slip in the barbarian world. (See? There I go.) Perhaps the words were clues to her society's still-secret identity.

WEIRD TERMS LYDIA DROPS

1) Packing, as in, "We should pack that Politics in Prose seminar together next semester. It's supposed to be really hard to get in, but we're seniors and it counts for both our majors." ← My theory is, it means band together and take it, or not, as one.
2) Jolling, as in, "I can't believe he'd actually make a statement like that in a class full of women. We almost jolled him on the spot." ← My theory is, it means jump someone.
3) Gunned, as in, "The dining hall was gunned tonight. Did you like those potatoes?" ← My theory is, she thinks the cooks were on their game.

Either that or it was the new hip-hop slang. Still, I wanted to get to the bottom of it. After all, she knew I was in Rose & Grave; it seemed only fair I at least learn what society she'd joined. And how funny would it be if the tomb we broke into for our annual crooking expedition was Lydia's?

I crossed Chapel Street and headed under the Art History building arch spanning High Street. And that's when I saw him. Micah Price, standing right beyond the arch on the tomb side of the street. I froze and flattened against the wall, thankful for the dark cape that no doubt shielded me from his sight. What was he doing there? As I watched, the door to the tomb opened, and Jenny stepped out. I thought she'd gone ages ago, and it was so not kosher to have your boyfriend waiting right outside like that. He watched her come down the steps and met her on the pavement. They kept their heads together for some time, whispering to each other, but I couldn't make out a word they said.

I rolled my eyes. Yeah, she was definitely using an imaginative interpretation of the secrecy oath. And I would definitely be bringing this up at the next meeting. I didn't care how angry she was at me already.

I arrived back at the suite to find that Lydia and Josh had started the party without me. Even more surprising: George was also in attendance.

"I assume you don't mind that he showed up at our door?" Lydia asked me slyly as she handed me a shot glass. "Drink up, we're running late."

Lydia was dressed in riding wear, complete with velvet hat and a crop, which apparently amused Josh to no end. For his part, Josh had chosen the time-honored James Bond costume (i.e., tuxedo, martini glass, and plastic Walther PPK), and George, who never missed an opportunity to be a) disaffected or b) dirty, was wearing a T-shirt that read, I AM THE MAN FROM NANTUCKET.

Together, we made our way across the campus to Memorial Hall, warmed only by our suite's official drink of Gumdrop Drops and (in my case, at least) flimsy costumes. The whole way over, George entertained himself trying to lob candy corn into my corset-enhanced cleavage, and I did my best to ward him off with flicks of my cape.

"I'll fish them out later," he promised in a whisper.

The concert hall was a zoo, the way it was every Halloween. The enormous mezzanine was already nearbursting with students who, drunk and costumed, were running from aisle to aisle, showing off their outfits and sharing inebriated conversations and dramas. Above us, two successive balconies teemed with people in devil outfits, Princess Leia costumes, streetwalker-wear (whorish togs being an evergreen Halloween choice at college campuses across the nation), and obscure interpretations of abstract ideas. This last is an Eli special. The point is to dress as a sort of walking rebus in hopes of inducing everyone around you to marvel at your brilliance and beg you to tell them what the hell you're dressed as. These clever little toolboxes were dotted about the audience, puffing out their chests and trying to stump passersby. I spotted four singing-group types wearing aprons and holding clippers and hair dryers (Barbershop Quartet), a chick with a pair of stilettos hanging around her neck (Head Over Heels), a man in a velour suit with numbers stuck all over him (Fuzzy Math), and a woman—who had me stumped for three straight minutes—wearing a bikini made out of two dining hall dishes and a computer keyboard, and carrying a bottle of Schweppes. Finally, I nailed it: Plate Tectonics.

We were trying to squeeze past a freshman in one of those purple balloon bunch-of-grapes getups I thought no one wore outside Fruit of the Loom commercials and a guy in full Mark Rothko body paint (and little else) when I felt a hand on mine.

"Amy!" Brandon cried. I turned to find him seated at the end of an aisle, dressed in a really kick-ass rendition of Alex from *A Clockwork Orange*—bowler cap, fake eyelashes, and all. At his side, Felicity looked as if she'd just stepped out of a U2 video in her belly dancer/genie outfit. A belt made of gold coins clinked around her hips and her long dark hair was piled artfully on top of her head. "Are you looking for a seat?"

He tried to scoot down the row a bit, but Felicity appeared to need more room than one would have imagined, considering how slim she was. I saw her take in my outfit, her eyes lingering extra-long on the scarlet letter on my chest.

"Amy." George appeared at my side. "Lydia found us seats. Come on." He looked over my shoulder at the space Brandon had created and shook his head. "I don't think that place is big enough for all of us."

Brandon only stared at me with mismatched, heavily made-up eyes and nodded slowly.

George leaned over the seat. "Hi there, I think we met last year. I'm George Prescott."

Felicity's eyes widened, though whether it was at the name or the corresponding reputation, I wasn't certain.

Her boyfriend took George's hand and rallied. "I'm Brandon, and this is Felicity."

Dimmesdale, meet Chillingworth.

"Well, have fun at the show." George put a hand on my waist. "C'mon, Boo. It's about to start."

"Nice costumes," I said to the seated couple.

"Thanks," Felicity replied. "I'm fascinated by yours."

"Did everything work out for your math tutor?" Brandon asked quickly. "I mean, did you take care of it?"

No, I hadn't. I'd been too busy taking care of my libido. And when I did try, Jenny had been a complete bitch. "It's fine," I lied, vowing to search out Jenny first thing tomorrow, as long as she wasn't busy with some sort of All Souls' Day cleansing ritual. Fight or no, I had an obligation to her.

But for now, I intended to enjoy my evening as one of the thousand or so "devil-worshipping" souls who fought to drive off the soon-to-be November chill by listening to a world-class symphony orchestra in weird outfits. I failed to see how college students dressed up like geological theories were somehow paying homage to underworld demons. I thought we were just having fun, and Halloween was the name we gave to this brand of fun.

How's that for not overthinking?

George pulled me onto his lap as the lights went down. The ESO puts on a phenomenal show every year. Not only were the members master musicians, they had a wonderful sense of whimsy, setting each year's live program to a home-made movie that usually followed plotlines that wouldn't be out of place on *The Simpsons*'s annual spooky special. And the show always began the same way: with an organist rocking the hell out of "Toccata and Fugue in D Minor" on the antique pipes embedded in the building's walls. The lights slowly rose on a trio of fiddlers who circled a glowing cauldron spilling over with mist and tossed their dreaded hair in time to their otherworldly music. The Weird Sisters.

Man, I loved Eli.

Okay, maybe Jenny had a point about the holiday's ties to Satanism, but she was one to talk. After all, she spent a few nights a week wearing robes in a room lit by candles inside skulls and professing allegiance to a goddess of the underworld. If anything, Rose & Grave had far more guilty-as-charged moments when it came to hellish activities.

The last strains of Bach overlaid these reflections, and then, incredibly, I wasn't thinking about music, or Halloween, or even the way George's hands were slowly creeping up my corset, no doubt in search of stray candy. Instead, I was remembering a conversation I'd once had with Jenny. It was the night of our Rose & Grave initiation, and we were hiding out from the other taps, who'd decided to go for a midnight swim in the indoor pool at the mansion where we had our party. I'd been trying to make getting-to-know-you chitchat and she'd been raving about the "Brotherhood of Death" and their "devious intentions." A few days later, she'd claimed she wanted to change the organization of Rose & Grave from the inside out.

She'd shown enough contempt for our traditions over the past few weeks to convince me she hated our current setup. I really did suspect she'd told that Micah guy what I'd said at my C.B. (if not others as well), breaking her oaths and undermining the fabric of the society. The only reason the Diggers felt comfortable talking so freely in the tomb was because they knew the others would never betray them. And yet Jenny was probably doing exactly that. Who knew what other secrets could do my fellow knights serious damage if they were out in the world? I sneaked a peek at Josh and Lydia, who were canoodling at the end of the row. Even I, who had an airtight reason to spill some secrets (roommate bonds being thick as blood after three years), had managed not to break my oath.

And how realistic was it really that a computer genius, a woman who'd made several million dollars by her eighteenth birthday selling off software to Silicon Valley, couldn't do something as simple as track down a little IP address?

And then tonight, why had she gone back to the tomb after we'd left? We hadn't even known she was there, and she didn't look like she was leaving until we came out onto the staircase. Had we caught Jenny in the middle of something? Had she gone back later, after she knew we were gone, to finish it?

"George," I said over the crash of the cymbals onstage, "I think I know who's leaking the information."

"What?" he shouted, as the crowd began to scream. On the screen above our heads, two band geeks dressed in *Matrix*-style black leather navigated their way through the ultra-modern landscape of the rare book library on their quest to get... well, I hadn't been paying attention, but the sound-track rocked.

"I said, I think ..." I checked the surroundings and re-membered Malcolm's standard reminder to use discretion when it came to all things Rose & Grave. Plus, it wasn't as if George would care. He'd remained completely disinterested in the whole traitor issue since it came up. George could ei-ther take Rose & Grave or leave it. He'd only joined as a fa-vor to his father, and it had taken a good deal of cajoling and even a bit of manhandling on the part of the elder Prescott to accomplish that.

But Josh was right down the row. I'm sure he'd want to hear my thoughts on the matter. Still, a glance at the couple indicated neither would welcome my interruption, and George had decided to go after the candy corn in earnest.

I'd see Josh in our room after the performance. It could wait.

Except we didn't go back to the room. From the smash-ing ESO performance, we hiked up to the Eli Film Society's yearly showing of *The Rocky Horror Picture Show*, and watched folks in skimpy costumes running around onstage throwing bread at one another and engaging in other wild, drunken revels, until George and I made the command decision to head back to Prescott and re-create some key scenes, sans alien transsexuals. On a night like this, I truly did love Eli. And it was such a nice send-off for the good times.

Because November sucked.

I hereby confess:
Discretion is the better
part of vice.

9.
Current Affairs

I was running late the next morning, and as I scurried over to my entryway and up into our first-floor suite, there wasn't anything on my mind except for: toothbrush, change of underwear, hair comb, check face for stray sparkles from my costume (which was currently balled up in the corner of George's bedroom). I flew blindly through the common room and made a beeline for my bedroom door.

"Good morning, Amy," said a male voice at my back. I whirled to find Josh sitting on our couch, laptop on his lap. He closed the cover and set it aside. "We need to talk."

"Crap. Yes, we do, I have something to tell you, but I'm running so late—"

"You have enough time for this. Sit down."

I blinked at him. Excuse me? *Sit down?* This man was my age, in my common room, on my couch, and he was telling me to sit down like he was my father? "Where's Lydia?" I planted my feet.

"At class."

"Well, much as I love having you here, Josh, I really do have to run. However, I want to talk to you. I think Jenny's the leak."

He looked incredulous. "No, she's not. Trust me. We've been working pretty closely on this and she's put a lot of effort into tracking this guy down. No one would be trying so hard if she were secretly involved."

"Are you sure it's not a cover?" I said. "Keep talking while I change really quick." I ducked into my room and tore off my clothes. "I have reason to think she's been telling her boyfriend about everything that happens in the tomb, breaking the oath of secrecy."

"You have proof of this?" Josh's voice floated in.

I scrubbed at my face with a toner cloth, but the sparkles stuck. "No, but the day after my C.B., he looked at me as if he knew all of my dirty secrets. Plus, I saw him lurking outside the tomb last night."

"Where outside the tomb?"

"By the Art History arch."

Josh laughed. "Okay, that's technically outside the tomb—the same way this room is. This is that prayer-group guy we're talking about? He probably hates you for no reason. That's his gig, remember?" He kept talking as I threw on new clothes and pulled my hair up with a clip. "Look, I know how you tend to over ... um, how you attribute certain ..." He apparently thought better of his sentence, for it soon changed directions completely. "Believe me when I say it can't be Jenny. We've spent hours on this leak situation. Hours. You can't prevaricate that long. She's incredibly intense. I promise you're mistaken."

Great. Now I was the Boy Who Cried Wolf because I was always calling "Conspiracy." I emerged from my room. "Okay, but I'm *not* wrong about her telling Micah about my

C.B. And I'm going to confront her about it." I crossed to the door. "Good talking to you."

"Wait a second! I listened to you, now you listen to me."

"Yeah, you listened to me good. Look, I have to run. . . ." I turned the knob.

"What are you doing with George?"

I froze and turned to him. "Nothing."

"Don't lie to me, Amy. You're sleeping with him."

I laughed. "Like that's any of your business?"

"As Secretary of D177, it *is* my business."

I crossed my arms. "I don't think so. This has nothing to do with what happens in Rose & Grave."

"I know for a fact it has *everything* to do with what happens in our tomb." He met my eyes full-on, and my breath hitched. Was the Inner Temple bugged all along? Oh, God, how embarrassing. "I don't understand why you would choose this time, when everything is so fragile, to weaken us further."

"Are you kidding? Weaken the society? It's barbarian matters. What George and I—*George and I*, not Puck and Bugaboo—choose to do won't affect you."

"We both know that's not true. You don't expect this little fling of yours to go on forever, do you? You know George. And when it's over, someone is going to be hurt, and the Diggers will be the ones to suffer for it. Society incest is a terrible idea."

You know George? Yes, I did, and I knew the man in front of me, too. "I'm going to say this once, and since you're a smart guy who managed to snag himself not only a slot in Phi Beta Kappa, but also a PBK honey, I'm sure you'll be able to understand it. I'll fuck whom I want to, and neither you nor any other Digger gets to tell me otherwise. Unlike you, George and I are being perfectly honest about what we're looking for in our relationship."

"What's that supposed to mean?" Josh stood now.

"Exactly what you think it does. How dare you accuse me of being the type to break my oaths for personal reasons? If that were true, I'd have told Lydia about you a long time ago." I put my hand on the door. "But hey, maybe you're right. Maybe I should. I don't know about George and me, but I know your relationship isn't going to last forever, either. I promise you, if you hurt my best friend, and I stood idly by and watched it happen like a good little Digger, I *will* break my oaths. I'll do my best to ruin your life, and I don't care what kind of vows I took."

———

Suffice it to say Josh and I weren't exactly friendly after that. It bothered me more than I'd expected it to. After all, we were supposed to lean on one another in times of trouble, and instead I'd alienated one of my favorite brothers. Jenny wasn't returning my phone calls or e-mails, and George didn't want to talk about any of it. Due to the chilly, uncomfortable, and frustrating atmosphere, I was understandably relieved when Clarissa and Demetria called a meeting of the Diggirls the day before our next society meeting. I looked forward to the chance to chill with some of my friendlier compatriots (my suite had turned into a Cold War zone) and finally have it out with Jenny.

Except when I arrived at the campus pizza joint where the Diggirls were supposed to meet, there were only four knights waiting for me: Clarissa, Demetria, Mara, and Odile. The little sneak had opted out. Well, no matter. I'd share my suspicions with the girls and see if they took me more seriously than Josh had.

"You're late," said Clarissa, scooting over in the booth and taking her crinkle-plastic cup full of diet pop with her. "I got your usual small Greek salad. I don't know how you can deal with all that fat." ("Small" was a misnomer when it came to the Greek salad at Normandy Pizza. It was roughly the size and shape of a football and drenched in feta cheese bits, olives, and dressing.)

"Yum," I said, sliding into the booth. "Anyone know where Jenny is?"

Demetria shrugged. "This isn't the first time she's wimped out on us. Girl doesn't have her priorities straight."

Clarissa nodded her agreement. "Have any of you ever seen her tattoo? I think she didn't get one."

Mara shuddered delicately. "Can I express once more how happy I am I joined your merry band after the whole tattoo phase? Staining one's skin is a sign of barbarism."

The other four of us looked at one another and smiled. "In this case," I said, "it's exactly the opposite."

"I hope she shows up," said Clarissa. "But I'm not going to hold my breath. We've got a lot to talk about, so let's get started and she can catch up. This whole leak situation really has the patriarchs rattled. Frankly, you'd think they'd be nicer, considering we're the ones protecting their secrets."

"Spoken like someone who would sell secrets just to get back at them for being jerks," Demetria said with a smile. "But have you seen that website? Come on. I refuse to let myself get up in arms over something with a flashing tiled background and animated gifs. Real firebrands would go for something professional-looking."

"The issue isn't the website," Clarissa said. "It's who the website turns on to the story. Josh says—"

I rolled my eyes. "Josh says an awful lot, but just because he's the Secretary doesn't mean he's the boss of us. To listen to him talk, sometimes you'd think we should each be strip-searched upon entering or leaving the tomb!"

"Tell me about it," said Odile. "You should have heard the interrogation I got when I came back from New York last month. Some timing, huh? And he was all, 'Terribly convenient for you to be absent the day the leak is broadcast, Lil' Demon.' Right. As if I'd be selling my services to some conspiracy-theorist website the same weekend I'm hosting *Saturday Night Live*. Why the hell would I do something like that when I had a much larger audience just waiting for me to spill some Eli goss? I swear the only thing Lorne ever wants me to talk about is the seedy underbelly of this school." And then she coughed.

Were this a Dickens novel, this would be a signal that Odile had contracted consumption, and would die within a few chapters. But in my world, it meant something else entirely. Mara and I started in our seats and then, for the first time in our relationship, our eyes met in understanding. We looked from Demetria to Odile, and back again.

"What?" said Clarissa as Demetria ducked her head. Realization slowly dawned on Miss High Society. "Ohhhh."

"Did you two hook up?" Mara said with a gasp.

"No!" Demetria protested ... too much.

Odile shot her an incredulous glance.

"Eww," said Clarissa. "Society incest. Bad idea."

"It is?" I asked, then occupied myself with my salad. *Shut up, Amy, or the cat will really be out of the coffin.*

"Duh, of course!" Clarissa said.

"I don't think so," said Odile.

Demetria snorted. "Of course *you'd* say that. You're not really the type to concern yourself with taboos, are you? A regular George Prescott, but without the dick."

"I didn't see you complaining," Odile snapped.

Clarissa sliced her hand down between them. "Whoa there, ladies."

"Forget about it," said Demetria. "It was silly." She caught Odile's eye. "No offense, but admit it, it was silly."

Odile shrugged, Mara was looking more scandalized than I'd ever seen her (which is saying something), and I was constructing a little tower of lettuce, feta, olives, and tomatoes on my fork. *A regular George Prescott?*

On the one hand, I was wild to hear more about the juiciest Rose & Grave gossip in months. On the other, it seemed a bit hypocritical for me to indulge, since I was currently engaged in my own society affair. Best to downplay whatever had transpired between Demetria and Odile, lest the scrutiny turn into speculation about who else in the club had hooked up.

Of course, George had yet to give his C.B., which meant if he planned to adhere to his oaths (always up in the air with a guy like George), then everything we'd done would be fair game. Clearly, Josh knew at least part of the story already. Maybe I should admit it to the Diggirls, so as not to send them into shock when they heard it through official channels. They wouldn't judge me, right? I mean, the guy was gorgeous and sexy and infamous and I bet all of them, even the female-focused Demetria, had wondered at least once if all the rumors were true. Besides, we were Diggers, and we were supposed to love and support one another and stuff.

Though maybe I hadn't been doing that recently with one of my fellow knights.

"Girls ..." I began. But just then, our waitress, another Eli institution (she'd been working at the restaurant longer than our freshman counselors' freshman counselors could remember) stopped by with her little black leather portfolio.

"We're not ready for the check," Clarissa said.

The waitress put her hands up, palms out. "I don't get involved with you people." And then she departed.

Clarissa furrowed her brow and flipped open the folder. There, on a slip of receipt paper, were scrawled three words:

It Went Live.

I hereby confess:
I wish I were wrong.

10.
Disappeared

Before he graduated, Malcolm told me that it was a good thing I had my grade point average in shape before I joined Rose & Grave, because my society commitments would begin to commandeer a lot of my time. No joke. I don't think I thought about schoolwork for a moment after that fake check arrived at our table. No, it was all angry e-mails, emergency meetings, spin summits, and of course the horrific and constant scrutiny the entire student body suddenly focused on the tomb on High Street.

The campus tabloid, *The Ruckus*, jumped on the story first, printing a special one-page issue alerting the campus to the conspiracy website and all of the secrets it spilled. (No doubt they still harbored some bitterness over the World Clock fiasco.) Naturally, the political bloggers scented blood in the air, and from that point, the race was on to be the first major 24-hour news cycle outlet to report the story. Print media, from the *Eli Daily News* and the *New Haven Register* to the New York *Daily News*, the *New York Post*, the *Washington Post*, and the *New York Times* were actually a bit late to the ball game, given the hassle of working with an actual printed press. It wasn't safe to approach the tomb, what with Channel 8 News and CNN camped outside, waiting to get an exclusive interview with an actual, live Digger.

What did they expect, that the President was about to come up to New Haven and just stroll inside?

Luckily, any media outlet controlled by actual, live Diggers (and there were several) stayed as far away from this little news nugget as possible. And what, pray tell, did the traitor say? Detailed analysis of all our initiation rites, membership lists of certain clubs, and teases about juicier info . . . to come next week. Apparently, the individual was giving the patriarchs and their adolescent exploits one week's reprieve (the better to build expectation—and extortion—with, my dear).

The patriarch reaction, as assessed through Phimalarlico e-mails, messages on the tomb's voice mail, and infuriated phone calls to our Secretary, Josh, could be divided into three groups:

Standard: "I've called to express my disappointment with the current media coverage of our society. I stood by this new club, unorthodox though it might be, and was willing to give you the benefit of the doubt that your unconventional makeup would inject new blood into the organization. I'm beginning to wonder if my fellow patriarchs weren't correct in their original decision to invalidate the tap. This is an appalling turn of events and I'm reconsidering my choice to continue supporting this society until you get your act together."

Angry: "I knew we shouldn't have expected much from you people, but this takes inappropriate to a whole new level. Less than six months in and you're already doing your best to drive Rose & Grave right into the ground. You need to find the knight responsible for this leak and deal with him...or her. I did not spend the better half of my life protecting the oaths of my brethren to let you people destroy it. You'll never see another dime from me."

Kurt Gehry: "You incompetent sons of bitches, I told you to take care of this. Fine, since you either cannot or will not do what's necessary, we're taking matters into our own hands. Watch how *real* men, *real* Diggers, handle those who threaten us."

On Thursday afternoon, my path crossed with Genevieve Grady, ex-editor of the *Eli Daily News*, ex-girlfriend of Malcolm Cabot, and ex–person-of-interest to Rose & Grave. Last year, Genevieve, in a fit of woman-scorned pique, had threatened to blackmail Malcolm into giving her paper a peep inside the tomb, but I'd managed to talk her out of it. When she saw me coming, she threw her hands up in surrender.

"Amy, I swear! I had nothing to do with—"

I shook my head. "No, I know. Your paper is simply repeating what's already out there. It's fine." And no, I couldn't resist the jab about recycled content.

"So you do know who's responsible?" She went immediately into reporter-mode.

I gave her the evil eye. "Right, because I'm about to turn that info over to you."

She smirked. "Come on, Haskel. You're my secret source."

"Not this time. You've lost your hold on me."

Her smile faded. "Have you...heard from him?" Genevieve had been in love with Malcolm, but the poor boy was unable to return her feelings.

"Yeah, I have. He told his parents last summer and they, predictably, disowned him. He's living in Alaska for his gap year and then he's going to business school."

"Disowned him?" She bit her lip. "I think I'd like to e-mail him. I feel so bad about... last year. I think I went a little nuts."

You think? But I refrained from saying that. "I bet he'd appreciate it."

"Okay, then, I will. Oh, and Amy ..." She touched my shoulder. "In retrospect, I'm really glad they tapped you and not me."

I shook her off. Yeah, she certainly dodged that bullet, didn't she?

But the rest of us were feeling its bite. Thursday evening, we managed to sneak into our meeting through a very complicated system of visiting the Art and Architecture's sculpture garden while various and sundry delivery trucks pulled up to the tomb's supply door.

"This is why we need that secret entrance I was promised," I grumbled to Odile as we hid behind a stack of milk bottles.

"Word."

Dinner that evening was a dismal affair, despite Hale's masterful preparation of beef Wellington. We wandered in, one by one, and picked at our food. Since Sunday had been reserved for a presentation from a patriarch who had recently returned from Bolivia, we'd temporarily switched the C.B. schedule to Thursday—though, given the consequences of the leak and the possible future humiliation should further Digger information come to light, no one was enthusiastic about sharing their sexual history. At first, we thought we'd can the schedule and just engage in a little old-fashioned Rose & Grave political debate, but state issues were not on the forefront of anyone's mind—not even Soze's, who was in full spin-doctor mode.

"Let's look on the bright side," he said, scooping up a forkful of mashed potatoes, then letting it plop back onto his plate. "What did the stupid site really say? A bunch of crap about our initiations and a floor plan of the tomb. They didn't actually release any of the info in the patriarch's Black Books."

"No," said Frodo, who had finally arrived. So far, only eight of us had made it through the gauntlet. "They're saving that for next week's big reveal. We gotta track this guy down before it gets any worse."

I took a bite of beef and looked at Soze. "Heard from Lucky, perchance? I haven't seen her in days."

"Drop it, *'boo*," Soze snapped. And if Puck noticed the use of his special name for me, he didn't show it. Unlike the rest of us, my lover didn't seem particularly morose about the recent turn of events, and was digging into his dinner with gusto. He'd already finished two servings of beef, and was eyeing the slice on my plate as well.

But Lil' Demon jumped to my defense. "Why should she drop it? You were on my back about being in New York when the announcement was first posted. No one here has seen Lucky since it went live. She skipped our last Diggirls get-together, she skipped all of our recent powwows, and I bet you a bottle of Cristal she skips tonight as well. Doesn't that seem far more suspicious to you?"

Soze narrowed his eyes in my direction. "Who else have you been sharing your suspicions with, Bugaboo?"

"They aren't *her* suspicions," Lil' Demon said. "They're mine. You're not the only one who gets to make accusations around here, Soze."

"Though I'm apparently the only one who realizes what

doing so might mean." He threw his fork down. "Has no one else been paying attention to Gehry's threats? He's out for blood, and we all know from personal experience the man doesn't bluff. I also know from political circles he's a leap-first-look-later kind of guy. If he thinks he can pin this on someone, he'll ruin them without a second thought. He'll do it even if it's only to make an example of the person."

"And he'd probably love to pin it on a Diggirl." Angel slumped in her chair, her blond hair tumbling over her shoulders.

"So what?" asked Big Demon. "He tries anything with Lucky and she'll crash his whole system."

"Not Lucky," Puck piped up at last. "Something tells me she's a turn-the-other-cheek kind of gal."

I set down my fork. "Look, I'm the last person who would turn her over to that asshole. What do you take me for? I just want to talk to her. That's all. I haven't seen her for a while. She hasn't managed to make it over here and I want to know why. Is this too much to ask?"

Apparently so. Of course, as it turned out, Lucky wasn't the only no-show on that fine November evening. Graverobber (of course), Kismet, Shandy, Thorndike (who you'd think would have experience running blockades), and Bond all failed to make an appearance, and when it became obvious we had nothing even approaching a quorum, Frodo, the evening's Uncle Tony, called a recess.

"We'll talk online," Soze suggested as we began to sneak out, "and make sure we can meet on Sunday. This should all blow over by then."

Here's hoping. And to that end, I decided to accompany Ben back to Edison College, which just happened to be my favorite missing knight's home. Josh may think Jenny's absence was more correlation than causation, but I'd decided to beard the computer hacker in her den of CPUs.

Edison is located on the far end of campus, near the gym. It's one of the so-called ugly colleges. While the rest of us dwell in Gothic or Georgian splendor (a little cramped, but hey, lead-veined windows, enormous fireplaces, exposed brick, and wood paneling), the residents of Edison College enjoy spacious singles from sophomore year onward and spend their time at Eli in an ultra-modern architectural example of abstract art. The building has no right angles. Those of us who were lucky enough to draw into one of the older colleges don't get the appeal.

"How do you like this place?" I asked Ben as we traversed a wide courtyard ringed with towering monoliths of glass and jagged stone. "I can't imagine living here. Half the reason you come to a place like Eli is because of how beautiful the campus is. What did you think when you were assigned into Edison?"

Ben blinked at me. "I came to Eli because I was recruited onto the team and it was the best academic program of the schools recruiting me. And, no, I don't think it's ugly at all. I think it's great. I transferred into this college, and so you know, it wasn't because I'm a jock and wanted to be close to the gym. I happen to *like* modern architecture."

Around that time, I remembered Ben was an Art History major, and wondered if I'd gain any points by offering to cut out my cruel tongue as punishment for my ham-handed remarks. Just because I preferred the Georgian style of Prescott College didn't mean I knew the first thing about the value of modern art. Never much one for Kandinsky, either.

But it was par for the course in our conversation. Ben was harboring some unnamed grudge that evening and only offered limited assistance. I needed his college key to activate the tower elevator that would take me up to Jenny's room on the eighth floor, but as soon as we stepped into the elevator, he begged off accompanying me to her door.

"It's bad enough I spend two nights a week with her," he said. "Negativity like that totally messes with my mojo, and Coach says . . ." He sighed. "It doesn't matter."

"What do you mean?"

"You aren't interested in the state of my game. You just need me to get to Jenny."

"That's not true." I touched his arm. "Of course I'm interested. If you're having a problem, you're supposed to come to one of us. Why didn't you bring it up at a meeting?"

Ben looked skeptical. "There's always some crisis going on down there. The patriarchs are rallying or failing to rally or everyone is threatening to quit or blah blah blah. I don't want to add to the whining."

"You think that's what it would be? Maybe it would force us to refocus on what we're really about."

He snorted. "We're not really about anything, Amy. Not this year. We never had a chance. We're nothing more than a bunch of cliques and factions. You girls and your tattoos. Think about it. The rest of us were in the city, too—hell, I drove the damn van—but were we invited to get tattoos? No." He stuck his hands in his pockets. "It's like last month when you wanted us all to track down Jenny and ask her what was bothering her. Right, like that was going to happen. How am I supposed to feel comfortable opening up to everyone if they don't open up to me?"

I swallowed. He had a point. Was I guilty of contributing to the fractious nature of this year's club? Had I, perhaps, not been listening when one of my brothers needed help? "Someone needs to start," I said at last. "If you want to talk to me, Ben, I'll always listen."

"Yeah. Whatever." The elevator arrived at the eighth floor, and he nodded toward Jenny's door. "Just not now."

I glanced out at the narrow hallway lined with doors.

The Edison College setup was so unlike the usual Eli dorm design that for a moment I felt as if I were at another school entirely. "No, if you want to talk, now is—"

"Nice try." There was the hint of a smile. "Let's go for Sunday."

"Really—"

He held up a hand that palmed basketballs. "Amy, this was supposed to be my C.B. night. We couldn't even have a meeting, because all the drama meant half the club didn't show. I'm in a bad mood, and I just want to take my anger out on the treadmill. Tell you what will really make me happy: You find the bastard responsible for wrecking my society experience. That's how you can make it up to me."

Then he pressed the *Door Close* button and departed, and I turned my back on one brother in need in order to confront another. *I'll try, Ben. I'll try.*

Jenny's door, unlike the others on the hall, was devoid of all decoration, signage, or even a whiteboard. I knocked, and then, receiving no answer, tried the handle. Locked. A quick scan of the bathroom showed she wasn't in there, either. Just as well. I didn't want to get caught in her hallway if the girl was about to emerge from the shower wearing a towel and a scowl. Maybe one of her more outwardly humanoid (judging by décor) suitemates knew where she was.

Still, it was Thursday, and if they, like Lydia, suspected Jenny's involvement in Rose & Grave, they'd be unlikely to spill her meeting-night whereabouts to a total stranger.

Three of the other six rooms on the floor were also no answer. Number four told me she never paid attention to when the rest of her suitemates arrived and departed, and wasn't even sure she knew all their names, having been added to the suite merely to round out to the required seven. Number five told me she hadn't seen Jenny in a few days and number six went Trappist monk on me. *Bingo.* She was clearly reacting to the day—Thursday. Unfortunately, I knew society commitments were not what kept this girl's suitemate away from home tonight.

Me: "Have you seen Jenny?"
Roommate: …
Me: "Do you know when she'll be back?"
Roommate: …
Me: "She didn't leave you a key, did she?"
Roommate: *(closes door in my face)*

Well, that was short and useless.

"Enough of this," I said to the empty hallway. I might be a mild-mannered Lit major, but even I had a few tricks up my sleeve. Or on my carabiner, as the case may be. I pulled my proximity card out of its plastic holder, knelt at Jenny's door, wiggled the card into the space near the catch, and prayed that a) Jenny hadn't upgraded average dorm-room security and b) I remembered how to do this. I hadn't broken into anyone's room since Thanksgiving Break freshman year, and even then, it had only been Lydia's. She'd called, hysterical, claiming her Sociology professor hadn't received her e-mailed final paper and she was stuck in some hellish layover in Detroit, sans Internet access, and would I please please please find her paper on the computer and e-mail it again. We've been best friends ever since. Nothing like a little larceny to cement a bond.

Several perspiration-inducing moments later, I heard a *click.* I blew on my fingers, a little smug, then pushed the door open, praying Jenny was indeed absent and not locking me out of some illicit tryst or other private moment. C.B.s were one thing. Actual visuals were most definitely another.

But the room was empty. At least, I think it was. Kind of

tough to tell at first glance, what with the five metric tons of electrical equipment piled about the place, and the blanket of paperwork covering everything.

Was this normal? I'd never been in Jenny's room before, so I had no idea if the bedlam that lay beyond the doors was indicative of her current state of mind or if the chick was simply a career slob.

I crossed the threshold and picked my way around endless piles of paper; random bits of wiring; labyrinthine, snaking cords; and the odd T-shirt or flip-flop. Most of the room was given over to a vast console of computers. There were a trio of monitors on her desk, and the shelves behind it were stacked with CPUs, speakers, and what looked like unused laptops. A long folding table had been set up, extending the desk so it wrapped around half the room, and there were more monitors arranged there—large, small, flat screen— and at least three keyboards.

It looked like the set of *Sliver*. What possible use could someone have for fourteen computers? Or did she collect them the way I collected blue pencils? I edged forward, keeping the corner of my eye on the door. I hadn't yet figured out how to excuse my presence should Jenny return.

But where was she? Her tall-backed ergonomic desk chair was situated in front of one computer terminal, and on the surface of the desk in front of it sat three things: Jenny's keys, Jenny's wallet, and Jenny's cell phone. She couldn't have gone far with such essentials left behind. Crap. That meant I didn't have much time.

In one unused corner of the room there was a squat table covered in red cloth, on which was a sort of makeshift altar topped with votive candles, a neatly curled rosary, and a figure of the Virgin, all looking a bit on the dusty side. A small pillow rested before the table, cushioning a thick book with a cover made of duct tape. A Bible, most likely. There were a few posters on the wall, mostly of the inoffensive Monet's landscape-and-lilies variety, and a portrait of some Victorian woman with Princess Leia hair.

Envelopes were strewn across her bed, along with file folders, textbooks, computer magazines, catalogs, stacks of CDs, jewel cases, and more of the ever-present wiring. It didn't even look possible to sleep on the thing. Of course, maybe Jenny didn't sleep here. Or at all. Maybe she was a raging insomniac who subsisted on No Doz and mocha lattes. Maybe she never took her keys with her anywhere. Maybe whatever intuition I had telling me this didn't seem like Jenny was utterly wrong. Did any of us really know what *did* seem like her? She'd always been the most secretive Digger, and not in that good, institutionalized way. Her secrecy, I was beginning to understand, was a front. Something she could hide behind while she sought to betray us. I just didn't know why.

I glanced down at the nearest paper-strewn flat surface, as if its contents would give me an insight into my brother's mysterious personality, but found nothing I didn't have lying on my desk back in my room. A handout from class, a few Post-it notes scribbled over with phone and room numbers, and junk mail, half of which wasn't even addressed to Jenny, but to "resident" or random names. I got the same sort of crap in my university Post Office Box every day. The spammers apparently thought the owner of my box was a Korean Chemistry grad student named Jungsub Byun. Jenny's prior occupant appeared to be one Ada Lovelace.

Ugh. What was I doing here? Even if there were proof of Jenny's treachery, I hadn't the faintest clue how to find it. Not in this mess. I pulled out the ergonomic chair—the one empty spot in the room, and sat down. Dead end.

Or at least, a dead end here. I could still try to track down Micah and see if Jenny was with him. Though she'd never talked to me about the confrontation I'd witnessed, I assumed she was still dating the guy, asshole or not. After all, I'd seen them together on Halloween. I felt a twinge of guilt that I'd never been able to get through to her on that issue, but forgive me if I was lacking in sympathy at the moment. Was that unbrotherly of me? After all, I'd once sworn to *bear the confidence and the confessions of my brothers, to support them in all their endeavors....* But did that mean supporting Jenny in her endeavor to become an oath-breaking bitch?

Methinks it's not what our forefathers had intended with that oath. Plus, we had other oaths to think about, like the ones saying we were to *further the society's friends and plight its enemies, and place above all others the causes of the Order of Rose & Grave.* Not to get all Kurt Gehry here, but I think it was safe to say Jenny was an enemy of the Order. Thus, she must be plighted.

Whatever that meant. Was "plight" even a verb?

On the floor at my feet there was a blinking red light. I reached over and pushed aside a few papers. Yet another keyboard, this one obviously a wireless. Look at the way Jenny treated her equipment! I picked it up, and flipped it over, accidentally jostling the tracking ball as I did so. One of the screens flickered to life.

So much for security. The monitor displayed a web-browser window open to the Phimalarlico webmail page. A "Compose" window lay open. I leaned into the screen.

From: Lucky-D177@phimalarlico.org
To: D177-Knights@phimalarlico.org
Subject:

I'm so sorry. By now, I know you are all very angry and I think you have every right to be. I don't know if there's any explanation for_ help help help help help help help help help

help help help help help help help help help help help help
help help help help help help help help help help help help
help help help help help help help help help help help help
help help help help help help help help help help help help
help help help help help help help help help help help help
help help help help help help help help help help help help

The words filled the page. I pressed *Return* and they
started up again—help help help—filling every screen in the
room.

I sat there for a moment, blinking at the screens. The
chaos around me took on a new, sinister meaning. Maybe
Jenny *wasn't* usually so messy. Maybe someone had been
here before me, rifling through her stuff. Maybe Jenny
wasn't hiding. Maybe she'd been disappeared.

*He's out for blood, and we all know from personal experience
the man doesn't bluff.*

No doubt about it: We'd found our leak. Now the only
problem was finding out what had happened to her.

I hereby confess:
He was the last person
I wanted.

11.

Friend-in-Law

I grabbed Jenny's cell phone and keys and got my ass out of the room. Who should I call? The campus police? The dean? The FBI?

First, I called Josh. "Jenny's gone," I gasped into the phone as I ran across the Edison College courtyard. "She's not in her room and it's been—trashed. She's definitely responsible for the leak. Come quick."

"How were you in her room?" Josh asked.

"I broke in with my prox card."

Josh was quiet. "You broke into her room?"

"Josh! I think something bad has happened to her."

"And you broke into her room? What were you thinking?"

I was thinking that if no one believed me about Jenny, I was going to get some proof. And now I was thinking she'd been kidnapped. "What does it matter? The point is, she's gone! We have to do something. Should we call the police?"

"And report your breaking and entering?" he scoffed.

"Amy, unless there's blood all over the floor, I don't think you've got much of an argument."

The only people who leave blood on the floor are your girl-friend's society, I wanted to snap, but held my tongue.

He went on. "She's probably just studying somewhere. Have you tried calling her?"

"I've got her cell phone in my hand." But that was a good point. I pressed the button for *Recently Dialed Calls*. Micah, Micah, Micah, Home, Sally's Pizza, someone named Grace, two numbers in New York, and two more here in Connecticut. I'd call those later.

"You *stole* her cell phone? Broke into her room and stole her cell phone. Are you crazy?"

"You're right." I stopped running, and stared down at my contraband. "I shouldn't touch anything until the police get here."

"You need to go put her stuff back. And then you need to write a note to have her call you. Go home, wait for her, and hope she doesn't get you in any trouble. Just because you're a Digger doesn't give you free rein to start breaking laws. I'm not a lawyer yet, but I'd say nothing you did tonight is cool."

"But Josh, you're not listening to me. I think she's in trouble. There's this half-finished e-mail on her computer and it says 'help' all over it. You said Gehry was out for—"

"Amy, I can see you're really upset, but you need to chill out for a second and think. Where are you right now? Why don't you come home so we can talk about this—"

"*Come home?*" I cried. "My suite is not your home, Josh Silver! My best friend is not your latest romantic mistake. And you are *not* my superior. I was there. I saw what her room looks like. You have to believe me that she's in trouble."

"I can't talk to you when you're like this." And then he hung up.

I walked back to Prescott, stewing. Maybe I should just call the cops, but Josh's words echoed in my head. The last thing I needed was to be arrested on counts of breaking and entering. And, like he said, I doubted they'd take me seriously anyway. So a college student was a slob. They'd laugh me out of the station if I tried to file a missing persons report when the person in question had been gone for maybe a few hours. For all anyone knew, she was still at the library, "help help help" or no.

That opinion was buoyed by the next ten calls I proceeded to make. Mara and Omar were appalled that I'd even think of breaking into someone else's suite (Mara, like the stick in the mud she was, even threatened to go to my dean with the information, until I reminded her of her Digger oaths); Kevin and Harun laughed and asked how many cracked-out conspiracy theories they could expect from me before this whole thing was over (Kevin even jokingly warned me that if I persisted in arguments along these lines, he'd start to suspect it was me behind the website); Odile said that no matter how angry I was at Jenny, there was no cause to start committing felonies; Ben was out jogging off his ire; and Nikolos, Greg, Demetria, and Clarissa told me little other than to leave a number after the beep.

I stood in the Prescott courtyard. No way was I going to go back to my place and let Josh lecture me. But I had one Digger left, and maybe I could get him to listen. I took the stairs to George's room.

Light spilled through the crack near the floor, and I heard music, but I had to knock twice before he answered. And when he did, as soon as he saw me, George burst into a grin. "Hey there, cutie," he said, and pulled me inside. "You ran off so quickly earlier, I thought I wasn't going to see you tonight."

His T-shirt was soft and hugged his chest and shoulders,

and his similarly well-worn sweatpants sat low on his hips. His hair was tousled and he was wearing his glasses. I love George's glasses. I love him in his glasses. As soon as we were inside, he crossed to his desk and closed his laptop. Sign of a guilty conscience if I've ever seen it. But I didn't have time to worry about that now. "George, I was at Jenny's."

"She behind this whole snafu?" he asked. He was rummaging in his mini-fridge now, and retrieved two beers. "Figures as much. That girl's a menace to the society. No pun intended."

"Yes, but that's not all. She wasn't there."

He popped the caps off and handed me one. "I'd be hiding out, too, if I were her."

"I think she's been kidnapped."

He raised an eyebrow over the rim of his glasses. "Really. Why? Find a ransom note? Someone holding her for a million shares in Microsoft?" He chuckled and took a pull on his beer.

"No, I found a half-finished e-mail covered with the word 'help.'"

This shut him up for a second, but then he regrouped. "Come on, Boo. Who do you think would kidnap her, aside from your average cult deprogrammer?" He leaned back on his futon. "And to them I say, have at it."

This was beginning to get frustrating. Why would no one take me seriously? I'd been right about the patriarchs last time, but no one had listened until we all lost our summer jobs. "I think it was the patriarchs. I think they discovered she was behind the leak and had her disappeared."

At this, he really started laughing. "Right. We'll find her with cement sneakers at the bottom of New Haven Harbor. That's not those guys' style."

"What about last spring?" I argued, though my pique

was fading fast. Eight discouraging conversations were about as many as I could take.

"Wrecking a couple of undergrad internships is about as criminal as these dudes get. I thought you were over this whole Rose & Grave mythology thing."

"I was until I went into Jenny's room."

He pulled me down beside him on the futon and started rubbing my neck. "Just relax for a second. You're freaking out."

I felt his thumbs dig into the tightness near my shoulder blades and bit my lip. Okay, I was. Freaking out again, just like they expected me to. I'd been named Bugaboo for a reason—I was the one who knew the least about how the society worked, who would be most prone to paying attention to its carefully cultivated legends. But I'd been proven correct during Reading Week last semester. A bunch of the patriarchs had banded together to ruin our newly tapped club, and they'd almost succeeded. However, George was right. They hadn't been doing anything illegal. Just unethical.

Still, the deeper George kneaded my flesh, the tighter my throat grew with unspoken words, and yes, even unshed tears. The rest of them hadn't seen what I saw.

George pushed my hair to the side and began to kiss the back of my neck. "Listen," he whispered between nibbles. "My dad was a Digger, and so was his dad and his dad and his dad, and the closest anyone ever got to breaking the law was a couple of campus pranks. Kurt Gehry and his gang like to talk big, but they'd never do anything dangerous. They're a bunch of punks with power, that's all."

Man, did I want to believe him. I hadn't been with George since the day the site went live. We'd been too preoccupied to get . . . occupied. And it did make a lot of sense. The professional bullying of a bunch of undergrads sounded a lot more realistic than actual cloak-and-dagger stuff. And now that I was sitting here, half in George's arms, the idea that Jenny was in danger—that she was indeed tied up in someone's trunk or sitting in a dark room with an interrogation light swinging overhead—well, it sounded patently ridiculous. No wonder everyone had laughed at me. "You really think it's okay?"

"I know it is." He took me by the shoulders and swiveled me until I faced him. "Relax. This is all going to blow over. It's just the latest in a long line of society scandals." He lowered me until I was reclined against the futon. "Let's get your mind off of this."

Strange and unnatural forces must be at work, for here I was in the presence of George Harrison Prescott, yet I found myself *not* in the mood. Okay, maybe some of my suspicions were over the line, but that didn't mean I had to disregard all of my instincts. I sat up. "What were you doing before I came in?"

"Working. Why?"

"Working on something so private you needed to shut your screen?" I folded my arms. "Do you think I'm an idiot?"

"Boo—"

"It's okay, you know," I said quickly. "We have no *understanding*."

"So then, why does it matter?"

Because I was curious. "IM-ing with some chick? Surfing MySpace profiles for pretty young things?"

He laughed. "Come on, now. I'm a player, not a pervert."

I shook my head. "You're so ready to claim that title."

"I don't need to claim it, baby," he said, leaning in. "The Diggers already dubbed me Puck."

But I was temporarily immune. "What were you doing?"

He collapsed back against the futon. "Are we really going to start doing this? I thought you were cool."

"I am."

"Then, what?" He studied me. "Is this some kind of turn-on? You want to know what other girls I'm with?"

An enumerated list? Hardly. "I want us to be honest."

"And I want things not to change."

Translation: He was seeing other people, but thought telling me would make me mad. Right now, I couldn't be sure what I was feeling, since I was *already* mad. "George, if I decided to stop sleeping with you, how would you feel?"

He considered this for a moment. "I don't know. Why, are you going to?"

"I don't know."

We sat there for a moment, not looking at each other. Finally, he spoke. "The truth is, I'm not seeing anyone else, and I haven't since we first got together."

Probably a lie. And I was picking a fight with him because he wouldn't help me. What a screwed-up relationship this was.

"Boo, look at me." When I didn't, he cupped my chin in his hands and turned my face toward his. His copper eyes burned right into mine. "I'm not lying. I haven't been with anyone but you. But that doesn't mean I won't. And if you want me to tell you, I will, and then you can make any decision you want."

It didn't get much fairer than that. "What do you want me to do if I start seeing someone else?"

He grinned. "Hide him." And then he kissed me.

But for the first time ever, I spent the night in George's room without any sex involved. I slept poorly, and early the next morning (okay, around 8 A.M.) I left and headed back to my suite. As expected, Josh was either gone or asleep.

I paced for a while in my room, as unable to sleep there

as I had been in George's arms. Sure, I was angry at Jenny, but underneath it all, she was my brother, and what's more, she was in all likelihood in serious trouble. But if Jenny Santos, who was about a hundred times smarter and better connected than I was, couldn't help herself, how was I supposed to do anything?

I couldn't, but then again, maybe I wouldn't need to. I'd call in the big guns. I sat down at my laptop, pulled up my Phimalarlico webmail, and dashed off a quick e-mail to Malcolm.

From: Bugaboo-D177@phimalarlico.org
To: Lancelot-D176@phimalarlico.org
Subject: Emergency

Lance, I need your help. Lucky betrayed us, and now she's gone missing. The others think she's hiding out because she knows how angry we are, but I suspect foul play. I saw her room. If she left, it wasn't planned. I need your help. We need to find out what happened to her. Call me ASAP.

My big sib must have been on his computer, because I got an answer two minutes later.

From: Lancelot-D176@phimalarlico.org
To: Bugaboo-D177@phimalarlico.org
Subject: Re: Emergency

bad timing, little sis. leaving now for fishing trip. (what are you doing up at this ungodly hour?) this is quite the mess. i understand your predicament, but you know what to do: call poe. he'll help you.

Yeah, right into my grave he'd help me—roses not included. I shot back:

From: Bugaboo-D177@phimalarlico.org
To: Lancelot-D176@phimalarlico.org
Subject: Re: Re: Emergency

Poe hates me and I'm not too fond of him. He'd never help me. Please, Lance? I need you!

This time, it took less than thirty seconds to get a response.

From: Lancelot-D176@phimalarlico.org
To: Bugaboo-D177@phimalarlico.org
Subject: Re: Re: Re: Emergency

gotta run. call poe. ☺

You know that bit about banging your head against the keyboard? In real life, it's not actually all that effective as a stress reliever. Plus, it's a bit impractical, what with all the accidental shutting down of programs that results.

Once I rebooted, I considered my options:

1) Forget the whole thing. Jenny must be okay.
   ← Yeah, so not my thing.
2) Go back and beg some of the other Diggers for help. ← Right, because I'm a veritable glutton for punishment.
3) Deal with it myself. After all, I'm a smart, capable sort of girl. I could surely get to the root of a suspected kidnapping all on my own. ← Except,

what do I know about kidnapping? I'm a Lit major, for crying out loud. The last abduction I read about was *The Rape of the Lock*.

4) Call the cops and explain to them that I was worried this girl I didn't actually know all that well and wasn't really all that friendly with and who is also, by the way, a computer millionaire, may have been kidnapped as part of a vast conspiracy reaching all the way up to the Chief of Staff to the President of the United States because she'd threatened to tell the world who a bunch of middle-aged men had slept with in their teens. ← *Res ipsa loquitur.**

5) Suck it up and contact Poe. ← After all, he's every bit as paranoid as I am, and much more experienced at dealing with it.

Of course, it wasn't going to be easy. Not only was there the aforementioned mutual hatred, but I'd managed to avoid ever learning the bastard's real name. That would be step one.

Cue *Mission Impossible* theme and commence stealthy journey back into the tomb. Once there, I took the stairs to the room of records. There'd been a motion to seal off the room until we'd located the leak, but no one thought it would be much of a deterrent. The person already had their info. Now I was glad for the access.

Along the wall of the room of records hung a group portrait for every club as far back as daguerreotypes were in vogue. I checked the wall for D176. The men were clustered around the grandfather clock I knew was in the Firefly Room, and before them lay a low table with the etching of

---

**"The thing speaks for itself." Though never a Classics major, the confessor does know a little Latin.*

Persephone on top. Each wore a formal tuxedo with tails. There was Malcolm in the front row, his hand resting on the shoulder of the knight I knew as Poe. I looked at the list of names beneath the photo.

James Orcutt.

What a ridiculously normal name. I'd half been expecting Darth Vader. But, no matter. The Grand Library had a computer terminal (because, honestly, how *grand* would it be otherwise?). I entered Orcutt's name into the student directory, and a few moments later had his home number. Bingo. I exited into the hall and approached the tomb's only phone.

Point of no return, Amy. Are you honestly going to do this? Go to Poe? I took a deep breath, and dialed.

"Hello?" My Pavlovian response to his voice has always been fight-or-flight, but I steeled myself and tried to sound cheery. Or at least amicable.

"Hi. James?" The name sounded bizarre on my tongue. "This is—"

"Amy Haskel." Not a question. "What do you want?"

I hesitated, still reeling from the shock that he'd recognized my voice. "I . . . Malcolm said— I need your help."

Silence, and then, "Figures. What is it—wait, are you at the tomb?"

"Yeah."

"Meet me at my place: 27 Danbury, number 3. Come now." And then he hung up.

What choice did I have? I was the desperate one. I'd work on his timetable. So I hoofed it across town. All the law students live off-campus, but when I got to the address Poe—sorry, *James*, but old habits die hard—had indicated, it was clear my nemesis was living as disreputably as possible. I stood for a moment on the tree lawn and debated whether or not the trash heap before me could possibly be the right address.

The front yard was a mess of weeds, hemmed in by a sagging chain-link fence emblazoned with a black-and-red BEWARE OF DOG sign. But there was no dog to be seen as I opened the catch and picked my way up the cracked front walk, and no mangy mutt chased me as I put my first tentative steps onto the team-of-termites-holding-hands that passed for a stoop. The steps creaked beneath my feet, and the front porch practically screamed "Skirt the edges," with all of its saggy spots. I reached number 3 and rang the bell.

A few moments later, the door beyond the screen opened, and there stood Poe—I mean, James—in his usual uniform of grubby white undershirt and worn dress pants. He leaned against the jamb and regarded me through the screen.

"You actually showed."

"I actually need help."

"And you *actually* think I'm going to give it to you... why, exactly?" He tilted his head to one side. "Let's forget for a minute that you've never been anything but a bitch to me. As far as I can see, you've been doing your level best to grind my society into dust since we handed you the reins. And now you want my assistance?"

Let's *not* forget that the first time I met this dude, he threatened to have me drowned and/or forced into sexual servitude. Not exactly getting off on the right foot. So what if it was hazing? Still hurt. But no matter. I had one card to play. "Look, I don't like you, and you don't like me. No surprise to either of us, I'm sure. But what we both like is Rose & Grave. And it's in trouble. It's in trouble because of this current scandal, and if my suspicions are right, it's about to be in a lot more trouble than that. I'm here for the society, nothing more."

He swallowed. If there was one thing I knew about this boy, it was that he was Digger, through and through. I'd gotten to him this way last year as well. Malcolm was right; Poe would help me. He'd hate it, but he'd help.

"What are you talking about?"

"Jenny Santos is the one who leaked the information to that website. And she's gone."

"Hiding out?" His voice dripped with anger. Like I said, Digger through and through.

"I don't think so. Her room looks trashed, and she left her wallet, keys, cell phone—everything—behind. There's a half-finished e-mail on her computer. I think she's just . . . gone."

"What do you mean? Like, kidnapped?"

"Kurt Gehry said he was going to deal with the matter *his* way, and make an example of the culprit. You know him better than anyone else. Do you think it's possible—"

Poe—James—oh, screw it, *Poe!*—pushed open the screen door. "Come in." He hustled me inside, took a quick look around the yard, and shut the door.

"Thanks. I don't think I was follow—"

He whirled on me. "You're serious about this. You think the *White House Chief of Staff* arranged for a college student to disappear. Do you have any idea how ridiculous that sounds?"

"Yes. People have been telling me all night. But you let me in."

"Because I didn't want anyone on the street to catch you raving."

I shook my head. "No, because you think I might be right."

He stabbed his fingers into his hair. "Wait here while I change my clothes."

I didn't ask him *Into what?* but I sure wanted to, as I'd never seen him in anything else (except, of course, for the times he was dressed up like Death). He trailed into his bedroom, yanking his shirt up over his head, and then slammed the door behind him.

"So does that mean you're going to help me?" I said to the closed door. No answer. I sighed, then looked around his cramped living space. Probably should make myself as comfortable as possible while he conjured up a new wardrobe.

In the middle of the room was a lumpy couch, upholstered in fraying, pale blue fabric that had been out of fashion since 1985. We were sporting something similar in our dorm room and I wondered if he'd salvaged his furniture from his undergrad years. I knew little about Poe's family background, but judging from the environs, he wasn't one of the wealthy Diggers, and the rumored post-grad gift of thirty thousand dollars was as mythical as our assumed total control of the world. He had a nice laptop, though. It lay closed on top of a scuffed coffee table piled with thick law textbooks. I raised my eyes to the bookshelves lining the wall. Curiouser and curiouser.

FIVE THINGS THAT ARE ABOUT TO SHOCK YOU ABOUT POE

1) He's a vegetarian. At least, he has a ton of vegetarian cookbooks. That can't be an accident. (But then, how he's friends with Malcolm Cabot, the great white hunter, is beyond me.)
2) He has *Harvey* on DVD. (Doesn't exactly seem like the giant imaginary rabbit type.)
3) And plays the harmonica.
4) And gardening is very good for the shoulders. (I can admit that, right?)
5) He also has a pet snake.

Actually, that last bit probably doesn't surprise you at all. But standing there, looking at this six-foot beast in a glass tank definitely made me a little uneasy. There was a wooden partition between the snake's cage and another aquarium. I went to peek inside the second. There, in a little nest made from cedar chips, near a tiny wheel and a lump of moist cheese, sat a white mouse, surrounded by five tiny, naked, bloody, albino bundles.

"Awww," I cooed. I couldn't help it.

"There were originally eight, but she ate the runts," Poe said.

"Gross." I looked at him, and bit my lip. From whence did he obtain such rocking duds? Now he was dressed in a soft burgundy sweater that must be at least cashmere blend, and a pair of charcoal gray cords. "What are their names?"

"I don't name food," he said. "They're all for him." He pointed at the snake cage.

Gross again. "You're feeding them to the snake?"

"Eventually," he said. "It's the food chain. Most of her siblings got fed to him, too."

Forget all that stuff about how cool it was he was vegetarian. Forget anything I said about his shoulders, too. "That's awful! You fed her whole family to that snake, and now you're feeding him her children?"

"Don't you want to know *his* name?" Poe smirked.

"No!"

He cocked his head at me. "Amy, are you a vegan?"

I crossed my arms. "You're the one who has all those files on me from deliberations. You know I'm not."

"Then don't act holier than thou about Lord Voldemort, there."

Voldemort? Figures. And the attitude explained his continued friendship with Six-Point Buck Cabot. But it wasn't why I was here.

"Enough niceties. I'm here about our problem. Are you going to help me?"

"In a manner of speaking. I'm coming with you, and I'm going to help you track down this girl. But it's only to prove how wrong you are."

"If you're so sure I'm wrong, why even bother?" I asked. "Everyone else has just been ignoring me."

"Everyone else doesn't know how much trouble you can be. Besides, I want to get my hands around her throat just as much as the next Digger."

"Works for me. Shall we start now?"

If I didn't know better, I'd think the smile he gave me was sweet. "The sooner we do, the sooner I get you out of my sight."

Trust me: The feeling was mutual.

I hereby confess:

I never took Interrogation 101.

12.
Sacrosanct

"First step: We call the Santoses," Poe said, power-walking back to campus.

"Do you have their number?" I was practically skipping in order to keep up. I'm sure we made quite the picture. Of course, Poe already thought I was a lightweight. An unintentional gambol or two wasn't going to significantly lessen his opinion.

"It's at the tomb, along with all her other records. We needed it during the deliberation process."

"I thought they burned that stuff."

He flashed me a look. "Yeah. *They* do. Amy, are you forgetting? You're one of *them*."

I skipped another step, hurrying to catch up. "Okay, fine. I thought *we* burned that stuff."

"We burn the records of the discussions. The new club doesn't need to know everything the knights who tapped them thought. But the actual files we amass on each of the taps, we keep. They'll be in the room of records, filed under my year's club."

But when we got to the tomb, Poe froze. "I had no idea it was this bad."

I peeked over his shoulder. Actually, it had settled down somewhat since earlier. The CNN van was still there, but Channel 8 News had departed, and so had most of the roving reporters. "This is nothing. You should have seen it the other day."

He pursed his lips. "I believe I'm persona non grata at the tomb right now."

Not right now. Just during the C.B.s. But I wasn't about to get in a fight with him over semantics. I still wanted his help. Besides, if he wanted to avoid the tomb, I was cool with it.

"This seems a little overboard," Poe said. "Given the information actually leaked."

"Maybe they're gearing up for next week," I said. "Why, aren't the initiation rites sacred enough for you?"

"For me, of course." Of course. "But I don't see it as earth-shattering to CNN."

We sidestepped any unnecessary interviews, and entered the tomb, though I couldn't see how we'd gotten through without being photographed from several angles.

"We were definitely nailed," Poe said.

"And the Diggers have to realize this was always a possibility. If they were so worried they'd have built us a secret entrance." Like I used to think they had.

"Always a possibility?" Poe scoffed. "They didn't have telephoto lenses in 1831, Bugaboo."

Up in the room of records, Poe quickly uncovered Jenny's file. He skimmed through it looking for a phone number while I entertained myself snooping through the files on my fellow members. It may interest you to know that Puck was once suspended from high school for being caught in the girls' locker room. With a girl. Seems his penchant for dangerous places is not a new one.

I moved on to my file. Wow, they had everything in here, from photocopies of my kindergarten report card to my father's IRS returns. "How the hell did you guys get your hands on this stuff?"

Poe looked at the folder in my hands, then slammed it shut. "Later. Let's call her folks."

Naturally, we didn't use the tomb's telephone. "Just in case," Poe whispered, and I was relieved to know I was not alone in what the others clearly thought were my more outlandish neuroses. Instead, we used my cell. Poe leaned in to listen, and I suppressed my instinct to pull away.

Mrs. Santos answered on the eighth ring. Her tone was cautious, halting.

"Mrs. Santos, I'm a friend of your daughter, Jenny. I was wondering if—"

"Who is this?"

I hesitated, and Poe jabbed my shoulder. But what if Jenny was at home, and had warned her mother not to take calls from society members? She might not have made a list of every possible patriarch, but I'm sure she'd guard against the current club, especially the Diggirls.

"It's Amy Haskel, Mrs. Santos. I'm a friend of your daughter's from Eli." Poe was now holding up two fingers. The jerk actually planned on fining me for this!

"I don't know you," Mrs. Santos said. "Are you in Edison College? Where's my daughter?"

"That's why I'm calling. I think your daughter went out of town for the weekend and she has . . . my notes for a project we've got due on Monday. I'm trying to track her down to get them back. Has she been at home?"

"She has your notes? That's not like Jenny. What project?"

This lady made my paranoia look like amateur night. "It's an English project. Shakespeare."

"Jenny isn't taking Shakespeare this semester. And she certainly wouldn't leave campus without telling us in advance. She must be at the library."

"No, Mrs. Santos. She definitely left. None of her suitemates have seen her for almost a day and a half." Poe was scribbling on a notepad. He held it up.

Don't scare her.

Too late. The other side had gone quiet. "Her roommates?" There was a catch in the woman's voice. "Have you notified her dean? Why hasn't anyone called us?"

"I'm calling you now, Mrs. Santos." But now that I did have her mother worried, I was afraid of what it would mean if I was wrong. Maybe Jenny was on her way home, or staying at a friend's, or even holed up at Micah Price's apartment. Maybe the rest of my club had been correct, and I was getting everyone stirred up for nothing. "You're in the Bronx, right?"

"Who is this?" There was a new voice on the phone, one I assumed to be Mr. Santos's. "Why are you scaring my wife? What happened to my daughter?"

"I'm so sorry, Mr. Santos, I'm not trying to get you upset. I've just been trying to get in touch with Jenny, and I haven't—"

"You're not the only one."

Poe and I exchanged glances.

"For the last two days, all we've gotten is phone calls, phone calls. 'Where is Jenny, have you seen her, have you talked to her.' We haven't, and she hasn't answered the phone in her room."

I thought about her cell phone, still nestled in my bag. It hadn't shown any missed calls. Wouldn't her parents try that number as well?

Professor Burak hadn't accused me of trying to cheat my way through my thesis, but the concern was obvious. So now I could add another task to my already overloaded To Do list.

I found Poe loitering outside the Edison College gates, waiting for someone with an Eli College undergrad proximity card to let him in. I swiped my card at the gate and held the door open as he passed through.

"Is it annoying not to have access anymore?" I asked as we crossed the courtyard.

He clenched his jaw and glowered at me. "Yes, it's annoying not to have access anymore."

But I didn't take the bait, and after a moment, he dropped the hostility.

"Actually, the most frustrating thing is that I've always charted my course through campus based on where the prox card let me go. Now I have to go around a lot of buildings I used to walk straight through." We took the steps up to the dean's office and he held the door open for me. "On the plus side, I can get into the all-night Law Library."

Touché. Eli's lack of an all-night study spot was a source of endless frustration for its students. Most of the university's libraries closed early in the evening, the main stacks at Dwight closed at midnight, and even the underground study carrels located beneath Cross Campus closed by two A.M. If you wanted to pull an all-nighter, you did it in your room (or, if you were lucky, your tomb). I knew a few people who had sweet-talked law-student friends into purloining them passes to the forbidden zone, and in general, the Law Library was considered a sort of mecca for the serious academics. A space where the faucets issued hot and cold running coffee and all the chairs were ergonomic.

I'd never been there myself. I'd never pulled an all-nighter, for that matter. My inability to stay up has been a constant source of amusement for my friends throughout my

"Oh, Carlos!" said Mrs. Santos. "Why didn't you tell me?"

"I didn't want you worried."

Poe was scribbling again. He held up another note. *You think the patriarchs knew she was gone?*

"So I want to know who you are, and why you're calling us. You're not in her class, because we know what classes she's taking, and you're no friend of hers, because we know all her friends."

Maybe you don't know your daughter like you think you do. But I couldn't say that any more than I could say, *I'm a fellow member of her secret society.* "I know her through Micah Price," I tried, because that was the only barbarian name I knew.

"That boy," Mrs. Santos spat, "is no friend to our girl."

Sometimes I don't get parents. They either go to extremes assuming you're getting yourself into trouble, or they completely underestimate what their children are doing behind their backs. The Santoses appeared to be the latter kind. They were about to get shocked out of their complacency.

"Ever since she started hanging out with him, she's been different. She used to come home on the weekends, come to our church. Now she won't even speak to our priest."

Or maybe they understood the situation better than I gave them credit for.

"Have you talked to this Price?" Mr. Santos asked. "All her other friends have been calling, but from him, not one word."

"So you've been hearing from her other friends," I said. "No one else?"

Silence.

When Mrs. Santos finally spoke, it was in a whisper. "You're one of *them*, aren't you? The Brotherhood of Death."

Abort! Abort! read Poe's pad.

"So it's true," said Mr. Santos. "She joined with you."

Poe grabbed my arm and squeezed, but I wrenched away. Protecting the secrecy of the society was not my main goal at this point. So far, the Santoses had given me good info. I wasn't going to let a little thing like discretion stand in my way. "And if I am?"

"Maricel, hang up the phone."

"Where is my daughter?" the woman pleaded. "If you are so powerful, you can find her, right? You can help her if she's in trouble?"

"Hang up the phone, *cariña.*" This time the man's voice sounded farther away, as if he was at her side rather than on his own extension. "Don't talk to them."

"No! You don't tell me people are calling after Jenny, and I have to hear it from some stranger. So I don't care what they say about the Brotherhood." She spoke into the phone now. "You'll find her, right? You'll find her for me?"

"I can try," I said, but the phone had gone dead. I looked at Poe.

His expression was grim. "That was a mistake. The Edison dean won't presume malfeasance in the case of a girl who skipped town for the weekend, but if parents call and start raving about the 'Brotherhood of Death,' especially given the current media scrutiny, then there might actually be some police pressure put on this case. There's definitely going to be more media attention. All undesirable circumstances."

"Speak for yourself," I said. "If there really is foul play going on, how can it hurt?"

"And if there isn't, then we just committed treason."

"How about this: My oaths to the society only pertain to the law-abiding parts?"

"If only it were that easy."

"For me, it is." I studied him. "Not for you?"

He was quiet for several seconds. "Ask me when this is over."

"So you can decide after the choice has been made for you." Digger, through and through. Would he consider his oaths sacred even if there were felonies involved? What the hell would that do to his political career?

"There's no filter on that mouth of yours, is there?"

"I call it like I see it."

"You don't see everything you think you do."

"Perhaps not," I said, "but at least I discovered it wasn't the patriarchs who have been calling looking for her. Maybe it's because they know where she is."

"Maybe it's because they assume, and rightly, it seems, that the Santoses *don't*." And then, as if to keep whatever threads of rapport we'd created from completely disintegrating, he looked down at the pad in his hand. "So now *we* assume the Santoses will be alerting the school, the police, and the media."

"Hope they have better luck getting people to care than I did."

"I hope they don't. And as for us?"

"I think it's clear."

He snapped the pad closed. "Micah Price."

———

Jenny had crap timing. I really needed to work this weekend. I had a meeting that afternoon with my thesis advisor, at which I'd promised I'd have him a topic at last, and I had a paper due tomorrow morning that I hadn't even started.

Technically, the paper was due today at five, but everyone knew Professor Szyska never came into the office on

Friday afternoons. That was the day her girlfriend came in from the pied-à-terre she kept in the city, to kick-start the weekend. Standing Szyska date night. As long as you slid the paper under her door by 10 A.M. on Saturday, when she showed up to work, you were golden. Which was good, because I hadn't even picked a topic for the six-pager I had to write on *The Expedition of Humphrey Clinker.* I was considering doing something about the current obscurity of Smollett in the modern collegiate academic curriculum. A well-placed film adaptation or two (perhaps written by Emma Thompson or Richard Curtis) would do wonders for the entire ostler subgenre of comedic 18th century English epistolary fiction.

As for the senior project: I was screwed. But I'd skip the bout of self-flagellating lectures about how I'd spent the last month distracted by George and worry about the issues at hand. Namely: tracking down Micah Price.

Which, it turned out, was not as hard as you'd think. Poe had been planning on working some Digger magic on the registrar's office, but that wasn't necessary after I plugged Price's name into Google. Search results turned up a good dozen news items from the *Eli Daily News* in the past few months. Apparently, he'd been running an ongoing protest outside the Bible as Literature lecture all semester. The class met Mondays and Wednesdays, with sections on Fridays at 10:30. As it happened, we were smack in the middle of Friday section time.

We found the protest, such as it was, on the Cross Campus lawn. I wondered if the scraggly bunch of protesters had enjoyed more popularity earlier in the year. Now the group consisted of Micah, a half-dozen signs, and three freshmen (one of whom was sitting cross-legged on the half-frozen, half-dead lawn and working on his linear algebra problem set). From the stack of protest signs lying abandoned near the group, I could tell Micah had expected more participants. He was shouting into a megaphone, with the result that many of his words were obscured, especially as you closed in on the "blockade."

"The word of God should *not* be analyzed!" he shouted, echoed by a halfhearted "Yeah" from two of the freshmen (Linear Algebra merely pumped his fist in the air). "It should *not* be subjected to comparison!" ("Yeah.") "These are not *stories*, to be dissected by the *heretics* who have signed up for this class. These are not *myths*, to be encapsulated and dismissed by the God-hating *atheists* who control this institution!"

His followers waved their signs, which bore slogans like DON'T TELL ME ABOUT *MY* GOD, THE BIBLE IS NOT A FAIRY TALE, and, oddly, I AM NOT A MONKEY. (That last one was probably left over from his Tuesday protest of the Geologic Basis of Human Evolution seminar at the Anthropology department.)

"I wonder," said Poe, "what Bible, particularly, they are up in arms about. The King James? The New International? The Catholic Bible? I wonder if he thinks it's okay to study the Apocrypha?"

"When I took the class, the text we used was the New Oxford Annotated," I said. "The big controversy in my class was due to issues of translation. I had a Jewish classmate who argued every week about vowels and alternate meanings, et cetera. I learned more than I ever thought I'd have to about the Septuagint."

"Maybe they should have a Bible as History class?" Poe asked.

"If possible, that would cause *more* controversy. The problem with teaching the sacred text of a living religion is that some people in the class are going to view it as sacred text. No one gets up in arms about the World Mythology Survey unless they worship Zeus or Odin. But trying to teach using text some people feel has been perverted from the start is bound to cause problems."

"So why bother teaching it in the Lit department? Why don't they stick Bible study in the Religious Studies department and be done with it?"

"Because we're not necessarily discussing the religion. Just the stories for the purpose of context. Some of us want to understand Faulkner and Borges and Steinbeck and have never read the Bible before."

"And whose fault is that?" He smirked. "This school was founded by a bunch of Puritans who didn't think Harvard was holy enough. Not in order to teach people who don't read the Bible."

"This school wasn't founded for women either, but look: Here we are," I snapped. "A lot of things work that way." I shook my head at the scene before us. "I don't know how they manage to lecture with this going on all the time."

"I imagine it becomes white noise after a while."

We headed across the lawn to Micah's not-so-merry band. He'd laid off the editorial in favor of quoting scripture. I tapped him on the shoulder during a particularly rousing rendition of Leviticus 26.

" '. . . *if you reject my decrees and abhor my laws and fail to carry out all my commands and so violate'*—What?" He whirled on me.

"Pardon me for interrupting," I said. "But you haven't seen Jenny recently, have you?"

Micah glared first at me, and then at Poe, but he didn't get very far with that. Poe was a Jedi master when it came to a good glare. He brought down walls.

"Well, well, well," Micah said, lowering his megaphone. "If it isn't the Brotherhood of Death, come to shut me up."

"Not at all," I said. "Carry on with your protest, by all means. But let me know when you last saw Jenny, first."

"Haven't seen her in days." He turned back around and lifted the megaphone to his lips. " '*I will destroy your high places, cut down your incense altars and pile your dead bodies on the lifeless forms of your idols, and I will abhor you.*' "

"Skipped a few verses," said Poe. He reached over and snatched the cone from Micah's hands. "Now answer the lady's questions, and you can get back to your rant."

The three freshmen froze. Linear Algebra even looked up from his graphing calculator, and I may have been imagining this, but in the sudden silence, I thought I saw a bunch of faces pressed against the glass in the classroom door. Poe waved for me to go on. Clearly, he did not adhere to Malcolm's constant admonishments for *discretion*.

"Right." I tugged at the hem of my sweater. "Again, when did you last see Jenny?"

Micah's expression gave Poe's a run for the money and I felt the sudden need to step back. But I ordered my feet to stay rooted to the spot and lifted my chin. I reminded myself that this was the guy who had threatened Jenny, the one who had almost fought Josh, and who, for all of his claims to piety, was the only person close to Jenny who hadn't bothered looking for her.

He leaned in close to me. "That bitch," he hissed, "betrayed me."

Get in line, buster.

But Micah wasn't done. "So I don't care where she is, and I don't care what happens to her. She deserves whatever punishment is inflicted upon her. Jennifer Santos is a worthless whore of Satan," he went on, "and you know it, because you are, too." He spat in my face.

I stood there in shock. So did the freshmen, the students in the classrooms (who most definitely were watching), and everyone else on Cross Campus.

Poe simply stepped forward and handed the megaphone back to Micah.

And then clocked him in the jaw.

I hereby confess:
I'm just as shocked
as you are.

13.

Hypotheses

"I can't believe I just did that," Poe kept saying, over and over, as we hightailed it off Cross Campus.

I looked over my shoulder as we raced up the steps near Maya Lin's Women-at-Eli Memorial Fountain, which bears more than a passing resemblance to her better-known Vietnam Veterans Memorial. (That lady has one schtick, but it's a good one.) Yep, Micah was still down for the count. The three freshmen huddled around his prone form. We *so* needed to get out of town.

"I can't believe I just did that. Why did I just do that? I can't believe I just did that." Poe reached into his pocket and pulled out a handkerchief. Oh, for Persephone's sake! What was he going to do, mop his brow?

But instead he handed it to me. "Did he get you in the eye?"

Too surprised to stop myself, I took it, and wiped Micah's spittle off my cheek. "No. Thanks."

"What was I thinking?" Poe leaned against a bulletin board near the library and dropped his head into his hands.

"I'm going to get arrested. I'm going to be suspended. If they charge me with a felony, I'll never pass the bar."

"I might be a bit biased," I said, "what with the defending-of-my-honor and all, but I thought it was wicked cool."

"I just . . . as soon as I heard him talking about—Rose & Grave like that . . ."

"Rose & Grave?" I cocked my head at him. "Don't you mean Jenny and me?"

He slid down the wall and studied his sneakers. "Oath of fidelity. Oh, I'm in trouble."

Okay, so maybe not so much defending my honor. At least, not any further than his oaths required. But even if the thought didn't count, the action sure as hell did. "Come on." I held out my hand. "Let's keep moving."

Poe dropped both hands to the pavement and pushed himself to his feet. "Right, because running from the scene of the crime is always the correct course of action."

"He's not going to report you," I said, as we took refuge in the nearest college's common room. "Because then he'd have to explain how he was a big pussy."

We sat on a leather sofa hidden from the door by a grand piano, and Poe flexed his hand. "It hurts," he said, his tone one of surprise.

"Well, you hit him pretty hard." We sat there for a moment, neither of us speaking, as our adrenaline levels dropped and we each caught our breath. It had been a good long while since I'd seen anyone in a fistfight—if this could even be counted as a fistfight. After all, there'd only been one punch. And yet . . . I glanced at Poe, who was still examining the damage to his knuckles. I think I've made a new entry on my list of things that surprised me about Poe.

Malcolm would be so proud.

Finally, I broke the silence. "What exactly do they mean when they call us the 'Brotherhood of Death'?"

Poe rubbed his sore fingers. "It's a barbarian term," he said. "It's really popular among the conspiracy theorists who think we're secretly Satan worshippers. Go look on that website, you'll see it all over."

Hmph. Right now I was pretty sure secretsofthe diggers.com was experiencing a bit of a deluge. Hey, there was an idea. Keep hitting it until the bandwidth overloaded and the site went down. If we crashed it, there was no way they'd be able to post anything else. I'd have to remember to tell Josh. There was, after all, more than one way to skin a paranoid conspiracy theorist. Of course, there could be a number of other ways to stop him (or her), too. The person doing most of the heavy lifting the past few weeks had been Jenny after all. Who knew if the information she'd been feeding us about how to find this guy had been false all along? Surely there was someone else in the club with enough computer knowledge to do some damage.

"It's because of the death and underworld imagery—all that stuff we use during the initiation," Poe was saying, while I pictured the whole scandal ending in a whimper, not a bang. "In the Christian tradition, the underworld is always hell, always the realm of the wicked. That wasn't the case in the Greco-Roman tradition. There was no value judgment placed on afterlife location. Heroes went there, too. Bad people were punished in Tartarus, heroes wound up in the Elysian Fields, but everyone went to the underworld."

"Thanks. I'm not clueless on the mythology, you know."

He shrugged. "It's another way they try to explain away our influence. Same as those nuts who think we're all controlled by reptiles from outer space. We're powerful, so we must be in league with demons, see?"

I nodded. I suppose I could understand the confusion. "Jenny called us the 'Brotherhood of Death,' " I said. "On Initiation Night."

"Does that surprise you, knowing the company she keeps? Note that her parents called us that as well."

"No, it doesn't surprise me." I leaned back on the couch and folded my feet up beneath me. "But it does make me wonder."

"What?"

I bit my lip. If I spoke my thoughts aloud, Poe would dismiss them, the way he dismissed every one of my so-called conspiracy theories. The way all of the Diggers had. But I was used to it by now, so what did I have to lose? "Just how long she may have had this planned. I know she dislikes being a Digger, and I've had reasons to suspect for some time that she's been breaking her oath of secrecy. I think she's been telling her boyfriend back there what's been going on at the meetings."

Poe's eyes widened. "Did you tell anyone about this?"

"Josh," I said, "but he brushed me off. I'm the uninformed, hysterical one, remember?"

"Amy, if you think you're a second-class citizen in your club, it's only because you're acting like it."

"No, it's because no one listens to me."

"Which is because—" Poe stopped himself, and sighed. "Never mind. Go on."

"Anyway. What if Jenny had been planning on exposing us since the moment she joined? Was that something anyone in your club feared? I don't know what kind of deliberations went into tapping her, but you do."

"That stuff's a secret."

"Apparently, a lot of things are secret, until they get out. Maybe keeping these secrets isn't very good for us."

"Or maybe the problem is that the info *was* leaked . . . to the patriarchs you seem to believe kidnapped her."

"So it *was* a concern!" I pounced on the hint. Poe winced. "What did you debate?"

"Jenny's big sib was a computer programmer," he said.

"Is he around?" Maybe he could help us.

"I've been waiting to hear back from him since the story went live."

Ugh. Seems all the recent patriarchs had moved on and washed their hands of us ...except Poe.

"Jenny was the best option to replace him, and everyone agreed." Poe hesitated. "I shouldn't be telling you any of this." But then he came to a decision. "Yes, we wondered if she would have difficulty dedicating herself to the society, considering her strong religious views, but you couldn't argue with her credentials. She's a genius. Remember, we were trying to tap a class of super-women."

And they had. Everyone except me, of course. I was the bugaboo, tapped at the eleventh hour after Malcolm's first choice had a) been dumped, b) gone vicious, and c) lost her shit.

The carillon one block over began to strike the hour.

Poe rose. "I have to go. I've got class. Can you meet this afternoon?"

"I have to see my thesis advisor at one."

He bit his lip. "Okay, then, after that. I'll try to get an appointment with the Edison College dean and see if we can't get him to look in Jenny's room—legitimately, this time. Maybe the Santoses have already called. And ..." He took a deep breath. "I'll see if I can remember anything else about Jenny's delibs. Deal?"

"Deal ... There *is* something else you can do," I said, and met his eyes. "Maybe get a straight answer once and for all about Gehry's involvement?"

He swallowed. "I don't have connections there anymore."

"You were going to be his intern!"

"Yeah," said Poe. "And then I listened to you."

I used to fantasize about my senior thesis, back before my brain got sidetracked into fantasizing about boys instead. In my imagination, I'd be seated in some picturesque collegiate setting—either a library stack study carrel surrounded by lead-veined windows and lousy with green-shaded table lamps, or on a carved granite bench beneath a weeping willow in a cloistered stone courtyard overlooked by gargoyles—and I'd turn a page in a musty book, read for a moment or two, then leap up, scattering foolscap and maybe even my non-existent reading glasses, pump my fist in the air, and shout, "Eureka!" Then I would rush to the office of my favorite professor (who, I'm vaguely embarrassed to admit, in my vision was always elderly, white, and male), where he would no doubt be lounging on a leather wingback chair in a spacious, bookshelf-lined office, having his secretary serve him tea in fine, translucent china. I'd be shivering with excitement to tell him all about the amazing gap in canon I'd discovered and how I—yes, I—would be the first to argue cogently that—

Well, the dream always broke before I actually got to the point of describing what I'd be writing about, though it conveniently picked up again around the time I was awarded a Fulbright and a Rhodes and published in the pre-eminent journal on the topic and was called all manner of things from *wunderkind* to "the discipline's brightest new star."

So much for that.

I stood in the elevator on the way up to my thesis advisor's office, which was oh-so-inconveniently located in the top-floor attic space of the—wait for it—Physics Administration building, devoid of secretaries of any kind, and populated by a professor who wasn't elderly and white so much as mid-forties and Middle Eastern. I quickly brainstormed.

WHAT TO SAY TO PROFESSOR BURAK

1) An apology. This had to come first, of course, since I'd already canceled three similar meetings and been granted two extensions on the department's unofficial deadline for formulating a topic.
2) Ask after his wife and kids, natch.
3) Another apology, for not being prepared with the annotated bibliography he no doubt expected at this meeting.
4) A topic.

Number four was the tricky part of the equation. The digital readout above my head reported that I had eight more floors to think of something.

The problem was, there was only so much multitasking I could handle. The Lit Magazine hadn't been a huge time commitment, and it paled in the face of the hours and hours I was devoting to Rose & Grave every week. (Howard had been right about that.) Add classes and my feeble attempts at a social life, and my table was groaning. I'd been promising myself that I'd dive into my thesis full time next semester, when it was an actual credit in my course load, and—with any luck—after all the Rose & Grave drama had died down.

Because, let's face it, it was tough to think about a good paper topic when you spent your days deciphering encoded anonymous e-mails, tracking down the owner of a ludicrous nutball website, or wondering if your ersatz friend had been kidnapped by "The Brotherhood of Death." If Persephone really was our patron goddess, it was time for her to start handing out miracles.

The elevator shuddered to a stop and a bell dinged to signify I'd reached my destination, but it barely registered.

Instead, I almost squished my hand trying to keep the doors from closing again, so lost was I in my reverie.

I had found a topic, at last.

I strode into my professor's office, ebullient.

"Miss Haskel," he said, gesturing me to a seat. "Have we finally settled on a project?"

"Yes." I beamed at him. "I would like to write my senior thesis on the permutations of the Persephone myth in modern literature."

He steepled his hands on the desk and seemed to digest this information. "Interesting. Any particular modern texts in mind?"

Crap. I mentally flipped through my repertoire of possibilities. Would *Tess of the d'Urbervilles* be too obvious? Too English? Too . . . well, *not modern?*

"I haven't yet whittled down my main texts," I said. "There are so many options."

"Indeed."

"I'm not sure whether to discuss the ramifications in English literature or maybe study some turn-of-the-century American choices. Or perhaps even focus strictly on texts from the period of the rise of feminism."

Professor Burak nodded, slowly. "Sounds good. Well, Miss Haskel," he said, standing, "it looks like you're off to a good start. I'll meet you in a month and see how you've progressed."

I also stood. That was it? He reached across the desk to shake my hand, but when I took it, he folded his fingers in an all-too-familiar way and, before I could stop myself, I was doing the countersign. The, um, Rose & Grave countersign.

I couldn't stifle the shock that registered on my face, which no doubt dug my—no pun intended—grave a little deeper. Dr. Burak was not a patriarch.

He'd been testing me, and I'd failed. Oops.

"Thought as much." He returned to his seat, and leaned back. "Shall we start again?"

Deny, deny, deny. "Sir?"

"Come now, Miss Haskel. Do you think you're the first student to come in here mysteriously itching to write a paper on Persephone?" He snorted, rolled over to his bookshelf, and pulled down a stack of bound manuscripts. "Let's see here. What have we got? 'Persephone and Demeter in the work of D. H. Lawrence' "—the paper plopped onto the desk—" 'An American Goddess: Pre-Feminist Persephones in *My Ántonia* and minor works of Willa Cather' "—*plop*— " 'Don't Eat the Pomegranate: Rape and Rejuvenation in Harlem Renaissance Poetry' "—*plop*—"and, lest we forget, no fewer than *seven* senior projects on the Persephone motifs in Thomas Hardy's *Tess of the d'Urbervilles.*" *Plop, plop, kathunk*.

Busted.

"It's not that I don't think it's a valid field of study, you see," he said as I stood there, staring stricken at the pile before him. I even recognized some of the writers as patriarchs. "But the field's a little crowded at the moment. At least, at *this* particular temple of learning."

I remained speechless.

"And of course," he added, "there's the ongoing issue with not being able to access and vet some of your sources, seeing as they are part of a very, *very* private collection."

I regained my tongue and remembered my oaths. "Professor Burak, I don't know what impression I may have given you earlier, but I assure you I—"

He raised his hand. "Look, I'm in favor of students exploring the traditions that speak most strongly to them. Passion is always a positive when it comes to charting courses of study.

But it's time to start getting creative. It's been, what, two hundred years?"

One hundred and seventy-seven. But that was none of his business.

"And I know you guys must have many rules and rituals that have origins in any variety of myths. Why the Persephone monomania?"

"Sir, I—"

"Right, right. 'You have no idea what I'm talking about.' Of course. I've been teaching at this university long enough to know the drill. But that doesn't change my take on the matter. We in the Literature department have been dealing with this for longer than you've been alive, Ms. Haskel. I doubt you're going to come at this topic from an angle we haven't seen. Back to the drawing board with you."

Defeated, I rose, and turned to go. I looked down at the stack of papers on his desk. "Were any of these written by a woman?" I asked him.

He considered. "No. As far as I know, you're the first woman to try this particular trick. But don't think that makes it acceptable."

"So how far does it get me?"

He chuckled. "Another week to come up with a topic."

———

Poe had text-messaged me to meet him at the office of the Edison dean at three-thirty, so after a short stint at a library computer terminal confirming that indeed the field of undergraduate Persephonial study was a bit crowded here at Eli, I wandered up that way, still shaken from the smackdown I'd received from my advisor. But seriously, what kind of idiots were we Diggers to think the academic bigwigs at this school wouldn't eventually catch on to our predilection for a certain myth? *From within doth Persephone rot,* indeed!

college career. When they're taking midnight study breaks and grabbing patty melts at the Buttery at midnight, I've already been hard at work for several hours, because I know by two A.M.—or three at the latest—I'm useless. I've been hitting the wall ever since I was tapped into Rose & Grave as well, starting on Initiation Night, when I passed out somewhere in the wee hours, only to be carried home, undressed, then tucked into bed by Malcolm (a situation that caused more than a little confusion when I first woke up, let me tell you), and continuing every meeting night. My club wraps up official society business around two, and then wants to hang out in the tomb and party, but all I want to do is snuggle into my duvet.

I'd be testing my condition tonight, as I struggled to get my as-yet-unformed treatise on *Humphrey Clinker* in shape by break of day.

"Did you manage to get through to anyone this afternoon?" I asked him as we entered the outer office.

"I'll tell you later." Poe gave our names to a secretary, whose desk was an altar to the union movement, and she announced our arrival to the dean. He appeared forthwith, ushered us into his office, and shut the door.

"You're friends of Jenny?" the dean asked.

We nodded. White lies, since I'm pretty sure Poe ranked right up there on the list of Jenny hatahs, and she didn't seem to think too well of him, either. As for me, I didn't know where I stood on the issue. I was furious with her, of course, but she was still my brother, and what's more, I felt bad for her. Hanging out for any length of time with an asshole like Micah Price had to suck.

"Here's the situation," said the dean. "I've received a call from the Santoses, indicating her friends do not know her present location. Her parents haven't any idea where she might be, and neither do her suitemates, each of whom I've contacted. I've been in touch with the campus police, and according to policy, without any evidence of foul play, there's little to show this is anything more than a case of a twenty-one-year-old girl taking off for the weekend. She could be at Foxwoods playing poker, for all you know. She could be raring for a night at the clubs in Chelsea. I can't call out the dogs because a senior with no classes on Friday decides to skip town."

"Have you met this girl?" Poe asked. "I can guarantee she's not playing poker."

"What do you mean, no evidence?" I asked, trying to keep on topic. "Have you seen her room?"

The dean eyed me. "Have you?"

I offered a weak smile and a shrug.

"I was up there earlier with two officers," he continued. "Nothing appeared out of place."

Nothing out of place? Was this guy saying that disaster zone looked normal? He'd obviously grown cynical from too many years living with messy college kids. I opened my mouth to speak, but Poe laid his hand over mine.

"We're so sorry to be a bother, sir," Poe said, as I steeled myself not to snatch my hand away, "but Amy here is a little worried about her friend. They had some kind of spat the other day and she's been beating herself up about it." He looked at me and shook his head slightly, his expression full of patronizing concern. I clenched my free hand into a fist. "What you've said makes a lot of sense, and I'm sure Jenny will be home by Sunday night."

"I'm sure she will, too," said the dean.

"Honey," Poe said to me, and I flinched, "why don't you leave Jenny a note? It can be the first thing she sees when she gets home. And much more personal than some e-mail or a scrawl on a whiteboard." Yeah, especially since she didn't even have a whiteboard. "Maybe the dean will let you put it on her desk, you know, *near her keys and cell phone.*" He looked at the dean. "That would be okay, right?"

"Sure," said the dean. "I'll get the skeleton key from my secretary."

Two minutes later, we were in the Edison College Tower elevator, and the dean and Poe were expounding on the virtues of modern architecture while I scribbled a missive to Jenny.

> *Dear Jenny,*
> *Pardon my language, but where the fuck are you? You have some serious answering to do, chica! Anything that results in protracted tête-à-têtes with James Orcutt is not easily forgiven. You'd better be in actual trouble, or you're dead meat.*
> *Love,*
> *Amy*

There. That should take care of it. We arrived on Jenny's floor and headed to her room, which now, shockingly, sported a freshly cleaned whiteboard on the door the dean unlocked. I stifled a gasp.

The room was clean. Like, *brochure* clean. Sure, Jenny's overload of computers were still in evidence, and there was a pile of unopened mail on her desk, but the cascade of papers and tangle of wires were nowhere in sight. The floor was swept and smelled faintly of lemon Pledge. Her bed displayed hospital corners.

"See?" said the dean. "Everything's fine. Go leave your note."

So I did, and while Poe distracted the dean with more chitchat, I dropped off her keys and phone and furtively searched the desktop for any clue as to what may have happened in this room in the last eighteen hours. Nothing. Not an illegible Post-it note, not a stray syllabus, not a scribble on the latest page of her Scripture-a-Day calendar (which, I might add, was turned to Friday's date). There was a neat mug filled with pens, a neat tower of library books, and a neat stack of the aforementioned junk mail. Her walls held the same posters of Impressionist art and Victorian portraiture. The altar in the corner looked fresh and shiny. Shivers flew up and down my spine, and didn't neglect my extremities, either.

What had happened here?

"Ready to go?" the dean prompted, and, like a zombie, I toddled out.

Wait. Wait, stop. Guys, something really weird is going on. Listen to me! Listen to me! The words welled up in my throat and I opened my mouth.

Poe grabbed my elbow.

At the base of the tower, Poe bade the dean a cheery adieu and steered me down the steps and across the courtyard. As soon as the dean vanished into his office, I whirled away.

"How...dare...you ..." I spluttered.

"I got us in the room, didn't I?" he said.

"Yes. By treating Jenny and me like idiot girls! It was humiliating."

Poe sighed. "You know, Amy, if you'd just step back for a minute in the middle of all your feminist ranting, you'd see that sometimes acting like an idiot—girl or otherwise—in matters of espionage can be a good way to get things accomplished. You're the Literature major. Did you skip *The Scarlet Pimpernel*?"

"Then *you* act the fool, Sir Percy."

He shook his head. "Not in that situation. Had the dean

been a woman, I'd have been happy to play the worried lover to your concerned Cupid, but it wouldn't have budged that guy."

Yeah, especially considering one would first have to buy Poe as boyfriend material (nice shoulders aside).

"Don't tell me you've never put on an act to get what you wanted."

He had me there.

"Maybe your problem was that the chosen act hit a little too close to home."

"Maybe my problem was that it gave you another chance to act chauvinistic and superior."

And apparently that remark hit a little too close to home as well. Poe was silent for a moment, then regrouped. "Amy, grow up. I did a little good-old-boy talk, and we got in. Get over your indignation."

Poe stuck his hands in his pockets and kept walking. I stood there for a moment, seething, my mouth opening and closing like a fish. Easy for him to say. Easy for him not to get up in arms every time he was taken for a moron, because he *chose* when it would happen. When you deal with dismissive attitudes every day, playing the fool grates a hell of a lot more. I was treated like a lesser being several times a week when I *wasn't* feigning stupidity, merely by virtue of... of what? In the general population, it was because I was a woman, in the world of Eli it was because I was a "soft" Literature major, and in my own secret society it was because I held a slight historical tendency toward paranoia.

But I was not an idiot, and I was not wrong about this. Any of it. There was something monumentally weird happening in the case of Jenny Santos, and I was going to prove it.

I caught up to Poe as he headed down the steps into the graduate school's main building. "Okay, fine," I said. "I agree to put aside our partisan politics in favor of the greater good. Yes, we got into her room. Thank you. And I know you aren't going to believe me, but that place was a disaster last night. It looked like a bomb had gone off in there."

Poe closed the door behind us and stood there for one long moment, his hand on the knob, his faced downturned. Then he looked at me, his gray eyes sad and full of concern. "I believe you," he said at last. "I think she may be in danger."

I hereby confess:

I'm not above feeling smug.

14.

Commission and Omission

Why did Poe's proclamation chill me the way it did? After all, I'd been saying as much all day. But by this point, I'd gotten used to people not believing me. So when someone did—someone who, up until this point, seemed to have one purpose in life and that was proving me wrong—I didn't feel vindicated. At least, not right away. No, my immediate reaction was terror.

Then triumph. Natch.

"What?" I exclaimed. "If you believe me, then we should be running to tell the police what we know."

"Not without any evidence of wrongdoing. Not for an adult who's been gone one day. No one would see a clean room as a sign of a kidnapping."

"When were you going to tell me about your change of heart?" We'd been together for the past half hour and he'd given me no indication he felt any differently.

"How about not in front of the Edison dean?"

"How about *yes* in front of him! How long were you planning on keeping me on the hook?"

"I wanted more information first. I wanted to confirm the facts."

Because he couldn't just believe me. "Why wouldn't you let me speak back in the tower? You saw that room. You know that's not the way it was."

"That's not the only thing I know." Poe checked the surrounding area, then backed me into a tiny chantry, leaned his head close to me, and started whispering. "After class today, I called Mr. Gehry."

"You did? I thought you said he wouldn't speak to you."

But apparently it was a matter of what, exactly, the disgraced Poe had to offer. "I told him we believe Jennifer Santos is responsible for the leak."

"And?"

"He didn't act surprised. Which in itself is not noteworthy. But then he said he'd 'taken care of it' and 'seen to it that people like her were no longer a threat to the organization.' " Poe pushed off the wall and turned away. "I thought I knew what he meant by that, but . . . her room! It's like it had been sanitized."

I didn't know how to deal with this Poe. The angry, smug, holier-than-thou Poe I was used to. Not the one who looked worried, or friendly, or . . . frightened. This was the Poe Malcolm actually liked. And I had no idea how to react to him.

He sat down on the bench and folded his hands before him. "You said that last night you thought her bedroom had been trashed. Maybe they were looking for something. And after seeing the room today, I'd say they found it." I digested this, and Poe watched me with clear, gray eyes. "Amy, are you sure there was no one else in that room with you last night?"

Oddly enough, the *of course* response failed to fall from my lips. It might be because I'd suddenly started shivering.

This stone enclave was cold, and dark, and a little damp. And I may be in serious shit.

"I don't know. There was so much crap in there. I don't know where someone would have been hiding—" Except behind the computer table, or in the closet, or even under the bed, blocked from sight by the balled-up duvet. I rubbed my hands up and down my arms. "If someone was there, and they saw me . . ."

"Then they probably think you have the info, too. They may be following us right now. They may be searching your room next."

"But that doesn't make any sense!" I realized my voice had gone up an octave and a few decibels, and I brought it back to a whisper. "Who would be following me? Every Digger on the planet knows the information Jenny's been spilling to the site. Of course I have the info. We all have it. That's never been of concern."

"They know what's she leaked so far. Our initiation procedures and similar information. To tell the truth, I'm pretty sure most of that stuff has been leaked at various times in the last century or so. But unless you read the Black Books, you don't know substantive information about the day-to-day of clubs that you didn't belong to. Maybe they're interested in discovering what she knows of those kind of details." He paused. "Or maybe it's even more than that." Poe closed in and took me by the shoulders. "What else do you know?"

I brought my hands down on his forearms, karate-chop style. "Nothing. I only know what they've been saying at the meetings."

He narrowed his eyes. "Are you sure?"

What the hell was he talking about? "Of course I'm sure. It's me you're talking to, remember? I'm the most clueless Digger of them all!"

Poe didn't respond, simply stood there for a moment,

studying me. "You keep saying that, but you must know it's not true." His tone was soft, almost conciliatory. Or maybe it was just that he was whispering. "You have this way of... weaseling information out. Like last year ..." He returned to the bench, and sat, staring at his shoes for several seconds.

Yeah, it was just the whisper. *Weaseling information out?* Please. Right after my initiation, when the patriarchs had barricaded the tomb, Poe had made an obscure slip of the tongue, and I remembered it long enough to figure out he'd do anything to support his club. It's not like I'd had him locked in a room, interrogating him with water boards and finger screws. *Weaseling!*

Finally, he lifted his head, "Amy, there's something ...after you kicked me out of the tomb last month ..."

"I'm not your confessor, James," I said. The last thing I wanted was to fill in for his graduated Digger friends. "Once upon a time, I found your weakness, and I exploited it. End of story."

Ah, the patented glare was back. Good. I was on firmer footing if Poe reverted to form. He lifted his chin. "Yes. You did. So now I'm not going to have any more weaknesses."

"You're still a devoted Digger," I said. "You know it, and I know it. You'd do anything to protect the sanctity of this organization."

He smirked. "Shows what you know."

Yep, back on solid ground.

———

When you become a Digger, you take three oaths to the society. They go like this:

1) *The oath of secrecy:* I do hereby most solemnly avow, within the Flame of Life and beneath the Shadow of Death, never to reveal, by commission or by

omission, the existence of, the knowledge considered sacred by, or the names of the membership of the Order of Rose & Grave.

2) *The oath of constancy:* I do hereby most solemnly avow, within the Flame of Life and beneath the Shadow of Death, to bear the confidence and the confessions of my brothers, to support them in all their endeavors, and to keep forever sacred whatsoever I may learn beneath the seal of the Order of Rose & Grave.

3) *The oath of fidelity:* I do hereby most solemnly pledge and avow my love and affection, everlasting loyalty and undying fealty. By the Flame of Life and the Shadow of Death, I swear to cleave wholly unto the principles of this ancient order, to further its friends and plight its enemies, and place above all others the causes of the Order of Rose & Grave.

And yes, I know those second two sound like synonyms. I didn't name the darn things; I just swore by them.

After Poe and I took our rather chilly leave of each other, I grabbed dinner then headed off to the library to get started on the *Humphrey Clinker* clunker. But the words wouldn't come, and the rereading-significant-passages phase failed to uncover any paper-worthy insights. This was going to be a painful one. After a few hours, I packed up and headed home. If I wasn't going to be working hard, I might as well not be doing so in the comfort of my own suite. Persephone willing, I wouldn't come face-to-face with Josh, because, frankly, ain't exactly feeling the brotherly love at the moment.

Instead, I found Lydia, who'd clearly been waiting for me a while, to judge by the way she pounced the second I crossed the threshold. "Do you have a minute?"

"*A* minute." I took off my bag and sat. "What's up?" My

roommate was looking rather less than happy at the moment. I hadn't been hanging with her much lately. Things at the tomb had been so hectic. But were those dark circles under her eyes?

"Something weird is going on with Josh. He's been acting strange all week."

All week? Not since, oh, Wednesday? I nodded and looked thoughtful. "Hmm ..."

"And I think I know why."

I clapped my mouth shut. She did? She what? How? We'd been so *discreet*.

Lydia took a deep breath. "I—um—kind of let the L-word slip. The real one. Not the 'I love your hair, I love your laugh, I love spending time with you' one, but the non-qualified version. I think I freaked him out."

Honestly, I thought so, too, but I remained unconvinced that this was the root of his personality shift. Unless ... He had gone on the attack right at the beginning of the week. Could our little confrontation a few days ago have been caused by his own relationship woes? But I tried to keep my tone neutral. "Wow. When did you say it?"

"After Halloween."

Bingo. "And the response?"

Lydia blushed.

In my opinion, there are several families of response to this statement:

1) "I love you, too." (Or some variation thereof.) And you mean it.
2) Same, but you don't.
3) "Thanks."
4) An upfront admission that, no, you don't love them, and you don't think it's a good idea they expend much energy loving you.

5) The coward's way out. (Full disclosure: I'm very
   familiar with this strategy, having most recently used
   it on Brandon. He said he loved me, I zoned out, he
   caught my attention, and I insisted I'd been listening
   the whole time. And, at the risk of sounding like a
   hypocrite, it sucks.)

"Lydia," I prompted. "What did he say?"

"He didn't say anything. He, um, did something. Something R-rated."

Oh. I guess there was also a number six. "Was it an
R-rated thing done with *love*?"

"Amy, I said it freaked him out. I don't think he was trying to return the sentiment."

Neither did I. And if I knew anything about Josh's romantic history, which I did, I'd guess he was out trolling for
some chick to turn into his escape clause. Dammit.

"You know, Lydia, I have heard some rumors...."

"What?"

"That Josh has a bit of problem...remaining faithful."

She laughed. "Oh, that. There are rumors about that?"

I shrugged. "Well, you know, I did some digging, just to
make sure you wouldn't get hurt."

"You did, huh?" She hugged me. "That's sweet, but
we've already talked about it. I know what I'm getting myself
into."

Wow. I'd been beating myself up all this time over
nothing. Josh had told her himself. Maybe I hadn't given
this guy the credit he deserved. Telling the other Diggers
didn't mean *he* was barred from telling the woman he was
dating.

Or maybe he told her because he was afraid I would.

"Nobody's perfect," Lydia continued. "Not me, not you,

not Josh. If we had perfect track records, we wouldn't be single and available for new relationships, would we?"

"Well, yeah, but considering recent events...do you trust him?"

"Yes. I guess I trust him. I trust him until he gives me a reason not to. That's how love works, right?"

Maybe that was our club's problem, as Ben had hinted at last night. We weren't hanging out because we loved one another, and letting the trust grow from that. We were hanging out because we'd promised to, and were expecting it to turn into love. None of the Diggers had been acting very trusting of late. It was because, ever since the rumors of the traitor surfaced, no one had trusted anyone else.

Actually, it had started even earlier, when the Diggirls had first received those rhyming e-mails, telling us to beware of danger right under our noses.

Like Ben said, too much drama and intrigue. Why couldn't we spend our time in Rose & Grave actually engaging in the things the society had been created for? Camaraderie and the exchanging of ideas. No wonder I felt ten times more comfortable chilling with Lydia in our suite than I did at meetings. Our Salvation Army–furnished common room may lack the cachet of star-studded dome ceilings or wood-paneled Grand Libraries, but it was utterly devoid of intrigue. Okay, *mostly* devoid. We still held the secrets of our respective societies pretty close to the chest.

"What's your plan for tonight?" I asked my roommate. "I'm overdue on a paper I have to turn in first thing tomorrow morning, so I'll probably be up late. I vote Chinese food."

"I'm working, too. That sounds great." She grabbed the phone. "Shall I order?"

"Please. I'm going to run to the bathroom. Get me my usual." I ducked out of the suite door and up the landing steps to the entryway restroom. And it was there, in the stall, with my pants around my ankles, that I heard the scream.

Lydia's scream.

I finished up my business in record time and bolted out of the stall, pulling my clothes together as I went. I heard the entryway door slam open, but by the time I reached the landing, there was nothing but darkness outside. I flew down the steps and back into my suite, where I found Lydia standing by my bedroom door, the phone clutched in her hand. The irate voice of the Chinese-food delivery man could be heard, faintly, from the receiver.

"Crazy girl!" he shouted, and slammed the phone down.

"Lydia, what happened?"

"Oh, Amy, there was someone in your room!" She leaned against the bookshelf, as if for support. "I opened the door to grab a menu from your bulletin board, and this guy—he leapt out at me!"

"Are you all right?"

"Yes. He just ran out. Didn't touch me or anything."

"Thank goodness. Did you see what he looked like?"

She shook her head and pressed her hand against her chest. "No. Tall. Dark clothes. White. Older...than us, I mean. I couldn't see if he took anything, either. Amy, your computer. Your stereo."

But I wasn't exactly worried about my subwoofers—at least, not with Poe's warning still forefront in my mind. *They may be searching your room next.* I slowly stepped toward my bedroom. Was there anyone else inside? Probably not, but I still felt violated. Ironic, huh?

"How long do you think he'd been in there?" Lydia said. "I was sitting in the suite for about ten minutes before you came home. I hate to think he was in there the whole time."

Plenty enough time for him to ascertain that I had

none of the mysterious information I could have supposedly swiped from Jenny. I peeked in the door. My computer was still there. Probably with keystroke recording software installed, and maybe a bug or two. Tell me my society isn't into spying!

"Should I call the police?"

"Yes. Wait. No. Call Josh."

She looked at me curiously. "Josh?"

This would be tricky. "Look, you're obviously distraught. Don't you want him nearby? Give him a call. Or I will." I grabbed the phone out of her hands and dialed Josh's room. "Hey, Josh?" I said when he answered. "It's Amy."

"Committed any felonies today?"

"Too busy dealing with people breaking into our suite."

"What!"

"Look, can you come over? Lydia just found a man in my room. He's gone now, but we're pretty shaken up."

"Yes. I'll be right there. Tell her I'll be right there. Are you both okay?"

"We're fine." He may not have provided the right response to Lydia's proclamation, but he had it down pat now. "Do you think we should call the police about this man who was *suddenly* in my room tonight?" I asked, hoping he got my drift. "I don't know *what* he was looking for."

Josh considered this. "Wait until I get there. I'm leaving right now."

I pressed the *Off* button and looked at Lydia. "Gosh, I don't know, hon. I think he cares very much."

But Lydia showed no reaction. Instead, she asked, "How do you know Josh's number?"

Uh-oh. "I think I looked it up one time when you were over there. I can't believe I remembered it."

She stared at me, a curious expression playing across her face. "I can't believe you did, either."

I forced a laugh. "Come on, Lydia. I'm not seeing your boyfriend behind your back."

Thankfully, Josh arrived a few moments later (he must have sprinted all the way from his college) and enfolded Lydia in a huge embrace. "Are you all right?"

"I'm fine, I'm fine," came the muffled reply. "He didn't do anything. Just ran past me."

Josh looked over Lydia's shoulder at me. "Did you see him?"

I shook my head. "I was in the bathroom. I heard Lydia scream."

Lydia disentangled herself from Josh's arms. "I think we need to call the police."

Josh took off his coat and threw it over the back of the couch, then strode into my bedroom. "This place looks okay, I mean, not *trashed* or anything." He shot a glance at me over his shoulder. "Do you have any idea what this person may have been looking for?"

"I wish I did," I said, and joined him in my room.

"Guys, the police?" said Lydia.

"Things have ... progressed somewhat since I spoke to you last night," I whispered. I needed to get Josh alone and share what Poe and I had discovered about Jenny's room. "The room is much *cleaner* than it was *yesterday*." I wagged my eyebrows at him.

"I really think we ought to call ..." Lydia tried again, then clearly gave up.

Josh moved until he was behind my bedroom door. "There's no sign of forced entry. Do you lock your door?" He mouthed at me, *You went back there?*

I checked the common room, but Lydia had moved out of sight range. "Yes, but since this is so vital to you, I want you to know it was *legal* this time. I was with her dean."

"Her dean?"

"Yeah, her parents called and were concerned."

"Because you called them?"

"Because James Orcutt and I called them, yes."

"Who?"

Poe, I mouthed.

Poe thinks there's a problem?

Yes. We're not all as skeptical as you. At this rate, we'd have to take out additional student loans to cover our society name fines. Although, I suppose the jury was still out on whether it counted if we didn't speak them aloud.

"I knew it!" shouted Lydia. Josh and I jumped, and then, stricken, spilled back into the common room.

Lydia was standing by the sofa, Josh's navy peacoat balled up in her hands. "You *liar*!" She lobbed it at his head and he caught it. His Rose & Grave pin shimmered from the left-hand pocket.

"Whoa, whoa, what lie? Sweetie—"

"You know exactly what lie. I can't believe you two, all this time, acting like you'd just met. I can't believe I never noticed. I can't believe—"

"What?" I said. "That Josh is a better secret keeper than I was? You really find that a tough one to swallow?"

She turned to me. "How much have the two of you been laughing behind my back about this?"

Josh and I exchanged glances. "Believe it or not," I said, "not at all. We've been too busy being at each other's throats."

"Why?"

"Because," said Josh, "we both love you and don't want to see you hurt."

My mouth fell open. Lydia, to her credit, kept her composure. "You . . . love me?"

Josh looked at her and sighed. "Yes. I do."

Around this time, I decided to go back to the bathroom

and, oh, I don't know, wash my hands, brush my hair, maybe pluck my eyebrows. Stuff.

When I got back, Josh and Lydia were snuggled up on the couch. "All better?" I asked.

Lydia smiled, gave Josh a quick peck on the cheek, and hightailed it into her bedroom.

"Well, that's one less secret I've got," Josh muttered.

I shrugged. "She's known about me since last year. World still hasn't ended."

"Indeed. So, fill me in on what's going on."

I told Josh what Poe and I discovered today (careful to always call Poe "James") and what we suspected was going on.

"And you have no idea what the person in your room may have been searching for?" he asked.

"No. If Jenny was sharing her information with anyone, it wasn't me. She was angry at me, remember? Do you know what they could be after?"

Josh shook his head. "Until a few minutes ago, I still wouldn't have believed Jenny was involved. But after hearing all of this, how can I doubt it anymore? I feel like a moron."

He looked at Lydia's closed bedroom door. "I don't want to call the police yet, but I don't want you two staying here tonight. I've talked Lydia into coming back with me."

"That must have taken some real effort."

"I take it you have someplace to stay?" He raised his eyebrows. "Still keeping it in the family?"

"I'll be fine." I changed the subject. "Don't you think it's about time to go to the authorities? Two break-ins in two days?"

"One break-in, one alleged, and we'd have to come out with the society involvement to show there's any connection at all. I'm not ready to go there."

This was the same spiel Poe had given. "So when *will*

you think they've gone too far, Josh? When it turns out the patriarchs have hurt Jenny?"

Josh frowned. "I don't know. I'm still hoping this is all some mix-up. I'm going to try to get ahold of our truant tonight. I'll call Po—what's-his-name—and let him know I want to help. Lydia says you've got a paper due anyway, and I feel like an asshole for not helping earlier. Tell you what: If Jenny doesn't contact us by tomorrow morning, we'll go to the police. Deal?"

One more night. And if Josh was willing to meet me halfway and take on some of the responsibility, then maybe I ought to let him. "Deal." I stuck out my hand, as if to shake on it.

"Amy," Josh said, and he took my hand. "I'm sorry. I should have trusted your instincts."

"You should have."

"Want me to call George and tell him to expect you?"

I thought about that for a moment. "No, that's okay. I've got a better idea."

———

Twenty minutes later, I met Poe outside the entrance to the Law Library with my copy of *The Expedition of Humphrey Clinker* in one hand and my laptop case in the other. Change for the soda machine jingled in my coat pocket as Poe guided us past the metaphorical velvet rope with a wave of his Law ID and a proprietary hand on the small of my back.

This time, his touch didn't make me ill.

"This never should have happened," he said, almost as if to himself. "Are you sure Jenny didn't pass anything on to you? Anything at all?"

Jenny was barely speaking to me. I was hardly her ally. But I'd come up with another hypothesis while gathering my papers. "Do you think there's a chance the guy in my room could be behind the website? That if Jenny has been, uh, *incapacitated*, he's trying to get his info from somewhere else?" If so, Josh's or George's rooms would be no safer than mine.

Poe scowled. "I'll put out the word to everyone in your club to double bolt their doors and report back any suspicious activity. But to be honest, I don't think this conspiracy theorist is the type that leaves his house much. And he'd be trying to get into the tomb, not your place. No, I think you were targeted because you were nosing around Jenny's room. And if so, then all of this has gotten out of hand."

He left me at his assigned study carrel, which came complete with a bag of Doritos. "Don't say I never did anything for you."

"I wouldn't," I said. "You've been helping me all day. I really appreciate everything you've done."

He frowned. "Don't mistake me, Amy. It's not for you, it's for Rose & Grave."

As if I'd somehow mix that up.

———

Nine hours, seven pages, and twenty-five hundred words later, I had a completed paper and a pounding headache, both of which I attributed to the four cups of Law Library coffee I'd consumed throughout the night. I'd also managed to stay up later than I had in the past three years, which I attributed in equal parts to panic and fear. Ever try to write a paper when you're certain someone is watching you, waiting for a chance to strike? Was I about to be snatched wholesale from Poe's study carrel, leaving behind little more than the dregs of my last latte and a half-eaten bag of Doritos? (Yes, I ate his Doritos. I owe him fifty-nine cents.) At least, in this case, they'd know straight off it was foul play. The library may be populated solely with zombies at this godforsaken hour, but even they would rouse at signs of a struggle.

Probably. If only to debate the ethics.

I was sick of being awake, of being paranoid, and of eighteenth-century stable-men. Unfortunately, due to the caffeine swirling through my system, I was not about to enjoy oblivion any time soon. Nor would I be returning to my cold, empty, recently violated room. There was safety in public places. I put my head down on the table and tried to breathe deeply, hoping that, if not sleep, at least I'd be able to meditate.

When it began to grow light beyond the windows, I gave up, packed my things, and began my academic walk of shame over to the English department to drop off my paper before my professor showed up at her office to collect.

Admittedly, I haven't spent a lot of time enjoying the early morning during college (or, you know, *ever*), but you'd think that on the few occasions I'd managed to rouse myself at the butt crack of dawn, the least Eli University could do was make it worth my while. But today the only discernible difference between night and not-night was a sickly looking glow behind the dark clouds that had engulfed the campus and, from what I could tell, the entire eastern seaboard. The air was frigid and wet, and the sky hocked loogies on anyone stupid enough to venture outside.

I found the English department locked, if "locked" was an accurate description of a catch that hundreds of students forced open every day in order to use the front entrance to the building. (Because Eli's Old Campus is gated and closed every night except to the students, the powers that be aren't as interested in security on the quad-facing side of the building as on the streetside.) I took the stairs to my professor's office, checked the floor for dust bunnies, and slid my paper under the door. There.

Maybe Hale had some bagels in the tomb. Since I was down on High Street, it was worth a look. The media had gone home, or at least weren't yet out, having no doubt been exhausted by the non-stop excitement of their stakeout of a windowless building with negligible landscaping. I skipped across the deserted street and entered by the open gate, which in society code meant there was someone in the tomb. At this hour? Clearly I wasn't the only Digger behind on my work.

I crept through the hall, fearful of waking another survivor of the all-night push, and into the Grand Library, where I found Juno, Bond, Angel, and Puck seated on the couches, drinking Earl Grey and eating cornbread.

" 'Boo!" Puck cried. "Come and join us."

"What are you doing here so early?" I waved off Angel's proffered teacup (no more caffeine for me, thank you very much) and grabbed a slice of cornbread.

"You mean so late," said Puck. "I got word late last night that my stepmom had to go into surgery, and they were worried about the baby. I just heard that everything's fine, and we're celebrating. I'm going to be a big brother!"

"The earth trembles at the prospect," said Angel. She beamed at me. "I just got back from the best date of my life. I think I've met The One."

"I'm trying to convince her there's no such thing," said Puck.

Careful, Clarissa. That's how he got me.

"I fell asleep here," Bond admitted, pointing at a nearby desk strewn with paper. "The first draft of my senior project is due before your national Puritan/Native celebration, and I haven't even started."

"I'm fresh from Tai Chi," said Juno. "Sad turnout today. I guess too many people thought their energy wouldn't be flowing in the frozen mud pit we usually call the New Haven Green. And you, Bugaboo?"

"I wrote seven pages about horseshoeing."

Angel choked on her tea. "I think you may need brandy."

But instead I got a mug of chamomile and settled in to listen sleepily to the rest of their conversation. Angel was wired, still fairly floating from her dream date; Bond seemed ready for a break from poetry translation; Juno worked her heretofore unknown Zen facets; and Puck set aside his usual contemptuous attitude toward his father and stepmother and exchanged it for obvious relief and good wishes. Over the next hour, the conversation meandered easily through a variety of topics: from Juno's opinions on new spring fashion (gleaned from a swiped copy of Angel's *Vogue*), to a debate about the all-important and upcoming Game between Harvard and Eli (Eli was up for the Ivy League Championship), to the various and contradictory historical accounts of the Black Hole of Calcutta. And no, I can't remember how they all connected. Can anyone when they've got a good vibe going on?

Magic. I almost didn't want to go to sleep. This should be what Rose & Grave was like all the time. Diggers, sitting in a room, sharing ideas and jokes and stories, without all the inner-society politicking and rancor that had hampered us since the start of school. This was what my club had been like in the beginning, or even over the summer, before we started worrying about missing funds and traitors.

But all good things must be spoiled by someone, and in this case that person was Angel. "So, has anyone heard from Lucky yet?"

Puck chuckled and nodded at me. "Ask Nancy Drew over there. Soze tells me she spent all yesterday investigating Lucky's 'disappearance.' "

"I'd disappear, too, if I were her," said Juno. "Everyone's so angry with her. What I can't figure out is why she'd pull a stunt like that. Isn't she a millionaire from some program she sold? It's not like she needs the money."

"Maybe she didn't do it for the money," I said, stifling a yawn.

"Then, what?" asked Bond.

I shrugged, because *She hates us* would totally smash the current lovey-dovey atmosphere in the room. But what would *Also, I think her disappearance is more like a kidnapping, and I'm not the only one* do to the energy? "Did Soze contact any of you last night?"

They all raised their hands. "Something about Lucky's room being searched," said Angel.

"And how you guys think it was arranged by a patriarch," said Juno. "Sounds likely to me. They want to see what other dirt she's got."

Angel shuddered. "They creep me out, going into people's rooms like that. Total power trip, if you ask me. They shouldn't be allowed to get away with that crap. Soze told me there was someone in your suite, too."

"Poetic justice?" Bond asked. "After all, you broke into Lucky's room first."

Puck winked at me. " 'Boo's growing into quite the fine little Digger. Look at all the neat tricks she's picked up."

"I was talking to Poe yesterday, after you guys ditched me," I said, keeping the snark to a minimum, "and he agrees these people might have gone a damn sight further than just breaking into some rooms. We think she may be *missing* missing." *You know, like I said to you people the night before last.*

Everyone sobered up quickly, even Puck. "Come on, 'boo," he said. "You don't really think the patriarchs would have anything to do with—"

"I do," said Angel. "My father is a corporate raider. You wouldn't believe some of the shit he's pulled. I bet he's the ringleader."

"Not the honorable White House Chief of Staff?" asked

Juno. "Maybe a little CIA action, since we're toying with the idea of a massive conspiracy?" She rolled her eyes.

But I was too tired and too unwilling to get into another argument. Let Poe or Soze come in and pick up the debate. "We spoke to her dean yesterday. He can't file a missing persons report without evidence of wrongdoing until she's been gone for more than forty-eight hours. We're not there yet. Soze promised me that if she hasn't contacted anyone by this morning, he'd tell the police about Lucky's link to Rose & Grave."

That shut up everyone. "He'd break his oath?" said Juno. "He really does think something is going on, then?"

"Yes. And thanks, by the way, for taking it seriously only when *he* thinks it. Guess who convinced him?" I poked my thumb at my chest. Okay, I was a little cranky.

"I'm sorry." Juno's expression went contrite. "I guess . . ."

"What?"

"I guess I'm not familiar with what these guys do," she said. "I wasn't here last year. You were. I didn't see her room. You did. I didn't—"

"Have some weirdo hiding out in your suite last night?" I prompted.

"Exactly," said Juno. "I should have paid you more attention. I'm sorry. It was just—everyone in the club was going on and on about what the patriarchs were going to do to the traitor. It was getting a little hysterical in here. My bullshit meter was on high alert."

"You weren't alone," I grumbled.

Juno came over, sat down beside me, and then, shockingly, gave me a hug. "I wasn't being a good brother. *Support them in all their endeavors*, right?"

Finally, she gets it.

That, of course, led to group hugging, and—I think (I

hope)—Puck copping a feel. And then another round of tea and cornbread.

After a while, Puck said, "I'm still not with you guys that she was kidnapped, but I do think she's telling tales about us. I never could trust her. I'd always thought we should bond— you know, because of our names."

"What do you mean?" I asked, fighting another yawn. I needed to go to sleep soon.

"Lucky's a traditional name, like Puck, and Big and Little Demon," said Angel. "They always come in pairs. Lucky goes to the tap with the *least* amount of sexual experience."

Juno grinned. "So she's a virgin. What kind of bonding were you considering, Puck?"

Yeah. What kind? I raised my eyebrows at my lover.

He shot me a look. "Nothing like that. Just pointers and stuff. Try to help her 'get lucky.' It's a terrible name to deal with."

"I'm sure *you'd* be embarrassed to have it." I wanted another slice of cornbread, but was too tired to reach over.

"I think she was, too," said Puck. "At least, that's the impression I got from her."

"I never got the impression she spoke to you at all," said Angel.

"She did. We had the same History of Science section freshman year. Not that we knew each other. I barely went to the class. She, of course, rocked it." Puck smiled. "If I were in charge of naming the club, I would have done Lucky better. Given her something appropriately kick-ass."

"Like what?" asked Greg.

He leaned his head back on the couch. "I don't know. Trinity, maybe? Deep Blue? Ada Lovelace?"

Ada Lovelace. My eyes were drifting shut. "That's too long for a society name."

"No longer than Tristram Shandy," said Angel. "Who's Ada Lovelace? I only know of one Lovelace, from literature, and he wasn't an Ada."

That's right. Lovelace, the villain of *Clarissa.* Of course Angel would remember.

"Not literature. History. She was the first computer programmer. Or something like that. Lucky did a report on her for one of the few class sessions I did attend." Puck looked proud of himself for remembering. "She was Byron's daughter and a mathematician." He looked up at the bookshelves. "I bet we've got something on her."

"Byron had a daughter named Lovelace?" Angel asked as Puck leapt up and began scanning the collection.

"Oh, yes," said Bond. "I remember reading about that. Some story about how his estranged wife raised their daughter to be logical and scientific to contradict the Romantic influence of the girl's father."

Ada Lovelace. Yeah, it was cooler than Lucky. I yawned again.

Bond pulled down a book and opened it to the index. "I think it was her married name. Here she is." He opened the book and placed it on the coffee table. I roused myself to look. There, on the page, was a very familiar-looking portrait of a Victorian woman with Princess Leia hair.

"I've seen this," I said. "Lucky's got a poster of her hanging in her room."

"Hero worship, huh?" said Angel.

"Ada Lovelace" sounded so familiar to me. I yawned again and Puck caught me. "I think I need to escort 'boo home," he said. "I'll make sure there are no monsters or CIA agents in her closet."

"Maybe I should do it instead, to make sure 'boo gets

some actual sleep," said Angel with a meaningful glance at me.

"Maybe 'boo will just stretch out here," said I, doing so. "This couch is comfy."

"Suit yourself." Puck stood. "I'm going home, then, before the news trucks arrive." He waved to us all and headed out.

A moment later, we heard his voice in the hall. "Mail's here."

"Is it FedEx?" said Juno. "That's weird. But who else would deliver here? Bring it in before it gets wet."

"I suppose," said Angel, "the nice thing about having an unlisted address like the tomb is you don't see a lot of junk mail."

I fought back the waves of sleep. *Junk mail. Ada Lovelace.* That's where I'd seen that name.

"Guys," Puck appeared at the door to the Library, clutching an open manila envelope, his face devoid of all color. "I think Lucky's been kidnapped."

He held up a long black braid.

I hereby confess:
I had no problem getting people
to believe me after that.

15.
Pied à Terre

I was also not getting back to sleep.

"Oh my God," cried Angel. "Don't touch it! Finger-prints."

"That envelope has been through too many hands," said Juno. "And getting fingerprints off hair—"

"What are you," said Angel, "*CSI?* No? Then shut up. And, George, for fuck's sake, put that down!"

Nobody, I'm proud to report, thought of fining her at that moment.

"What should we do?" said Puck, holding the braid away from his body as if it were a live snake. "Call the cops?"

"Yes. Then call Soze," said Juno. "And that Poe guy. You said he'd been helping, right, Bugaboo?"

I nodded dumbly. "What—what else is in there? Is there any kind of note?"

Puck shook his head. "I'm almost afraid to look." But look he did, and to our collective relief, the envelope was devoid of any additional body parts.

"Well," Juno reasoned, "at least it isn't a finger."

But this provided little comfort. I called Soze (who was still asleep) and Poe (who wasn't—but vampires hunt at night, right?), and they both told me to wait until they arrived to phone the cops. Puck offered to call his dad, though we all thought that maybe Mr. Prescott needed to stay by his wife's side this morning. I called Gus Kelting on the TTA board, who'd arranged my internship last summer, but his voice mail said he was away on business. We tried to brainstorm other sympathetic patriarchs, but the list was a bit thin at the moment.

"Who could have done something like this?" Angel said in a shaky voice. "Her hair was so beautiful. . . ."

"Right, because *beauty* is the issue," said Juno.

Puck moved from seat to seat. "I don't believe it could have been—I can't—it's just a stupid society, right? A frat? I mean, shit, I don't like her very much, but she's a good kid, you know? They wouldn't . . ."

We all spent a lot of time looking at the braid, which Puck had finally dropped on the coffee table.

It seemed to take Poe and Soze forever to arrive, but in actuality, it was probably closer to twenty minutes. Considering Poe's apartment was a good twenty-minute walk from campus, I was impressed.

"How did you find it?" Soze asked.

Puck gestured to the envelope. "It was on the porch. Like, in the mail."

Poe picked it up and studied the address label. "It was mailed? Here? How odd. The postmark says Manhattan. Thursday."

"Well," said Bond, "that narrows it down."

I raised my hand. "Guys, the other day, when I took Jenny's phone, there were some phone numbers in New York City. I called them, but there was no answer."

"Again, not so helpful," said Angel. "When are we calling the police? I think we've got evidence here."

"But evidence of what?" asked Poe. "If it was the patriarchs, why leave the trophy on the stoop? Shouldn't they be sending it to the guy running the website? Or even to Bugaboo or me, because we were the ones tracking them?"

"Evidence of *what*?" Juno asked incredulously. "Of a kidnapping, that's what!"

"Okay." I tried again. "Before we were interrupted with the Locks of Not-so-much Love, I was thinking about Ada Lovelace—"

" 'Boo, what does that have to do with anything?" Puck asked.

I ignored him. "And I remembered that in Lucky's room she had some mail addressed to Ada Lovelace. I thought it was junk mail, but now . . ."

"She probably used a fake name on some Internet site," said Puck. "I do that."

"Porn sites?" Angel asked. Puck shot her a look.

"You wouldn't put a fake name and a real address, though," said Poe, and turned back to me. "Do you remember what kind of mail it was?"

I shrugged. "I thought it was junk mail. It was still there on her desk when we were in her room yesterday. It's probably nothing, but it's weird. We should tell the cops—"

"Let's go check it out," said Poe.

"How?" I said. "You want me to break in again?"

Poe smiled. "Won't be necessary."

Soze stepped in. "What does this have to do with anything? We need to call the cops, right now. Lucky could be in trouble."

"I called them last night," said Poe, avoiding my eyes. "I was getting worried. But they backed up the dean."

"But now . . ." Soze pointed at the hair.

Poe shrugged. "Try it again, see what happens. But I'm sorry to admit they may be mildly accustomed to lunatic phone calls about the Diggers. I don't know if a hank of hair is going to convince them of much." He looked at me. "Coming?"

I sighed. "Yeah."

Angel picked up the envelope. "I'm going to look up this zip code, see what neighborhood it comes from."

Soze shook his head. "If someone checks our Internet search records, don't you think it will look suspicious that before we called the police, we checked up on the evidence?"

Poe laughed mirthlessly. "We're Rose & Grave, junior. Everything we do looks suspicious."

———

Poe was a man of mysterious talents. Unbeknownst to either the dean or me, he'd sabotaged Jenny's lock yesterday while we were up there visiting. A small piece of tape held the catch in place. Now we slipped inside and collected the Ada Lovelace mail.

"This isn't addressed to an Eli P.O. Box," I said. "It's all been sent to someplace in New York City." And it was weird stuff, too. An electric bill, a cable notice . . . not your usual college loan consolidation crap. Of course, Jenny being a millionaire and all, she probably didn't have any loans.

Clarissa called. "The zip code 10002 is for Union Square and the Lower East Side."

"Thanks," I said. I looked at the envelope. "Hey, where is Ludlow Street in Manhattan?"

I could practically hear her wrinkle her nose. "The Lower East Side."

What were the chances? I hung up and looked at Poe. "What does this mean?"

"It means that Miss Goody-Goody's got a secret crib."

I considered this for a moment. "Is it possible that everyone was right all along? That Jenny did just go away for the weekend, but now maybe she's run into trouble down in New York?"

Poe gave a determined nod. "I'm going down there."

"I'm coming with you."

He looked at me. "Amy, you haven't slept and you look like hell."

"So? I'll sleep on the train."

"And...it could be dangerous."

"Right, because you're the badass who freaks out when he punches someone?"

Poe took a deep breath. "You are very difficult."

"You set the curve."

———

Sleeping on the Metro North commuter train takes talent. Sleeping on the Metro North commuter train in the middle of a (possible) kidnapping investigation while your partner-né-nemesis sits across from you and marks up pages of his law textbook with a squeaky highlighter takes the kind of talent usually reserved for deaf, blind, and comatose Zen monks. I gave up before we hit Stamford.

According to Poe's curt update when I stopped pretending to sleep, Josh had called the police, who'd berated him for not contacting campus security when Lydia had caught an intruder in my room. If anything was stolen, we were to file a report—with *campus security*. But nothing had been stolen, and the second Josh dropped the words "Rose & Grave" in the mix, the cops clammed up. Either they thought we were Eli pranksters, or they didn't want to get involved. Either way, we were on our own.

I stared out the window for a while, and then, for a while

longer, I stared at Poe. He was back in his usual attire today: wool pants slightly shiny at the knees, and a pilled gray sweater under a black wool overcoat in dire need of a good lint brushing. But really, who was I to talk? I was wearing yesterday's clothes for my glamorous trip into the city. Maybe later we could catch dinner and a show.

You know, after we did our *Remington Steele* act.

Poe caught me staring. "Can I help you?"

"Sorry," I said. "I was just thinking—sorry, spacing out." I looked out the window. "This isn't what I imagine when I think about going to the city for the weekend."

He returned to his textbook. "I wouldn't know. I never went into the city for the weekend."

"Not even with Malcolm?"

He snorted. "I don't think we'd be interested in the same spots. Plus, I'd probably cramp his style."

Shocker. Poe had no style. I returned to my absent gazing out at the dreary rain-soaked landscape.

"It's so easy for you, isn't it?" Poe went on, and I looked at him. "You never have to worry about anything. You have no idea how rough it was for me at school. I was broke."

"I'm broke, too," I said. "Way over a hundred thousand dollars in debt. You've seen my files. You know my parents aren't rolling like Malcolm's or George's or Clarissa's—"

"No, Amy, I was *penniless* broke. Beyond loans. I didn't go into the city, I didn't go out, I didn't go . . . get pizza and a beer. A two-dollar slice of pizza! I had about five dollars of discretionary spending per week. Thank God for the coffee I stole from the dining hall." He looked back down at his book. "When I got into—you know—that was it for me. I suddenly had a social life. I couldn't go to the bars or the clubs or whatever, but I could go to the tomb. It was still tough, though. I had the chops, but not exactly the pedigree.

My dad's a landscaper. I think he practically starved these last four years so I could go to Eli instead of a state college. That's who I worked for this summer."

And it must have been nigh on impossible to go crawling home to his father and admit he couldn't get a job the year he graduated from Eli. Sudden contrition overcame my usual disdain for the man seated across from me.

I leaned forward. "James, I'm so sorry—"

He slammed the book closed. "For Christ's sake, stop calling me that!" He looked away, ran his fingers through his hair. "My name is Jamie. Always has been. Not Jim, or Jimbo, or James. Nobody calls me James."

Jamie? I sat back against my seat and digested this for a few moments. So Poe had financial issues at school. He was far from the first. Lydia's dad got laid off from work her sophomore year, putting the whole family in pretty rough financial straits, and she didn't become a misanthrope. She simply picked social activities that were free. Amazing how much fun you could have with some classmates and your college's cracked Parcheesi set. Still, it explained a lot.

"I still think of you as Poe, you know. It suits you."

He met my eyes and cracked a smile. A real smile. "Two dollars. And you don't want to know what I think of you as."

"I can probably guess." I watched him open his book back up. "So, are things . . . better now?"

"Law school gives me a more reasonable living expenses budget," he said, "but I'm not exactly carting around in high style." He gestured to his outfit. "It's okay, though. I'll make it all back when I'm out of school. I'm going to work for some big firm for a while, get rich."

"And then?"

He shrugged. "Politics. Provided I have any connections left after this little caper. Which looks unlikely. You still going to work in publishing?"

"I don't know. I thought about it a lot this summer. I was working for—"

"Kelting's think tank."

"Right. We put together a little book of memoirs. Ex-prostitutes, illegal aliens caught up in the sex trade.... It was pretty powerful stuff. But it also made me realize how limited my education really is. Smollett et al. are fine, but I think I've got a lot more to learn." I looked down the train car, at the gum-encrusted floor, anywhere but at Jamie. I hadn't talked to many people about this. "I was thinking of maybe going to graduate school. Not necessarily for Literature. Maybe something else."

"More school, more debt," Poe said. "I don't suggest going unless you have a clear plan in mind."

Right. Way to pop that little bubble.

"Unless you *do* know what you want to do, and pretending you don't is your way of getting around actually making the decision."

"Pardon me?"

Poe put his feet up on my seat. "In undergrad, there was this type. Drove me crazy. They would always act coy about it, but what they wanted to do was go into politics. And not the government-appointee kind like Josh or me or even Kurt Gehry. They wanted to run for office. But somehow, they believed that *saying* they wanted to run for office was some sort of ego trip that signified they shouldn't."

"I don't want to run for office."

"Not saying you do. But maybe you want to be a social worker, or a teacher, but won't admit it because you're afraid people won't think it's lofty enough for an Eli grad."

"If I thought that, you're precisely the type of person who I'd be afraid of judging me."

He put his hand to his chest. "I'm the son of a gardener."

"You're a Digger at the best law school in the country."

"You're a Digger at the best university in the country."

"Even more reason to aspire to greatness."

He laughed. "Someday, go look through the roster of the patriarchs. See what they all do for a living. You may be surprised. We've even got a garbageman." He opened his book again. After a page or so, he added, "My mom was a social worker."

"Did she retire?"

"She died."

And that pretty much killed the conversation. We rode the rest of the way into New York City in silence, and I even managed to doze off for a little while. I don't know how many pages Poe read, and I can't be sure, but I think the humidity in the car must have done wonders for the squeakiness of his highlighter, because it completely stopped making noise.

We arrived at Grand Central Station, and Poe deciphered the tangle of subway lines while I ran into a nearby shop to grab a couple of umbrellas. Though the tunnels were warm, to judge from the streams of icy water leaking through the cracks and dripping down the subway stairwells, it was a real bitch of a day outside. One switch to the F train later, and we were on the LES. (Lower East Side—I can swing the lingo with the best of them.)

"So what's the plan?" I asked Poe as we picked our way through the puddle-riddled streets.

"I don't have one. I thought we'd go up to the apartment and knock, see what happens."

"Sounds brilliant." I rolled my eyes.

"That I am." We turned the corner. Jenny's building was a grungy, graffiti-sprayed five-story job with a bodega on the first floor. Whatever gentrification may have swept through the Lower East Side recently had skipped this particular spot, which didn't mean Jenny had acquired it any more cheaply. I wonder if her parents, or even her ersatz boyfriend (you know, the one nursing his glass jaw) knew about her little hideaway. According to Poe, his club hadn't been aware of Jenny's apartment during their deliberation process, so it must be a relatively recent development.

We entered the vestibule and buzzed Jenny's apartment, but there was no answer. There was no name on the tiny mailbox slot, either. With nothing to lose, I pressed the other buttons. After a second, there came a muffled response.

"Delivery," I said, and the door buzzed open. I smiled at Poe. "You aren't the only one with little tricks up your sleeve."

A middle-aged man in a work shirt streaked with grease stuck his head over the banister. "Mind telling me what you want?" he said, lumbering down the steps and wiping off his hands with a towel. "You don't look like you got a package."

"Are you the super here?" I asked. "We're looking for the resident of 4A. Ada Lovelace?"

"Never met her." He shrugged. "She leased the place a couple months ago, when the new owner took over. But I don't think she's here much."

"Do you know if she's been in this weekend?"

"Look, girly, why don't you and your boyfriend—"

"We're not trying to start a fight," said Poe, stepping forward. "We merely wanted to leave this note for her." He held out a small card emblazoned with the Rose & Grave seal.

The man's eyes went wide, and he looked at us each in turn. "Who are you guys?"

"Who do you think we are?"

"Couple of punks." The super nodded at the card. "You're the second crew to come in here waving that symbol around like I should care. What are you, a gang?"

"You don't know what this symbol means?" asked Poe, a hint of defensiveness creeping into his voice.

The guy shrugged. "Some *Da Vinci Code* crapola. I don't give a shit. Now, why don't you get out of here before I throw you out."

Back on the street, Poe kicked at the cornerstone. "I don't get it. The D-bomb usually works like a charm."

"Maybe in New Haven," I said. "And *D-bomb*?"

"Drop the Digger name into a conversation and see how quickly your way is smoothed for you," Poe said.

"Isn't that against the secrecy policy?"

Poe lifted his shoulders. "What's the point of power if you can't use it every once in a while? The policy of the society is to fly under the radar, it's true, but they do occasionally throw their weight around."

"You mean like last spring when they made us lose all our internships?" I looked back at the building. "Well, we don't seem to have much influence here. Plus, I'm about to freeze or fall asleep standing up—possibly both. So let's continue this conversation in the nearest coffee shop, okay?"

Poe sighed. "Fine. Let me run around the corner real quick and see what the fire-escape situation looks like. If I can get up there—"

"Whatever, Spider-Man." But I couldn't help smiling.

"I have some skills you aren't aware of, Miss Haskel. Anyway, if I can't jimmy the window, I can at least peep inside."

"And get yourself shot and/or arrested?"

"Just let me look. I'll be back in two seconds. Don't drown while I'm gone, okay?" He winked and took off.

I ducked under the bodega's canopy and rubbed my arms through my coat. I should have brought gloves. I should be in bed right now, curled up with the fall issue of the Lit Mag.

Damn Jenny. Okay, that was it. I needed coffee *now*. I went inside the shop. Ghost town, like the rest of the street on this ugly day. The guy behind the counter was watching daytime television, and there was a young truant in a black windbreaker shoplifting candy in the corner. "Small coffee, please," I said to the attendant. "Actually, make it two."

The guy nodded and went to pour the cups. He looked over at the boy. "Buddy, gonna buy something?"

The boy picked up two PowerBars. "Yeah," he mumbled.

But it was enough. I turned my head toward the kid with the familiar voice, who looked up, facing me fully. "Oh my God ..."

"So," Jenny said, "you found me."

I hereby confess:
I'm not proud of myself.

16.
D-Bomb

"Where the hell have you been!" I cried.

"Amy—"

"What the hell happened to you!"

"Please, just calm—"

"I thought they fucking kidnapped you, do you know that?"

"I know," she said, and her eyes went from me to the attendant, to the door.

"How do you know? What the hell, Jenny? What were you thinking? Your *hair* was left on our *stoop*!"

"I wasn't . . . just—I wasn't, okay?" She lifted her hands. "Who is that with you?" she asked. "Poe?"

"You know what?" I said, walking toward her and stabbing my finger at her raincoat. "I'm not even going to say you're fined for that. You're a traitor!" Now that I saw she was safe (though shorn), all of my inner rage decided to have a coming-out party. "How could you? You manipulative, lying, oath-breaking bitch! How could you!"

"Whoa," said the guy behind the counter. "You're a

chick! Weird. Wait, is this some kind of butch lesbian thing?"

"Amy, wait a second!" Jenny grabbed my hands in both of hers. "I'm—" She took a deep breath. "I'm really scared. And I want to talk to you, but ..." She looked out the window. "Not with him there, okay? I can't stand that guy."

"Well, he can't stand you, either," I snapped. "And though I may have been on your side about that a few days ago, now I think I'm on his."

"Amy." She squeezed my hands. "Please. Help. Me."

Jenny may not pay attention to her oaths, but I still did. Okay, so I sucked at secrecy. So I didn't always completely trust or love my brethren. I was still there to help them out when they needed me.

And this chick needed me.

"Jenny, what am I supposed to say? That you'll talk, but only to me? That's a little *NYPD Blue*, don't you think?"

"No, you can't tell him I'm here at all. Please? I don't trust him."

This, coming from the traitor with the secret apartment and the false name. "I don't have a particularly high opinion of the people you *do* trust."

Jenny maneuvered herself behind the Cheetos display. "Right now, there's only one person who fits that description and she's standing in front of me."

"Then strike what I just said." I looked out at the street. Poe was probably already searching for me.

"Get rid of him, okay?" She thrust a restaurant postcard at me. "Then meet me here."

"Absolutely not!" I said. "You've been missing for two days and you think I'm letting you out of my sight? Forget it."

"Amy, I swear—"

"Bullshit. I don't believe anything you swear. Not after what you did."

She closed her eyes and took a deep breath. "I swear. I swear on the Bible." She reached behind her neck and unclasped her crucifix and chain. "Here. This was my grandmother's. Take it as assurance that I'll meet you. But don't tell Poe about me. Please. There's a lot going on you don't know."

I was getting a little sick of hearing that, and also, I wasn't entirely sure I hadn't just palmed some cheap trinket. But I'd seen Jenny wear this crucifix before. "Fine," I said, regretting it already.

Jenny walked up to the counter, whispered a word to the still-stunned clerk, then ran out the back door.

"So, girly," he said, pocketing a fifty, "you still want your coffees?"

———

Outside, I scanned the dismal streets for Poe while balancing two paper cups and an umbrella handle and brainstorming ways to, as Jenny said, "get rid of him." We'd been working together so well, too. I was still trying to figure it out when Poe rounded the corner, saw me, and came splashing up.

"Where have you been!" he said with a scowl. "I've been looking for you everywhere."

"Everywhere but in the store you left me in front of?"

He put his hands on my shoulders. "You have no idea what I thought."

"I have a pretty good idea, actually," I replied, shaking him off. I handed him his cup. "I'm the big conspiracy theorist in the group, remember?"

"Can you just lay off the backtalk for two minutes?

I wanted to show you something. I think we can get in through—"

But I'd stopped listening. "*Backtalk?*" I repeated, imbuing the word with as much venom as possible. "*Backtalk?* Who do you think you are, my great-aunt Amelia, wielding her wooden spoon?"

He rolled his eyes. "Sorry. It was just an expression. I was joking."

"Joking." I searched the memory banks. "Since when do you have a sense of humor? I seem to recall a certain individual who tried to drown me the last time I made a joke." Poe had been cruel to me during my initiation. Focus on that.

"Okay, now I *know* you're mocking me. I said I'm sorry. Can we get on with it?"

He wasn't going to make this easy, was he? "Not if you plan to keep patronizing me like this. I don't even get why you're still here, James. What's your plan? Trying to get in good with Gehry?"

"No, not anymore. I thought we went over this. It's Jamie, and I'm a gardener now, remember?"

"And unless you want to *stay* a gardener, don't you think you'd better get out of here? Keep it up, and you won't have any friends in politics left."

He placed his cup on a window ledge and stuck his hands in his pockets. "Wherefore the sudden concern?"

"It's not concern," I replied smoothly. "It's that pesky paranoia of mine. So here's my theory: You say you want to help. You feed me nice little bits of information, and then you make sure you tag along every step of the way. You're not here to help me. You're helping them. What better way to get back in their good graces?"

"Are you insane?"

Yes. "You knew I would track her down eventually, and you made sure you'd be right beside me."

"You *are* insane. Amy, you couldn't track a train by yourself." *That's right, Poe. Make it easy.* My eyes began to burn. "And in case you haven't noticed, we haven't exactly found her, either." *Ah, Poe, how little you understand.* "Is this how you get when you haven't had your nap?"

"Right. My nap. Always good to have the condescension as well as the misogyny in your arsenal, isn't it?"

Oops, maybe a tad too far. Poe reeled back as if struck. He stood there for a moment, in the rain, blinking at me. Then he raised his hands in surrender. "I fucking don't get you women."

Enter Misogyny. Or, at the very least, chauvinism.

He looked at Jenny's building, then shook his head. "This was a dead end anyway. I'm out of here. See you around, Amy." He turned and walked off.

I stood there until my coffee got cold.

––––––––

Jenny was seated in a tall-backed booth when I arrived at the near-empty restaurant. I stashed my dripping umbrella, wondered briefly what had happened to Poe's, and slid into the seat across from her.

"Where is he?" she asked.

"I pissed him off and he ditched me." I dropped her necklace on the table and waved to the waitress. "Double cappuccino?"

Jenny slid the menu at me. "Are you hungry?"

"Mostly for information. Now, tell me what happened before I'm tempted to commit assault with the pepper shaker."

She folded her hands in her lap. "Where do I start?"

"Anywhere. Your involvement with the website. Your disappearance. Your alias. Your fake apartment. How about explaining why the hell thirteen inches of your hair are sitting in the Grand Library right now?"

"I screwed up."

"I know that part. Tell me how. And start with whether or not anyone has been hurting you."

She worried her bottom lip, and her eyes grew glassy. "Not as much as I've been hurting myself. The Diggers are all bark and no bite, you know."

"Tell that to the man who broke into my room yesterday," I snapped.

"Someone broke into your room?" she asked.

"Yes. And yours." I was losing my patience. Where was that cappuccino? "Now, *what happened?* Begin with the part where you betrayed us, and then I'll see if I'm interested in sticking around for the rest."

She took a deep breath. "Okay. When I joined, I didn't know what to expect. I mean, I was told Rose & Grave worshipped the devil."

"Then why did you join?"

"I was a sleeper agent," she said matter-of-factly as the waitress arrived. The woman gave Jenny a skeptical glance, set down a cup of cappuccino, a milkshake, and an omelette with French fries and departed. "It was Micah's idea. When the Diggers started grooming me, we thought it was the perfect chance." She waved in the air with her fork. "To . . . get them."

"What went wrong?"

She dug into her food. "To start with, you did. And the other girls. You were really nice to me and I was kind of into the whole battle—you know, down with the entrenched patriarchy and all that stuff Demetria says. It made the society seem really human to me. Before I was in there, I pretty much thought it was all blood rituals."

"Like the initiation?" Mmmm…cappuccino.

Jenny snorted. "I thought the initiation was going to be much worse than it was."

Clearly, no one had threatened to force her into sexual slavery.

"I thought it would be real blood, for starters. And Persephone? Please."

I put my cup down. "You were prepared to drink real blood?"

"Gross, right?" Jenny slurped from her milkshake. "But it was for the cause."

"I'm trying to think of a cause that would tempt me to drink blood."

"Jesus died for my sins. I think the least I could do in return is drink something nasty. But I felt like I was being mocked with that initiation. So close, and yet so far from any real heresy. And definitely from any real evil. It was like walking through a haunted house at a carnival. I don't think anyone was taking the Persephone stuff seriously."

"I thought you didn't believe in haunted-house rides."

"I don't, but that doesn't mean I haven't been on them. I don't want them banned or anything. It's just silliness." She thought about it for a moment. "It's very complicated, what I believe. I mean, when I was younger, my parents loved Halloween and stuff. My mom, she's Filipino, and my dad is Puerto Rican. They both have a lot of traditions that go back to superstitions, and I remember them being really fun. I even carved pumpkins and stuff at the church I went to growing up."

"When did it change?"

"I've been kind of moving away from my parents'

beliefs—and from Catholicism in general—ever since I came to school. Micah says—" She broke off. "The point is, Rose & Grave wasn't what I thought it would be, so as it turned out, there weren't really any covens to destroy, you know?" She caught me eyeing her plate. "Want some?"

It did smell divine. I picked up a fork. "So you went Stockholm. Bet your boyfriend wasn't happy about that, huh?"

Jenny's expression turned grim. "Not exactly. I still thought you guys were evil. I decided I hadn't looked far enough. Like maybe they were saving the real stuff for later, after they thought they could trust us. I kept searching."

I clenched my jaw. "And then? When did you decide you hated us?"

"I didn't!"

"You acted like it." I glared at her. "You told your boyfriend about stuff we said at the meetings. You told him about my C.B. Don't deny it!"

"I won't," Jenny said softly. "I'm sorry."

I wiped at my suddenly misty eyes. "*Why?* What could my sexual history possibly have had to do with devil worship!"

"Micah was . . . impatient." Jenny scratched at the back of her neck, as if looking for her braid, for something to do with her hands. "He wanted to know more. He wanted to understand what I saw in you guys."

"And did he?" I fought to keep from shouting. "Did he understand?"

"No. And the more we talked about it, the less I understood, too. I think that's the real reason we're supposed to keep it all a secret. It doesn't translate well to barbarians." She laughed mirthlessly. "If Micah ever heard me refer to him as a *barbarian* . . ."

I could just imagine how he'd react. I rubbed my cheek.

"And then?"

"I'm not like the rest of you, that's for sure. I could see that once the C.B.s started. I was so afraid of doing mine— or not doing it, as the case would have been."

"None of us are like the rest of us," I said. "That's pretty much the point." Still, I'd been nervous as well, so it wasn't as if I could blame her.

"I started thinking maybe Micah was right." She dropped her chin. "I hated being there. Not you, but being there, because I wanted to like you guys, and I wanted to be like you guys, but I knew it was wrong."

"To like us or to *be* like us?" I shook my head. "No one's asking you to change who you are, Jenny."

"Well, the person *I am* dislikes people like you. She isn't supposed to go drinking with Demetria or think George is kind of cute and charming or want to confide in his most recent victim." She shot me a glance.

"Okay, one, I'm *not* a victim. Two, you're not supposed to know about that. And three, so we're nice people. Whatever happened to *love the sinner if not the sin*?"

Now she raised her head fully. "Oh, please, Amy. Everyone knows about you and George. We're not morons. Remember how I caught you two making out?"

Eep.

"And I'd kind of forgotten that last part. With Micah, everything was *You're either with me or against me*. I know that now." She picked up a fry, then put it back down.

I took it as a sign that she'd finished, and began scarfing her meal in earnest.

"And the longer I waited, the more he started dropping hints that I was against him." There was a catch in her voice as she said this. "I couldn't bear that. He's so—I've never met anyone like him. He's so amazing. So sure in his faith. So pure."

"The man spit on me and called us both whores of Satan," I said. "Purity ain't exactly one of his virtues."

Jenny burst into tears. Oops.

"I just . . . I just . . . What could I do? I couldn't lose him. And I thought he was right. You guys were pretty bad—I mean, not *bad* bad, but not what I— Never mind. It wasn't such a leap to go from there to evil. And Micah—"

"What? He said he loved you?" I asked in a mocking voice.

She nodded miserably, and grabbed a napkin to blow her nose. "He said people needed to know what kind of things the Diggers did. He said it would be such an act of . . ." She broke into sobs. ". . . *loyalty.*"

Poe hadn't punched him hard enough.

The waitress arrived. "Is she all right?"

"She's fine," I said. "Can I have another cappuccino? And do you think you could add a splash of Grand Marnier?" I needed a drink to get me through this.

"You got it."

"You see?" Jenny had seen to her Kleenex needs by now. "Micah would have had a fit if he saw me drinking this early."

"You're not drinking, though, Jenny. I am. And I'm not asking you to join me."

"Fine. *Being* with someone who would drink this early."

"Who cares what Micah thinks?"

"I do. I did. He makes me so happy. Every time I'm near him." She sniffled. "But I couldn't do what we'd planned," she said. "Deep down, I didn't want to. Maybe I knew how stupid I'd been. That's why I was so angry at you. It's as if you people, and liking you at all, was keeping me from what I really wanted."

"Micah."

She nodded. "I figured I had a choice: I could either be this good person, or I could be like you."

"Thanks."

"You know what I mean. I had spent my whole life working hard, being good, making the right decisions, trying to live the kind of life Christ wants me to, but I couldn't do it."

"I think I'm missing where you're falling short."

"It's tough to explain."

"It's tough to explain to a non-Christian, or it's tough to explain because the explanation doesn't sound very Christian at all?"

She hesitated. "The latter."

"The part where you destroy us for the glory of God."

"Yes."

"Vengeance is mine, saith the Lord."

She was quiet for a moment. "Hebrews 10:30?"

"Romans 12. I think. But it could be both. When He really means something, I think God says it a couple of times."

"Right." Jenny swallowed. "You read the Bible?"

"I took a class."

She let that sink in for a bit, then continued. "So you understand that I couldn't really wrap my head around it. I spent a lot of time praying for guidance, but the only answer I got was that betraying the society would be wrong. And Micah said it was because I'd been . . . corrupted."

"That asshole."

Her lower lip began to quiver again. "So I had a choice. And being good wasn't working. Hadn't worked. But you— you were perfectly happy."

"I was?"

"You looked it. And you had George and that other boy from the coffee shop. The way they look at you—"

Brandon?!? "You're mistaken, Jenny. I'm not involved—"

"If Micah ever looked at me that way, I'd be happy

forever." She met my eyes. "I'd do anything. You know what I mean."

"This is sounding like the beginning of *Faust*, but yes."

"So we fought—you and me—and then . . . I don't know. I wanted to prove you weren't right about everything, and that you didn't have it all."

Me? "How did you go about proving this?"

"I decided to seduce Micah."

I needed more than a splash of Grand Marnier. "Because of me."

She sucked in air through her teeth. "I know. It sounds dumb, right?"

"It sounds like *an excuse*."

"Which it was. I see that now. Anyway, it didn't work. He . . . didn't . . . want me."

She burst into tears again and I slid out of my seat and over to her side of the booth. I put my arms around her and she leaned into my shoulder, sobbing. "Hey, it's okay." Heck, it was more than okay, considering Micah Price was a bastard of the highest caliber. But that kind of logic doesn't go well with a broken heart.

"I was going to give him exactly what he wanted. Everything he wanted. Well, almost. I couldn't bear to give him the Black Books—not even then—but I compromised."

"Had the same effect."

She peered up from between damp eyelashes. "I know it doesn't make a difference. Betrayal is betrayal. But it felt like it gave me a little control. I could pick and choose the least damaging things. I didn't expect the media to latch on like that. It was all so innocuous, hardly secrets at all."

"Where did you find that website?"

"It belongs to one of Micah's friends. Very private guy. Very off-the-grid. He's never even told me his real name. I offered to help him redesign the site once—make it look a little more user-friendly, a little more...professional, and he freaked."

"And we're the weird ones?" I asked ruefully.

She gave me a halfhearted smile. "So we sent him a breakdown of the rituals and the club lists and stuff, and then Micah and I celebrated. It was going to be phase one. Everything was perfect."

"Until?"

"Until I kissed him. Even that was perfect, at first. And then I did something wrong, or got aggressive, or I don't know what." She pulled away from me, but kept her face cast downward. "He pushed me away. I fell on the floor. He started shouting at me. Terrible things. Awful things. He said I'd been ruined...that the...Diggers had... ruined me." She looked at me. "Amy, I was kissing him. That's all. He didn't even want to kiss me. What's wrong with me?"

Where did she want me to start? "Nothing is 'wrong' with you. Not like that anyway." It wasn't necessary for me to be explicit about how many issues her boyfriend had, was it? "Do what you want: Drink or don't. Have sex, or don't. It's up to you. Nobody I respect judges you for it."

"After he left, I didn't know what to do. I was crying like...like I've never cried. I couldn't take it. And I didn't have anywhere to turn. I don't have friends who aren't Micah's—not anymore. I couldn't go to you guys, not after what I'd done. And to listen to Micah, God hated me, too. I was all alone. So I ran."

"Here." I looked at her. "Why not home?"

"Right," she said, lifting her head. "My parents would be so thrilled to learn I was upset because my attempt to seduce the boy they hated and thought was turning me away from the Church after the two of us conspired to ruin the possibly Satanic secret society I'd joined had backfired. That would go over beautifully." She bit her lip. "I don't know if you noticed, Amy, but my folks are a little controlling."

I stared at her. "How do you know I talked to your folks?"

She smirked. "Please. I've had my home phone tapped for years. That's how I knew you were looking for me."

Would wonders never cease? "Of course I was looking for you! I thought something terrible had happened to you. That note on your computer screen..."

"Yeah." Her expression turned sheepish. "That was the idea."

"Why?"

"Because I wanted to see if he really loved me. And the answer is—he doesn't."

"What if the police had gotten involved? Jenny, you could be in big trouble."

"I know. And I know now that I wasn't thinking very clearly. I've had the last few days to calm down."

"And I've had the last few days to freak out."

She dipped her head again, but there was no hair to fall in her face. "I'm sorry. I'm so sorry. I don't know how to make it up to you. I don't expect any of you to ever forgive me."

"That's good. Keep your expectations nice and low," I said.

She blew her nose again. "I don't know what I'm going to do now. Everything is so screwed up. I've been praying a lot. I even went to church. Catholic church. Took communion. Haven't done that in a while."

"Why not? Oh, wait, let me guess, Micah doesn't like it."

Jenny banged her head a few times against the back of the booth. "I'm such an idiot. I'm such an idiot. Why?"

"I'm going to assume that's rhetorical. We all turn into idiots in matters of the heart."

"How about matters of the soul? All this time, I thought everything Micah was teaching me was bringing me closer to Christ. I really believed that. But now I think I've let Him down." (I'm assuming the capital here.)

I put my arm around her again. "I think He can handle it."

"Yeah. But can I? I've been going crazy these last few days."

"These last few days?" I slid my eyes toward her. "You have an apartment under a false name. I think you went crazy a while ago."

"That's fair."

"And your hair? Why did you do that?"

"Leviticus. Absolution."

Um, whatever. "I don't know if anyone in the club will accept it as a peace offering."

She knit her brows. "I didn't mean it for the Diggers. I sent it to Micah."

"It was on the front step of the tomb this morning, in an envelope—" I broke off. "God dammit." I cringed and looked at Jenny. "Sorry. But I bet I know who left that thing on our porch this morning." I pulled out my cell phone. "I'm calling Josh to ask if he can peel that address label off the envelope and see if Micah's address is underneath."

"Trust me, it is. Sneak move of his, though." She put her hand over mine. "Don't contact Josh yet. I'm not done with the story."

"I just want to tell him to call off the dogs of war. You're safe and . . . well, if not sound, then at least on your way there."

"Eh, I'd let that go for a minute. We're going to need those dogs."

I frowned. "What do you mean?"

"The unwilling patriarchs, chasing us down? Going through your dorm room and mine? Coming into the city?"

"Right. They're looking for you, to make you pay for releasing that information."

"Not exactly. I mean, I've no doubt they'd like to pay me back. But I don't think that's what they've been looking for. They want to know if I know what I know, and if I've told you."

"What do you know?"

Jenny sneaked a peek at the rest of the room. "Not here." She signaled for the check and threw some money onto the table. "Amy, it really means a lot to me that you tracked me down."

"Why? I'm pretty pissed at you, remember? I mean, all of this huggy stuff aside, I'm still furious at you for everything you did."

"But you also cared whether I was alive or dead. Which is more than I can say for anyone else. If I'd called you earlier this week, I bet you would have been there for me, no matter how mad you were. You really believe in your oaths, don't you? You believe we should love each other."

"Sometimes," I said. "But I wouldn't start preparing the application to beatify me just yet. Mostly, I think we should try to keep each other safe from danger."

"Well, you found me. So right now, you're my best friend."

"Poe found you, too," I reminded her. Fines, at the moment, were a bit moot. "Believe me, he's been working his ass off. Why can't you trust him?"

She pulled on her coat. "After what I'm about to tell you," she said, standing, "you won't trust him, either."

I hereby confess:
Confession, barbarian
or otherwise, is good
for the soul.

17.
Elysion

This time, the super merely gave me a curious look as Jenny swept us past him and up the landing. "Everything okay, Miss Lovelace?"

"Fine," she called.

"I still can't get over the idea that you have another alias," I said, as we climbed the flights.

"I've even got a few more online."

"You're a mystery, Jenny. I don't understand why all the pretending."

"You get used to it, I guess. I grew up on computers, where no one was who they said they were: not their age, or gender, or nationality, or name. Nobody knew who I really was except for kids at school or church. When I sold my software, they didn't even know I was fifteen until we were so far into the deal they couldn't back out. They didn't know I was a girl either, for that matter. After a while, it seemed weird to use my real name for anything. You're so vulnerable. Everyone knows your business. It's impossible to stay off the grid, but you can reduce your presence."

And somewhere between her cyber-background and her strict upbringing, she started hiding more and more of herself away. How come none of us had seen this? "But you have property under a false name—is that even legal?"

She frowned outside her door. "I don't know. Maybe I should ask my lawyers. I just assumed they had it covered. I don't think I *own* the property under the false name. I think my alias is 'renting' from myself. Whatever. I let the lawyers handle the paperwork."

She undid several locks on the door and stepped inside, but I was too busy trying to make sense of it to follow right away. "How can I possibly trust you?" I asked. "You've lied, you've *spied*, you've been throwing pseudonyms and fifty-dollar bills around for who knows how long, and to top it off, I don't think you like me very much."

"I know," said Jenny, relocking (and relocking and relocking) the door behind us, then throwing the chain for good measure. "I would have a hard time trusting me if I were in your position, but bear with me a little longer."

"I've been making a lot of allowances lately," I said. "I was even nice to Poe."

"I bet I'll be a cinch after him." She hung up her raincoat. "Welcome to my humble abode."

Humble was right. There was a lot of space, to be sure, and a lovely hardwood floor, but not much else. Wall-to-wall computers, a coffee machine, and a mattress in the corner. No new paint, no curtains, no decorations of any kind, and the only furniture was purely utilitarian: folding tables for the computers and a big ergonomic chair.

"I'd offer you something to drink but I think you may have had enough caffeine today, and everything I've got falls into the Jolt category."

"Jenny," I said, "when we get back to school, you're going into therapy. Or at the very least, sitting down with your folks and your priest and talking about some of this stuff." I sat on the nearest office chair. "I'd say you should take your problems to Rose & Grave, but—"

"You don't think they'll have me back?" She shot me a rueful smile.

Frankly, no. But aside from that . . . "I was going to say, it doesn't seem like you put a lot of faith in what we do."

"And you do?"

"I—"

"It won't matter pretty soon anyway. Take a look." She sat in front of one of the consoles and brought the screen to life. "Remember back at the beginning of school when we got those weird e-mails?"

"The rhyming ones?"

"That you guys made non-stop fun of? Yes, that one." She pulled up a few windows. "Well, I sent it. And in an unprecedented display of disinterest, you promptly ignored it."

"No, we just didn't understand it."

"I was trying to spark a little investigation, Amy. Thought if the Diggirls were worried about what was happening, they'd look into it."

Well, we'd tried to look into it. Even tried to get Jenny to do some research, but she'd washed her hands of the whole matter. "Jenny, please. What do you mean, 'what was happening'?"

"Your society is being pulled out from under you and you don't even know it."

"What? Why didn't you just tell us, then?"

"Hi, remember, secret agent bent on destruction? I couldn't really help you outright."

I rolled my eyes. "Like we'd run and tattle on you to your boyfriend? Jenny, I repeat: therapy. Sometimes it's okay to come out and tell a person something."

"I'm trying to do that right now. Look." She pointed at

the screen and I leaned in. "Certain members of the club have, since the beginning of school, been involved in a secret pact to form a society *within* Rose & Grave. A males-only version that they feel has been unjustly taken from them. I've been tracking their e-mails since shopping period."

Cut through the web in which you're caught. "Wait, you've been what?"

She shrugged. "It was an easy hack. Phimalarlico security is designed to keep outsiders out, not to keep insiders from snooping around." Kind of like the doors on Old Campus. "I can read anyone's e-mails if I want."

"I'll sleep better knowing that. Now, what are these guys doing?"

"Systematically disenfranchising you." She handed me a stack of printouts. "They meet in secret to discuss the details of their society, and have slowly been siphoning off money from the trust."

"They've been stealing our cash?"

"Through the help of interested parties on the TTA board. The unfriendly patriarchs? They aren't gone, they've just transferred their 'allegiance' to Elysion. If Elysion gets enough support, enough money, your society will be a joke."

I skimmed through the e-mails, all of which were addressed to people called things like Theseus-X1 and Hector-X1. Some of the conversations were little more than chatter, or harsh rundowns of what had happened at Rose & Grave meetings and how to avoid such "embarrassments" once the switch took place. They'd increased in frequency ever since the Straggler Initiation Night, and mentioned losing Howard as a catalyst to gain support. Many spoke of money, or how the movement within the patriarchy was gaining ground. "Elysion, huh?" I said. "Like the Elysian Fields, the heaven of the Greek underworld, reserved for heroes?"

"Exactly."

"So who are they?"

"I've been slowly putting together a key to their identities, based on timing and content of the messages. It would usually be easy, given ISP addresses, but the Eli wireless system makes that tough." Jenny looked at me. "This is all I've got so far. Brace yourself." And then she handed me a list:

ELYSION MEMBERS

Hades = Kurt Gehry

Hector = Nikolos Kandes

Theseus = George Harrison Prescott

Ajax = Benjamin Edwards

Orion = Omar Mathabane

Orpheus = Kevin Lee

Nestor = James Orcutt

I swallowed hard and leaned back against my seat. *Stay cool. You don't have enough energy left to indulge in rage. Deal with it.* "Who started this?" I choked out.

"I'm not sure. It hasn't been discussed on e-mail. But I bet it happened this summer. Nikolos appears to have been one of the first organizers."

No surprise there. *Learn of the thief who can be bought.* It was a reference to Graverobber. I was right again. Go, me. "And there are five of them. Every man in the club except—"

"Josh, Greg, and Harun."

George was on the list. And Poe. How could I not have known this? Of course, Poe was no big shock, though it did make my little street performance ring with a sudden truth. But George! How the hell had he made time for Elysion with all of our other activities? If he was involved in both societies, he definitely wasn't seeing anyone else. It wasn't a matter of desire, it was a matter of scheduling.

She picked up another sheet. "I've been trying to track the other patriarchs involved as well, but it's much harder to learn their identities. They don't send e-mails. Here's what I've got so far...."

But I never got a chance to look. Someone started pounding on the door. "Jennifer Santos!" an angry voice called. "Open this door. We know you're in there."

We both froze, but Jenny regained her wits quickly. "Put these in your bag," she whispered, and handed me a stack of papers. "We've got to run."

"What?" I said. "What if that's the police?"

Jenny was busy doing something to her computer. Within a few seconds, she'd closed everything down and was pulling out flash drives and unplugging little metal boxes. "Please," she said. "It's the Elysions. They're back, and this time, my super didn't hold them off. We can't let them catch us. We can't let them find out how much we know."

"I think they know exactly what it is we know," I said. "Why else would they be here?" Had Poe called them? Had he figured out that I'd ditched him because I'd found Jenny?

The pounding on the door gave way to a much more insidious sound—that of locks giving way. Apparently, some pockets ran even deeper than Jenny's. Wonder what bribe—or threat—had finally won over the prickly super? So much for all bark and no bite. "What are we going to do?" I said. "This is an apartment. There's only one exit. They've definitely got the fire escapes guarded."

"Got it covered. Let's go now." Jenny pressed a few more keys and all of the computers in the room began making a hideous grinding sound. She grabbed my hand and pulled me across the room to one of the windows. "Go!"

I looked out and down, and for a second wasn't sure what I was seeing. A ladder stretched diagonally from the window across a tiny space. I stared down into a minuscule courtyard ringed by tall, thin walls studded with windows. "What is this?"

"A light well. Go."

I swung my bag over my shoulder, gave her a look of skepticism, and went. The ladder was freezing, wet, and slippery. It also bent and popped with every step. I was sure that any second it would slip from its mooring on the lower ledge and send us both clattering to the refuse-littered ground four floors below. The only thing keeping me moving was the sound of the Elysions hammering at the door and trying to get the chain to break off.

At last, I reached the bottom, where the base of the ladder rested against another window ledge on the opposite side of the light well. I slipped inside. Jenny clambered down after me then swung the ladder away from her window. It crashed to the ground.

"They'll be back down any second," she said. "We have to hide."

She pulled me farther into the room. There was a narrow, steep set of stairs leading down into the floor. We descended, and I found myself in some sort of storage area. Giant crates of pop and pallets stacked with snack foods surrounded us. We were in the back room of the bodega.

Jenny leaned against the wall. "So now you see why I'm scared."

"Yeah. All this on-the-run stuff really does a number on your adrenaline levels." Speaking of which, I'd just about run out. All-nighters, too much caffeine on top of too little food, and thrilling escapes—not to mention I hadn't exactly slept well the night before last—and you had a girl ready to drop. "Explain why we ran?"

She blinked at me. "Because they were trying to break into my apartment."

"Then we call the police," I said. "We don't need to hide. What are a bunch of businessmen going to do to us in broad daylight on the streets of Manhattan?"

"This from the girl who a few hours ago thought I'd been kidnapped," she snapped. "I don't want to find out what they'd do to me. Hence, I don't want them to catch me."

"Fair enough," I said. "So what do we do now?"

"You mean what are *you* going to do, Amy. You've got the information now. Are you going to let them snatch your society out from under you?"

"It's your society, too, Jenny."

She looked down at her feet. "Not anymore. If it ever was."

———

So the fifty-dollar bill Jenny had slipped the bodega employee had nothing to do with overpriced Manhattan energy bars. Instead she'd charged him with taking her car out of storage. Within half an hour, we were on the highway heading back to New Haven. I spent the time text-messaging Josh and Clarissa that they could stop worrying about Jenny, but please don't spread the word until I'd spoken in detail to them both. After that, I tried again to get in touch with my old boss, Gus Kelting, member of the TTA board. Gus was on a business trip to Reykjavik, and according to his secretary, he wouldn't be available for several days. I was transferred to his voice mail and pressed the 312 code, which I'd learned last summer took me to his special Rose & Grave mailbox. I hoped like hell he was checking his messages from Iceland. If not, we kids would be on our own with this one—though maybe it was time to see if we could hack it without help.

I stayed awake as long as possible, watching to see if we were being followed and debating with Jenny the necessity of our thrilling escape.

"These guys' idea of being a badass is sabotaging a summer internship, not breaking kneecaps," I said, finally agreeing with the argument everyone had been throwing at me since Jenny vanished.

"How about hiring thugs to break kneecaps?" Jenny asked. "I'm from the Bronx. I don't take chances."

Fair enough.

I fell asleep soon after, and awoke only when Jenny parked in the York Street garage and turned off the ignition. Home sweet home.

"I don't want to go back to my room," she said.

"Why not? It's nice and clean now." I gave her a weak, sleepy smile. "Come home with me if you want. Josh will probably be in the room, and we can tell him the whole story. I promise he'll be more coherent than I am."

She bit her lip. By this point, I was surprised she hadn't bit it through. "I don't know how I can face Josh. I don't know how I can face any of them."

Frankly, I didn't know how she was going to do it either, but hopefully we'd be able to steer quickly past accusations and recriminations and straight on to the issue at hand: Elysion.

Speaking of people we didn't want to face at that moment, the first person we saw as we entered the gate of Prescott College was none other than George Harrison Prescott himself.

"Hey there, Boo," he said, his tone jovial and not at all indicative of his months-long duplicity. Cold, man. Ice cold. "Back from New York?"

"Looks like it," I replied, while Jenny pulled down the

brim of her baseball cap, exposing her boyish, shorn nape, and pretended to read the bulletin board.

"Find anything?"

I shrugged, because I couldn't trust myself to lie to him. I wanted to wring his neck. And what would be the point of making conversation anyway? It was entirely possible he was toying with me, that he and the rest of his Elysion cronies already knew about the break-in at "Ada Lovelace's" apartment. No doubt the super had told the men about Jenny's visitor before he'd let them have his keys. "I'm really tired. I'm going to try to grab some sleep."

"Can I see you later?" He slipped an arm around my waist. Jenny's back stiffened, echoing, no doubt, my own sudden relationship with good posture.

George noticed my decided lack of thrill when it came to his touch, and dropped his arm. "You okay?"

"Fine. Just tired." Which was true, or at least half true. I *was* exhausted, only not "just exhausted."

"Well, give me a call later if you want to get together. I probably won't be in until late."

"Okay," I mumbled.

Jenny and I continued on our way, through the courtyard and up the steps to my suite, which glowed with warm yellow lights. I could see the door to my bedroom standing slightly ajar, and my eyes grew heavy again. *Come on, Amy, buck up. Miles to go before you sleep.*

"I don't think he recognized you," I said, swiping my card at the entryway door.

"I don't think he recognizes anything he doesn't classify under the category of possible sexual partner," Jenny snapped. "So we have that going for us. You aren't going to call him later, are you?"

"Just tell me you're not enjoying this."

Josh and Lydia were seated on the sofa of our common room, digging into a box of pizza. They looked up, and Josh's mouthful actually fell onto his shirt.

"Oh my God," he said. "What happened to you guys?"

"Amy," said Lydia, "you look like shit."

"Thanks, hon. I'll love you forever if that's pepperoni."

"You loved me forever years ago, but yes." She grabbed another paper plate.

I checked out my reflection in the glass. Sure enough, there were bags under the bags under my eyes, and my face was streaked with dirt. And this was what George had wanted to get together with later? Blinded by lust, perhaps? "Never mind. I think I need a shower first."

"Your bedroom's clear," said Josh. "I've been checking regularly." Only then did he choose to recognize Jenny's presence. "Hi."

She adjusted her bag on her shoulder. "Hi."

Pleasantries aside, I left the not-so-merry group and took a shower. Say what you will about dorm life, there's very little to compare with the glory of a scalding hot, elephant-strength Prescott College bathroom shower. Twenty minutes of steam seeping into my pores later, I emerged, reddened and relaxed, shrugged into my robe, and headed back to the suite.

Jenny had clearly related the whole story to Josh by this time, and he, naturally, had mobilized. Lydia had kindly taken her leave of the suite (the note on my whiteboard read: *Okay, fine. You get one free pass for turning my common room into your clubhouse. I understand emergencies. Luv, Lyds*).

"Do you think she's going to go tell her society our business?" I asked Josh. "You know every other society on campus is going to crow with delight if they hear about this."

"Hear about what?" said Josh. "She left before Jenny

said a word. That roommate of yours is one classy dame. Can I pick 'em, or what?"

"You're dating Amy's roommate?" Jenny peeked her head out of my bedroom, then looked at me. "And you allow that?"

"Shut up, Jenny," Josh said, following me to the door of my bedroom. "Lydia's not the only one who knows how to give people the benefit of the doubt. You're lucky we do."

"I believe her," I said.

Josh sighed. "So do I. Everyone's on their way."

"Everyone?"

"The non-Elysions," Jenny said. She returned to my desk and showed me what she'd pulled up on my laptop while I'd been gone. "There's been more activity on their e-mails. I think there's a meeting tonight. I just need to find out where it is."

"Tonight?" I said. "On Saturday?" *I probably won't be in until late,* George had said. No kidding.

"That's why we're concerned," said Josh. "It must be important if people are giving up their weekend for it. It may be about the information they think Jenny has passed along."

Soon after, the rest of the group arrived.

"This had better be good," said Clarissa. "I'm supposed to be on another date with Mr. Wonderful."

"Two nights in a row?" said Mara, picking over the pizza. "Wow, it's true love."

Greg snatched the last slice of pepperoni out from underneath both of us, and began chomping. "We all canceled plans to be here," he said. "I expect there's a reason."

"I canceled nothing," said Harun. "And yes, I own my loser status. If you all had parties to go to, the least you could do would be to take me along. Whatever happened to supporting a brother in all his endeavors?"

"We were supporting you in your loserdom," said Clarissa.

Odile and Demetria arrived and stood on opposite sides of the room. Lover's spat, perhaps? I raised my eyebrows at Demetria, but she ignored me.

"How long is this going to take?" Demetria asked. "If we're waiting around for George or Nikolos to get home from the bars, we'll be here all night."

"That's not where they are," said Josh through clenched teeth.

I'd gotten dressed in Lydia's room while Jenny worked on my computer, and now the door to my room stood closed.

"I'm getting kind of sick of these constant powwows," said Odile. "I thought we signed up for two meetings a week, not seventeen."

"Don't worry," said Josh. "This may be the last. Of any kind." He opened my bedroom door. "Come on out."

Jenny came forward, and everyone in the room gasped.

"Holy shit, it's *Boys Don't Cry*," said Odile.

Jenny gave a halfhearted wave. "Hi, guys."

Only Harun returned her salutation. Everyone else looked pissed.

"So you found her," sniffed Clarissa. "Great. Can we string her up now?"

"Not quite yet," said Josh. "Give her five minutes."

So we listened as Jenny gave a very abbreviated history of her sleeper agent scheme. She didn't sugarcoat her involvement, or place any blame on Micah. She stood there, upfront and honest (and under her actual name), and admitted to everyone that what she'd done to them was wrong. I don't know how many points she earned, but I was proud of her.

And then she segued into the true purpose for the meeting: Elysion. We passed around the printed e-mails and list of participants. To most of the girls, it came as a shock. Mara didn't look too dismayed, and the boys greeted the news with more disappointment than surprise.

Josh looked at Harun and Greg. "I take it your experiences were pretty much like mine?"

Greg shrugged. "Some of the guys would make these offhand comments," he said. "I thought they were merely taking the piss out of the girls, and never paid much attention."

"I think they were judging our responses," said Josh. "And when we didn't seem to express any interest in the idea, they didn't invite us in."

"I got invited," said Harun, softly. "At least, in retrospect, I think that's what they were trying to do."

All eyes turned to him.

"It was a few months ago, just after Straggler Initiation Night. I went out for drinks with Ben and Nikolos and we were shooting the shit, talking about investment banking, things like that. I didn't understand how the society worked yet. I thought they were trying to recruit me into some sort of Digger fund-raising committee. I didn't have time for it—not with all of my other activities. So I said no." He looked around at all the stricken faces. "I didn't know what it was. I thought they were trying to get me to volunteer. That was the last I heard of it."

"So if you'd known, would you have joined?" asked Demetria.

"Hell, no," Harun said. "I don't roll with that sexist crap."

"Really?" said Juno. "I'd have thought—"

He narrowed his eyes at her. "Thanks. I seem to have left all my burkas in my other bag, or I'd give you one."

"Peace out," said Demetria. "Can we do the racist commentary later?"

"For your information," Juno said with a sneer, "it has nothing to do with race. I was going to say that Harun told me he didn't know they let women in until he arrived in August. I got the impression he wasn't pleased."

"It was you who weren't pleased, if I remember correctly," said Clarissa. "Hypocritical, sure. But you weren't pleased."

"Just because I don't agree with the principle behind a tax cut doesn't mean I'm not going to pay anyway," Mara replied.

"All right, guys, leaving behind the sticky logic for a moment, let's move along to the point where we figure out what we're going to do next." The sooner this was decided, the sooner I could go to bed.

Mara eyed Jenny. "Why should we do anything? She's admitted to lying to us, to using our own fears against us, to tricking us into casting suspicion on one another. How do we know this isn't Phase Two?"

Now who was the paranoid one? Of course, if I'd had a few moments of sleep the previous evening, maybe I'd have ruminated on the possibility as well. "That's awfully diabolical of her, wouldn't you say?"

"Takes one to know one," Clarissa said. "What plan to take down a diabolical organization wouldn't be equally diabolical?"

"You're speculating," said Josh, "that these last few days have been part of an elaborate plot to convince us to trust her when she presented information showing a third of our club has been conspiring against us? Wouldn't we have believed her more readily *before* we knew she'd betrayed us all?"

Clarissa pursed her lips. "Okay, you're right. When you put it like that it does sound a little unlikely."

Greg snorted and held up one of the Elysion e-mails Jenny had printed. "Those bastards. Listen to this: 'We've gotten a lot of support for our cause from the willing patriarchs, especially those from whom donations in general have been way down. The only remaining concern is what to do about the balance of the trust. It would be easy enough to redirect a portion of appreciation/dividends into the new account, but this is hardly a worthwhile trust. Yours under the rose, Hades.' They're stealing our money."

"Well," Jenny said, "they think it's their money, too."

"They can't do that, though, right?" I asked. "Even if it's all part of the Tobias Trust Association, they can't just decide on a new budget that includes secret funds to Elysion without the vote of the board, or of the club. Right?"

"Definitely," Josh said. "And I doubt most of the board even knows about this. You haven't been able to contact your guy, have you, Amy?"

"He's in Iceland," I said. "I left him a voice mail, but . . ." For all I knew, some Elysian with access to Gus's Digger inbox could be erasing any message clueing him in on the plot.

"Listen to this," said Demetria, holding up another e-mail. " 'I doubt the club will meet Sunday night, due to the current atmosphere of scrutiny. Now is the perfect time to decide upon our next move. Why delay? This is our moment. The old order is crumbling. Let's not get caught in the rubble. Yours under the rose' . . . et cetera."

"Who wrote that one?" Mara asked.

"Um, someone named Hector."

All of a sudden, Odile straightened. "Wait. I've heard of this before. Elysion."

Demetria eyed her. "Don't tell me you got an invite."

"No, I read about them. In the annals. They existed once before, when the club first began accepting non-white and non-Christian members. Some of the old guard were upset, so they formed a *secret* secret club."

"Gross," said Jenny. "What happened to it?"

Odile shrugged. "I don't remember the details, but it's in the Black Books. I guess the rest of the club discovered it and flipped out."

"So now history is repeating itself," I said.

Demetria put down the e-mail. "Okay, I'm ready. Let's go nail these jackasses to the wall."

"First we've got to find them," said Clarissa. "Where do we think they're meeting? It's not at the tomb. I was just there."

"Did you go all over?" Josh asked.

"I didn't search the place, if that's what you mean, but it was definitely empty. I was upstairs, downstairs—I even went into the kitchen, because someone left the light on down there. Total ghost town."

I picked up another sheet. "Does it say anything about location in these e-mails?"

"Precious little," said Jenny. "Which I suppose means they always meet in the same place, since they never feel the need to announce location, only time."

"When do they meet?" asked Josh. "Maybe we can narrow it down based on that."

Jenny began flipping through the pages. "Wednesday, Wednesday, Wednesday, here's a Monday, a Tuesday, a Friday, another Wednesday. There was a Saturday the first weekend in October—"

"I remember that night," said Odile. "It was the Jane Fonda marathon Kevin insisted we all go to and then he disappeared in the middle of it."

"George wasn't there, either," I said. We'd gotten in a fight about it.

"Do you think they were trying to keep us busy?" Greg said. "If we were all at the theater, then we couldn't be—"

"In the tomb," said Clarissa. "But they weren't there just now. I swear I would have noticed."

I looked at the e-mails Jenny had discarded. I'd spent so much time with George in the last few weeks. Where had I seen him? One of the Wednesday meetings caught my eye. Like I'd forget *that* night. George and me, in the tomb. But it made no sense. He hadn't been at any Elysion meeting. He'd been with me.

But I hadn't heard the door open when he'd come in. And his skin hadn't been cold from the outside. And he'd *guaranteed me that everyone had gone home for the night....* Oh, God.

"They meet in the tomb," I said. "I'm sure of it."

Josh's eyes met mine and a flicker of understanding passed between us. "But where?" he asked. "Not the Inner Temple, surely."

Is that how George had known there were no cameras? I couldn't bear to think of it. "And not the Firefly Room or the Library." I would have heard them. "I think it's unlikely to be anyplace on the main floor. Are there any rooms in the tomb I'm not aware of?"

"Considering it's you, probably," Clarissa said with a smile.

"Who knows?" said Odile. "The blueprints are missing from our archives."

Everyone turned to her. "What?"

She shrugged. "They're listed in the card catalog, which, by the way, is a total disgrace, but they aren't on the shelves. I wanted to use them back when we were planning the Straggler Initiation, but I couldn't find them."

Jenny lifted her hands. "I swear that wasn't me. I drew my own floor plan."

Time to change the subject. "What do you want to bet they went missing right around the time the Elysians came up with this idea?" I said.

"But how is it possible that none of our big sibs bothered to tell us about some other room in the tomb?" Greg asked.

"Maybe they didn't know about it," I said. *Oh, Amy, how could you be so stupid?* "Maybe the only big sib who knew was someone very well versed in Digger history. Someone on the side of the Elysians."

Someone like Poe. Man, I almost had him in that alcove after we'd visited Edison College. He was obviously trying to figure out if I knew anything about Elysion. He'd practically told me himself. But, like always, I'd resorted to trading snark rather than actually *listening*.

I picked up one of the earliest e-mails from "Nestor." I will give the Elysion boys this: They sure knew how to pick their names. I'd read Homer. Nestor was the wise old warrior who'd advised all the young heroes in *The Iliad*.

From: Nestor-X1@phimalarlico.org
To: Elysion-X1@phimalarlico.org
Subject: Re: next time

I think the complaints are unfounded. Naturally, our space does not have the grandeur of the Inner Temple, but it is far better suited to our purposes. Recall the temples of Mithras and other spartan assemblages. We're warriors. What do we need of luxury? Besides, if you wish to split hairs, our entrance beats the crap out of theirs, and shares its history with the most glorious artifact in the Inner Temple.
Yours under the rose,
Nestor

Their entrance? But if everything in the tomb was built at the same time, why would an entrance have anything to do with the antiques we kept in the Inner Temple? And what "artifact" was he talking about anyway? The oil paintings? The engraving of Persephone? The elaborately carved throne?

The only thing I'd ever seen that looked like the throne was the carved wood frame on the diamond-dust mirror hanging in the basement. I faced the group. "Clarissa, you said someone had left the light on in the kitchen?"

"Yes. So what?"

"I think they're meeting in the basement."

"Where in the basement?"

"Behind the mirror."

En masse, the nine of us headed over to the tomb on High Street. Discretion was a thing of the past. During the trip, I berated myself for ignoring all the signs. Poe and George, appearing in the kitchen out of nowhere. Poe, grilling me for what else I'd found out in Jenny's room. George, making excuses for times he'd bailed on me and hiding secrets on his computer. I'd been sure it was about another girl. Clever, clever—any devious action on his part surely related to sexual, not societal, betrayal.

I was so clueless.

Josh and Harun threw open the tomb door and we strode in, completely mindless of who might have the street staked out. We took the stairs down to the basement and crowded into the narrow hall—nine little Diggers, staring up at the tall, mildly warped mirror.

Soze slipped his fingers around the edge of the frame and tugged, but the mirror didn't move. "It's not this side," he whispered. He tried the other. "Still nothing."

"Maybe there's a catch," Thorndike said. She ran her hands up and down the frame. "I can't feel anything, either." She dusted her hands off on her cargo pants. "Hate to say it, Bugaboo, but I think you got it wrong."

"Let's search the rest of the tomb," said Juno. "They have to be here someplace."

"No," said Lucky. "I think she's right. Look."

She backed up a few steps and pointed at the mirror. The frame's intricate carvings detailed the rape and imprisonment of Persephone, her seduction-by-pomegranate, and her eventual subscription into the royal family of the underworld. And there, at the top, sat a large carved rose.

Lucky looked at me and smiled. "Under the rose." And then she leaned forward and pressed on the glass.

It swung open like a door, revealing a set of stairs.

"Hurry," said Thorndike. "They had to have heard that."

We rushed down the stairs, only to hit a set of double doors at the bottom. Thorndike flung them open, revealing a small, barrel-shaped room beyond. Old-fashioned hurricane lanterns illuminated seven figures in long red robes around a long table. They leapt to their feet, and I saw shock and dismay on every one of their faces. Most of them bolted away from us, to the far end of the room, where there was another door.

"Follow them!" I heard Thorndike shout, as chaos erupted in the corridor.

But I didn't think I had the energy to run. I stood there watching as one of the two remaining figures pushed back his hood, to reveal Poe. The other, still seated, leaned forward in his seat, rested his chin on his hand, and sighed. "Sorry, 'boo," George said.

My eyes began to burn. Okay, I was wrong. I turned and ran.

I hereby confess:
There are days when I think
it's not worth the trouble.

18.
Benefits

I ran as if I hadn't been awake for more than twenty-four hours. I ran as if the burn in my legs would somehow erase the need or the ability to cry. (It didn't.) I ran as if Cerberus himself were chasing me. But it wasn't a three-headed hound of hell who caught up moments after I slammed the Prescott gate behind me. And it wasn't George, either.

"Amy, wait!"

I stopped. I clenched teeth and fists. And then, slowly, I turned.

Poe put his hands on the bars. "Open the gate."

"There's a reason," I began in a choking voice, "they don't let graduates keep their proximity cards. It's because we don't want you in our lives anymore!"

"Amy, I want to talk to you about this. Please, can't you just calm down?"

"You lied to me! You betrayed us—again!"

"*I* lied to *you*?" His voice rose a few decibels. "Who was the one who pulled that act in New York today? You knew where Jenny was, and instead of telling me, after everything I did to help, you conned me!"

Yeah, and I'd felt bad about it at the time. But clearly it had been misplaced emotion. I stepped closer to the gate. "Jenny pleaded with me not to tell you. And she was right. You were working against us! What a lucky guess on my part, huh?"

"No, Amy! That's not how it was."

"Tell that to the goons the patriarchs sent to break into her apartment."

He slammed his hands against the bars. "I *was* trying to help. I *was* worried about her. Believe me or don't, I don't care."

"No. You don't," I hissed, getting even closer. I wrapped my hands around the bars as well and peered at him through them. "I was such a fool. This whole time, I've been telling myself that no matter what I thought of you personally, I could trust you to do what was best for the society. I was sure you of all people believed Rose & Grave came first." I leaned in, until we were practically nose to nose. "You're so good at making me look like an idiot, James. All along, you were trying to ruin us."

"That's not true!"

"No?" I dropped my hands. "Then explain the point of Elysion. Explain the point of stealing from our trust, of bogarting our members, of carrying on your own secret meetings in our tomb until you had compiled enough influence to go it on your own!"

For a moment, he said nothing at all.

I nodded, pursing my lips in an effort not to cry. When I'd regained enough confidence in my self-control, I went on. "You, who knows everything about the society. You know enough of the history to see what a bad idea this was. You know what they once used Elysion for. You know the kind of racism it represented." I looked into his eyes, which were wide and gray and probably every bit as bloodshot as my own. "How could you start it up again?"

"I didn't start it," he said. "I swear. I didn't know about it at all until the day you kicked me out of the tomb. I just—I missed Rose & Grave so much. It was the best time I ever had. The best friends. And it was gone. So when Nikolos came to me with an invite, yes, I went along with it. It wasn't Rose & Grave, but I was welcome there."

"But don't you see?" I cried. "You're *destroying* the society in your bid to cling to it. Grow up! Leave us alone!"

"If you didn't keep begging for my help, maybe I could!" he shouted back.

"Hey!" George arrived at the gate. "Stop yelling." He looked from Poe to me, then back again. "Mind stepping aside?"

Poe did, and George swiped his prox card over the sensor. The gate unlocked and Poe put his hand out to pull it open. George stopped him. "No, dude," he said. "You're not coming inside."

"I just want to talk to her."

"Well, I don't want to talk to you," I said.

"You were talking a few seconds ago," he replied.

George slipped inside and closed the gate behind him. He came up to me, a small frown marring his perfect, gorgeous features. "This is really about me, isn't it? Come on, Amy, let's go someplace and discuss this."

I wasn't entirely sure it was about him, but I wanted a few words with Prescott here, too.

Poe pounded the gate. "No, Amy, wait!"

I glared at him. "Drop dead, James." George put his arm around me and began to lead me away.

"For the last time," Poe said in hushed tones, "it's *Jamie*."

I shrugged George off and looked over my shoulder. "Fine. Drop dead, *Jamie*."

————

I went to George's room without complaint, but once I was there, I unleashed plenty.

"How could you do this? Why did you lie to me?"

"I didn't lie."

"Another one! God, you're good! How can you ever expect me to listen to you, to trust you, to feel comfortable around you, to ..." Okay, I'd already said *trust you*, right? "... to sleep with you again!"

He looked hurt. "Not sleep with me?"

"George, our whole relationship is predicated on the idea that we, unlike all of those boyfriend/girlfriend idiots, were actually going to be honest with each other. Want to talk about the many, many times you've lied to me? How about what you were really doing on your e-mail on Thursday when I came over here? How about where you really were before you found me that night in the tomb? How about what you were doing the time you were supposed to meet me at the film festival? You weren't writing a paper about Berlin! All this time, I thought you were lying to protect me from sordid stories about other women. It's crazy; *that* I could have dealt with. But lying about Rose & Grave? No. The only promises you've ever made are about that."

"You're taking this way too personally."

"No, George, I'm not. This isn't about you and me. This is about you and the rest of the Diggers. I'm pissed at you as a *brother*. How could you do this behind our backs?"

He plopped down on his futon and took a deep breath. "I don't know. I was hanging out with Nikolos a lot. He's a cool guy. We've been talking about getting a boat this summer, cruising around the islands."

And picking up chicks, no doubt. I gave him the "get to the point" signal.

"Next thing I knew, I was down there with the red robes. Nikolos seemed into the idea, and I thought, what the hell, right? Pretty ironic."

"How so?"

"I didn't even want to be a Digger, if you remember," he said. "And here I am, a member of the Super Diggers. Still, I had no idea this would upset people so much."

"You're not supposed to keep secrets from us. You're not supposed to be in another society."

And yet George just sat there, shrugging the whole thing off. "Honestly, it didn't even cross my mind that it would be an issue until this morning. When I found out that Jenny knew about us and that's why everyone was so freaked by her disappearance, it did occur to me that you might be angry."

"But you didn't think to let me in on your little secret? Not even when I was going nuts thinking Jenny was in trouble?" I shook my head. "If you didn't care about Elysion, then why did you bother?"

He shrugged. "It seemed fun. What more reason do I need?"

"For deceiving me? Plenty!" I cried.

He laughed then; the kind of laugh that's about eight parts snort, one part chuckle, and one part sneer. "I knew this was going to happen," he said, as if to himself.

"What? That we'd finally figure out this charade you guys were pulling? No kidding."

"No, I mean I knew you couldn't handle the parameters

of our relationship. No strings, remember? I don't owe you special treatment."

"I'm not asking for it," I said, while inside I seethed. How dare he accuse me of that! You'd think he'd know me well enough after all this time. "Right now, I'm asking for regular old honorable treatment, Digger to Digger. I'm asking you to think for a moment about how you might be hurting people, before you just go along with something for the hell of it." Asking him to pretend he could care about someone besides himself.

He rolled his eyes and stood. "Come on, Boo," he said, as a smile began playing around the corners of his beautiful mouth. "Don't act like you have a good reason for every single thing you do."

"I don't," I admitted. "Sometimes they're really horrible reasons. But I have to take responsibility for them anyway. That's part of growing up—putting away childish things."

He raised his hands in a gesture of acceptance. "That must be my problem, then. I still like to play." I scowled, which only made his smile widen as he came toward me. "But there's more to this. Tell me you aren't just a little bit more upset with me than you are with the others. Stop kidding yourself."

"You're right," I said. "I'm more upset with you. Because we were close, and I trusted you more."

He spread his arms. "See? It is about you and me."

Oh, *hell* no. "You misunderstand, honey. It has nothing to do with sex and everything to do with the fact that I spend more time with you than with Kevin or Nikolos or Omar. We're *friends*. I'd be every bit as mad at Josh, or someone else I cared about out in the barbarian world. Do you think I'm in love with you?" I scoffed. "I'm not so shallow as that!" I turned toward the door. "And I'm not so stupid, either."

His hand hit the door just above my head and slammed it

closed. I barely had time to gasp before he grabbed me, whirled me around, and pushed me up against the wall. And then he was kissing me, hard. They weren't the usual George kisses. All elements that could be considered languid, seductive, or charming had been given their walking papers. These *hurt*.

I turned my face to the side, but he followed me. "George—" I pushed at his shoulders, and he leaned in, crushing me with his body weight, insinuating his knee between my legs. "George!" I shoved him away.

We stood there, two feet apart, panting and staring at each other. George's hair was mussed, his glasses slightly askew on his face, his permasmile completely absent. But I recognized his expression. He was turned on. He was turned on because I was fighting with him.

I closed my eyes. Just like his parents. *I couldn't become that.*

"I'm leaving," I said. "And I don't want to do this anymore."

His voice was cool and calm. "I think you should stay."

"No." I held my arm out, as if warding him off. "This wasn't foreplay, George. I'm angry at you. I don't want to be with you when you act like this. We may only be having fun, but we're not playing games."

This time, he didn't stop me when I opened the door and got my ass out of there. I made it all the way out of his suite, all the way down the stairs, all the way across the Prescott College courtyard, up the steps to my entryway, and inside. All I wanted was to get home, go to my room, and go to bed. All I wanted was to cry myself to sleep. All I wanted was to be alone.

I entered my suite, closed the door behind me, then slid down it until I sat on the floor, my knees bent in front of me.

I leaned my head back against the wood, and felt the tears building up behind my eyes. I hated men. I hated all men.

I heard the sound of a throat clearing, and opened my eyes.

Josh stood at my whiteboard, uncapped marker in hand. "Is this a bad time?"

I hereby confess:

Politics is always personal.

19.
Uncle Tony

It is a truth very rarely acknowledged that no matter how long you sleep, your issues are still there to smack you upside the head as soon as you get up. And so, ten hours later, I crawled my way up through oblivion to respond to the pounding on my door.

"What!"

"Amy, it's Josh. Can I come in?"

"No." He'd narrowly escaped having his face torn off last night, and only because I was too tired to do any tearing. I'd simply brushed past him on the way to my bed, closed the door behind me, and locked it. Mr. Phi Beta Kappa got the message.

But now he was back. "You'd better be decent," he said, as he opened the door anyway and traipsed around the messy piles of my clothes. You'd think, after the stellar cleaning job the patriarchs did on Jenny's room, they could have afforded me just a bit of the same treatment. Josh sat on the edge of my bed. "I brought you some orange juice."

"I hate you mildly less." I grabbed the proffered cup and went back to hiding under my duvet, drink and all.

"We need to talk."

"I beg to differ." I sipped at the juice. Wow. The first non-caffeinated beverage I'd had since I can't remember when. And I was starved as well. "Unless, perchance, you also brought a bagel?"

I heard a wrapper crinkle. Okay, I hated all men sans Josh.

"Amy, it's important."

"It's always important. It's been important for weeks. I can't take any more importance right now. I think I made that clear last night. What more do you want? I found the leak. I brought her to you. I uncovered a massive conspiracy. I brought you to that. I survived the fallout, even. I'm *so* done."

"It's about Lydia."

I pulled the covers down. "What?"

"I got home really late, obviously," Josh said. "But I had an e-mail from Lydia, and she asked to come over. I suppose all of the honesty about Rose & Grave opened the floodgates for her to talk about her own society experiences. . . . Amy, I'm really worried about her."

"What do you mean?"

"How much has she talked to you about her society?"

I began wolfing the bagel. "Zilch. It's verboten in the suite. Back last year, around tap, we argued about it a lot."

"I've been getting the impression that whatever she's involved in, it's pretty intense."

"More intense than Rose & Grave?" I asked, skeptical. "How is that possible?"

"I'm getting the idea she was hazed pretty badly."

Oh. That. "I was a little worried about that after Initiation

Night. When I came back, it looked like she'd been through a real ordeal. Her room was covered in feathers and cow blood. It was disgusting." I wrinkled my nose, remembering. The whole common room had smelled like bile, and there was mud tracked all over the place. I thought the Rose & Grave initiation had been bad, what with all the being-shut-in-coffins and imminent-threat-of-drowning, but it was clearly nothing to whatever Lydia's society had done to her. "It obviously wasn't pleasant, but she seemed to weather it okay. Why the sudden concern?"

"The way she talked about her meetings—they're brutal. Do you know she has to stand naked on a pedestal and re-count her sexual experiences?"

I stopped chewing.

"Rules infractions are apparently repaid with corporal punishment."

I blinked at him. "Like, she's whipped?"

"Well, she must not have broken any rules, because I haven't seen any marks on her. But can you imagine?"

"No! That's terrible." I'd dreamed up a lot of wild stories before I understood the truth about Rose & Grave, but I'd never imagined anything like that.

"She told me about one of the other members. He or she—she wouldn't say—is on the swim team. They stick the society pin *into their skin* at practice."

I put down my bagel. "Stop. This sounds horrible. Did you find out what society it is?"

"No, but I want to. I bet we have some sort of records on them in the tomb. I want to kick these guys' asses."

"I can't believe she'd submit to stuff like that," I said, but the truth was, I could. Lydia had always viewed society membership as a crowning achievement to her time at Eli.

"I bet it's a newer society," Josh said. "Maybe one of the

reconstituted ones. They tend to be much more hard core because they want so badly to have the same sort of reputation as Rose & Grave."

"That's possible. Although really, who'd want Rose & Grave's rep right now?"

He shrugged then became quiet for a moment. "I wanted to ask you last night why you disappeared."

"Had to. I'd had enough. I was dead on my feet. What happened?"

"The room leads into a tunnel that empties out in a corner of the sculpture garden. So you were right all along when you said there was a secret entrance to the tomb."

"Score!" I took a swig of orange juice.

"They'd basically scattered by the time we all made it out. Not that it matters. The confrontation was the important thing. I take it you had a couple of your own?"

I didn't answer, and Josh, to his credit, didn't spend any time saying "I told you so." But I'd learned my lesson. Society incest is a bad, bad thing.

"The big question is who's going to show up to the meeting tonight," he said.

"You think they won't show?"

"I'm afraid of what will happen either way," Josh said. "Amy, you know it's your turn to be Uncle Tony."

I caught my breath. No, I'd forgotten.

"I talked to some of the others. I was surprised by the variety of opinions on the issue. Some of them thought we should simply forget the whole thing happened. Say it's bygones and go on with our lives. Some think we should kick their asses out of the club for breaking the oath of fidelity."

"What do you think?" I asked him.

"What do *you* think?" he replied.

I leaned back on my pillows. "I say fuck 'em all. I can't deal with it anymore."

He was very quiet. "Some people say they should be allowed to go on as they have been. That their little faction is no different than the Diggirls."

I sat up. "That's bullshit."

"I'm just saying some people have said this."

" 'Some people' named Mara?"

He didn't answer. Instead, he said, "So we can talk more later about Lydia?"

"Sure. I'll see what I can get from her. But I'm warning you, she's pretty tight-lipped about stuff like this."

He nodded. "And a bunch of the, uh, 'good' Diggers are getting together before dinner to discuss the situation. Will you be there?"

I considered this, then started scooching back beneath the covers. "I'll be there for the meeting," I said at last. "I think I've devoted enough of my time to the Order of Rose & Grave for one week."

"Ah, you forget." Josh stood. "It's Sunday now. Whole new week."

Curses.

———

When I finally did arrive at the tomb, shortly before dinner, I was greeted almost as you'd expect: as a conquering hero by the "good" Diggers and with cold silence by the disgraced Elysians. Fortunately, I only had to bear a moment or two of the juxtaposition before Lucky showed up. The reaction she provoked was unanimous.

"Wow, so you do have the *cojones* to show your face," said Angel, raising her glass. "I salute such extraordinary chutzpah."

I was busy saluting such an extraordinary combination of foreign tongues. We convened in the dining room for the most awkward meal I've ever attended. Actually, "awkward" isn't the word. Neither is "uncomfortable," "intolerable," "ill-at-ease," "strained," or even "torturous," though really, dinner was defined by all of the above and more. It was tough to eat, what with the giant woolly mammoth of issues arm-wrestling the enormous King Kong of unresolved tension right there in the room with us. Hale had cooked salmon in what I'm sure was a scrumptious creamy dill sauce, but I couldn't swallow a bite. Nobody met the eyes of anyone else, the room remained more silent than the Stacks at exam time, and Puck appeared to have been body-snatched, to judge by his utter inability to crack anything resembling a joke.

Not that I would have laughed.

Twenty-nine painful minutes later, I gave a little cough to get everyone's attention. "Shall we get this show on the road?" I said. Murmurs of assent replaced the choked stillness, and we adjourned to the Temple. I started the meeting with the usual rituals, but skipped right past the song-singing and hair-ruffling part. Who were we kidding, really?

"Tonight, in lieu of the usual discussion of fines for minor rule transgressions, let us skip straight to the real issue." I paused for effect. "What the fuck, people?"

Everyone looked at me. I shoved back the hood of my robe.

"Seriously. I spent the last few days running around this campus and a good portion of the tri-state area, trying very hard to hold this society together. I'm tired. I'm angry. And I want to know why I should keep bothering, other than the obvious reason that I swore I would. From what anyone with the sense God gave a goldfish has been able to gather, some of you aren't happy with the current incarnation of the society—and some of you aren't happy with the society, full stop. So what we're going to do now, if it's okay with everyone, is let each knight speak in turn on the following topics." I counted them off on my fingers. "The existence of Elysion, the perceived failings of this year's club, the recent leaks, and what, if anything, should be done about these things. Right to left. Go."

I sat on the throne, folded my arms across my chest, and waited.

And one by one, people began to speak.

According to Thorndike and Angel—who, stop the presses, actually agreed with each other about something— we should ride the lot of them out of the tomb on a rail, including Lucky. Oath-breaking is oath-breaking, and they'd each committed some serious oath-breaking.

Bond's stance was that we should give the lot of them a "right good titching." Being a bit behind on Eton slang, it wasn't until Soze gave me a meaningful glance that I realized that whatever it meant, it was the kind of behavior more often practiced by Lydia's society than the Diggers. Bond also suggested we follow that up with several months of probation. Except he didn't say "probation." He said we should "gate them." Same thing, apparently.

Juno said we should accept the new status quo (but still kick Lucky out). As Soze had intimated earlier, she saw Elysion as not materially different from the informal gatherings the Diggirls participated in. Others (and I include myself in that number), however, argued that the Diggirls weren't keeping any secrets—especially about our existence— from the rest of the club, nor had we formed any kind of formal parameters or rituals for the group, like the Elysions' red robes, nor would we exclude any knight who wished to join us at whatever pizza place/coffee shop/bar we were frequenting, *nor* were we doing anything that could be remotely interpreted as "skimming from the top" of the

Tobias Trust, so that argument didn't hold much water. Juno merely retorted that our tattoos were rituals of the oldest and most traditional sort, and just because Elysion had thought of the dedicated meeting space and special subtrust first didn't mean the girls wouldn't have come up with it later. It was her recommendation that, henceforth, all Rose & Grave initiates, depending on gender, be granted simultaneous entry into either Diggirls or Elysion, much in the same way that, until recently, female students at Harvard received diplomas proclaiming them graduates of Harvard *and* Radcliffe.

In a move that shocked pretty much everyone, including perhaps herself, Lil' Demon agreed with many of Juno's points. "Not the stuff about the Diggirls and the tattoos," she was quick to add, "but I don't think Elysion is the harbinger of doom we're making it out to be. Yeah, it was a bitch move to do it all behind our backs, but so what? We caught them; it's out now. At the risk of sounding like a walking stereotype, can't we all just get along?" She added that she thought Lucky should be punished for her actions, but she was certain we'd be able to find a suitable penalty without resorting to dissolving anyone's membership. "We can try that titching thing Bond mentioned." (Quoth Soze: "Um, no.")

Graverobber reiterated his old chestnut of funding, expounding on his argument that Elysion was the last great hope of the Rose & Grave of the past. (At this point, Thorndike began to argue that the *Elysion* of the past was the last great hope of the Third Reich, at which point I pounded the gavel a few times to get her to shut up and let Graverobber finish his speech, when what I really wanted to do was shout "Hear, hear!" and fling said gavel at Graverobber's head.) He finished up by saying he was in complete support of Juno's suggestion as long as they contained a provision to keep Elysion money with Elysion, et cetera.

Big Demon begged off financial analysis in favor of focusing his discussion on the problems he'd been experiencing in the club. However, he admitted, since its inception, Elysion had, for his money, been spending too much time talking about Rose & Grave and not enough actually doing all the cool bonding stuff. "Just once," he said, "I'd like to spend some time in this society *not* talking about the state of the society. This is like a bad relationship."

Kismet and Frodo both expressed dismay that they hadn't been more well informed about the original incarnation of Elysion. "I'd probably have been loath to get involved had I known what the name stood for in Digger circles," Frodo said.

Kismet concurred, but added that he felt their main sin had not been naming their subsociety after the earlier one, but rather, keeping their true purpose a secret. "Had we approached you openly," he asked, "would we even be arguing about this now? What is your greatest complaint: that Elysion exists, or that it exists as a fait accompli?"

We all considered this in the silence that fell after his speech. Finally, Kismet elbowed Puck, who started as if he'd been dozing off. *Perfect.*

"Whatever you guys decide," Puck said, still not meeting my eyes, "I'm cool."

"That's not sufficient," I said.

And now, at last, he looked at me, his expression all casual and devil-may-care. "Of course it isn't. 'Boo needs more. Well, I'm sorry, but that's all I've got."

I took a deep, calming breath. "You have nothing to say

about your involvement in Elysion or your hopes for the future of the order?"

He tilted his head to the side, as if considering. "Nope. Can't say I do. As you may recall, I'm not so involved that my heart will get broken if it all just . . . ceases to exist."

Asshole. While I attempted to frame a calm response (not to mention keep an even expression), Jenny rose to her feet. The look she sent Puck bore the usual level of righteous hostility, but there was something noticeably different about its flavor. This time, she was angry on my behalf.

Jenny tugged on the hem of her shirt and began. "I don't know if I'm supposed to talk during this, and judging from what most of you have said, I'm pretty sure how this is going to pan out where I'm concerned. To be honest, I can't blame you. I made promises to Rose & Grave, and I broke them. And I'm very sorry. I'm sorry because I now realize how much it's hurt you—not only due to what you've gone through this week, but also because I think all the concern over the last month has definitely contributed to the lack of . . . cohesiveness in this year's club." She turned to Big Demon. "I'm so sorry for usurping your C.B. night. I feel especially bad because you're not only my brother, but before all of this, we were barbarian college mates. I should have made a point to become better friends with you." She turned back to the group. "And I know this sounds selfish, but I'm mostly sorry because I know I'll never have another chance like this. I should have realized it when, even as I was leaking info, I found myself picking and choosing what I'd let go of. I should have realized it meant that I didn't want to do it. I loved Rose & Grave, even if I wasn't willing to admit it. So now I am, and it's too late."

She sat down to resounding silence, and not the good kind, either. The Inner Temple began to feel every bit as uncomfortable as the dining room had. And then Tristram Shandy stood.

"I haven't said anything yet. In fact, I haven't really said much of anything all semester. I've felt pretty left out, to tell you the truth. Juno was the only other Straggler who actually made it into the society, and she was instantly gathered into the bosoms of the other Diggirls."

Angel let out a little, snorting laugh. *"Instantly?"*

"Bosoms?" Thorndike added.

I raised my gavel in warning.

Shandy went on. "I've listened to you all make your arguments, and you've given me a lot of food for thought, especially about the idea that we can go on in this manner—Elysion for men, Diggirls for women. But in the end, I think it's bullshit." He crossed to the pedestal near where I sat and took down the book of oaths. "I don't know if it was any different when I was initiated in Saudi Arabia, but I'm pretty sure my oath of fidelity said the same thing yours did: *to place above all others the Order of Rose & Grave.* As far as I'm concerned, that means above other societies as well. The very idea of subsocieties within the Order goes against the principles we swore to.

"Elysion does not represent me. Never has. And I won't be a part of it, because as far as I'm concerned, its very existence is a mockery of the type of brotherhood we're supposed to be creating. There's not supposed to be a hierarchy within the club. That's why we pick a new Uncle Tony every week. That's why we vote on everything. We speak as one voice. It's my understanding that our predecessors did the same when they chose to tap women. Why would we denigrate their efforts by splitting off into groups—the people who are girls, the people who are boys. . . ." He trailed off. "What happens to the people like me who don't want to be part of any subgroup?" He sat down, and once again, silence reigned. This time, however, I think it was because we were all shocked that Shandy, always so silent, had come up with the best argument of all.

Okay, then. "I suppose we all might want to take a few moments to think about—"

"Wait," said Lil' Demon. "You haven't said what you think."

What I think? What I think. Oh, where to start! All I'd been doing was thinking about this, all I'd been doing was fighting for it—for far too long—and I still had no answers. Hiding under my duvet began to seem like a permanent solution. "I think this club hasn't been living up to expectations. I think I've devoted a ton of time and energy to it. I think we've all been hurt and disappointed by what's happened ever since we joined. We lost jobs, we lost friends, we lost who knows what else. So there's got to be something keeping us here anyway. It's not the money, it's not the networking, and it can't only be Hale's cooking. I think one hundred and seventy-six years' worth of patriarchs would be devastated if we let it go to pot. But I think if we don't, as a group, make a decision about the next step, then we'll go down as the worst club—and possibly the last club—in all of Rose & Grave history."

I lifted my shoulders and then let them drop as the words sank in my own ears as well as those of everyone else in the Inner Temple. "And I think I'm tired of having this argument. I've been tired of it for at least a month, and I'm not the only one. If we can't get past trying to figure out where this society is going and actually start taking it there, then we might as well give up. Right now—and this may be my sleep deprivation talking—I'd almost be willing to take the position of Puck over there. 'Fuck it. I don't care what happens.' " He looked up at me, and actual surprise registered on his features. "But I do care. I just don't have an answer. I suppose I think we should do whatever is best for the society we've been swearing to uphold. But I can't decide that on my own, and I don't know if we're ready to decide it as a group." I stood. "So I propose the following: We adjourn this meeting and go home. We all know what our options are, and where each person stands on the issue. For the next few days, we'll try to come to some sort of agreement about where to go from here. And if we can't, then I say we make Thursday's meeting a time to admit we're hung. At which point, we'll vote to disband, and the Club of D177 will be no more."

———

There's something to be said for a dramatic exit. And actually speaking the words aloud added an especially nice touch, in my opinion. You thought the silence was pretty intense before, you should have heard it after my little decree. Or not, as the case may be.

We'd been pussyfooting around the issue all evening. I was just the one who actually put words to our worst-case scenario. Figure out how to make this work or be the ones responsible for waving good-bye to two centuries of tradition. Boom.

Plus, it's the truth. I'd devoted enough time and energy to the dramas of Rose & Grave. If we couldn't get it together, maybe we should give up. Even if it meant going on hiatus and letting the patriarchs pick a new class (who, I'm cynical enough to predict, would undoubtedly be all male) for D178.

I closed down the meeting and vamoosed, disrobing and departing the Inner Temple before I could be roped into any more conversations or debate. And I wasn't going to sign into my Phimalarlico account tonight, either. I'd given plenty to the society in the last few days. If it couldn't stand without me for a few hours, then maybe it didn't deserve to stand.

This time, as I left the tomb, no one followed me back to my college. (As if George wanted to get anywhere near me!) I anticipated a blissfully peaceful Sunday evening. Even Lydia would be busy with her own society meeting.

But as I turned onto York Street and Prescott College came into view, I caught sight of a familiar figure passing through the gate and turning toward College Street. It was Lydia, carrying her bag. What was she doing out here? She must be way late for her society meeting.

I began walking after her, keeping a safe distance. This was the perfect opportunity to discover what society she'd actually joined. I'd simply follow her right to the door of her tomb.

But instead of leading me to any tomb I knew of, she turned into Cross Campus and headed for the library. I followed her into the building and watched her make a beeline for the elevators in the back. As soon as the doors closed behind her, I rushed up and watched the number display. Floor seven. Freshman year, I'd heard rumors of a society that actually met in a secret room in the library stacks, though I'd never learned which one it was. I hopped in the next elevator. How hard would it be to find the entrance to the tomb in the Stacks? There wasn't anything up there but reading rooms and bookshelves. Of course, I'd recently been taught a lesson about how well a society could hide its rooms, if necessary. I'd have to keep an eye out for any suspicious-looking mirrors.

The elevator reached the seventh floor and opened onto a hall lined with doorways. Most were inset with panes of frosted glass, though a few of those panes had been covered up by layers of paint or even, in one case, pieces of wood. I held my ear against each door. Nothing. I touched the metal doorknobs. Still cold.

Maybe the entrance was actually *in* the Stacks.

At Eli, there are two different types of people: those who study in the Stacks, and those who don't. I've been known to do a bit of reading or even a problem set or two in the public reading rooms on the ground floor, but hang out for hours in the Stacks? Not on your life. Endless, silent rows of bookshelves, each illuminated by fluorescent bulbs controlled by individual electric timers. Going into the Stacks meant turning the dial, waiting until the light flickered into sickly life, and then rushing down the row, hoping to find the book you needed before the clock stopped ticking and the light went out. There was nothing freakier than wandering through these dusty rows and wondering, if something was to happen to you up here, how long it would be until someone needed a copy of *The Passion of Perpetua* or was interested in a little light reading on the life of Hildegard of Bingen. For instance. There were indeed study carrels to be found in this bibliographic wasteland, though I couldn't imagine the type of person who would frequent them. There's a decided difference between peace and quiet and fearing you're the only person left on Earth.

Or maybe I'd just been traumatized at an early age by the poltergeist librarian in *Ghostbusters*.

Whatever the cause, I remained on high alert as I picked my way through the abandoned floor. Most of the rows were dim, and I didn't turn on any lights, fearing discovery. When I reached the end of the row of shelves, I turned right and headed toward the interior wall. Any secret room would likely be found along that end. Of course, all I could see before me was a row of study carrels, each as abandoned and forlorn as everything else in this desolate fortress of learning.

"Amy?"

I froze. There, seated behind one of the tall wooden

dividers of a cubicle, sat Lydia. Her bag was open on her lap, and she hadn't even gotten out her highlighter yet.

"Amy, what are you doing here? Don't you have your meeting?"

I just stared at her, openmouthed. *"Don't you have yours?"*

*I hereby confess:
I so knew it!*

20.

Address and Redress

Lydia sat there for a moment, tapping her pen against her hand. "Does it look like I'm at a meeting?" she said at last.

"I don't understand," I said. "Was yours over early, too?" I'd latch on to any explanation at this point.

"I'm glad this happened," Lydia said. "I am."

I shook my head. "This can't be right."

"Were you following me?" She leaned over and caught the leg of another chair, scraping it across the floor until it was positioned across from her. I collapsed onto the seat.

"Of course I was! I wanted to see what tomb you went into!" I shook my head again. "Don't do this to me, Lydia. I honestly don't think I can take anything else this week. What happened with your society?"

She took a deep breath. "I'm not in one."

"No shit!" I massaged my temples. If your cerebral cortex explodes before graduation, do your parents get a refund? "But what about everything you told Josh?"

"Lies." She shrugged.

"What about everything you told me?"

"More lies."

"What about all that crap that happened on Initiation Night? What about the fucking blood on our fucking floor?"

"Wow, *language*, Amy. And this is a library. Keep your voice down."

"There's no one around for miles, Lydia. Talk to me! I don't believe this is happening. And if you knew anything at all about the kind of week I've been having, you'd know that's saying a lot." My best friend, a liar. My society brothers, my lover, and now my best friend. Any second now, my parents would call and tell me they were actually space aliens. Or European royalty. Or Republicans.

I considered scheduling a nice chat with the folks at Mental Hygiene. That's what the DUH (Department of University Health, and a more accurate acronym has never been employed) calls their Psych department.

"I know, Amy. There have been so many times I wanted to confess the whole thing. But I didn't even know how to start."

"Just start," I whispered. See? I can talk softly.

Another deep breath. "I didn't get called back after interviews. I didn't get tapped. And you did. By Rose & Grave, of all places. I didn't even know they do women."

"They didn't."

"And I was . . . jealous. You didn't even want to be in a society. Not like I did. I was also a little embarrassed. So I started doing research on secret societies, and then I kind of . . . made one up."

"You *made up* a secret society?" Maybe I wasn't the one who needed Mental Hygiene after all.

"Yeah. I wanted you to think I'd gotten tapped, too. I figured it would be pretty easy to pretend. All I had to do was fake a couple of Initiation Night rituals and then disappear every Thursday and Sunday. And sometimes I didn't even have to do that, since you weren't in the suite on those nights anyway."

"But, Lydia—the blood . . . the feathers . . ."

She ducked her head sheepishly. "Yeah, I think I went a little overboard. Still, you believed it. And it was kind of fun, having you think I was in an even more intense society than you were."

"What I was thinking," I corrected, "was that whoever those bastards were, they were hurting you. Nothing about it was fun."

"That dawned on me pretty quickly. Also, the whole ruse became tiresome. Lying sucks because it's much harder to remember. And it's completely ruined my social life, too. All our friends go out on Thursday and I'm stuck at home because I'm terrified people will say something in front of you about how I was at a bar with Carol or something. I can't even eat in the Prescott Dining Hall. I go someplace where no one knows me." She laughed. "I was almost relieved when Josh and I started dating. It was pretty obvious he was in a society, so at least I didn't have to come up with another excuse."

Unbelievable.

"And I started to recognize that I'd been acting a little crazy." (*A little*, she says.) "None of it seemed important after all the hype of Tap Night was over. But I'd built such a story, I couldn't just abandon it. It's what I'd always imagined for myself. I'd go to Eli, get tapped by a society, graduate into the exalted ranks of the Bilderberg Group."

"The who?"

She blinked at me. "You're serious? What kind of Digger are you?"

I shrugged. The bugaboo kind.

Lydia went on. "This fall, after I got into Phi Beta Kappa, I realized exactly how foolish I'd been. Here I was, in a real honor society, the oldest in the country, and I was whining about some stupid frat."

"They're not stu- . . ." I shut my mouth. Well, who was I to speak on that subject tonight? Occasionally, they were incredibly stupid. "If you were so over it, then why did you get mad at Josh when you found out his society was Rose & Grave?"

"Because you two had been pretending you didn't know each other. You played me so well." She started doodling on the cover of one of her notebooks. "It's fine, though. I understand now that you guys weren't talking about me behind my back."

This was crazy. We'd been so worried about her and all the time she was making shit up? "Last night, you told Josh about how your fake society had been beating you and sticking pins in your skin."

"He told you about that?" She smirked. "I guess I spoke a little soon about all the not-talking-about-me-behind-my-back. And it wasn't me. It was the fake swim team members in my fake society. But yeah, it got out of hand. It seemed like he wanted to talk about society stuff. Whatever hard time you guys were having, he just needed to vent a little. And I couldn't let him do it without giving him something in return."

"What did he tell you?"

"Nothing damning, I swear!" She tilted her head to the side. "Look at you, so loyal. I promise, he didn't tell me anything. Just that he was really stressed, didn't know how things would turn out, stuff like that. It wasn't really the time to come clean about my . . . um, tall tales. He needed me to be there for him. He can trust me. You both can."

"So you told him your society was torturing you to make him feel a little better about what was happening with his?"

"Pretty much, yeah."

The truth was, it was so adorable and so twisted that

I couldn't even condemn her for it. "But now the truth is out."

"Yes. And, Amy, I'm so relieved. The more involved my lie became, the more I felt like I was living in a bad sitcom. It's so embarrassing. Please forgive me."

"You're forgiven," I said instantly. "I'm not even going to ask you where you got those feathers." Lydia's society research left much to be desired. Where had she gotten her information?

"Old pillow." She looked at me through her bangs. "Will you let me tell Josh myself?"

I hugged her. "Gladly." Lydia's transgressions were minor in the scheme of things. Bizarre, to be sure, but ultimately harmless. Except, perhaps, to old pillows. A week ago, this might have put a pretty bad dent in our friendship. Now it seemed like little more than a foible. I couldn't afford to lose another friend. At this rate, who knew what kind of perspectives I'd be able to entertain by Winter Break? Still, I didn't want to be anywhere near Josh when he heard this one. "Though, if you want my opinion, his plate's a little full right now. Might want to wait a few days."

"Yes. Of course I will." Lydia pulled back and examined my face. "Amy ... is everything going to be all right?"

I couldn't say yes. I couldn't say no. I couldn't even say *I'd tell you, but then I'd have to kill you.* Not after the heaping spoonful of truth Lydia had just served me. The dam broke and tears started rolling down my cheeks. I watched Lydia's eyes grow wide as deep, heaving sobs rumbled their way up through my chest. She started holding me again and I cried, and cried, and cried. I cried until there were wet spots all over her shirt and my eyeballs felt like mosquito bites and my sinuses like cake batter.

Oh, thank God! I'd been waiting for this for days. I'd held out through the fights with Josh, Jenny's disappearance, no one trusting me, arguing with Poe, staying up all night, fighting with Poe in the city, dealing with Jenny, dealing with Elysion, dealing with George, dealing with Poe, dealing with dealing with dealing with. I was so sick of it. The tears were like vomit, like poison. I wanted this pain out of my system. I didn't care. No more secrets. No more Rose & Grave. What kind of knight was I?

"Oh, God, Amy, don't tell me they're flogging *you!*" Lydia said as the waterworks stretched on.

"You'd think," I sobbed. "Maybe they should. We messed it up. The alums said we would, that we women would ruin it, and they were right. It's over, Lydia. You should be very impressed with your roommate. I'm a goddess of destruction. I'm Medusa. I'm Kali."

"You're freaking me out is what you are. Calm down." She pushed some hair out of my eyes. "I don't even understand you. Is this some sort of society jargon?"

No. The Diggers had an entirely different pantheon in mind. "It's been very difficult this semester. I thought we were all on the same page, but apparently no one agrees on what we're really supposed to be about. Are we the sum of our traditions, even if those traditions suck? Or are we whatever the traditions were put there to protect?" I knew I was being too vague to get any real answer out of my best friend, but I was trapped by my vows of secrecy. Even now, I cared. "It's just really tough, because the decisions of last year's club blew apart the image of what the society has been . . . forever. And now we don't know what we're supposed to be."

"Do you really believe that?" she asked. "That they've always been the same thing?"

"Sort of." Though, come to think of it, those industrial barons and plantation gentry of the mid-1800s were hardly the kind of diverse population on the roster today. They'd even survived the infighting faction of Elysion once before.

"Here's a little lesson you learn in Poli-Sci," Lydia said. "Nothing is ever as stable as you think it is. What they called Republicans became Democrats who became Republicans who ended up deeding their ideology to Democrats...."

"I think I remember failing that quiz in A.P. History," I said.

"The point is, every generation chooses its own image, regardless of the mandates of whoever came before. You have to, or you'd lose all relevance."

"How much relevance can we have in a tomb, in silly costumes, singing old songs?"

"How much relevance do we have sitting here, in a 1930s rip-off of a medieval cathedral, surrounded by card catalogs?" She smiled. "Those are simply the trappings. The real tradition is us—the latest in the long line of students with the privilege of receiving our education at one of the greatest universities in the nation. And I don't know about you, but I'm not here to look pretty. The tradition I'm interested in upholding is the pursuit of academic excellence. Therefore, it follows that it may be a great honor to be tapped into Rose & Grave, but it's an even bigger honor to be granted the responsibility of keeping it going."

"Spoken like a woman who really belongs in a society."

"You don't think you belong?"

"It's not the best time to ask me that."

"Fine. I'll ask you this: What do you think of the others? You don't have to tell me if you think it will wreck your secrecy or anything. But think about it. I know Josh is in it, and you know how I feel about him. And I'm pretty sure that Clarissa chick is, too. If there were no tomb, no whatever marvelous mysteries you've been granted, whatever silver platter they've handed you—what would you be in it for?"

Lydia was right, of course. And it was the same argument Ben, Jenny, Mara, and Harun had been making, and even, to some extent, the same as I'd been making to George. What did being a Digger mean? The problem wasn't all the nonsense of underground rooms and money and rituals and secrets leaked to the press. The problem was, we'd been so busy thinking about the society as an entity, we'd forgotten about Rose & Grave as an experience. Hostility and competition between members was no way to run a society of people who were supposed to be brothers.

When we dropped all the politics, we did have an awesome time. Like the other morning, just sitting in the Library, drinking tea and talking. Or all the pickup Kaboodle Ball games. Or the political debates, even if most of the topics went way over my head. Even my so-called enemies evoked memories that had nothing to do with our arguments. Nikolos cataloged our art collection, Kevin rewrote the Digger anthems to hip-hop songs, Omar and Ben staged Kaboodle Ball death matches, and George ... George made a good time happen wherever he went. Whether it was setting up an impromptu chess tournament or reciting from his litany of dirty limericks (as if there's any other kind), he was our resident activity director, and he charmed the pants off everyone who knew him. Usually literally.

I belonged in *that* Rose & Grave, the one where no one thought it odd that your fellow knights went running off to New York City if they thought you were in trouble. The question was, could the knights of D177 ever be those Diggers?

It was Wednesday before I received the first hint that such a thing was possible. Josh—who was practically a resident by this time—Lydia, and I were having lunch in the Prescott College Dining Hall and I was enjoying a surprisingly good rendition of apple-pumpkin soup (go, dining hall chefs!) when I felt a hand on my shoulder.

"I'm sorry for bothering you at lunch, but can I talk to you?"

I looked up to see the (gorgeous, of course) arm attached to that hand, and beyond it, the rest of its owner, looking exceptionally scrumptious in a blue wool V-neck. I swear, autumn is made for boys as pretty as George. Handsome men look seventeen times more devastating when outfitted in L.L. Bean. You just want them to roll you in hay and have done with it.

Focus, Amy. "I'm not really ready to talk to you," I said, and returned to my soup. Which was when I noticed that George's other hand was resting on Josh's shoulder.

"It's about that Greek project," he continued.

Greek. As in, more Thucydides, less Persian barbarian. Josh and I exchanged glances, and Lydia began kicking me under the table.

"Sure," Josh said. "Lydia, would you excuse us for a minute?"

George led us out of the dining hall and up the stairs to the Prescott College Library. New Haven had taken pity on us today and bathed our campus in the type of sunlight that only exists in the autumn. Everything was brighter, as if both sun and brave surviving plants were throwing a last-ditch effort at existence. They'd fail, of course, but it was pretty while it lasted. The golden wood paneling and whitewashed accents practically glittered in the clear yellow light. Odile was squinting on the couch.

"The coast is clear," she said, as George shut the door behind us.

"What's this about?" Josh asked.

"We come with a proposal."

"*We* do?" I asked, looking from George to Odile and back again. "Did I miss the team draft?"

Odile came forward, her arms full of papers. "I'm the

architect of peace." She dropped the load on the table before us. "I'm here to do what it takes to get us back on track. And I think this is the right way to do it."

"We've all had time to think now," said George. "And most of the other Elysians and I agree we made a mistake. We'd like to disband Elysion and work to rebuild the unity of our club."

"*Most* of you?"

George ignored my crack. "But we also realize that treachery can't just be swept under the rug. If an act of disloyalty has the power to dissolve our bonds and threaten the order, then an act of extreme loyalty should have the power to renew them." He pulled forward one file. "And that goes for all of the knights. Even the—uh—traitors who *weren't* in Elysion."

Jenny. I raised an eyebrow at him. "What kind of act?"

"From our conversations with Jenny," Odile began, "we've come to the conclusion that there are certain factions—"

George coughed a bit.

"Fine. Certain *people* who claim to be enemies of the order."

They were talking to Jenny? Wow, maybe I had underestimated them.

"And we plan," said George, "to show this person what it really means to be an enemy of Rose & Grave. To give him a taste of what will happen if he ever tells anyone the things he may know of our C.B.'s."

"No way," said Josh. "I think I've had enough of conspiracies and crimes to last one semester."

"This is, like, barely a crime," Odile said, squeezing her thumb and forefinger together. "Total misdemeanor territory."

"Out of curiosity," I said to George, "how many people do you have going along with this scheme so far?"

He hesitated, then turned to Odile. "Well, Jenny, of course, and Ben and Harun, too. If we get the two of you in, that's seven."

"Fifty percent?"

"We have high hopes," said Odile. "We're really lobbying. I feel very sure that before tomorrow's meeting—"

"The fact is," George interrupted, fixing me with his copper eyes, "I think the holdouts are waiting to hear what you think."

"Me? Are you kidding? Why?"

"Because you made it all happen. You found Jenny. You uncovered Elysion."

I rolled my eyes. "Jenny uncovered Elysion, and I doubt most of the Elysians are happy about it." I noticed that Omar, Kevin, and Nikolos weren't part of the present support group.

Josh cut in. "Jenny doesn't count, though. She's in more trouble than anyone. After all your effort last week, Amy, it makes sense."

"Ah, that reminds me," said Odile. "The plan takes care of Jenny, too. See, according to my research, all the stuff she allegedly 'leaked'—"

"There's nothing alleged about it," I said. "She pleaded guilty."

"—had already been leaked in 1972 in an article in *Harper's*, in 1983 in an article in *Esquire*, and in 1990 in an exposé by the BBC. Certain details of our initiation rituals are no secret, and haven't been for quite some time."

"That's what she meant when she said she'd chosen carefully!" I said with a gasp. Anyone with even a vague grasp of Boolean searches could have figured out what had been leaked a long time ago. And Jenny was a girl who could Google.

"Gehry and the other patriarchs knew it, too," George said. "But the week of the leak, they played up the damage to the Elysians—told us this was an example of how far Rose & Grave had fallen—and we fell for it."

"You weren't the only ones," Josh said.

"Well, I should have ... been more responsible. Taken my own counsel. Been more—" he caught my eye "—adult."

"But if you look at it from this perspective," Odile said, "Jenny's crime wasn't really so heinous."

"I beg to differ," Josh argued. "Look at all the media attention. If it really was old news, why would everyone care so much?"

"Because memories are short and there's a 24-hour news cycle that needs filling," Odile said.

"Even though we would freak, in the end it wouldn't make a difference." I marveled at the deviousness of the angelic Jennifer Santos. I'd need to learn to watch my step around her.

"See?" Odile gave us a megawatt smile. "I think we can make this work."

George leaned in. "Trust me, Boo. This will fix us."

Trust him? Trust *him*? Now I knew I'd entered Bizarro World.

"Come on, Boo. With one fell swoop we can pay back Micah Price, who's not only been working to bust open the secrets of our order, but has completely screwed over one of our own. And we can get the Diggers back on track. All three of our tenets. One little punk. What do you say?"

I looked at them. Smart move, putting the most beautiful people in the club on this particular campaign. Odile and George stood there, looking like a cross between a beer commercial and an ad for face wash, and silently encouraged me to let them do their worst.

Three oaths. One caper. And it would make Micah miserable?

"Have at it."

I hereby confess:
It's good to be knight.

21.
The Game

Those of us who have chosen to spend our college years within the Gothic, ivy-spattered walls of this New Haven institution, who have bathed ourselves in blue and baptized ourselves "the sons and daughters of Eli," who have aligned our academic and collegiate philosophies with this university, who have proclaimed our allegiance and sung, full-throated, our alma mater—to us, there is only one Game. *The Game.* Eli vs. Harvard.

Every November, on our campus or theirs, on the Saturday before Thanksgiving, we play the last football game of the season against them. Every time, it's epic. It doesn't matter if the results have no bearing on the championship standing. It doesn't matter if their record trounces ours all season long. We rally, and scream, and cheer, and sing songs for the glory of our team and school, as generations of Eli students did before us.

This year, it mattered, as Eli was up for the Ivy League Championship. If we won The Game, we'd take first place. It was my senior year, my last Game, and we had home field advantage. But on this overcast Saturday, my mind was focused on loyalty of a different sort: Today was the day the Diggers got their pride back.

In the week following our meeting with Odile and George, they'd done everything they'd promised, and more. (I spent the time hacking out a new thesis topic. Jury's still out on whether Burak will accept it.) We'd been told the revenge scheme would serve as penance for the disgraced knights. What we hadn't realized was that the planning process would do more to galvanize the club than a semester's worth of whining about devotion and brotherhood. Forget oaths—nothing bonds people together quite like the power of mutual dislike.

Today, that dislike was focused on the blond head seated seven rows down. Most Eli attendees in the stadium had been sectioned off into groups according to their college affiliation. Near the forty-yard line, I caught sight of the Prescott College contingent in their sunny yellow shirts. Lydia was the one sporting the yellow bandanna and the giant foam finger. My last Game, and I was missing cheering in the stands with my best friend. Still, it would be worth it. Above me, I could see a huge crowd of green-clad Calvin College residents, though thankfully Brandon was not in evidence.

At Eli, school spirit is every bit as valid in college colors as in Eli colors, unless, of course, your college colors happen to be Harvard crimson. Edison College colors were red, so the shirts of the people seated around me were gray with red accents, and everyone waved Eli Blue banners as well as the college flag as they shouted obscenities and college cheers across the rows to the other groups. I hadn't the foggiest what constituted an Edison College cheer, so I stayed quiet. I looked at Jenny, seated beside me and shielded from the sight of anyone nearby by the massive form of Ben, who was splayed out in the row below us wearing a giant bulldog-shaped hat.

"How's it going?" I asked her.

"Fine." Her thumbs moved beneath her anorak, which was letting off a series of very unanorak-like beeps. "Just keep your eyes on that scoreboard. He's still there, right?"

I looked over Ben's hat. "Yep."

Micah, of course, was not doing anything so dull as sitting with the rest of Calvin College. (Perhaps it was because they weren't behaving in a manner that could be construed as remotely Calvinist.) Instead, he'd gathered about him his usual groupies and they'd separated themselves from the surrounding madness. For once, he didn't appear to be attacking anyone. I felt a small twinge of guilt that we were about to reward such benevolent behavior with humiliation, but then again, I doubted it would be long before he pulled a dick move of some sort or another.

Above me, a brown-shirted member of Hartford College made a play for the Edison flag (flag stealing being a favorite pastime at The Game), and the whole section rose in revolt. Someone jostled Jenny, and she slammed into me, throwing us both off the bench and against Ben's broad back.

"Watch it!" he shouted at the squirming mass of Edisonians. "You okay?"

"I think I screwed up the sequence," Jenny said, rubbing the back of her head. "I knew I should be doing this from the tent."

"And miss the look on his face?" I asked. "Not a chance, hon. You deserve this more than anyone. This is the only part we can't catch on camera. So we're here."

"We won't be catching anything, camera or otherwise, if I screw up the sequence." Jenny crouched in the space between the benches and started back in. "Okay, it's counting down. A little early, but it'll still work, right?"

Elsewhere, people paid attention to the action on the field, sang along to the school hymns the marching band banged out, or sneaked out flasks for a quick swig; all were oblivious to the chaos about to be unleashed.

Harun appeared behind us. "How's it going?"

"We started."

"Already?" He put his hands on Jenny's shoulders and gave her a congratulatory knead. "Great! How are you feeling?"

Jenny shrugged, but didn't pull away.

"Not guilty, right?" He smiled down at her. "Personally, we're all excited you've decided to hang on to your vengeance card for a little longer."

"Vengeance is a lofty goal," she said. "One I'd never think of usurping. I try to keep it simple." And then she smiled. "Just a little reminder that payback, when indeed it comes, is going to be a bitch."

A gasp rippled through the crowd and we all looked up. Here it goes. The scoreboard began to decay before our eyes, the digital numbers falling from screen to screen.

"Show-off," Harun whispered.

"This is hilarious," said an Edison junior nearby. "Someone hacked it. What do you think, MIT?"

"This wouldn't be the first time," said the guy's girlfriend. "But I bet it's one of our guys. Who else would have access to the scoreboard?"

All the Diggers hid their smiles.

The announcer called a pause in play as everyone in the bowl, from the players on the field to the students in the stands to the alumni enjoying the pricey seats in the boxes, stared at the scoreboard and wondered what would happen next.

This is what they saw:

MICAH PRICE
WE'RE WATCHING YOU
BEST BE CAREFUL WHAT YOU DO

And then the words exploded into a shower of tiny hexagons and roses.

"Nice touch," said Harun.

Jenny tried not to smile and we all ducked farther down in our seats as people in the audience began pointing to Micah. A knot of people had surrounded him, their heads close together as they whispered about the message. Laughs and jeers floated down the rows. Frat boys taunted him with sophomoric singsong rhymes. At last he stood and made a beeline for one of the exits. Harun picked up his cell phone and typed a message. As soon as Micah disappeared down the hall, we stood.

"Shall we?" I asked, and it took restraint not to link elbows as we strolled out of the stadium, leaving the Eli football team to fend for themselves. I'd like to say the game was going well for our side, but the Eli students had already started up the cheer of "School on Monday," which was only utilized when we thought we couldn't lord it over the Harvard students any other way. (Eli gave the whole week of Thanksgiving off, whereas Harvard kids only got Wednesday, Thursday, and Friday.) Things weren't looking good for Old Blue. I hoped it wasn't a harbinger of bad luck to come for Old Blue's most notorious secret society. Much as I loved my school, if anyone needed luck right now, it was the Order of Rose & Grave.

We spilled out of the stadium and into the shantytown of tailgating tents and vans. The Rose & Grave tent was a respectable yet relatively unassuming affair situated in alumni

central. Even in the midst of a massive conspiracy to start
civil war, the patriarchs knew to keep up appearances. Actually, the ones who arranged the tent (like Gus Kelting) probably weren't aware of what their fellow board members had
been up to. That would all end today.

The rest of the club was waiting for us inside.

"He's in his car," George reported, waving us over. We
gathered around the television set, and someone handed me
a beer. On the screen, a grainy image of Micah could be seen
driving back to campus.

"Come on, flip on the radio ..." George coaxed, and such
is the boy's charm that Micah, even from this distance, did.

"Man, I wish we had sound!" Josh exclaimed. But you almost didn't need it. You could see the shock register on
Micah's face as he listened.

"By the way, this is what he's hearing," said Odile, press-
ing PLAY on the iPod she'd plugged into a stereo. A jarring,
grinding sound issued from the speakers, followed by Micah's
name, whispered over and over in an ominous, evil voice.
"Micah Price ... we're watching you. You can't escape from
the Devil that easily."

Micah's face was a mask of fear as we watched him press
station after station on his radio control.

"Jammed," Omar said, and smiled slightly.

Finally, Micah switched his radio off and pulled in to
what I supposed was his parking garage.

Odile lifted her phone to her ear. "He's at home. Quick,
George, switch the channel. It's showtime!"

Odile had called in one more favor from her Hollywood
FX friends, Kevin had raided the Eli Dramat for the neces-
sary sound and video equipment, and Nikolos had D-bombed
Micah's landlord good and proper. The stage was set.

The television set now showed a four-way split screen,
each focused on a different section of Micah's efficiency

apartment: his kitchen sink, his bathroom mirror, the front hall, and the phone.

A few moments later, Micah entered by the front door. As soon as he did, he froze and put his hands up to cover his ears.

"The open door trips a wire that blasts death metal," Kevin explained. "Really Satanic stuff."

In the image, Micah ran from spot to spot, looking for a way to make the music stop. He paused to turn on a light, and the picture flooded with shades of red and violet.

"Wow, Micah," said Odile. "Are you using those new low-energy bulbs?" She giggled as Micah stuck his head under the lamp shade to get a look at his new lighting scheme, and got a face full of movie cobwebs instead.

From there, he rushed into the kitchen and turned on the sink tap, the better to wash the gunk off his face. Yet what issued from the faucet was not water, but dark red blood. (Actually, dye packs shoved in the faucet head.) As it splashed all over his hands and arms, he reeled back in shock.

"Please get a towel," Jenny said. "I'm begging you."

He knelt on the floor in front of the sink and went to yank open the cabinet. From that point on, everything happened too fast. All I saw were things spilling out on him and Micah scrambling back, practically climbing the walls to get away from the wave of little brown bodies . . . rats!

"*Well-trained* rats," Ben clarified. "Homing rats, if you will. And they were *not* easy to get in there."

The homing rats covered the floor and Micah dropped out of the frame. For a moment, all I saw were the squirming bodies of the rats slowly filling the floor of the apartment, and I hoped they actually *were* very well trained, because I couldn't imagine how much more freaked the landlord would be if he were to find out what the Diggers had done once they'd been granted permission to go inside his place.

All of a sudden, there was movement near the phone. Micah's feet. He was standing on a chair.

"Time for the coup de grâce, I think," said Odile, and whipped out her cell phone. On-screen, we could see Micah lean over and pick up his own phone.

"Hello," we heard him say over Odile's speakerphone.

"Micah Price," Odile said in her best impression of Cruella de Vil. "You have been judged and found *unworthy*. Prepare for your punishment at the hands of my minions, the unholy Knights of the Order of Rose & Grave."

"Holy shit, make it stop! Make it stop!" When hysterical, I noted, Micah sounded surprisingly like a six-year-old girl.

"Do you know what it means to have the Brotherhood of Death as an enemy, Micah Price?"

"I'm sorry. Please! Please! I can't stand these rats! Get them out of here!" Behind the sound of his voice, I heard more of the music and, yes, squeaking.

"If you know what's good for you," she went on, "you'll be more careful about whom you decide to target. We can always get to you, Micah Price. This is merely a taste of what you can expect." She stopped. "Oh, and for Christ's sake, stop picketing that Bible class." She clicked off. "That should do it."

We all burst into applause. On-screen, two figures entered the apartment, both enormous, burly guys dressed completely in black and wearing executioner-style hoods. One grabbed an unresisting Micah and threw him over his shoulder like a sack of potatoes, while the other proceeded to begin herding up the rodents.

We toasted our success, and were still laughing when the tent flap opened to reveal a half-dozen patriarchs, including Kurt Gehry. The good cheer died down at once, and he strode forward and took in the scene on the television set.

"I knew it! I was told there were shenanigans going on in this tent. You're making a mockery of this organization!" He looked over at Nikolos. "I expected better from you. What are we, a group of magicians playing parlor tricks?"

Nikolos did his best bored-rich-boy shrug and grabbed a handful of pretzels. "I thought it was funny."

"A bit childish, perhaps," said George, adopting a similar pose, "but then again, some of us are known for our immaturity." He winked at me, but there was nothing lascivious about it. Maybe we were all capable of growing up.

"Not childish," I interjected. "Good clean fun. Right, Mara?"

"The type of prank we've engaged in for centuries," she agreed. "Actually, sir, it's you who makes a mockery of this organization every time you seek to undermine our unity and turn brother against brother."

"You disapprove of parlor tricks because your method falls much more toward the bullying and threatening side of the equation," said George. "Which isn't cool."

Josh pointed at him. "Kurt Gehry, so-called Barebones: For breaking the oath of constancy, for your participation in the unsanctioned revival of Elysion, and most of all, for your totally whack lies and insinuations about patriarch involvement in the disappearance of one of our brothers, we knights of D177 disavow you as our patriarch. All in favor, say 'Aye.' "

A chorus of "Aye"s erupted across the room.

"You can't do that," Gehry spluttered. "I'm a trustee."

"Not a trustee whose opinions or orders will ever matter to this club again, God willing," Jenny said.

"We've entered your name and actions into the annals of the Black Books," I said. "Your infamous behavior toward this club is now recorded for posterity. At Rose & Grave, your name is mud."

He laughed. "I don't think so, girly. I'm one of the most powerful men in the country. Who do you think people care about? Me, or a bunch of silly college students?"

"You should be the one who cares about a bunch of silly college students," said Josh. "We've recently become quite adept at combing our archives."

"And we've pulled up a good chunk of dirt on you," added Odile.

"And, funny," said Jenny, "but since you've been dis-avowed by this club, I don't think we're under any vows of secrecy as far as *you're* concerned."

I smiled sweetly. "Watch your step, sir. You of all people should know what we like to do to outsiders."

At that, Gehry and a few of his cronies turned very red in the face and left. A few more stayed behind, watching us curiously.

"What's been going on here?" one asked.

Josh stepped forward. "I'll be happy to explain it all back at the tomb, sirs. But suffice it to say, it's been a very interesting semester. We admit the club has been plagued with certain problems, but we believe we've rooted them out, and now we're back on track."

"But . . . threatening a trustee . . ." another began.

"He almost destroyed us," I said. "He's lucky all we did was threaten."

Soon after, the cheers resounding in the stadium indicated that Eli had once again snatched victory from the gaping maw of humiliating defeat, and the parking lot began to grow quite crowded. As a group, we decided to adjourn to our home base to enjoy the fruits (hopefully fermented) of our success and explain the rest of our story to the stunned patriarchs. We headed back to campus, then fairly ran home to the ancient tomb on High Street.

Poe was seated on the stoop. He watched as most of the

members filtered past him, waving at a few, completely ignoring Jenny, and giving deferential nods to several patriarchs. At last, it was just the two of us.

"What's up?" he asked. "You look like you've had an interesting day."

I couldn't hold back my grin of triumph. "I've been cleaning house. Getting rid of all the trash we've been keeping around here."

"Quite the show back there at The Game." He nodded sagely and scuffed his feet against the step. "Good for you. Malcolm told me your plan."

"It was hardly *my* plan. We all came up with it." Credit where credit's due and all. But it must have given Poe a jolt when Malcolm told him what we upstarts had been scheming. "What did you say to him?"

"That you weren't like anything we'd expected."

"That doesn't sound like a good thing."

But he neither confirmed nor denied my assessment. "I guess you've got to go in there."

I tilted my head. "And you?"

He was silent for a few moments, and then, very quietly, "I'm not welcome. Unlike the rest of them, I've committed no great act of loyalty."

But neither had he set out to destroy us. "I beg to differ. You commit them all the time. I'm sure you're still well in the plus column."

"Even after Elysion?"

"Even after everything. You were the only patriarch who cared enough to find Jenny, regardless of what it meant for you. You're the go-to guy—the patriarch I think most understands what it means to be a knight of Rose & Grave." I walked over to the door and gestured to him. "Come on, old man. Shower us with your Diggerly wisdom."

He followed me, his face full of hope. "You're sure?"

I put my hand over my Rose & Grave pin. "Cross my heart. Besides, if you don't get in there, I have to call you Jamie. Don't do that to me."

The ghost of a smile flickered across his face as he yanked open the door and stuck one foot inside. "After you, Bugaboo."

And, together, we entered the tomb. Though maybe I should have thought better of it.

After all, Puck still had to give his C.B.

Acknowledgments

My appreciation goes out to every reader of *Secret Society Girl* and *Under the Rose*. Your e-mails and letters have meant so much to me. I especially want to thank the amazing booksellers in the D.C. area, in Tampa Bay, and in Connecticut, who were so enthusiastic about my book and helped me set up rocking signings. You're the best. Also, thanks to the Random House Get Lit team for choosing my book and helping to spread the word.

Lots of credit is due to those who helped this novel find its way into print: my genius editor Kerri Buckley, savvy copy editor Pam Feinstein, tireless publicist Shawn O'Gallgher, Brant Janeway, Cynthia Lasky, Gina Wachtel, Kelly Chian, Paolo Pepe, Lynn Andreozzi, Lynn Newmark, Tracy Devine, and, of course, Nita Taublib and Irwyn Applebaum. A special shout out to Pamela Testa, who makes a very beautiful Amy. Luanne Rice, Lauren Baratz-Logsted, and Cara Lockwood, thank you for reading advanced copies of my debut. Also, to Mike Gibson, for working so hard on my website. And I can't forget the "regulars" on my blog— you've made so many of my days.

More gratitude is due my agent, Deidre Knight, and her entire staff for their boundless energy and hard work. I'd also like to thank the agency sistahs and the members of my writing organizations, both official and those as secret as any society: the RWA Tampa chapter and the Chick Lit Writers of the World, the Non-Bombs, and the *other* group with the initials NB.

To my fellow writers Marley Gibson, Cheryl Wilson, Kelly Remick, Justine Larbalestier, and Julie Leto, thank you for your advice, critiques, and support. I am so lucky to have colleagues as talented and generous as you.

I am overwhelmed by the support I've received from my coworkers, friends, and family. I love you all. Mom and Dad, I can't tell you how much your excitement and plans have meant to me in the past two years. That party was incredible. Everyone says so. And to my future mom and dad, thank you for sharing so much with me. And to Dan, thank you for listening to every word, calling me on the crap, and making the night of my launch party utterly unforgettable (as if it wasn't already)!

Amy owes many of her turns of phrase to the classic works of literature she studies; I applaud the teachers who introduced me to them. And last, but not least, I am in debt to my fellow sons and daughters of Eli for inspiring my stories, and to my secret sources, for allowing me inside their wonderful world.

About the Author

DIANA PETERFREUND graduated from Yale University in 2001 with degrees in geology and literature. A former food critic, she now resides in Washington, D.C.; this is her second novel. Visit the author's website at: http://www.dianapeterfreund.com.

Watch for

The Rites of Spring (Break)

by

Diana Peterfreund

On Sale Summer 2008

I hereby confess:
Even the secretive and the powerful
need vacations...

Please turn the page for a special advance preview.